THE CRISTOS PARCHMENTS

By

CRAIG DIRGO

PROLOGUE

HE MOVED through the dark streets like a wraith, aware of the danger lurking on every corner. Passing through the central portion of the town, which was elevated and surrounded by block and dried mud walls for defense, he listened carefully for footsteps of soldiers. It was quiet, with only the sound of a waning wind. For now the man was ahead of his pursuers.

In the last few decades the town, comprising some fifteen thousand inhabitants, had outgrown its original defensive perimeter. Buildings sprawled across the desert highlands like a blot on a dusty canvas. Skirting the ruins of a fallen king's palace, the lone man turned down the side street that led him past the oasis housing the main water supply. He could hear the sound of water dripping down to the pool twelve feet below street level. He stared overhead at the dusting of stars. High and to his left was the thick band of the Milky Way. Slightly to his right, the stars formed what looked like a dipper that one would use for water. The two stars forming the end pointed north, toward the guiding star. The night was clear and cold with a light breeze that carried the sounds of the few people still stirring at this late hour.

Hearing a noise ahead and to his right, he slipped into a doorway and hid in the shadows. A junk man pulling an ox cart came close. The junk man stopped to scavenge in a pile of rubbish for treasures, then, finding nothing of interest, continued on. The man in the shadows remained as still as the dead. When it was safe, he sneaked from the doorway and resumed his journey.

Staying to the edge of the great square, the man stared across the open space with hatred. Rising like an erupting boil from the city sat the administrative offices of the Roman overlords. The man felt fear and revulsion for both the building and its inhabitants. They ruled his people with an iron fist. Twin torches, their yellow light casting pools on the packed earth, framed an arched stone doorway leading to the puppet court. A pair of Roman soldiers on guard duty stood unmoving at the edge of the doorway, their long thin spears upright and ready. He continued along unnoticed, his worn sandals barely making a sound as he passed. Once safely past the hall of horror, the man said a silent prayer.

Someday his people would rise up and crush the hated usurpers, just as they had freed themselves with God's divine help from the pharaohs in the land to the east. The man just hoped he was still alive, for the thought of killing a hated Roman soldier gave him solace and comfort. All things come in God's time, he thought to himself.

Quickly he ran past the great gardens where pomegranates, plums and figs would bring sustenance to the lucky this summer. He continued past the edge of the temple, where the holiest of holies sat in an inner sanctum. Now he moved into the area where the homes of the inhabitants were clustered together. He could still catch the smell of smoke from evening cooking fires now gone to coals. It was scent of people banded together, living and sharing a common goal. He was close now. Approaching the house, he paused to be sure he was not being followed. Once he was certain he was alone, he climbed the worn stone steps. Then he hesitated for a moment in respect.

***

Two sharp raps sounded suddenly on the wormwood-planked front door.

Inside the house a woman rose onto her elbows, stared out the door of the sleeping room and waited. After a pause, three more raps came from the door. That was the signal. All was not well.

For months, the woman had waited in fearful anticipation for this sound, praying and hoping it would never come. But now it was here—and there was little she could do but answer the call. Shrugging off the thin woven bed covering, she rose and slid her feet into a pair of thick camel hide sandals then wrapped a robe tightly around her body. She walked toward the front room but paused, lit a punk in the fire pit, and touched the flaring end to a beeswax candle set in a tarnished silver holder. The candle cast a flickering glow in the entry way as she cracked the door open.

"The Romans have come for your husband," the man whispered. "I am here to take you and the young ones to safety."

The woman stared through the dim light at the messenger, a short man bowed from years of hard labor. He was dressed in tattered tan robes held in place by a woven rope, his left hand held a wooden staff like that used by herdsmen. His left arm was deformed from a birth defect and lay unmoving across his stomach. His hair, full beard and mustache were long and black. His nose was large and hook shaped, with a prominent bump midway between his eyes. The eyes. Only the eyes showed any emotion. They burned with equal parts fear and fury. They were the eyes of man ready to kill or die.

"Please," the man whispered, "time is short."

"I must awake the children," the woman said as she opened the door and allowed him entrance. "Please give us a few moments to prepare."

The man took a step across the threshold just as a hoot like that from an owl rang out.

Instantly a dagger appeared in the man's hand, the jewel embedded in the hilt glinting in the candle light. He raised the blade vertically near his mouth to signal silence, then slid back out the door silently. A few seconds later he reappeared.

"They are with us," he said quietly when he reappeared.

"Wait here," the woman said before disappearing back into the back of the house.

Outside there was another hoot then a whistle like that from a whip-o-will. A few seconds later the cooing of mourning doves—the answering signal. More had arrived, six, eight, and ten. Now the man was less afraid. His remaining fear came not from the most natural fear of dying. He was more than willing to die for his cause. But his greatest concern tonight was a fear of failure. He had been tasked with the most important of duties—to protect with his life the most important facets of the uncrowned King's life. His was a sacred obligation.

The man would not fail. Indeed, he could not fail. He prayed for strength as he looked around the front room. For the home of royalty the dwelling was far from plush. A few pieces of sandalwood furniture, a clay fire pit with a hammered-iron smokestack leading into the open air, a fur rug from a desert beast, an altar built against the far wall.

These were humble surroundings for so great a man.

***

The sergeant of the Roman soldiers stared around the hall as his men attached iron shackles to the wrists and ankles of the leader of the radicals. A long table sat on an elevated section of the room near the far wall. On the opposite wall a thick bed of coals glowed in undulating shades of red in a thick round clay fire pit.

Most of the light in the room came from dirty brown candles set in a candelabra in the middle and each end of the table. Earthenware platters and plates with half-eaten food shared space with goblets of gold and silver.

A feast had been in progress.

A feast for the radicals and defiant—a last feast for at least one of the men.

He walked closer to the man in shackles and unrolled a parchment scroll, then read the words he already knew by heart.

"You are charged with the crime of treason against the Roman Empire," he said to the man in shackles.

The prisoner stared directly into his eyes.

"Who are you to judge?" he said in the voice of a man used to being heard.

The sergeant took a step backward as his soul was taken by a cold stab of fear and loathing.

He had arrested at least a dozen radicals prior to this. Why this man so unnerved him, he had no answer. Taking a deep breath, he stared at the man, who, though shackled, seemed unbowed by the power of the mighty Roman Empire.

The prisoner's dark eyes continued burning a hole in the sergeant's skull.

"Truth is greater than swords swung by men who know naught," he told the sergeant.

The soldiers backed away from the man as palpable waves of power radiated from him. If the sergeant did not gain control quickly he would lose all face with those that he led. So with full force he backhanded the radical.

"Silence," the sergeant screamed. "You may make your statements at the court."

The prisoner stood firmly in place. Other than a growing red spot above his beard on the left cheek, it seemed he had suffered little from the assault.

"Take him to the jail," the sergeant said quickly before he again lost his nerve.

Two soldiers stepped forward and grabbed the radical, one to each arm, then dragged him out the door. As soon as the prisoner was safely out of the room the sergeant began to exert control.

"Chain the others together," he said a touch too loudly. "They are witnesses."

Once the others were chained and led away, the sergeant turned to the six remaining soldiers. He removed a sheet of parchment from his uniform and handed it to a soldier who could read.

"This is a map to the radical leader's home," he said. "Four of you are to take the family into control and bring them to the jail." The sergeant said, now reading from the note on the papyrus. "You other two secure a wooden box with poles attached. You are to carry that to the court as well."

"As ordered, sir," the literate soldiers said.

"Do it now," the sergeant said quickly.

The six men trotted from the room. Only a few minutes later, the Roman soldiers arrived at the radical leader's house and found both the family and the box were gone.

For two hundred decades, both have remained hidden.

1

IN A BOAT anchored in Matagorda Bay near Port O'Connor, Texas, a stocky man named Sam Walker wiped the sweat off his forehead with a red bandana.

"I don't know what them Venezuelans were thinking," he said to his partner.

Walker slid open the rear door of his seventy-two-foot sport-fishing boat, named *Darby*. A blast of cold from the air-conditioning hit him as soon as he entered the cabin. He smiled at one of the pair of high-class strippers he brought in from Houston.

"Can you fetch me a cold one?" he asked with a smile.

The strippers were dressed in bikinis comprising about as much fabric as the bandana he'd used to wipe his head, and were sprawled around the furniture in the main salon. One of them rose to go to the refrigerator in the galley to retrieve the beer. Another one batted her eyes at Walker.

"Can we go out and tan yet?" she asked.

The woman returned from the galley with the green bottle of beer and handed it to Walker.

"You girls can start oiling yourselves up. But give us five more minutes before you come out." He popped off the top using an opener attached to a leash on his pant loop.

Walker was missing the tip of one finger and the rest of his hands showed that he was a man who had once worked for a living. Sliding the door closed, he turned to look at his partner, Leland Hobbs, who was seated on the rear deck.

Walker and Hobbs were the owners of Hobker Petroleum Company, the largest independent oil-and-gas company in the world. Hobbs had won the honor of having part of his name first as the result of a drunken coin toss. It wouldn't be the last time a gamble had paid off for him. Though both men were competitive by nature, when involved in a business deal they thought as one. Since forming the company decades ago when both men were just twenty-one years of age, they built a behemoth that now operated on four continents and employed nearly fifty thousand people.

Both men had started out as the lowest roughnecks, called worms, when they came aboard the rigs at sixteen years of age. Through hard work, night school and a touch of luck, they moved up the ranks to motorman, derrick man and later to driller—the individual who is actually in charge of the drilling operation. There is one more person on the rig who is technically above the driller, the guy who serves as the tool pusher. But Walker and Hobbs never wanted that job. The tool pusher did most of the paperwork and coordinating with the main office, and both men were too much of the hands-on types for that kind of headache.

During the last oil industry boom, they bought an older rig and refurbished it to drill. Eschewing debt and carefully watching their expenses, they drilled a series of wells in Texas that paid off. Buying increasingly larger and more complex rigs, they moved into Oklahoma and into the deep-gas play. At that time, natural gas was a regulated commodity with the price set by federal and state authorities. There was a loophole, however. Gas found below a depth of twenty thousand feet was exempt from the pricing structure. A shortage of natural gas occurred at the same time Hobker Petroleum took delivery of a new rig that could drill to depths of twenty-five thousand feet. The first deep well they drilled in Oklahoma was a barn burner, producing so much natural gas it was as if Walker and Hobbs had placed a straw in the earth that led to the mother of all natural gas reservoirs.

While the other operators were receiving the fixed price for gas, Walker and Hobbs were allowed to charge market price, which rose four or five times above the regulated price. The expensive deep-drilling rig they bought paid back in months and the company coffers grew flush with cash.

Hobker Petroleum continued to build its reserves of oil and natural gas until the two men began to sense a top was forming. Based on that hunch, they sold out most of their holdings at the peak to the largest oil company in the world for just over eight hundred million.

Flush with cash and barely thirty years of age, the two men flirted with retirement. Both found it boring. Hobbs bought a large chunk of land in Southern California, where he raised racing horses. He sold the land within ten years to a developer for twice what he had paid. Walker tried to stay busy with RV parks, restaurant chains, and trophy wives. As for Hobker Petroleum, it continued to operate on a much smaller scale as the prices for oil and natural gas declined. There was scant profit to be had, and Hobbs and Walker had kept the business going primarily for the long-term employees and their families. By the millennium, both men were missing the old days. Shedding their other investments and returning to the rigs, they slowly started to rebuild their company.

Most of the money they received from the sale of the reserves was placed with an investment genius in Houston who'd bought stocks in a variety of companies. Both men became billionaires. Sensing a change coming again for the oil industry, they ordered their stock holdings liquidated and avoided the crash. With the cash from the stock liquidation, Walker and Hobbs started buying rigs along with hundreds of thousands of acres of drilling leases in Wyoming, the Barnett Shale play in Texas and Western Colorado. Overseas, they established operations in South America, Indonesia, Yemen and Africa.

As usual their timing was perfect. When the prices for oil and gas started climbing, Hobker Petroleum was in the cat-bird seat. Their only setback had come recently when their holding in one of the South American countries had been nationalized by the country's president. For a pair of men used to winning, that was simply unacceptable.

"He's a crazy man," Hobbs said, "a Commie through and through."

"Taking from an American oil company," Walker said. "What the hell was he thinking?"

"Short of having someone shoot that bastard," Hobbs said, "which we've discussed more than once, I don't know how we can even this up. I thought Chavez was bad. This guy is worse."

"The Dallas solution," Walker said, "but we would still have no way to know we'd get our rigs and leases back. The next guy might be worse. We need a bold move."

Hobbs took a long pull on his beer before speaking.

"I agree," he said finally.

"That salesman that visited us a few days ago and pitched that company in Miami?"

"According to him they are a private CIA," Hobbs agreed.

"I still don't know how their salesman found us," Walker said, "and knew about the rigs and all."

"Considering how it all came together, the nationalization and then him just showing up," Hobbs said, "it must have been divine intervention."

The two men stared at one another. Then burst out laughing. They had little use for God.

"What do you think it will cost?" Walker asked.

Hobbs said laconically. "Millions and millions. Shoot, whatever it costs it'll pale in comparison to what we'll make if it all works out. Considering they have the largest oil reserves in the world—we'd have an almost unlimited treasury."

"We've spent tens of millions on failed ventures before," Walker admitted. "Do you happen to remember the name of the man that approached us?"

The man had been like a character actor whose looks you remember but not the name.

"Doesn't matter," Hobbs said, "he left me the name of the president of the company. And since when do we deal with salesmen? We go right to the top."

"Then you want to give it a go? Call them and see if they can come up with a plan?"

Just then the door slid open and the first stripper walked out on the deck. She had dyed brunette hair stacked atop her head and sported comically large breast implants. Walker motioned her to walk over to him and then gave Hobbs his answer.

"Hell, yeah," he told his partner. "If they can come up with anything—no matter how far-fetched—let's give it a go. We're nothing if not risk-takers."

Once the brunette was standing next to him, Walker reached up to her neck and unfastened the ties holding the top of her bikini in place. The thin straps tumbled down to her side and a pair of mammoth white orbs appeared. Walker reached around to her back and untied the last strap holding the top in place.

"Let's give these kids some fresh air," he said, tossing the top to the deck.

A peroxide-blonde stripper walked out on the deck.

"Damn, you look just like Marilyn Monroe," Hobbs noted.

The blonde bent over slightly and slowly did a grind for Hobbs.

"I like this idea, partner," Walker said, "even if it came from some salesman. I like it a lot."

Hobbs was smiling too. "How dare a socialist pansy try to cross two of the biggest, baddest capitalists on the planet. Taking our rigs—don't they know?"

"I don't see why people just don't get it. We're in the oil business. We run everything."

The two men were quiet now that the decision had been made.

"Enough talking about work," Hobbs said, smiling. "It's time for play."

2

OUTSIDE THE smell of salt air was fighting with the smell of mangroves at low tide. On 79th Street causeway, cars with windows rolled up and doors locked made their way east from I-95 through the Little Haiti section of Miami. Once across a seedy section of Biscayne Boulevard, they passed over the drawbridge onto North Bay Island and the town of North Bay Village. Using sand dredged from the bay during a time where environmental concerns were nonexistent, the series of small islands, a few square miles in total, were a world onto their own.

With a drawbridge on the west side shutting off the dregs from the seedy area to the east and another on east end effectively creating a break from a formerly downtrodden area of Miami Beach, the islands and the town over the years had remained relatively crime-free. This status of a haven, in the midst of what for years before had been crime-riddled cesspools, could be traced to two factors.

The first, of course, was the bridges. If someone from outside robbed one of the handful of stores, restaurants or bars on the islands, the police could simply radio the bridge attendant to raise the spans, thus effectively trapping the perpetrator. The second was less obvious but perhaps better known to the criminal elements. North Bay Village had once had a rather large organized-crime influence. Even criminals needed a safe place to live, eat and drink. In years past, North Bay Village provided that safe zone.

Since the passing of most of the old Jewish and Italian crime types who resided or frequented North Bay Island, the town had changed some—as had all south Florida. More immigrants from Cuba, Central and South America resided in the high-rises and the small single-family-home section on the islands. There was more traffic and outsiders passing through on the road leading to the beaches a few miles east. Not everyone knew everyone anymore.

Some of the old landmark buildings, like the nightclub owned by Dean Martin and a home where Al Capone had wintered, had been torn down over the past few decades. Still, the lowlifes plying their trades on Miami Beach to the east and Miami to the west, continued to give the island a wide berth. Outsiders to the islands were still noted and watched.

Inside the only office high-rise on the island, a ten-story building abutting 79th Street, Burke Taylor switched off his computer. "I'm going to lunch," he told the receptionist.

The time was eleven fifteen on a Friday. The receptionist knew he was not coming back today. Walking to the elevator he rode down to the parking lot, and climbed into his car. Where Taylor was going was only a couple of blocks, and, quite frankly, one could walk from one bridge to the other and throughout all the islands in the town in a lot less than an hour, but Taylor was not one to walk where he could ride. Pulling onto 79th Street, he drove the two blocks then pulled around to the back of a decrepit-looking structure next to where the bridge led over to Miami Beach. A black man with a cigar in his mouth waved then waited until Taylor climbed out.

"Need it washed, Chief?"

"No, Eddie," Taylor said. "She looks okay to me."

Eddie had been on the island since most anyone could remember. He ran a hand carwash around the back of the building, and who knew what else he ran inside in the back corner of the business. Eddie nodded and puffed his cigar as Taylor opened the back door. Light flooded into the darkened bar room as a smell of sticky liquor, stale beer and mildew floated out. The door shut behind Taylor and the light grew dim once again.

The lounge was about as far from a trendy South Beach watering hole as the North Pole from the South. This was a place for hard-core drinkers. One side was the bar area, a crowded space with a pool table and juke box. There was a slightly larger space in the rear, where Taylor had entered, containing an old booth and a few games, and another room to the east where the package liquor store resided. A person, if so inclined, could drink at the bar as well as take a bottle home to finish the job later. The jukebox was playing Sinatra as Taylor made his way to the front of the bar.

"You're slow today," Taylor said as he stopped at the corner of the bar near the front door.

The bartender had started making his drink the minute he'd entered and she usually had it in front of him before he reached his usual place at the bar.

"Takes a while," she said sarcastically, "to get that much booze in a glass."

She tossed a paper napkin down and sat the tall glass of vodka with a splash of cranberry juice atop. The glass had barely landed before Taylor grabbed it in his left and drained down half. Without being asked, the bartender started pouring a backup.

"What's the word today, Doll?" Taylor reached to a pile of napkins and wiped his mouth.

Doll, whose real name was Dolinda, stood five and a half foot tall; her width was around a foot at her slim waist, and closer to two feet across her chest. Doll had been born in New Jersey but her father, a low-ranking mobster, had relocated to Miami in the nineteen sixties when she was a young girl. Her hair was black, and her eyes brown and highlighted with just a touch too much make-up. Doll's breasts were large, and as she didn't mind pointing out occasionally, real and not the work of a surgeon. Her legs were muscular and tanned where they showed between the bottom of her shorts and the top of her bright white socks rising out of her athletic shoes.

Just over the hump of forty years of age, she was cute but looked like she could hold her own if need be—a valuable trait in a bar like this. The lounge was unusual for people not familiar with Florida liquor licenses. It opened at ten in the morning, usually with a few hardcore drunks already waiting, and closed at five in the morning. During the day, people drifted in and out, some sneaking away from work for a snort, some hopelessly addicted to alcohol and needing a fix. As the day wore on the crowd got a little nicer. A few regular people came by and downed a few after work. Some people from the high-rise condos nearby would come for a quick drink before going to the liquor store and then home.

Then with nightfall, the customers changed. Local heavy drinkers reappeared. A few bagmen finished with their collections would come in, along with strippers who had worked their shift for the night. Often people who had partied on South Beach and were heading home would stop in for one more. They all filtered in and out. Doll and the other bartenders had seen and served them all: transvestites and Cuban drug dealers, people that smelled of gunpowder or vomit. Nothing much fazed those that worked at the lounge.

"Shooting down at the beach bar last night," she said.

The beach bar was what the locals called another bar that was located across the bridge in Miami Beach. Sometimes when the regulars got drunk and were bored with hanging out at the first bar, they headed over there for a while before returning to the safety of their nest.

"How many dead?" Taylor asked before draining the rest of his glass and motioning for Doll to bring the other one across the rail.

"Guy missed," she said as she started to fill another glass with ice for the next drink.

"Rookies," Taylor said. "Everyone talks about gun control but no one does anything."

A man who had been hunched over his drink a few seats down the bar piped up. "Gun control? What are you talking about?"

"Gun control, you know," Taylor explained. "It means you should always hit what you aim at."

The drunk chuckled as the jukebox switched to a Rolling Stones tune.

Taylor finished half of the second drink. So far for lunch he had consumed about twenty ounces of vodka and a little cranberry juice for vitamin C.

Taylor was a spy. Or, more accurately, he had been a spy in the past. While working for the CIA he'd traveled the world using the cover of a journalist. China, the Middle East and South America were all on his resume. He had left the agency after being caught brokering an arms deal after the fall of the Soviet Union. Since leaving his former employer, he'd joined a private intelligence service with an office in the nearby high-rise.

The company had a bland name:—Strategic Planning Solutions or SPS—but its work was far from ordinary. At first the company had specialized in a profitable niche—they were highly paid hostage negotiators for corporations who had executives kidnapped overseas. More recently, with the privatization of governmental agencies blossoming, the company had branched out into private intelligence work, including security, terrorist prevention, and strategic planning for despots and dictators. The company's field of operations was worldwide and most of the company employees were ex-intelligence and military types. It was a regular rogues' gallery of operatives whose moral fiber could be erased by money.

Consequently, Taylor's drinking problem was nothing unusual amongst his colleagues. Most of them sported a variety of personal issues, such as addiction, gambling and whoring. Taylor worked in the office writing analysis papers and operation plans, using the journalist skills honed by his former cover. And in performing those tasks, his alcoholism was somewhat of a benefit. Sometimes a drunken mind came up with solutions a sober man would never contemplate.

The jukebox changed to rock 'n' roll.

"Sinatra, then Stones," Taylor said, more slowly sipping the second glass. "Hemingway must have been here."

Hemingway was a pulp-fiction author who had suddenly appeared on the island about a year ago. The author had rented an apartment in a luxury condo building across the street. He had made a few bucks on his first book and now it seemed he was intent on drinking himself silly.

"He ran over to the bank to get some money," Doll said. "Said he'd be right back."

Taylor liked the author. Like the former spy, he was a cut above the bar's usual clientele. They both had money, for one thing. Taylor hated broke drunks angling for free drinks. In fact, the author seemed bound and determined to spend through the windfall from his first book. Just about any time the author was at the lounge, the place perked up.

Still, the author was not without faults. Sometimes late at night if he got real drunk, he would become bitter and angry, and pick fights. But he'd never tried that with Taylor, or for that matter any of the other regulars that mattered. Those people the author always treated with respect.

***

The front door opened and Hemingway walked inside. He was wearing khaki pants and a white button-down shirt. His face was tanned and he appeared healthy.

"Here," he said, handing Doll a hundred-dollar bill.

She took the bill, slid it into the cash register, then picked up a bar tab from the pile and marked the debt paid.

"You actually have credit on your account," she said.

"That's got to be a first for this joint," Taylor said.

"It won't be for long," the author said. "I'd like to buy everybody a drink on me."

"Big spender," Taylor noted dryly.

Hemingway glanced over. He had been studying the former spy since he had arrived in Florida.

Taylor was of medium height and weight. His facial features were nondescript—with the exception of his striking red hair. When Hemingway had arrived on the island, it had not taken him long to figure out Taylor's past. The revelation was explainable enough. Hemingway had been working on a book set in Beirut and had discovered that Taylor possessed a textbook knowledge of the city. Taylor had even corrected some of Hemingway's technical mistakes. Then there was the day they had spoken of Kyrgyzstan, a remote country that was barely a blip on the radar. Taylor had been drunk that afternoon and started reciting economic statistics about that part of the former Soviet Union. At that point Hemingway just asked him outright. Taylor never admitted to any of his past work. He simply didn't deny what Hemingway had surmised. Over the past year Hemingway had come to learn a lot of the details of Taylor's current occupation. He filed the information away.

In Hemingway's mind, the two men were both writers. Taylor's writing was just reality-based.

"Shaky Shakerson," the author said, noting the tremble in Taylor's hand. "You okay?"

"Yes," Taylor said with a hint of indignation. A drunk with the shakes prefers to shake in private.

Hemingway thought it best to change the subject. "What are you working on at the office?"

Taylor was a stone-cold drunk but he was still the best the company had. He told Hemingway with pride if something came to his company that was big, it went to him. Even so, most of his assignments were dull. A while back he mentioned that he'd prepared a report for a company wanting to know the economic impact of a new Indian hydroelectric plant on the citizens of the province. More recently he had worked up an analysis for the current government of Tonga, which was preparing to construct a new soft-drink bottling plant. These were usually dusty, dry reports—the sort that made reading the World Almanac seem interesting. Every now and then, however, his assignments were more interesting.

"Something big," Taylor said. "If I can pull this one off I'll be a hero."

The author smiled. That was the information he wanted to hear.

"Can you talk about it?" the author asked.

"I shouldn't," Taylor said, "and more importantly I really don't have anything good yet."

Hemingway nodded. His friend was still a little sober—but he could change that.

"I'm here if I can help," Hemingway said magnanimously.

Taylor nodded and took another sip. "So what about you? You disappeared for a few days. Where did you go?"

The author ignored the question.

"What do you want to hear?" Hemingway asked before turning to the jukebox.

"Cash," Taylor said.

"*Shot a man in Reno?*"

"To start with," Taylor said, downing the remainder of his drink.

3

TWO BLOCKS away in the high-rise fronting 79th Street, the men that owned the private intelligence company were sitting in a corner office overlooking the intra-coastal waterway. They were discussing the job that had just fallen into their lap. This one could prove to be the one that vaulted their company to the top of the private-intelligence game. In one fell swoop of what seemed like blind luck they could move from small-time to big-league.

"Who did you assign to the Texas contract?" one asked the other.

"Burke Taylor," his partner noted.

"This is a big-money deal, maybe our biggest ever, and that boy's still drinking like a fish."

"We don't have a lot of people to choose from—and as far as his drinking, what else is new?"

The first man nodded.

"I just got another call from the customers," the first man said. "They want something right away. Any idea how's he coming?"

"I haven't seen anything. But we only gave him the assignment yesterday."

The first man pushed a buzzer on the desk and summoned the receptionist. "Have Taylor come in here, please."

The receptionist had been involved in a relationship with Taylor a few years past. The relationship proved to be short-lived due to Taylor's excessive drinking. Still, like many who have known or loved a drunk, she still tried to protect him from himself. It is a fallacy, thinking that one person might be able to save another from themselves, but still people try.

As soon as she was asked about Taylor, her lies spilled out naturally.

"He went to lunch," she said, "then he said he'd be out of the office for the rest of the day doing research."

The two men stared at one another across the desk. Both looked skeptical. The first man bent down and pushed the intercom button again.

"Please contact him and let him know we need that proposal he's working on first thing Monday morning. Set up a meeting between us for nine. And tell him no excuses this time."

"I'll let him know, sir," the receptionist said. The intercom went dead.

Sitting back in her chair, the receptionist considered this. The signs of the owners' dissatisfaction with her former lover had been growing over the last few months. They had requested his personnel files a few months ago, and lately they seemed to be taking more interest in his comings and goings. Two weeks ago, she had been asked to set up an appointment with a lawyer. In doing so, she had learned the lawyer's specialty was human resources and employee contracts. It just might be the owners wanted to make sure they were sue-proof if they fired him.

She glanced at the clock.

It was one in the afternoon and this was not something she wanted to discuss with him over a cell phone. She had four more hours before she got off work and could talk to Taylor in person. By then she knew he'd be good and drunk. She just prayed she would be able to get through to him.

***

At four-thirty the lounge was starting to fill up. Hemingway and Taylor were holding court where they always did, in the L-shaped corner near the door. To one side was the jukebox and cigarette machine; behind them, on the way to the liquor store, the pool table.

"How's the new book coming?" Taylor asked.

"Surprisingly slow," the author said. "I seem to keep getting diverted."

Doll had just served some drinks farther down the bar and was walking back down to their end. "Might be you're in here getting drunk all the time."

Doll had broken up with her last boyfriend a month or so ago, just before he was sent upstate for a stint in prison for receiving stolen goods. Since then she had considered bedding the author but hadn't made a move. He was handsome enough—not pretty-boy cute, but handsome in a sturdy way. She also liked that he had money. She was becoming tired of supporting her men. The problem was his drinking. She was not a teetotaler; she downed a few herself. If he'd just rein it in, she'd consider taking him to heaven. If not, over time, his next stop would be hell.

"Get back in the knife drawer," the author said. "If I wanted a bitch I'd buy a female dog."

"Always with the words, never with the action," Doll said as she wandered off down the bar.

Warren Zevon started playing on the jukebox.

"I've been coming here for years," Taylor said, "and you're the only single man I've ever seen Doll been nice to. I think she wants to sample your wares."

"I don't think that will happen," the author said. "In the first place she's a little too rough for me. Her last boyfriend was sent to prison.

Her family is part of the Family. In the second place, she works here and that could seriously impact my fun."

Hemingway's statement sounded true but it was fiction.

"So rather than pound that hot piece of tail," Taylor said, "you'd rather be able to drink here."

"Crudely put," the author said. "But accurate enough."

The truth was Hemingway had a lot going on right now. More than enough.

"Quiet," Taylor said, "she's coming back."

"You ready to talk about your big news yet?"

Taylor just took a large drink and winked.

***

Just then the front door opened and the receptionist walked inside. In all the years she had known Taylor, even during the time they were together, she had yet to set foot in the joint. Taylor caught her reflection in the mirror behind the bar and turned. He flicked his head for her to follow him back outside. They walked a few feet from the front door and stood in the parking lot.

"What are you doing here?" Taylor asked.

The receptionist felt like she had invaded some secret club. She stammered at first. Then she just blurted it all out. Taylor listened without speaking until she was done.

"Shit," he said when she was finished, "so you think if I don't come through with something good, they're going to give me the axe?"

"I don't even know if goodwill do it this time," she said. "It had better be brilliant."

Taylor nodded. At this point a normal person would have run home, started drinking coffee and worked feverishly through the weekend. But those thoughts would never have entered the mind of an alcoholic. Taylor's first thought was to have another drink and think this new information over.

"Thanks for giving me the heads-up," he said.

She was silent.

"How long has it been since you've been to that spa you like?" Taylor asked to cut the silence.

The receptionist stared at Taylor. It was like he had forgotten all she had just said.

"I, ah," she stuttered, "not in a while."

Taylor reached in his pocket and withdrew a money clip. "Here's a fifty," he said. "Why don't you go treat yourself on me?"

She stared at the money. First of all, a trip to the spa would cost her more like two hundred. In the second place, it felt like her former lover was trying to pay her off for alerting him. Whatever the case it felt all wrong. She needed to distance herself from him.

"You keep your money, Burke," she said, staring at the neon martini glass flickering in the window. "You look like you'll need it tonight."

He stood there, mute, and she turned and walked away.

A sober man might have felt worried about his job, uneasy about the way he and his ex-girlfriend had parted, dissatisfied with the direction of his life and the role that booze was playing in his future. Taylor felt none of these things. He craved a drink more than anything else. He walked back inside.

"Problems?" the author said.

"Maybe," Taylor said quietly as a fresh drink was slapped down on the bar in front of him.

He took a giant gulp and his feelings lightened.

Taylor managed to make it home Friday morning at three. He slept it off most of Saturday.

***

By ten Saturday night, Taylor was pacing around his apartment racking his brain to come up with a proposal, any proposal, to be able to present Monday morning. He was edgy and suffering withdrawals from the alcohol. He headed down to the lounge.

"Bond," Hemingway shouted in a British accent when Taylor slinked in. "License to drink."

The author motioned with his hand for the bartender to set up his friend.

"Doll's got the night off," the author said, "Ted will be our guide this evening."

Ted was the lounge's other primary bartender. He'd drifted down from Wisconsin a few years ago seeking looser women and a warmer clime. Ted had found both. In spite of his small-town upbringing, he'd slid right into the South Florida lifestyle. The cheese state was now but a quaint memory.

"Hit at the horse track for six bills today," Ted said, setting the drink down in front of Taylor and starting to mix another right away. Taylor downed half of the glass in one gulp.

"Good deal."

He turned to Hemingway.

"Is that where the sunburn came from? Did you go to the track with the cheese-head?"

"Negative," the author said, "I did the beach today. In fact I was just getting ready to call you. I have a couple of babes that I met down that are supposed to be coming in here tonight."

Taylor finished the drink. Ted slid the other one over.

"Do you realize it's after ten?" Taylor said. "I think you've been stood up."

"After ten?" the author said loudly, "You hear that, Ted?"

Ted nodded and reached down on the lower shelf of the bar and removed a bottle of clear liquid. He poured two generous servings in snifters and slapped them down.

"Ted was instructed to serve me ouzo at ten exactly," the author said sliding one of the drinks over to Taylor. "That's when I crave a licorice taste."

It was almost as if Hemingway's drinking was a dramatic production.

The author downed his and motioned for Taylor to do the same. He complied.

"As for your negative comment about me being stood up," the author said, "the ladies are waitresses at a seafood restaurant on South Beach. I'm sure once they finish work they will need to go home and shower and change before coming here. I would expect they'll be here in the next hour or so. Stood up? Hah!"

Hemingway shivered like a dog coming out of the water from the burn of the ouzo going down.

"You're having them meet you here?" Taylor asked.

"My plan is to take them across the street to the nice place," the author said, "'until they are sufficiently drunk to be able to handle this madness."

Across the street and half a block east was a more respectable establishment. It served food, had a nicer clientele, and shut down at two a.m. On this island it passed for a high-class establishment. The author and Taylor used it as sorbet during their meals of debauchery.

The ouzo had an immediate effect on Taylor. He perked up and started feeling better.

He said, "Before the night's madness starts, I've got something to talk to you about."

The author glanced around the bar. It was crowded with people going to and from the front door and the jukebox.

"Wall-of-silence stuff?" the author asked.

"Probably better if we step outside."

"Watch our spots," the author yelled at Ted, who was down at the other end of the bar. The barman waved in agreement. With drinks in hand, the two men stepped out the door and walked over to the side of the building. Since the appearance of the receptionist Hemingway had been expecting this.

"Hit me," the author said.

"This is between you and me."

Hemingway and Taylor exchanged a look of trust, then Taylor started explaining the requirements of the proposal he had due Monday morning. The author stood quietly sipping from a bottle of beer. When Taylor finished, he burped and nodded. Finally he'd gotten around to what was on his mind.

"I need a couple hours and a dozen more drinks," he said, "but I've got a got a plan that might help. If fact, the more I think about it, it's exactly what you need. As I get drunker, I'll flesh out all the details in my mind."

"Hum," Taylor said, "I'd like to…"

***

A Honda Civic pulled into the parking lot. It drove over near them and the window rolled down electrically. A brunette and a strawberry blonde were seated in the front.

"Ladies," the author said, making a sweep with his arm down to where there was an open parking spot, "tie up that horse and get in here." Once in awhile Hemingway would blurt out a Western saying.

The brunette who was driving nodded and smiled and slid the window back up. She steered the Honda over and slid into a spot.

"The brunette is for me," the author said quietly, "unless they decide differently."

"Got it," Taylor said quietly as the two women climbed from their car.

From the waist down the two women were dressed the same, in black slacks and strappy sandals. From the waist up they differed. The strawberry blonde was wearing a flowing blue top that opened a few inches in width and downward to just above her belly button. Her breasts were medium-sized and the edges were barely visible next to her breastplate and ribs. The brunette was a different story. Her breasts were at least DD cup size and were crammed into a stretch sleeveless top with a turtleneck collar. Both were wearing make-up that bordered on dramatic.

Just two women out for a night on the town wanting attention but not cash proposals. The brunette walked up, smiled and spoke.

"They kick you out of here?" she said, laughing.

"No," the author said, "we were having a confab."

The brunette reached over and kissed Hemingway on the cheek as if claiming the territory.

"Good to see you again," she said easily.

The strawberry blonde, not to be upstaged, took a step closer to the author and did the same.

"You got a little burned, today," she said.

From their actions it looked like the pairings had not yet been decided.

"This is my friend, Taylor," the author said.

The two women reached out and shook hands and introduced themselves.

"So, they got any booze in there?" the strawberry blonde said a second later.

"We could have a quick one here," Taylor noted, "but the place across the street is a lot nicer."

"Let's wet the whistle, here," the brunette said, starting for the door, "then decide our plan of action for the rest of the night."

***

An hour passed with the four drinking at the bar. Taylor learned the brunette was a native Floridian while the strawberry blonde had moved down here a few years before from North Carolina. The two women had met at work and had become roommates a year and a half ago. From what Taylor gathered, both were sowing some wild oats before the right men came along and they settled down. They also both knew their way around a bottle.

"Do you know James Patterson?" the strawberry blonde asked, turning to the author.

"Can't say I do," Hemingway said, "but then being a writer is not like being an actor. We don't meet one another on movie sets or such. We all pretty much work alone."

Hemingway motioned for Ted to bring the ladies another round. Since the last drink, the blonde, who was on his left, had taken to clutching his left arm in hers and pulling him close. The brunette, who was seated to his right, was retaliating by repeatedly turning and poking his other arm with her massive and firm front bumpers. Now she decided to up the ante by reaching up and running her fingers through the hair on the back of his head.

"You've got a lot of hair," she said seductively to the author.

That was true. Hemingway had wavy hair that was blond when younger but now darkening.

The strawberry blonde caught the signal. She decided to back down. She turned and engaged Taylor in conversation. This was not worth losing a roommate over. The all settled in to drink and never made it across the street to the other bar. By four that morning they were all more than reasonably drunk. The lounge would be closing in another hour so the author decided to move the party home.

"Ted," the author said, "tab me out for the night."

The bartender totaled up the bill but didn't collect. The author would settle up tomorrow.

"Ladies," the author said next, "let's leave your car here and go across the street to my condo. I have a great view of both the bay and the lights of Miami Beach."

"You have anything to drink over there?" Taylor slurred.

As the night had progressed, he had become very drunk and his eyes were droopy.

"Not anything everything," the author said.

"Away we go," the strawberry blonde said happily.

The four of them stumbled across the street and through the lobby to the elevators. Riding up to the penthouse level, they exited the elevator and down the hall to one of the corner units. The author unlocked the door and they paraded inside. The author got some music going, directed the women to the bathrooms, then started to fix drinks. Taylor opened the glass doors leading to the balcony and slid into one of the chaise lounge chairs. By the time the women had returned from the bathrooms, his head was slumped over and he was snoring lightly. The author put his finger to his lips for the women to be quiet and slid the glass door closed.

"I think he's a done deal. Let's let him sleep," he said.

The women walked into the kitchen and retrieved their drinks, then walked around the two-bedroom apartment inspecting the furniture and floor plan.

"This is nice," the brunette said as she walked through the rooms.

"Can we turn down the lights and fire up some candles?" the strawberry blonde asked.

"Sure," the author said.

He walked into the kitchen and removed a long fireplace lighter from a drawer. Next he made his way through the apartment, lighting candles and turning off the lights. To the east through the full-length glass windows that made up one entire wall of the units, the lights of Miami Beach twinkled. The music played softly.

On one side of the author's apartment was the master bedroom and bathroom, and he had lit the candles there first. The center section was the large living room, dining room and kitchen he made his way through lighting candles as he went. On the other side of the condo was another bedroom that shared a bath in the entry with the living room. This bedroom, the author used as an office. As he finished lighting the last few candles in his office, Hemingway reemerged into the living room. Taking a seat on the couch, he sipped his drink.

The strawberry blonde was fiddling with the music. The brunette was nowhere to be seen. After she'd finished changing the music to light jazz, the blond sat down on the couch next to him.

"Where's your friend?" the author asked.

The strawberry blonde reached over and unbuttoned his shirt while speaking.

"I don't know." She rubbed her fingers over his chest.

The author reached up and placed his hand around her neck he pulled her closer. Then he slipped his tongue in her mouth. Just then a voice sounded from the bedroom.

"Come in here," the brunette said.

Hemingway finished the kiss and stood up. His master bedroom had a king-sized bed and dresser along with what designers call a fainting couch alongside the windows. Similar to a padded chaise lounge without arms, the author bought it thinking that he'd like to recline on the couch in the morning and drink coffee. In reality he found out that he rarely used it. The lights of Miami Beach twinkled in the distance and the candles he'd lit sent flickering light through the room.

The brunette was leaning against a pile of pillows stacked next to the headboard. She'd removed her stretch top and she was not wearing a bra. The round orbs usually covered by her bikini covered shone white against the rest of her tanned skin. Around her waist was a red satin garter belt connected to black textured stockings that led down to her sandals still on her feet.

"That is dangerously sexy. Have you been wearing that all night?" the author asked.

She smiled and nodded slowly.

"Shoes on the bed?" the author said. "Didn't your mother teach you anything?"

"Oh," the brunette said, "I'm bad."

The strawberry blonde came up behind the author, who was still standing in the doorway.

"I'm watching this," she said.

As the author led the strawberry blonde to the fainting couch, Taylor lay sound asleep on the deck. Alcohol was secreting from his pores and the back of his neck was sticky with sweat. His body trembled and his ankles swelled from alcohol poisoning. He was twenty-nine hours away from his meeting. Twenty-nine hours away from unemployment.

Hemingway seated the strawberry blonde and helped her remove her top. He loved it when a plan came together and he felt powerful and aroused. The strawberry blonde was completely naked and reclining on the chaise with her legs bent. The tip of her finger was dancing around down below and her breathing quickened. The brunette was doing the same but alternating with squeezing the white flesh higher up her body.

Hemingway kissed the blonde then walked stiffly toward the brunette. Since he needed to be in Miami, he might as well play the part. At least that's what he told himself.

Sunday morning, Taylor awoke just past nine. He sat on the chaise unsteadily for a moment then rose and walked down the deck. Peering into the bedroom window, he could see the author atop the sheets with his arms draped over both women. Walking back down the deck, he slid open the glass door, and walked through the living room into the kitchen to brew coffee.

His hands were shaking as he poured some in a mug. Setting the steaming mug back down, he reached into the cabinet and removed a bottle of Irish whiskey and filled up the rest of the mug.

Using both hands, he held it to his lips and drank. A few minutes later the shakes started to moderate. He was still standing in the kitchen working on his second cup of half coffee-half whiskey, when the bedroom door opened and the author padded out in a robe.

"Shssh," he whispered, "the girls are still sleeping."

Pouring himself a cup of coffee, he grabbed the coffee pot and the bottle, and then motioned with his head toward the office.

Once the door shut and they were seated, he spoke.

"The last of it came to me last night," the author said carefully. "Let me go through it with you. I'm sure it will work."

Taylor took a yellow pad from the desk and made notes as the author spoke. Twenty minutes later when Hemingway finished, Taylor looked up from the pad.

"I think it might just work."

"Take this," the author said. "It's a prologue of a novel I was working on—I made the mistake of telling my editor about it. Problem was, I then had to switch over and co-write another book for some cash before I could get this completed. During that time the editor then told one of the other authors he works with about my plot. Part of my plot was used for what became that big best-seller. In short, I was jacked over."

"Damn, that little bit of deceit by the editor cost you a pile," Taylor said, "No wonder you become bitter when you drink."

"I figure a hundred million," the author agreed, "but the bitterness has been dissipating as of late."

Taylor made another Irish Coffee and took a sip.

"If what you've outlined here works. I'll owe you a big one. I have a few stories from the old days that might make a good novel."

"While that is appealing, I'm working on righting matters in my own way," the author said, pouring some more straight coffee into his mug. "Big corporations like those in publishing have no conscience—they only recognize money. I realize now that is the way of the world and no longer have pie-in-the-sky illusions."

Taylor nodded. He had lost his innocence decades before.

Hemingway said, "You need to pull this off. Believe me when I say this is a winning plan. If I were you I wouldn't go down to the bar until Monday after the meeting. Pull it together and convince them this will work."

"Good advice," Taylor said, "and thanks. I think you really saved my ass."

Hemingway nodded. Taylor stared at the prologue the author had given him.

"Revulsion?" Taylor asked, pointing to a word in the manuscript.

"It's a good word," Hemingway noted. "Lots of impact."

The two men rose.

Leading Taylor to the front door, the author let him out. He walked down the hallway to the elevator with the prologue and notes in his hand. Shutting the door, the author took a shower in the hall bathroom near his office. When he was finished and had dried off, he walked naked back to the master bedroom and quietly slipped inside. Lying down alongside the strawberry blonde, he took her slowly from behind. Once that was done, the author walked into the kitchen and began making stacks of pecan pancakes with turkey bacon. The brunette cut up fruit for a fruit salad. The three ate their breakfast on the deck. Not far away they could see the ocean just behind the high rises of Miami Beach. The day was crystal clear with bright blue skies.

"Pool?" the author asked, pointing down to the pool deck below them.

The women nodded.

"Did you ladies bring swim suits?"

"Nope."

"Go look in the closet in my office."

The pair walked into the office and found a half-dozen women's swim suits in different styles and colors along with some beach sandals and a stack of fluffy towels. They each selected several to try on, then once they had made their selection they walked back onto the deck.

"Perfect," the author noted.

"I have to hand it to you. You are prepared for everything," the brunette asked.

"Well," the author said, "I was a Boy Scout."

"You sure don't act like one," the blonde said easily.

***

The women stayed until Monday morning. They left about the same time Taylor started explaining his proposal. Just as Hemingway had predicted, the owners of the company loved the proposal. Since the hit novel with Hemingway's stolen plot had already broke the ground, all SPS had to do was convince the clients—then till the dirt and turn fiction into fact.

4

HALF A COUNTRY away from Miami at the Walter Reed Army Medical Center, a doctor was observing a chart showing the patient's vital signs for the last twenty-four-hour period.

"Since we reduced the meds," the doctor said, "he appears to be coming out of the coma."

They say that no one fully heals from a traumatic injury, and for John Taft this would prove true. Although his body had been seriously injured perhaps a half-dozen times with other lesser injuries so many times they were too numerous to count, this time was different. Most likely it was the massive charge of electricity that had passed through his body that made this unusual. Maybe it was the electricity combined with the injuries, years of stress and decades of training his mind to perform his job. Whatever the case there was detachment. While Taft's body lay in the hospital bed, his mind had been traveling far and wide.

"Is there going to be permanent damage?" Martinez was asking.

Taft had returned and was hovering above the bed.

"Won't know," the doctor said quietly, "until he's awake and can be tested."

Martinez bent over the hospital bed and moved his face close to Taft's.

"Come on, buddy," he said to the silent patient. "It's time to return to the real world."

The scene was touching but the doctor was immune to much emotion.

"I'll check back later," the doctor said, "I have another patient to tend to."

Martinez nodded, then settled down in a chair and picked up a magazine.

Taft hovered above the doctor who stepped out into the hall, checked his phone for a text, and walked toward an elevator. After ascending two floors, the doctor went into an empty room and mounted a waiting nurse. Taft was seeing true reality for the first time. He knew the doctor was not seeing another patient as he had told Martinez, knew he was married and cheating, and knew the doctor had herpes which he had failed to share with the nurse. Was it all a dream?

What bothered Taft the most during his out-of-body journeys was seeing that the government and system that he had served with his heart, soul and damaged physical body was not what it appeared to be. Maybe it had always been different than he thought. Taft had no way of knowing the past. What he realized now was that unless the massive bolt of electricity had made him insane, the world he inhabited was a vastly different place then he had understood.

***

Often the fierce fist of reality strikes a man unannounced. Like when he thinks all is going great with his spouse and then he arrives home one day to a Dear John letter or an empty house devoid of furniture, or to a legal summons. Sometimes it happens when a man or woman has served a company faithfully for years only to arrive at work one day to find themselves unemployed through no fault of their own. Occasionally when stock markets or real estate markets collapse, and a person realizes there is one set of rules for them and another for the rich and powerful they see the truth. Less frequent but more disturbing is when young men and women return from war with a jaded cynicism that can only come after killing an enemy then realizing the war had achieved nothing.

Taft had spent years at war. In secret wars between states. Secret wars against individuals seeking to harm his country. Wars against unseen enemies whose very ideology was considered dangerous.

Taft was now realizing he had been a warrior for a king that had no clothes.

Back at Walter Reed, Martinez was engrossed in his magazine. The sadness that swept over Taft traveled from his spirit flying free, and his physical shell lying unmoving on the hospital bed. Tears sprang from his eyes and dripped down his cheeks. They were the salty tracks of the ideological beliefs and jingoistic slogans, and the false pride Taft had taken in his job.

He cried for those he had killed and injured as he now knew they too falsely believed their own personal reality. He cried for the time he had missed with his family and friends. As his years as a spy rolled forward, he came to believe that there was no way anyone could understand what he was facing and he had withdrawn slowly and steadily from all others in the human race.

And then, slowly, with no one as a witness, the tears began to dry.

***

Taft was coming back to life and returning to his physical shell. As this process occurred, his mind started to play tricks. He began to question. Only man of all the creatures would ever ponder if he was sane or insane and Taft did this. As the minutes passed he started to make excuses for his thoughts, to justify what he had seen and heard and felt. Taft's memory returned and as his memory came back so too did the past programming, habits and behaviors.

As far back as a cellular level, human are programmed to do certain things. If not, how could we be born with a fear of fire and a fear of falling yet we have never yet seen fire or been dropped? How much of what we know and believe comes from preprogrammed responses to cellular memory or things drilled into our heads as infants and beyond?

How much of what we think we know is in fact completely wrong but since it is pounded into our brain, it becomes like a song lyric that we cannot shake, or akin to the daily ritual of bathing in which we wash ourselves the same way each morning, never deviating but never questioning either?

Taft, like most people, was so used to his methods of thoughts, his justifications and his personal realities, that as his mind and physical shell began to reunite his old beliefs and habits came rushing back together like a bowl of stirred ice cream. He fought to hold onto the truth but the task became harder and harder.

Martinez flipped the page on the magazine and pondered a trip to the cafeteria.

Unnoticed on the far side of the bed, Taft's left hand twitched.

Since Taft's electrocution while stopping an attack on the U.S. electrical grid, Martinez had spent a good deal of time at the hospital watching over his partner's recovery. Their boss at the National Intelligence Agency, General Earl Benson, had made his desires clear.

"Either you," Benson had noted, "or another NIA agent remains with Taft at all times. I'll have Dick handle the scheduling." Dick was Richard Albright, Benson's second-in-command. And true to his word, Martinez or a series of junior agents had sat by Taft day and night since the accident.

Nearly ten days had passed with Taft comatose from the shock and the drugs the doctors had administered. None of the doctors were sure how much longer it might be until he awoke.

Martinez flicked through the channels on the television. Finding a Travel Channel show that rated the swimming pools in Las Vegas, he settled in to watch. A few feet away in the hospital bed, Taft's mind was awakening. The realities he had seen were receding. Now he saw only bright flashes of light from deep in his brain like someone was holding a strobe light next to his eyes. When that sensation abated, a round circle with static appeared in his mind. The circle was large at first, but it gradually collapsed in on itself.

Finally Taft began to feel his arms and legs. The muscles on his left arm and right leg, where the electricity had passed through his body, drummed with a deep twitching soreness that came from inside. His right foot hurt the most. The muscles were cramped and, although Taft didn't know this, he was missing the toenail on his big toe. As Taft continued awakening more sensations returned. His left hand felt strange as if the fingers were a single unit. Eyes still closed, Taft tried to move the fingers. They could bend, but the fingers seemed glued together.

Something else Taft didn't know was that the fingers on his left hand were taped together. After the shock, the muscles in his hand and arm had been contorted with the index finger and second finger separated from the third finger and pinkie like he was attempting to form a Vulcan salute. The doctors had taped the fingers together to see if that would relax the muscles. Taft's mind moved up his body. His midsection felt okay, but higher up his chest was tight. Again, Taft had no idea he'd cracked a pair of ribs and that the doctors had taped his chest. Taft's thoughts moved up to his neck. Here the muscles felt like cords and his jaw on both sides of his face felt like he'd been punched by a heavyweight fighter. Taft flexed his lips and opened his mouth slightly. Then he managed to open his eyelids a tiny bit. His scalp felt like it was infested by lice. The hair follicles itched and the skin beneath tingled. Taft concentrated and raised his right arm to scratch. An alarm attached to his body let out a loud beep.

***

Taft opened his eyes and returned to the present. At the sound of the beep, Martinez turned away from the television and glanced over. The alarms had sounded occasionally in the last ten days and it had always been a malfunction.

Looking over at his partner, Martinez saw one of Taft's eyes was open and for a second he couldn't comprehend what was happening. As soon as it registered he jumped from the chair, pushed the call button for the nurse, and then stood alongside the bed at Taft's side.

"Can you hear me, John?" Martinez said loudly.

Taft concentrated and opened his other eye halfway.

"Well, yeah," Taft said quietly, "they can probably hear you up the hall. Why are you yelling?"

Taft's voice sounded strange to his brain. After the quiet of the last ten days the words echoed.

A nurse walked quickly into the room. She glanced once at Taft, noting his condition, then reached over and called the desk at the nurses' station, telling who answered to summon the doctor. Next the nurse started pinching Taft's toes and working her way up his body.

"I think we should meet first," Taft said quietly, "before you begin feeling me up."

The nurse smiled and made notes on a chart. All the nurses on the floor knew this patient was to receive V.I.P. care, even though they did not know his real name and the particulars of how he had been injured. Whatever had brought him here for treatment was important enough to warrant the finest care. No mistakes would be allowed.

"Sir," the nurse said, "I called for the doctor. Is there anything I can do for you right now?"

"Scratch my scalp," Taft said.

"I'm not sure...," the nurse started to say.

"Just give me a scratch," Taft implored.

The nurse hesitated, then reached up and ran her gloved hands through Taft's thick crop of blond hair.

"Have you got any nails under those gloves?" he asked.

The nurse smiled and peeled off the left glove to reveal a set of manicured fingernails painted in crimson. She started to run them through his hair.

"Up there on top," Taft said, "dig in." The nurse resumed her scratching, a little harder now.

"Oh, yeah," Taft said. "That's it."

Right then the doctor walked into the room.

"This sounds irregular," the doctor said walking over to the side of the bed.

"He wanted me to scratch his scalp," the nurse said defensively.

"It's fine," the doctor said easily. The doctor bent over and stared down at Taft.

"Some of the drugs we gave you can create a tickling sensation. Once I finish here, I'll have a nurse brush your hair and massage your body to increase your circulation. Right now, however, I need to ask you a few questions."

Taft nodded slightly.

"Do you know the date?"

"Last I remember," Taft said, "it was August."

"Close enough," the doctor said making a note on the chart.

"Can I have a Coke? I'm parched."

"Go ahead, nurse," the doctor said.

The nurse walked out and up the hall to where the vending machines were located.

"Could you recite the alphabet for me?"

Taft ran through A to Z.

The doctor gave Taft a few math problems which he solved, some history, both American history and about Taft's family. Next he quizzed him about his current location.

"I'd imagine I'm in a military hospital," Taft said. "Which one, I don't know."

Taft looked over at Martinez.

"You're at Walter Reed," Martinez said.

"Well," Taft said, "there you go."

The nurse returned with the can of soda. She slid a straw into the hole. The doctor nodded for her to go ahead. She maneuvered the straw into his mouth, and he took a long sip.

"Damn," he said when finished, "sometimes nothing hits the spot like good old American Coca-Cola."

"You okay for now?" the doctor asked.

Taft smiled and nodded.

"Good," the doctor said, "I'll resume. Tell me what hurts."

The doctor poked and prodded Taft, who indicated with a yep when the doctor hit a tender spot. While the doctor was doing the examination Martinez stepped into the hall and reported to Benson that Taft had awakened and was undergoing tests. The doctor was just finishing the examination when Martinez reentered the room.

"Okay," the doctor said finally, "I need to analyze all this data."

"I hear you," Taft said, "but for right now I'd like you to take the tube out of my penis."

"I don't want you on your feet quite yet," the doctor noted.

"Doc," Taft said, "you're military, right?"

"Navy," the doctor said.

"What's your rank?"

"Lieutenant Commander," the doctor stated defensively.

"Larry," Taft said, "are my papers here?"

Martinez walked over to the closet and removed a folded sheet of paper from the inside pocket of the jacket Taft had been wearing when he was injured. He unfolded it and handed it to the doctor who glanced down.

There were several seals and embossed logos.

TO ALL OFFICERS, MEN AND WOMEN OF THE UNITED STATES MILITARY

The person holding this document maintains the equivalent rank of flag officer. He or she works directly for the National Intelligence Agency (NIA) under direct control of the National Security Council and the President of the United States. Any aid or help you can offer this party is to be considered as a request from the office of the President and Commander-in-Chief.

usgov-natlsec.ammended 09-01,04-06,07-13.ratified.

The doctor glanced up at Taft.

"Sorry, doc," Taft said, "I don't want to pull rank. But get this damn tube out of my dick and unhook me from these machines."

The doctor nodded and turned to the nurse.

"You heard him," he said, "let's get him unhooked."

Ten minutes later, Taft was disconnected. The doctor left the room and the nurse started brushing his hair. The sensation was so pleasing that Taft's eyes welled up with tears.

"Thank you," Taft said quietly.

"If only all men were so easy to please," the nurse said.

"You want some more Coke?" Martinez asked, as the nurse prepared to give Taft a massage.

"Damn straight," Taft said happily.

5

IN A FARM HOUSE atop a mountain on the outskirts of Caracas, a just and noble man was slowly rocking in a chair on the screened-in back porch. He poured tea from a silver samovar on a nearby table, then added two sugar cubes. Placing the delicate cup to his lips, he tasted it and smiled.

Venezuelans are a mix of peoples including the indigenous people, settlers from the Canary Islands of Spain, German settlers and others mixed together into a joyous pot of humanity. The only country to have two successive Miss World winners, it is a country blessed with beautiful people. The national pastime is baseball but sports run the gamut from Formula One auto racing to soccer. The first of the Spanish American colonies to declare freedom, Venezuela abolished slavery in 1854, before the United States. Although the country is located entirely within the tropics, it has 16,000-foot Andes Mountains and Amazon Basin rainforests along with a long tropical coastline. Most of the population resides in urban areas and the people of Venezuela can be as cosmopolitan as any capital of Europe. They are a people who celebrate life.

The smiling man was tall, fair of complexion and light of hair. Six-foot-plus in height and just under two hundred pounds in weight, he was a handsome man blessed with a prominent jaw line and straight white teeth. His eyes were a blue-green color that drew people closer. He had a calm and confident manner to go with his good looks and a natural air of leadership that made people want to follow. While the opposite sex was attracted to him, he had remained single all his life.

The man neither smoked nor drank, an aberration for an adult Venezuelan male. His only vice, if one could call it that, was the sweet cakes and tea in front of him now. Placing the cup back on the table, he selected an almond-dusted pastry from a silver plate and took a bite. When he finished, he wiped his hands together to remove the powdered sugar, then rose from the table.

If by chance he was ever elected to office the first thing, he would do was ban government subsidies on liquor. The second thing would be to start an anti-smoking campaign.

The smell of rose and jasmine wafted through the air. Walking a short distance away, he made toward his private sanctuary, a garden grotto built off to one side of the swimming pool. Had the trees, shrubs and flowers not surrounded the man-made waterfall, he would have been able to see the city in the distance. As it was, only the sound of the trickle of water and the smell of the plants invaded his prayers. He was a spiritual man. Perhaps the most spiritual of all.

Away from the place of peace, screeching noises from the tires of a half dozen vehicles racing up the curves on the mountain road to the house filled the air. The windows on the vehicles were tinted dark and their license plates were attached with magnets to allow for quick change-outs. Had anyone looked under their hoods someone versed in the mechanical arts would have noticed the myriad of modifications designed to increase the performance. The bodies of the vehicles were bulletproof and had hidden gun ports that opened when needed.

Taking the final corner, the lead vehicle slid to a stop and a medium-sized man with black hair and a thin mustache jumped out with an automatic handgun. He cocked the slide and started running for the house. More men jumped from the other vehicles and followed. Still others set up a defensive perimeter that blocked the street. At the sound of the approaching vehicles, two bodyguards ran from the house. They were met with muffled shots, which were followed by their groans and the sound of their bodies hitting the ground. Security cameras would film it all.

The intruders raced through the house, rounding up the cook and housemaids. Quickly the men spread out, searching for their target. Room after room was searched without avail. Their leader knew the clock was running and by now someone had reported their intrusion into the neighborhood. This was an area with more than a few important and influential residents. Soon the helicopters would arrive, followed by the dreaded Federal Police. They had only minutes to find their target before beating a retreat back down the mountain.

The man had finished his prayers and was refreshed. He had heard none of the racket and knew nothing of the commotion in the house. His mind was relaxed and filled with awe. The human mind is an amazing instrument and is equipped with safeguards. One of these is the mind's refusal to accept that which is too far outside the norm. As the man exited his sanctuary and started around the pool, he was unable to fully comprehend the meaning of the men running toward him with handguns. He stood watching the approach as if he was watching a movie. The scene did not become real until the men wrestled him to the ground, bound his hands behind his back with plastic ties, then quickly placed a cloth bag over his head. He was taken through a side gate to the lead vehicle and roughly placed in the back seat.

At the same time the man with the mustache made it clear to the cooks and housemaids that they were never to speak of what just happened.

"If you tell anyone," the man said, "we will kill your patron."

The women nodded quickly. They loved the man they served and understood in their country kidnappings were as common as bank robberies. Once the ransom was paid their boss would be back—as long as they remained quiet and said nothing about what they had witnessed.

***

Hours later and not far away an electric light flickered then went dark.

Marty Thompson walked over to the window in his hotel room, moved aside the stained drapes, and stared out. Since the United States had imposed the sanctions against Venezuela for the gradual nationalization of its oil industry, the entire country was suffering. Venezuela should have been flush with cash from the high price of oil, but most of its infrastructure was American-made and they couldn't buy parts to keep it all running. The country was replacing critical components with French, German and Chinese-made products but the process was slow. Nothing short of a new president who would play ball with the Americans would quickly solve the problem.

Since arriving in Caracas three days ago, Thompson had become accustomed to such adversities. Sometimes the electricity returned. Usually not. Two nights ago, Thompson had been down at the front desk attempting to send a message to his office when all went dark. Just as the hotel manager had secured a few candles and lit them, the power suddenly returned. Thompson remembered how the sudden power surge had affected the aging computer—the unit started smoking and burned his documents before they could be retrieved. Now there was no computer at all—and the manager honestly told him there probably would not be for some time. Perhaps you have a satellite telephone, the manager had asked seriously. No, Thompson had answered politely, that was stolen minutes after I arrived.

"This is insane," Thompson said to the empty room.

Taking a candle from his suitcase he struck a match and lit the wick. Thompson had thought the front office was kidding when they gave him a survival box containing candles, medicines, canned meat and other items before he left. He'd even joked with his company receptionist.

"I'm not going to the end of the earth," Thompson had said.

"No honey," the receptionist had said, smiling, "this is worse."

Right about now, he wished his company would have included sleeping pills.

Melting wax in a puddle directly on the dresser where the non-functional television sat Thompson plopped the squat candle in the puddle until it stuck. Then he unzipped the portion of his suitcase where he'd hid a few pints of good old American Jack Daniel's whiskey. The pouch was empty. He'd been robbed right out of his suitcase, which had been kept in what passed for one of the finer hotels in Caracas. But years of business travel had made Thompson nothing if not creative. Reaching down into the toe area of one of his pairs of extra shoes, he retrieved two airplane bottles of Wild Turkey.

Score one for the home team.

Thompson thought back a few days. This trip had been bad almost from the start. Well, at least from Miami, where he'd boarded the flight to Caracas. Pausing at the jetway, Thompson had stopped and stared at the airplane through the window. The wing flap on the right side was a different color—as if some mechanic had just stripped it from a parts plane and slapped it on to make the flight. The plane's tires—those most critical circles of rubber that support the plane when landing—were bald. Right then Thompson had watched as a man who he assumed was a member of the maintenance team lean a ladder next to the jet then climb up to wash the windshield with a dirty rag. He had smiled to himself as the guy finished, stowed the ladder on the ground, then climbed the stairway onto the jetway. The window seemed dirtier than before.

At that instant the attendant called for last boarding, so Thompson walked down the way.

As he neared the plane's door, a side door to the jetway opened and the man that had cleaned the windshield walked in, wiping his hands. Then he'd nodded at Thompson, reached over to a podium in the hallway, picked up his pilot's cap and made his way to the cockpit where he climbed into the right seat. He was the pilot for today's flight.

Thompson had counted his blessings when he safely arrived in Caracas.

At the airport, Thompson had faced a two-hour wait before he could find his bags. Then, once he'd managed to find a taxi with enough gasoline to take him to the hotel, he'd opened one of his bags to find that someone had absconded with his satellite telephone. Luckily, the Argentinean cabbie taking him into Caracas barely spoke English, so he was unaware of the stream of curse words Thompson was uttering from the rear. Then four miles from the airport the cab ran smack dab into a wall of humanity that stretched back for miles.

"What's this," Thompson asked, reading from his English-Spanish phrase book.

"Gathering," the man answered in English.

"Gathering?"

They went back and forth for a few minutes, each saying the word gradually louder until finally the cabbie tried a different approach.

"Revolve-alution," he said.

"A revolution?" Thompson said in astonishment.

"Little one," the cabbie answered.

Two hours later, Thompson had finally arrived at the hotel.

By this point Thompson was starting to have doubts. If it wasn't for the money, he would have taken the next flight out. He opened the second mini-bottle of Wild Turkey and took a sip.

At just that instant the electricity returned with a vengeance. The returning power surge caused one of the pair of operational light bulbs in the room to burn out with a blinding flash. After waiting for the bulb to cool and finishing his mini-bottle, Thompson removed the bulb to take down to the front desk and beg for a replacement. If he was successful with that chore, he was planning to treat himself to a sumptuous meal in the dining room.

Last night he'd heard that there was meat if you were early enough.

6

SPECIAL AGENT John Taft was sitting across from the Caracas McDonald's restaurant on a park bench. This was his last assignment. Since leaving the hospital, Taft had been unable to fully erase his memory while in the coma. If even a sliver was true, then the world was a different place than he one he had always imagined. Taft had been leaving anyway—his retirement papers had been filed and were being processed. Due to the injuries he'd suffered and his time in service, his responsibilities would soon be over. Taft was a man with a foot in two doors. The foot leading to civilian life was much more firmly planted.

The last month, Taft had been content with his lot. He'd fallen into a routine of going into the office, usually at nine, not five or six, like he had when he was young and gung-ho. There he read a few reports, adding his analysis. After that he ate lunch did a little more reading and left early.

This was how the National Intelligence Agency transitioned their agents into retirement.

Taft would not even be in Caracas had not two things occurred. The first was that his partner Larry Martinez, who had been assigned this duty, had slipped on his pool deck and sprained his knee. The second factor was that Taft was becoming bored—very bored—with the light duty. The retirement papers should have come through three weeks ago, but there had been some bureaucratic delay. Until the president signed off on the document, Taft still belonged to the NIA.

Going into the office every day was beginning to feel like a jail without bars, so General Benson did not have to work hard to convince him to accept a different assignment: a quick and simple three-day look-see at the current state of the Venezuelan economy so the NIA could add their observations into a report to the National Security Council.

"I'll do it, boss," Taft had said. "You make it sound perfect for a man on the way out."

"Just a quick in-and-out," Benson agreed. "So we can have an agent's firsthand account for the report. By the time you get back we should have the papers signed and you will be a free man."

Taft was sipping a strawberry shake and composing the report in his head when his watch beeped with the code for him to call the office immediately. Taft quickly made his way to the U.S. Embassy and waited while the communications officer established a secure telephone link to the NIA.

"I'm sending a burst transmission with your new orders in five," Benson said.

"New orders?" Taft had asked. "I'm here to write a report. Easy in and easy out, remember?"

"I'm sorry, John, this comes from the top," Benson said. "National Security Council."

"Boss, whatever it is, I think it would be better if you just stick an active agent on a fast Air Force jet and they could be here in a few hours," Taft said wearily. "I'm quitting this business, remember?"

"John, you know Venezuela won't let the Air Force land a jet in their country," Benson said. "So that means we'd have to land the agent in Aruba or the Netherlands Antilles and then boat them over to Venezuela or fly to Columbia or Brazil and transport them overland. We don't have time for either one of those options."

"Just when I thought I was out...." Taft started to say.

Benson interrupted him. "Just call me after you've read the orders."

Taft handed the telephone to the communications officer, who disconnected the voice link and reconfigured the device to receive the burst transmission. A few minutes passed until the packet arrived and was unscrambled. Taft read the orders, memorized the contents, and then handed them to the communications officer.

"Class-one destruction protocol," Taft said, "but put me back to voice first."

"Same number?"

"Yes," Taft said. The communications officer went through the process and reestablished a link with Benson in Washington. Then he went to a corner of the room to destroy Taft's orders.

"Boss," Taft said to Benson, "'this sounds like a job for CIA or DIA, maybe Army Intel."

"You're probably right," Benson said, "but none of those agencies has anyone nearby."

"Well I just...." Taft muttered. "Shit."

"Call me when it's done," Benson said.

7

GENERAL JOSE Albornez had reached his limit. He'd served thirty-two years in the Venezuelan military, the last twenty-seven years with the Venezuelan Military Intelligence. For a lifetime of decorated service to his homeland, for a lifetime of toil and duty, Albornez earned the equivalent salary of what a unionized bellhop received in the United States. But salary wasn't the reason he was ready to change sides. His reason went deeper than that. It was honor—or more accurately, lack thereof. In the last few years the Venezuelan military had been decimated by budget cuts, sweetheart deals and, more recently, orders to spy on his own people. The past year it had gotten worse. Just the effort to get his men paid took most of his workday.

Forget the job he was trained to do—external intelligence. Albornez had not launched any real intelligence operations for nearly three years. At first the general wanted to believe that things would get better once the former president had died and there was a new man at the top. But in fact the situation had grown worse. There was even less funding and more domestic-spying demands.

And then there was his daughter, Marguerite.

Twenty-two and newly married, Marguerite had gone into the hospital for a burst appendix. While it was a serious condition, it was also something the surgeons should be able to handle. And they handled it as best they could. They operated and removed the appendix and all should have been fine. But it wasn't. A simple staph infection had arisen after surgery. And because of the sanctions there had been no antibiotics to treat the infection. Albornez still remembered how the doctor that performed the surgery had cried in his arms when Marguerite had died from something that could have been easily treated had the proper medicine been available.

"I can take no more," the doctor had wailed.

Albornez couldn't either.

While still grieving for his daughter, his wife had died suddenly from a heart attack. Now the general was truly alone—alone with his thoughts and his rage for a system that had failed him. He had come to the conclusion if this continued, his country would be too far gone to be saved. Venezuela was a dying beast—and if the information Albornez had in his head could shorten the misery, so be it. As for him, he wanted nothing more than to spend his last few years on this planet in relative comfort.

Once approached by the American, it was a simple choice. He made a call and offered to join them.

***

In spite of his irritation at the situation thrust upon him, Taft quickly morphed into his agent mode. Standing on the street where the orders indicated, he scanned his memory for the picture of Albornez. He had just formed an outline in his mind when the man suddenly approached.

"If you dream it," Taft muttered quietly, "you can achieve it."

Albornez was four feet from Taft and would soon walk past.

Taft rose unsteadily from the bench. He had quickly dressed in tattered clothes and rubbed dirt on his face. Still, if anyone got too close, they could easily see he was not a bum. In the first place, Taft had all his teeth. In the second place, real bums have an aroma of rotting garbage impossible to duplicate in the laboratory. Taft stumbled toward Albornez as if drunk, then placed his hands on his shoulders.

"She's so fine my four-oh-nine," Taft whispered.

As soon as Albornez heard the Beach Boys lyrics, he winked and recoiled.

"Away," he said in Spanish.

There is a time in every operation—the moment of truth—when there can be no explaining away to the authorities as to intentions. That time comes when you cross over the line of no return. Once that point is reached, no amount of excuses will set you free. It is the moment of treason. The time must come when the party being extracted places himself and his future in the hands of the other agent. Because the timing is so critical, the handoff must be instituted by the side taking delivery.

All Albornez had to do now was continue walking. It was up to Taft to make the move.

8

LESS THAN a dozen miles away, inside Central University, Dr. Claudio Ponce was carefully removing wooden slats from the peaked top of what promised to be a most interesting artifact. Once the one-foot-wide by two-foot-long slats were removed and carefully catalogued, Ponce placed lighted magnification goggles atop his head and adjusted the focus. As soon as the image was defined, he bent over and peered into an opening.

What appeared to be an ancient parchment book lay inside.

Ponce studied the writing on the outer page for a second, and then leaned back away from the box. He sat quietly for a few seconds before reaching in his pocket and removing a pouch of tobacco. Then he slowly rolled and lit a thick cigarette.

The writing appeared to be ancient Aramaic script.

Ponce turned to the graduate student off to his side.

"Go ask Dr. Romer if he could come in here," he said slowly.

The object that would soon be known as The Cristos Parchment had been found.

***

Nearer the center of Caracas, the leader of the far-right party was holding a planning session. His party headquarters was a two-story mansion built of stone a hundred years prior. The main dining room held a long formal table surrounded by tall-backed chairs, fine tapestries on the walls and an ornate chandelier. It was a fitting venue for the man who was leading in the polls and was believed to possibly be the next President of Venezuela.

"The count from the last protest was nearly one hundred thousand," his campaign manager reported proudly.

"You have done well," the possible future President said.

"The anti-American message combined with the virulent outsider rhetoric seems to play best," a squat man added.

The squat man was a hired Venezuelan pollster tasked with monitoring public opinion and adjusting the party message. After each speech he polled the crowd to find which part of the candidate's message carried the most impact. He was a student and scientist in the formation of public beliefs.

"Make note of that," he said to a speechwriter farther down the table, "and adjust the message accordingly."

It was a game for the puppeteers to find the weakness and fear and fuel those fires with hatred. Politics in every country had become a tussle to convince a trusting population they were not being manipulated, when they were. Big lies worked better than small ones.

***

Dr. Santo Romer stood alongside the box, which sat on a cluttered table in the archaeology laboratory. Romer was nearing sixty and his hair was a shock of white. In his mouth was an unlit briar pipe that was older than the graduate student that had summoned him. Six decades on the planet had taught Romer patience, and his movements were slow and calculated. He examined the construction of the box and the method used to fasten the wood together, then he lightly ran his finger over the surface.

"It looks like it was built sometime around the first century," Romer said finally.

"My thoughts exactly," Dr. Ponce noted. "Inside is a parchment with what I believe is Aramaic writing. As that is your specialty, I wondered if you might decipher the words on the outer page before I remove the tablet from inside."

"Most certainly, Claudio," Romer said, accepting the magnifying glasses from Ponce. "I would be quite happy to help."

Minutes passed as Romer sat peering into the opening unmoving. Finally he raised his head, removed the glasses then stood back. Then he lit his pipe and puffed the bowl to life before speaking.

"It appears to be a genealogy record," he said quietly as a cloud of blue smoke encircled his head, "of the royal family Benjamin."

The words took a moment to register with Ponce. Then all at once they hit the archaeologists mind with full force.

"You don't mean to imply..." Ponce stuttered.

"I imply nothing," Romer said slowly. "I am a scientist. However, if I was to hazard a guess—and it is only a guess—this box may hold the genealogy records for the family of the man who became known as Jesus Christ."

9

ALBORNEZ CONTINUED straight ahead while Taft made his way along a side street. The spot Taft had chosen was three blocks away from the square, on a quiet street away from prying eyes. Taft needed to make his way to the location without detection, then approach Albornez and order him to get aboard. Taft was not thrilled with his choice of transportation but he'd had little choice. His contact at the American embassy had made it clear that all the automobiles they had available were already well known to local authorities. If he used one of those he would be almost certainly tailed and detained. That little glitch required Taft to make other arrangements.

Two hundred dollars and a packet of penicillin had secured the short-term rental of an untraceable Vincent motorcycle with a sidecar. The Vincent, of 1950s vintage, was parked down an alley with the spark plug wire removed. Taft had the spark-plug wire in his pocket to keep the motorcycle from being stolen. Taft approached the motorcycle, reattached the wire then gave the kickstarter a few good pokes.

Nothing.

"Damn," he said under his breath.

The Vincent looked like it had been through a war, and in fact it had served with the army before being sold to its current owner. Taft stared at his watch—six minutes had passed since initial contact. If Taft could not get the motor started in the next few minutes he would have to abort. The rules were clear. After first contact, the grab must be made within ten minutes. Anything longer than that and anyone following would have time to call their office for further orders.

Just then a pile of cardboard and newspapers near a trash bin in the alley stirred. A grimy head poked out and the man began to rise to his feet. Taft slid a carbon-fiber knife taped to the small of his back into his hand. Now came decision time—how he handled this sudden complication could have international implications. If the guy in the trash was actually Venezuelan Intelligence and Taft chose to kill him, he could be caught, and there would be no chance of a later swap for him and freedom for Albornez. Venezuelan Intelligence would simply even the score. Neither would it be safe to let the guy go free if he were an agent. Taft decided he would not surrender without a fight.

The man in the trash opened his mouth to yawn. The few teeth he had were only dirty stubs.

"I have a thousand Bolivars if you will help me push start this cycle," he said to the bum in Spanish.

Taft slid the knife back under his belt and reached in his pocket to proffer the bill as an offering. The bum said nothing, but stumbled toward the rear of the motorcycle. He stood at the rear on unsteady feet. Taft handed him the money.

"When I say 'Go,' you push as hard as you can then run along with the bike and continue pushing," Taft said. "Once we get rolling, I'll pop it into gear."

The bum nodded then bent over and placed his filthy hands on the back of the sidecar.

"Get ready," Taft said.

At just that instant, the bum raised his hand, staggered a few feet away and vomited onto the pavement. After wiping his mouth with the grimy sleeve of his coat, he stumbled back over.

"I'm ready now," he said quietly.

Taft took a deep breath.

"All right," he shouted, "now."

The bum was drunk but he was strong. The Vincent began rolling faster and faster down the alley gaining speed. Halfway down the alley the Vincent rolled over a thick patch of mud.

Taft looked back and saw that the bum slipped and had crashed to the ground. The motorcycle continued to gain speed as it approached the street. Ten feet before exiting the alley, Taft said a prayer and popped the clutch.

The ancient engine coughed and sputtered. For a brief second Taft thought all was lost. Then the magneto sparked, the fuel ignited, and the engine found compression. With a roar from the rusted exhaust pipe, the Vincent began running just as Taft reached the street. Banking with the weight of his entire body, he forced the Vincent around the corner and raced up the block.

There was less than a minute of safe time remaining.

Around the block and over then down the side street just as Albornez crossed.

Taft slid to a stop.

"Get in," he shouted in Spanish.

10

THE MINISTER of the Interior for Venezuela, Antonio Herrera, sat behind a massive desk in the government building across the square from the Capitol. He was dressed in a black wool suit with a vest. His tie was red, silk and perfectly knotted. On his desk blotter were a pack of Winston cigarettes, a silver lighter, and a can of mango soda. Dr. Ponce sat across from him. Herrera was a career bureaucrat who had long ago learned how to play the game. First, he would get the facts straight in his mind. Then he would plan how best to exploit the information for his own gain.

"Start from the beginning again," he said. "Where were the objects found?"

"Under the palace of Bolivar," Ponce said. "We were performing an excavation in the basement to study the construction of lower levels, so my students might better understand older masonry techniques."

"Is this your field of expertise?" Herrera asked.

"No," Ponce admitted, "my specialty is medieval armaments, but I am a professor of archaeology. Masonry just happened to be the class I was teaching."

"I understand," Herrera said.

"On the second day we were digging around the footings when one of my students hit wood. We dug around the objects...."

"So there is more than one box?"

"Yes, we uncovered a total of three but the other two were of more recent lineage."

"So you have the one box with poles that you think have Christian religious records—what about the other two?"

"Well," Ponce said, "we opened the oldest first and found the parchment. After that I was curious and dismantled the other two."

"And what did you find in them?"

"The second one has documents written in Greek text," Ponce said, "and I date the container to the year eleven hundred."

"And the third?"

"The box itself is less than few hundred years old," Ponce said. "The text is Latin, French, English and Cyrillic."

Herrera nodded, reached over and removed a Winston from the pack, then lit it. He paused, then slid the pack toward Ponce, who tapped out a cigarette and leaned over for it to be lit.

"And what is contained in those boxes?" Herrera asked.

"More genealogy records," Ponce admitted. "We believe they trace the family line of Jesus Christ almost until the current day."

"If my memory is correct," Herrera said, "neither Christianity nor history has ever recorded Jesus as anything but a single man. In fact what you suggest would be interpreted by most anyone of the Christian faith as blasphemy."

"I am very aware of that," Ponce said quietly, "but that is nonetheless what we have found."

***

"Allende," a man in a black felt fedora said, answering the telephone.

"I was told you are the finest reporter in Caracas," a firm voice said.

"You wouldn't know this from my salary," Allende said. "What do you need?"

Gustavo Allende tapped a pencil on one of the few clear spots on his crowded desk inside the newsroom of the Venezuelan media giant TSS. Allende was twenty-eight years old, possessed a degree in English from Caracas University, and was the popular anchor of the evening news. Usually his calls were screened by his secretary, but she was at lunch. As much to stop the noise as anything, Allende had grabbed the telephone. Now he was sorry he had—he hated fawning from fans.

"I thought you might be interested to know the Ministry of the Interior has recovered some ancient genealogy records that may prove enlightening."

Allende sat upright. He could smell a story a continent away. There was more to this than the caller was saying. The hair on the back of his neck rose.

"Genealogy records of which family?"

"Well," the caller paused, "I think that is what you need to find out."

The telephone went dead in his ear.

Allende tapped the pencil a few more times. Then he reached for his card file to see who he knew at the Ministry of the Interior.

11

JOHN TAFT waited as the Venezuelan customs official slowly read the declaration. The man's eyes widened slightly when he reached the last page and found the bribe taped to the bill of lading. Four feet from Taft, a long plastic crate with a temperature gauge on the outside sat on a cart with rollers. In Spanish was stamped the words: PERISHABLE FOODSTUFFS and a decal of a fish. On each side of the top was a decal of a false company.

The box did contain frozen fish—at least the top few feet, which were chilled by cooling blocks. Beneath that layer, however, in a hermetically sealed chamber complete with padding and tanks of compressed air and oxygen for the higher elevations, lay a drugged General Jose Albornez. A pair of microcomputers would control airflow and temperature as Albornez slept. Once he was on United States soil, another agent would revive him.

Taft stared at the official, who was discreetly pocketing the bribe.

"The cargo flight to Miami that is leaving in twenty minutes?" the customs official asked.

"Correct," Taft said in Spanish.

The man screamed at a pair of workers slouching against the far wall. They walked over to handle the crate. Taft watched until it was wheeled from sight. Then he stayed outside the cargo terminal with binoculars until he saw it loaded into the cargo hold. As soon as he watched the plane lift off, Taft waited an additional thirty minutes in case there were aircraft troubles. When he was sure the aircraft had not turned back, he left the airport. Less than an hour later he was back in Caracas, checking into a hotel room, when his watch beeped with a message.

The NSA satellites showed the cargo flight out of Venezuelan airspace and over the Caribbean Sea. Taft's job here was finished. General Albornez was now someone else's problem. Now all Taft had to do was await his orders to withdraw.

His wait would be longer than he imagined.

**

Vincente Cristos was running dead last in the race for Venezuelan President. Leading the pack was Jose Sanchez, head of the radical far-right party. Second, and ten points down, was Royo Matos, pro-military and national industry, who had also finished second in the last election. Third was the dark-horse moderate candidate, Jose Caldos, whose campaign favored further belt-tightening while reining in the now-powerful Venezuelan military. Fourth and falling lower was the current President.

The current President's first claim with the voters was being the handpicked successor of the popular former President, who had died. Second was that he'd strengthened his ties with Communist China, something that helped those in the population that sought handouts, but also a move that had scared most of the Western money-center banks from loaning his beleaguered country further funds. Third, that he was close friends with the regime in Cuba, which was a longtime supporter of Venezuela.

It appeared the choices for voters were increased right-wing politics, more nationalization, further austerity, or more of the same from the man already in power. It was like picking between being stricken with cancer or hepatitis. Not surprisingly, the citizens were reacting with rioting and unrest.

Over thousands of years, man had demonstrated that force can hold a group in bondage only for so long. For a society to effectively function requires three things: an economy that would sustain their needs, a feeling of safety, and a source of patriotic pride.

Currently Venezuela was lacking in all three.

It had an economy on the road to collapse, a military disenfranchised and fractured, and a national pride battered by repeated failures of man and industry. In society, if these conditions persist, man has proven he will rise up and revolt against those people and systems in power.

Even those that ruled with an iron fist, like the Shah of Iran, Ferdinand Marcos, Nicolae Ceausescu and Czar Nicholas could attest to these truths. Anyone, no matter how diabolical or cruel, can be removed by the people. And the process can start and end in days.

***

The Venezuelan economy might have been short on money but not on grease for its wheels. That came in the form of American green backs. Reporter Allende had gotten nowhere with his attempts to talk to Antonio Herrera. The Minister of the Interior had rebuffed all efforts at a meeting and instructed his underlings not to speak to any media. But Allende had not risen to his current position without developing invaluable skills. He was a relentless reporter that held on to a story like it was a rabbit in the mouth of a rabid Alsatian. He spent five hundred dollars in a bribe to the cleaning woman and that got him into the desk of Herrera's secretary, where he copied the minister's visitors log for the prior week. A full day's hard work after that had narrowed the search down to Dr. Ponce. To get inside the archaeology laboratory to view the artifacts had taken another twelve hundred dollars, a figure reached after much negotiation with a graduate student. Still more cash plus the promise of untold fame convinced the reluctant professor to speak on camera.

Allende already had an hour of raw tape and was almost finished. A few moments before, Dr. Ponce had asked for a break. Allende sat on a stool in the laboratory, still tethered to his microphone. The reporter was dressed in all black: black pleated slacks, a black Henley pull-over, black Swiss leather belt and shoes. This gave him an "on camera" look that was equal parts western Hollywood producer and bookish seriousness. It also made his blue eyes stand out and Allende had taught his eyes to tell the story to the camera.

Ponce returned from the restroom, wiping his hands with a towel. Sitting in the stool across from Allende he sipped a cup of coffee handed to by a production assistant, then waited while his microphone was reattached to his lapel.

"All okay, now?" Allende asked when Ponce had settled.

"Yes, fine. Thank you."

"Roll tape," Allende ordered. The reporter continued exactly where he'd left off.

"So in interpreting these documents, you began to believe you'd found records tracing the blood line of the royal family of Jesus Christ."

"Yes," Ponce said easily, "at one point the family name became Kingov."

"Kingov?"

"Yes, Kingov."

"And the significance of that?" Allende asked.

"Kingov means King," Ponce said, "as in, Christ is King."

"Amazing."

"Yes I thought so too," Ponce said, "but there is more. Reading through the record we were able to follow the growth of the family line. The descendants moved frequently as if to avoid detection. From the Holy Land, they moved first to Greece, then to France, followed by Austria and finally to their current location."

"And where is that?" Allende said, barely able to contain his growing excitement.

"Here," Ponce said, "here in Caracas."

"So we have the head of the Kingov family residing in Venezuela?"

"Yes we do," Ponce said, "but over time the family name has changed once again."

There it was—the time in each interview when the truth surges forth. It was the climax for Allende, when hours of work and preparation yield the diamond of discovery. This was going to be another gold-medal moment—not just a race well run. Allende paused, then asked the question carefully.

"And what is the family's current name?"

"Cristos," Ponce said directly.

The studio was deadly silent. Allende was unraveling the greatest story of his career.

"Cristos? The same name as Vincente Cristos, the presidential candidate?"

"Exactly," Ponce agreed.

There was the money shot. The camera panned from a reverent-looking Allende back to the archaeologist.

"You are saying..." Allende said, leading.

Ponce cut in.

"According to the documents we uncovered," Ponce said seriously, "Vincente Cristos is a descendent of the family of Jesus Christ."

12

THE RALLY was scheduled for eight that evening, a full two hours after the story was due to air on the TSS six o'clock news. Vincente Cristos dressed carefully in a white banded-collar shirt that gave him an air of religious righteousness. A traditional black suit was perfectly tailored to his frame. He glued his hair in place so it would not blow in the wind—the weather forecast called for a windy night—and carefully applied stage make-up so his face would not appear pale for the television cameras.

When his primping was finished he sat quietly for an hour to collect his thoughts. Then at five thirty he walked out the door, and into his limousine. Cristos would spend the remainder of the time until his speech at an office in Caracas. There, his handlers would monitor the news broadcast and gauge the reaction to the bombshell. From here on, everything he did would be controlled and deliberate.

***

"Have you arranged my extraction?" Taft asked. Thirty minutes before, his watch had beeped and he'd made his way to the American embassy for his new orders.

"We have a development," General Benson said quietly. "'You need to stay where you are for the time being."

Shortly after Allende had concluded his interview with Ponce, a transcript had found its way out of TSS and over a secure satellite link to the CIA headquarters in Langley, Virginia. The raw tape that had been shot would soon follow. Within an hour the leaders of all U.S. intelligence agencies were apprised of the contents. The National Security Council was due to convene within the hour. The President had been made aware of the developments in Venezuela and he wanted answers.

"What about my retirement?" Taft asked.

"The papers are on the President's desk," Benson said, "but since you are still an agent as of now I have assigned you and Martinez a new case."

"What now, boss?" Taft asked.

Benson explained about the Cristos Parchments.

***

"We go in five, four..." The news anchor straightened his tie as the assistant counted the rest of the numbers on his fingers then pointed, indicating they were live.

"The lead story tonight is one sure to have interest for the entire world. Joining me in the studio is reporter Gustavo Allende. Gustavo, what have you uncovered?"

"Thank you. A two-thousand-year-old mystery may now have been solved and what we have uncovered may cause worldwide alarm"—he paused—"or untold joy."

"Documents recovered by a Caracas archaeologist contain the genealogical records of the man known to the Christian world as Jesus Christ. While the portion of the Bible known as the New Testament never indicate that Jesus was married, biblical scholars have sometimes challenged that assumption. On the question of marriage and family, the New Testament is curiously silent. Why, they have asked, if God wanted to experience life as a man, did he exclude that most precious of times—the experience of marriage and fatherhood and the joy of siblings? In addition, more radical biblical scholars have noted that if Jesus was indeed a rabbi in his faith, and many believe he was, it is almost a requirement that he married and fathered offspring."

"Sounds like a question for biblical scholars," the anchor said on cue.

"Yes it is," Allende agreed, "and that is what makes these documents all the more interesting for Christians and for the world. If someone from the family of Jesus still lives, where are they now? We believe we may have discovered the answer to that question."

"Incredible," the anchor said, building the tension.

"Very much so," Allende agreed. "After exhaustive research by this reporter and examination of the ancient records, we traced the bloodline through the centuries to Venezuela and to one of the men currently running for president of our country."

"Unbelievable," the anchor chimed. "First, someone of the family of Jesus Christ walks the earth as a man," he said, reading carefully from the Teleprompter, "and second, he seeks to lead Venezuela forward?"

"It is truly an amazing story."

"Which candidate?" the anchor asked.

Allende stared at the camera with his most studious face. "Vincente Cristos."

They both paused for dramatic effect. Then the anchor spoke.

"Polls have him last. I'm sure that changes now."

"One would think." Allende said, resuming control of the broadcast.

"What else do you have for us, Gustavo?"

"We are now going to a panel of biblical scholars we have assembled in the studio."

Allende rose and walked across the set to where the religious leaders sat. For the next few hours Gustavo Allende was the most watched man on earth. His broadcast was translated in dozens of languages and aired on every continent.

***

The people of Caracas stopped in their tracks. So did many citizens of Miami, Jerusalem, London and New York. People simply ceased what they were doing and clustered around their televisions as translated versions of Allende's show aired worldwide. On Antarctica, the workers at the science outpost watched over a satellite link. Ships at sea carried the broadcast and people at remote locations received updates via computer and even radiophone. Churches opened their doors and people flooded inside. Worldwide commerce slowed then ceased.

In the United States, both the cellular and land-based telephone circuits could not handle the traffic of people calling one another and went silent. Worldwide, the revelation had the effect of a mechanical bomb that disabled travel. As the news came across the radio, many people in their cars simply pulled to the side of the road. Trains ran late as the engineers listened for more news. Airline flights ran hours behind as the air-traffic-control systems suffered from the lack of telephone lines available for data transmission. Children playing outside were asked to come inside. People of all faiths clustered together, and sought answers from the newsmen and religious leaders.

There are a handful of times in history when everyone can recall where they were when they heard certain news. The news today about Cristos would prove to be the largest yet. The disclosure of his lineage was a bombshell wrapped in a revelation. It seemed most people in the world felt not fear but hope as they digested the news. Others felt that the world had been yanked from under their feet.

***

Adolpho Fiorini was as close to the Pope as any man alive. Fiorini ran the apparatus that handled the business end of the Roman Catholic Church. Though it is hard for most to imagine, religion is in fact a business. Almost all religions collect and dispense money, pay wages and have employees. They own property, have investments and sell a product—belief. Where it differs from many businesses is that their intent is not profit, but answers and salvation.

Fiorini was the fourth generation of his family to serve the church. His offices handled funds, planned the trips the Pope would make, and monitored worldwide opinions toward his employer, and kept track of the mood of Catholic followers, among other tasks.

Fiorini was a moderate and had welcomed the changes the Catholic Church had made in the last few decades toward modernism. He had agreed with the decision prior his time to retire Latin as the language for Mass. As an adult he had agreed with the choice for the church to express misgivings about its role during World War II. Currently the church's slow but steady acknowledgment of the abuses their priests had inflicted on young men was warranted and long overdue, he felt. Fiorini believed that which does not adjust to the times, even a church, is doomed to become extinct.

Still, the revelation from Venezuela disturbed him.

In his office in Vatican City he sat quietly. A light knock sounded from his door.

"Enter," he said.

A priest in robes opened the door and entered. In his hands he clutched a thick file folder. Walking over to the desk, he held them out in his hands.

"These are the latest transcripts from television, radio and the internet."

Fiorini nodded glumly.

"How are our followers?" he asked the priest directly.

"The Italian people seem to be handling the revelation well," the priest said easily. "They seek answers, of course. But don't we all."

"As long as we can provide guidance," Fiorini said, "we will have done our duty."

The priest paused, unsure how to ask the question he was dying to know.

"Sir," he said quietly, "there are some rumors circulating that the church has always been aware of the existence of descendants. Do you know anything of this?"

Fiorini felt he knew the answer to the question but he could not comment.

He raised both hands in the air. The question was not his to answer.

13

NO BREEZE blew through Houston, and the air was thick and heavy. The trees outside the ten-story office building sitting just off the Interstate 45 had lost their leaves months before. Rain was predicted for today but it had yet to fall. The clouds to the north over downtown were black and advancing. On the interstate, nearby cars whizzed past. At the Cracker Barrel restaurant near the exit, people hurried from their cars for a hot meal.

J. Thomas Melton stared out the window with detachment. He had larger issues on his mind.

Next to the tall office building was a university campus, a large church with the tallest spire in the Southwest and a full television production studio that beamed his sermons and shows to a massive audience. Melton had built it all from scratch. It was named it the Evangelical Church of Believers, and Melton ran it.

Melton had started as a rural preacher in Shreveport, Louisiana, fresh out of divinity school. After building that church from eighty regulars to four hundred, he turned it over to a trusted aide and left for greener pastures. The bigger market of Houston followed, where the church he took over with a change in name increased its membership thousand-fold during a time of economic ruin. Melton rode the wave out of recession to prosperity with the same formula he'd used since the start. People now attending church wanted entertainment with their message. So Melton entertained his flock like no other in organized religion.

His worship services were practically a Las Vegas show. Sometimes Melton preached a message of love and redemption. For others, like the scourge of homosexuality, Communism and labor unions, he preached a certain burning hell. His church was a method of mind control designed to form the opinions in his followers but his flock didn't see it that way. They thought Melton was right—the only right—and it is hard to argue with a person filled with righteousness. Righteousness breeds passion and passion can breed love or hatred. Melton both knew this and was willing to use this to further his own base of power. The riches had poured in over the years.

The band at the Evangelical Church of Believers comprised musicians that could have worked for any studio in the United States. They might have, but Melton paid them better. His singers had the voices of angels—and well they should, for an average starting salary of fifty thousand dollars a year plus retirement benefits. He had sixty ministers under him, a twenty-four-hour-a-day face-to-face counseling service available at the church, and provisions for servicing those who could not travel. Recently he'd even franchised his message, selling territories nationwide. Those trained in the Melton system were in all fifty states, all U.S. territories and forty-two foreign countries.

The total take in the coming year was projected to reach the $400 million mark.

Melton paced his office as he tried to form the sermon for his flock. How was he to explain that a real man might be walking the earth borne from the seed of the basis of their beliefs? A religious man would have kneeled down and prayed. But not Melton.

***

To his last rally, Vincente Cristos had drawn fewer than two thousand people. Just before he walked on stage tonight, one of his new advisors had pegged this crowd at one hundred times that number and growing. It was impossible to drive anywhere near Central Caracas. And the distance between where the busses could pass and the center stage was ever widening. Many passengers faced walks of miles to reach the square. Luckily the men now managing the Cristos campaign had planned well. Four dozen trucks with loudspeakers were spread out at equal distances from the podium. Cristos's voice would be beamed through the air to the masses.

Slipping from behind a black curtain, he was met with a roar of applause that grew and grew in volume until it mimicked nearby thunder. Cristos raised his hand and surprisingly, dead quiet followed. Then he paused for effect.

"Thank you," he said in Venezuelan. "I am Vincente Cristos and I want to be the next President of Venezuela."

Pandemonium erupted.

Just this opening statement brought clapping and screaming and stomping of feet. The raucous din could be heard five, six and seven miles away. It was the sound of joy, anticipation, rapture. He raised his hands again and the noise died instantly as if a switch had been flicked to off.

"Please hold your applause," Cristos said reverently.

The crowd remained silent.

"Some two thousand years ago a Messiah came to earth. Today I ask that you allow me to be the Messiah for a new Venezuela. Our country has faced a series of what seems like never-ending challenges but I stand before you today to say they are at an end. Though I come from royalty I do not seek to return us to the dark days of kings and queens. Though I come from religion I do not seek a movement to a religious state. Though I come from politics I do not seek a continuation of politics as they are."

Cristos paused again for effect.

"Instead I stand before you today and pledge a return to greatness for Venezuela by a combination of divine guidance and common sense. We will rebuild our economy and make it the marvel of the world. We will rebuild our military to standards beyond all others. We will feed our starving, heal our sick, and nurture our young. We will move forward not back, and look to the future with fond anticipation not national disgrace and ridicule. We will embrace our rightful place as a world leader. We will, we will, we will."

In spite of his earlier instructions, the crowd erupted. He let the applause wash over him like a balm. Two minutes later he raised his hands once again.

"In a week you will have a choice at the polls. I ask that you choose me—someone who was born to lead you forward. Choose someone who calls on the greatness of a divine power for help and guidance—someone who knows right from wrong."

Cristos paused again.

"Now let us pray," he said.

Hundreds of thousands of heads bowed at once.

"Oh Great One, he who rules the heavens and earth, we ask that you shine your power and favor upon these people who have faced so much hardship and toil. We ask that you bring forth for us a time of prosperity and good tidings. We ask that, through me, you lead us forward into the future. We ask that you strengthen this country and restore us to greatness. Amen."

Then Cristos stepped back through the curtain to a round of applause that rattled windows and was felt throughout Caracas. The King had come to claim his throne.

14

THE PRESIDENT of the United States entered the briefing room, followed by the Secretary of State. He took his place at the head of the table while the Secretary slid into a seat to his immediate right. Smiling a thin smile, the President turned first to the National Security Advisor.

"You can begin when you are ready."

"Thank you, Mr. President. We have convened here to discuss the implications of the discovery of the documents now being known as The Cristos Parchment."

"First," the President asked, "what is a parchment, exactly?"

"Mr. Albright, could you field that question?" the National Security Advisor asked.

Richard Albright, second-in-command to General Earl Benson at the NIA, opened a folder and consulted his notes.

"Mr. President, the simple answer is a parchment is early crude paper."

"Early paper," the President said, "and I thought we were a paperless world."

The crowd laughed politely. Most did not care for the President.

"So," the President continued, "my early briefing disclosed the Venezuelans have recovered documents that indicate that Jesus Christ had children, and a descendant of his is now running for the President of Venezuela. Sounds like shades of that Da Vinci novel. Is that about where we are?"

"Yes, sir," the National Security Advisor said.

He motioned to the head of the CIA.

"What's the psychological read on Vincente Cristos?" The President asked.

The CIA director read from his file.

"Vincente Cristos was born..." he began.

"Not his biography. How does he feel towards the U.S.?"

"None of his speeches so far have indicated any anti-American sentiment. In fact, if I was asked to characterize I would say he favors continued relations with us while at the same time forging a stronger sense of Venezuelan pride through internal growth."

"So he doesn't hate us," the President summarized, "but he might want to be left alone."

"It would seem that way," the director said.

"What is his chance of winning the election?"

"Although it is impossible to accurately predict because this development is so recent," the director said, "our people on the ground in Caracas have noted an immediate and massive surge in his popularity. If this continues then he's a shoo-in to be elected President."

"Pro-military?" The President asked the head of the Defense Intelligence Agency, a three-star army general dressed in full uniform adorned with ribbons.

"He's not anti-military," the man noted. "If I was to sum him up, I would say he wants to return the Venezuelan military to glory as much to create a source of national pride as anything else. If I was to hazard a guess I would say he would take a defensive, not offensive, posture."

"Sounds like he's everything to everybody," the President noted. "A true politician."

The President sometimes came across as a lightweight. Those close to him knew it was not an act.

He pointed to the CIA director. "What about China? The current President strengthened his ties with the Communist Chinese government. If he is elected, will Cristos continue on that path?"

"That is one good thing," the director said. "Cristos has called Communism 'a godless institution,' and I think he might sever ties or at least reduce the relationship."

"That sounds like saber rattling," the President said. "China in the last decade has become about as Communist as Japan. He's might just be making those statements for further use."

"But the statement is anti-China," the director noted, "and we don't see much of that these days."

Everyone seemed to be assuming Cristos was a politician and not of a higher calling.

"True. Then I'd have to say we like him," the President said. "All of you know how China has become a thorn in our side."

Almost from the start of the President's term, China and the United States had been at odds. It started when a disabled Navy submarine detection plane was forced to land on Chinese soil. The situation was exacerbated by U.S. arms sales to Taiwan. Right now, the U.S. Navy was playing a game of cat and mouse with the Chinese in the water close to the disputed Spratly Islands near Vietnam.

"Where did this guy come from?" the President asked, "and why didn't we know about this before?"

"From what we can gather," the head of National Intelligence offered, "Cristos and his family have always kept a low profile. It is strange he even filed to run for President—it was a last-minute affair with no real plan we can ascertain. If the parchments had not been discovered it is almost certain he would have been dead last."

"Odd," the President noted.

The President knew more than he was letting on.

"What about the threat of terrorism from this development?" He pointed to Benson.

"Mr. President, the threat from the common sources of Iran, Iraq, Libya and the radical Arab states should be nonexistent. Their religion has always claimed Jesus was a prophet and not the son of God. Quite frankly, Islam is happy about the revelation. There is another threat, however, and that is both internal and external. We have not yet been able to accurately gauge the reaction of Christian fundamentalists to the news. This could bear significant social and political impact."

"I can see how they might be taken aback by the news," the President agreed. "The Messiah has come, but in a decidedly different form—that of an ordinary man."

"We're not sure how it will play," Benson said seriously.

The President sat for a moment before speaking.

"I'm worried about our own people," he said quietly. "I spoke to a minister before coming in here. The members of his congregation are unsure how to handle the news. On one hand, if Cristos is a descendant of Jesus, it goes to some of their core beliefs. On the other hand, Jesus coming at all offers them hope if they can just change a few major points in their tenets."

The President's religion was a front to be elected—he was just seeking an angle for when he needed it. Most in the room knew that.

"Sir," Benson said, "if I might present another idea."

"Please, General," the President said.

"Before we form any plan I think we need to examine the proof," Benson said.

"What do you mean?" the President asked.

"My best agent, John Taft, is currently in Caracas on another mission," Benson said.

"Taft?" the President said. "The agent that was electrocuted. Wasn't he in a coma?"

"That's him," Benson agreed.

"I thought he put in for retirement?" the President noted.

"The papers are awaiting your signature," Benson admitted.

"Should I hold off on that?"

"For right now," Benson said quietly.

"What are you proposing?" the President asked.

"Most of us here today have one function for this country. To provide accurate information, so policy can be formed. Right now, all we can offer is speculation as to the possible consequences of something out of our control."

"What are you proposing?" the President asked.

"Maybe Taft can steal the ancient parchments," Benson said, "so we can determine if Cristos is actually *is* the true descendant of Jesus. Or if this is a clever scam."

"Hum," the President said. "What you're proposing is to have one of our own scientists weigh in on the issue."

"Exactly, Mr. President," Benson said.

"What if Cristos is a fake?" the President asked.

"What if he is not?"

15

"I CAN DO it," Taft said, "but it has to be tonight. Tomorrow might be too late."

Taft had gone through a complete reversal of attitudes in the past three hours. When he had first been contacted, he'd assumed stealing the parchments would be simply impossible. But the initial wave of contempt had eroded with investigation. After some surveillance, he managed to determine the three boxes and their earth-shattering information remained in the laboratory under loose guard. Quite simply, with all that had happened, no one had yet perceived the need for increased security. Soon, very soon, someone would wake up to the fact the documents needed to be protected. Right now, however, the precious parchments were being watched over by a single nighttime guard.

Back at the NIA headquarters, Larry Martinez had his injured knee propped up on his desk.

"There's been a change in the plans. CIA magicians have created duplicates of the boxes from images taken from the taped interview with Ponce. The wood that was used to construct the boxes is of the appropriate age. The boxes are on their way to Venezuela along with a trio of technicians who can forge anything," Martinez said.

"I'm taking in duplicates to replace the originals?" Taft said. "So the Venezuelans never realize there was a robbery?"

"It's more involved than that, John," Martinez said. "There is no way for us to forge the documents themselves. All that showed on the tape was the top pages. We need to copy them in a lab we've set up nearby. And then we'll return a duplicate set."

"Copy them?" Taft asked in amazement.

"Yes, it's a special process—not quite as simple as scanning and reprinting. The CIA has a stock of aged parchment along with forgers trained to write in any style and script with ink that will hold up to a carbon-dating test. They plan to copy the documents, one forger to each box, then you will return the faux parchments and boxes and retain the originals."

"I'm going in twice?" Taft asked. "I hoped I could just steal them and be out."

"The powers to be think this is the way to go," Martinez said quietly.

"That doubles my risk."

"Sorry, about that partner," Martinez said. "That's the way they want it done."

"That's easy for you to say, old buddy, you're safe in Virginia," Taft said laconically. "This was your mission, not mine, if I remember right."

"Field work is for studs like you," Martinez laughed. "You know I'm more of an office geek."

"Good for you," Taft noted, "Bad for me."

"What are you going to do with the guard?" Martinez asked.

"Happy sauce," Taft answered. "I'll serve him a Super Roofie through skin absorption."

Taft was referring to a refined version of the date-rape drug mixed with the chemical used before surgery to block memory. The liquid chemical was developed by U.S. intelligence and could be slipped into a drink or absorbed on the skin. Whoever received the dose would sleep for a prescribed period, then awake without memory.

"Good news is we have enough agents on the ground in Venezuela now to provide limited coverage around the building."

"Makes it better," Taft agreed.

"Here's the address to the duplication site." Martinez read off the street name and number. "As soon as you have stolen the boxes, proceed there."

"When will I know the fake wooden boxes and the forgers have arrived at the laboratory?" Taft asked.

"Two beeps on your watch."

"Okay, pal," Taft said easily, "Here goes nothing."

"Good luck, John."

***

The three CIA forgers sent to Venezuela came from all parts of the globe. One was stationed in Morocco, one Singapore, and the last and closest was from Germany. Each man had been trained to quickly churn out any documents, visas, passports or other credentials an agent might need for an operation. Each also had a specialty. The Singapore-based officer was a master of counterfeit currency. The Morocco-based officer was an expert in fake art work and statues, while the officer stationed in Germany was trained to fake government documents from multiple countries. The team quickly assembled.

"Phantom series machine," the agent from Morocco noted. "That should work."

"Did anyone have any problems with Venezuelan customs?" the officer from Germany asked.

"Slid right through," the officer from Singapore commented. "You do good work."

"A little extra effort for my friends." The German smiled. "In a week, the ink dissolves off the applications and no one will be able to prove we were ever here."

A senior CIA officer who had personally transported the fake boxes and blank parchments from Langley, motioned for the trio to cluster under a large, round illuminated magnifying glass built on a folding frame so it could be raised or lowered over the work table.

"Here is the paper," he said, offering it to the men for inspection.

"Will it date?" the German asked.

"It should," the senior officer said. "It's authentic, two thousand years old. We removed it from a shopkeeper's ledger that was excavated in Jerusalem." He pointed to a series of marked cardboard boxes on the table.

"The others are also authentic documents scraped clean by the technicians at the Magic Shop. They date two hundred years apart," said the senior agent, referring to the main laboratories at Langley.

"Good. Two hundred years is closer than carbon dating is accurate," the officer from Singapore noted.

"Check your tools," the senior officer noted, "and see if anything is missing."

The three men pawed through wooden boxes with quills, dated ink and chemicals to discolor and stain paper to match any situation.

"It looks good," the agent from Morocco noted. "There is just one more thing we need."

"What's that?" the senior CIA officer asked.

"Black coffee. It was a long flight."

The senior agent turned to the rookie agent that had accompanied him.

"You heard these men," he said, chuckling. "Get them some coffee."

"And a bottle of liquor. Peppermint schnapps if you can find it," the German officer said. "Schnapps quiets our nerves."

***

If this was the movies or television, Taft would have needed to avoid motion sensors and laser beams. Instead he simply waited until the single guard had left to take a restroom break and then dotted some Super Roofie on the doorknob leading back inside. Hiding in the next room, he waited until the man returned. The liquid was absorbed through the guard's skin, and ten minutes later he was sound asleep in his chair. Taft slipped inside the laboratory and stared at the boxes.

Lit by a single fluorescent tube above the work bench, each box was slightly different. The first was two feet by one foot ,and one foot high. It was capped with a peaked lid like a mini-ski lodge and had a pair of poles on each side. The second and the third were more similar in appearance and without poles. Slightly larger than sheets of typing paper, the first was made of rougher wood and finished with faded yellow paint showing mildew. The second was polished walnut that closed with a tarnished brass clasp. Taft carefully placed them into a Venezuela army duffel bag. Then he adjusted the shirt of his Venezuelan army private's uniform and slipped past the guard.

***

The makeshift duplication lab was only four blocks away and Taft made quick time. As he passed each side street, unseen agents radioed his progress to the senior agent. A Marine embassy guard dressed as a local met him at the lower stair, led him up the stairs, and opened the door.

Taft walked over to the work table, untied the duffel bag, and removed the boxes.

"Hey, Lee," he greeted the officer from Germany, "long time no see."

"Taft, you old son of a gun. I haven't seen you since Yemen."

The other two forgers began unpacking the boxes.

"You two know each other?" the senior CIA officer said in astonishment.

"Yes," Taft said, "I rented the other half of his duplex when I first went to work for the NIA."

"Small world," the senior CIA officer remarked.

The officer from Singapore was already copying the first stack of parchments and the light from the machine was flashing like a strobe. The rookie agent carried them to a table where the officer from Morocco was sitting, quill in hand.

"I'll be back stateside in another week or two," Lee said. "Why don't you call Mary and we get together. Right now, I'd better get this done so you can high-tail them back into place."

"Sounds good. I'll wait over here." Taft made his way to a chair.

He sat and watched the operation. First the original was fastened underneath a strange-looking plastic oblong device. The top section stepped down, like the sides of a pyramid minus the facing stones, or somewhat like a deck of cards in which the top layers had been slid lengthwise along the deck. That allowed the forgers to see the original while working on the fake. In fact, they could almost trace the lettering.

The inside of the plastic frame held polished glass under which the originals and the copies were sandwiched and outlined in a glowing red light. Once the lettering was added, the technicians removed the fake and studied the original under magnification. Then freehand, like a fine artist, they added the appropriate marks and stains using tools from the toolbox.

They worked quickly and precisely.

"Who has got the green mold?"

"How does this look?"

Nearly forty minutes passed. The senior agent walked over to Taft.

"I just checked the bug you left," he said easily. "The guard is still snoring."

"Thank you, sir," Taft said.

"I've also got a man watching the front door of the archaeology building. He says no one has come in or out."

"Perfect," Taft said. The forgers were now doing a final check to insure the ink had dried. Seconds later, they were reassembling the packets into the appropriate boxes. When each man had finished, he slid the box he had worked on back into the duffel bag.

"Sir," Lee said finally, "we're a go."

Taft rose from his seat and slid the bag over his shoulder.

"Good thing you're not paid by the hour," he said, starting for the door.

"You just get inside and back out again," Lee said to Taft.

"Piece of cake," Taft said with a wave to Lee as he left the impromptu laboratory.

A Marine led him down the stairs and saluted him at the landing.

"Good luck, sir."

Taft nodded slowly, and then peered out. Seeing no one, he walked out the door.

***

There is no precise way to accurately gauge skin absorption of chemical outside a controlled environment. Taft had placed a quarter-sized spot on the doorknob, an amount that should have kept the guard sleeping for hours. But the guard must not have placed his palm completely on the knob—that or he had the drug tolerance of a rock star. He awoke just as Taft was placing the boxes back on the bench.

Two seconds later he was on his feet and running at Taft.

When doing fieldwork, the ability to improvise is often times more critical than brute strength or firepower. So is planning. Taft had rehearsed what he would do if this happened.

Taft took a punch in the jaw.

There were a hundred ways Taft could have disabled the man if he needed to do that. Instead, his plan was to fight with the guard just long enough for it to appear real. He let the guard grab him from behind. But then the man bit him on the neck.

As quick as a flash of light, Taft elbowed the man in the ribs, cracking three. As soon as he released his hold on him, Taft turned and punched the guard in the nose. Blood flowed from the guard's nostrils and he staggered backward. Taft slipped past him and raced for the door.

"He is not the true Messiah," Taft screamed as he ran out.

Five minutes later, the University building was surrounded by police and a military unit. Taft was long gone by then and the fakes were safely in place. The police and the military would put it down as an aborted robbery by a religious zealot. They would not allow that to happen again.

16

EARLY EVENING, a pair of men wearing disguises sat on a bench on the west side of a public park in Caracas wearing disguises. Even with the fake beards, mustaches and hats pulled low, they were still wary.

"The robbery attempt makes things much more complicated," one said quietly with a slight accent.

"We need it done."

"We are good but we cannot do the impossible."

"I'm willing to pay more."

"Where are the documents now?"

"We understand they are still at the University but security is very tight."

"So we do it there?"

"I've learned from a follower that tomorrow night they are due to be removed and taken to Caracas Museum so the curators can determine if they are stable enough to be displayed."

"That cannot happen," the man said seriously. "Once there they will be well protected."

"My man on the inside has given me the security arrangements and the intended route. The switch is scheduled for two in the morning when the city sleeps."

"In that case my team can do it," the taller man said. "But it will cost more—a lot more."

"Money and religion," the other man said, rising. "They always go together. You just be sure and have someone remember to do the writing. It is critically important."

***

"How's it look, Doc?" Taft asked the doctor at the American embassy.

"The human mouth is packed with deadly bacteria," the doctor said easily.

"Thanks. You have a pleasant bedside manner," Taft said.

"I washed the wound and stitched it closed," the doctor said, tapping Taft's inner elbow to raise a vein. "Once I shoot you up with this antibiotic, you should be just fine."

The doctor administered the injection.

"Did you take a dental impression?" Taft said. "I want to find this guy and beat him to death."

The senior CIA officer rose from a chair in the examination room.

"You'd better do it fast, Mr. Taft," he said easily. "The last communication I received said you've been ordered to return home with me shortly."

Taft rose from his seat and touched the cotton ball the doctor had taped to his arm.

"Can I have some pain pills, please?" he said to the doctor, who was washing his hands.

"Something to knock you out would be more appropriate," the doctor muttered.

Taft walked to where the CIA man was holding the door open.

"Bill my insurance," he said.

"Just get out," the doctor said, shaking his head and laughing.

17

THREE HOURS later and thousands of miles away, Larry Martinez was knee deep in biblical research. Taft had called a few minutes prior to say he was in Tampa, waiting while the CIA jet was refueled. Martinez had assured his partner that he did not need a T-shirt from Tampa, and that he would meet him when the plane landed. Then he returned to his work.

Martinez had already read a book discussing the possibility that Jesus might have fathered children. He was now halfway through a second book on the same subject. The idea was not as far-fetched as he'd first believed. Still like many Mexican-Americans, Martinez was raised Catholic. And while he had come to question many church practices over the years, the very idea that Jesus may have been more man than God was somewhat disturbing to him.

He wondered to himself if this question was one best left unanswered as the telephone rang.

"Hi honey, it's me," his wife, Marie, said sweetly.

"Hello, dear," Martinez said. "John's safe. He just called from Tampa."

"Did you ask him about a spoon?"

Marie collected spoons etched with the names of cities, states and countries.

"Has he ever forgotten?"

"No, he never has," Marie said, laughing.

"Is this about dinner?" Martinez glanced at his watch.

"Yes. Do you want us to go ahead and eat?"

"Can you give me a half hour or so?"

"However long you need dear," Marie said. "I gave the kids a snack an hour ago. They're doing their homework now."

"Need anything else?"

"Just you at home, love," Marie said.

"I hear that."

Martinez cut the connection, then dialed another number.

"Karen, this is Larry Martinez," he said. "Is my research finished?"

Two floors above in the analysts' section, Karen the receptionist flipped through a stack of padded manila envelopes on her desk and read the cover sheet before answering.

"It looks like it, Mr. Martinez. I can send the packet down the chute to the front desk right now, if you'd like."

"Thanks, I'm just getting ready to leave."

"It's already been vetted for secrecy," Karen said, "and stamped for out of the building. As long as you have your security briefcase, you should be able to grab it and run."

"Thanks a bunch," Martinez said. "Have a good rest of the night."

"You too," Karen said pleasantly.

After locking his desk, Martinez walked out the office door and punched a code into the keypad on the wall to the left. He made his way to the elevator, carrying his briefcase, and rode down. At the front desk, he signed a log that stated that he was taking material home, and a second log that showed he was leaving for the night. Then he walked through the lobby and out the front door. He smelled rain in the air as he unlocked his minivan and climbed inside.

His mind was full of troubling thoughts and he drove down the road like a robot.

***

Popular support for Vincente Cristos was not growing in Venezuela, it was exploding. Less than forty-eight hours after Allende had broken the story the polls were showing his chance of being elected at greater than eighty percent.

"He'd need to be found with a young boy in a compromising position not to be elected," Allende's female assistant cracked.

"And the young boy would need to be dead," Allende said.

"I doubt even charges of pedophilia, homosexuality, or necrophilia could stop him now," Allende's producer noted. "His election is a lock."

The three men were sitting in the producer's office at TSS drinking champagne and smoking Cuban cigars. Once in a reporter's life, if lucky, he'd have a chance to break a story with such far-reaching implications. The men all knew this. Unless Allende screwed up, he was set for life.

"We've recreated the attempted robbery for tonight's broadcast," the producer said.

"Excellent," Allende said, smiling.

"I've almost reached an agreement with Diane Sawyer's people for the interview," the assistant noted. "They have met all of your demands."

"Good," Allende said. "Then add some more."

The phone rang.

"I said no interruptions," the producer said into the speaker.

"It is the Artist Agency of America calling from California for Allende," the receptionist said. "They would like to speak to him about representation."

"I'll take it at my desk," Allende said, rising.

The producer raised his eyebrow as Allende walked out. He wasn't finished with this meeting. Since the story had broken, his star reporter had negotiated a pay raise, a company car and driver and a wide-screen television. He hated to think what he might ask for if someone else was handling the negotiations.

The producer's concern was well founded. In the next few hours the story would explode once again. He poured himself another glass of champagne and stared at the assistant.

"So," he said. "If you want him, I'd move quickly. This story has made him a star."

She nodded. Her intentions must have been obvious.

18

THE BATTLE would be between two unequal opponents.

A pair of two-and-one-half-ton Venezuelan army trucks rumbled away from the Caracas University archaeology laboratory. Tufts of dry rain danced over the asphalt like Mississippi cotton blown from the pod. The trucks were old and their electrical systems were failing. Only a pair of dim yellow beams from the headlights illuminated the road ahead.

There were eight soldiers in the rear of each truck plus one driver per—eighteen men in all. The soldiers carried carbines and wore sidearms, but they would prove to be no match for the highly trained force about to descend.

One block ahead a lone man stood along the road. In his hand was a simple-looking plastic device with a single switch. Hidden under a cardboard box at his feet was a more elaborate device with magnified battery power. His other hand held a wooden picket with a paper sign attached. He waited patiently until the trucks approached.

Just a protester, the driver in the lead truck thought as he came near and read the sign.

The phony protester flipped the plastic switch, sending a massive surge of electricity under the hoods of both trucks. The jolts were so powerful they melted the distributor caps and shorted out the trucks' electrical systems. The truck engines ceased firing and the drivers steered the now-dead trucks to the side of the road. A pair of black Chevrolet Suburbans with Orliken fire cannons perched above the roof line and slid to a stop at an angle behind each of the truck's rear openings. Spotlights blinded the soldiers inside as four men from each

Suburban jumped out and pointed into the trucks with their American-made assault rifles and loaded grenade launchers.

"Move and you die," one of the men shouted in Spanish.

Hands went in the air as the crack team from the Suburbans formed an offensive perimeter around the trucks. Then the captors moved forward. With two men covering, the others disarmed the soldiers inside the trucks and took their weapons to the Suburbans.

A lone man, taller than most, walked over to the lead truck and removed the cargo boxes. He quickly examined the documents inside each and shouted in Spanish, "They're real."

"Move them now! Go, go," he shouted as the crack team loaded the document boxes into the Suburbans.

Then a second later, in what approached a ballet of movement, the forces began retreat to the Suburbans, leaving a single man guarding each truck. A few seconds after that a pair of thumps was heard as gas grenades were launched into the rear of the trucks. Then the last two members of the crack team ran to the now-moving Suburbans and jumped into the open doors.

The entire operation had taken less than three minutes. The screams of the Venezuelan soldiers lasted a lot longer.

The tall man in the lead Suburban shouted to go faster through the streets. It was hot in the Suburban and the tall man began to sweat under his black Kevlar bulletproof vest. He flicked the fan higher and looked ahead through the windshield as they raced the few blocks from the Central University area to the Jardin Botanico, or botanical gardens, directly ahead. Both Suburbans slid to a stop, but only the tall man jumped out. He moved quickly into a Venezuelan-made limousine. Two other men transferred the boxes to a helicopter on the botanical grounds. The helicopter lifted off and flew a short distance into the countryside outside Caracas to a crude landing strip.

Already in place was a transport plane, propeller turning and engine revving. The boxes were transferred and the plane slid along the packed dirt, then lifted into the air. He flew low to avoid detection on radar.

By the time the disabled trucks were reported, the boxes were eighty miles east of Caracas, one hundred feet in the air. The pilot had a long way to go and he stared at the digital fuel meters to check his burn rate. The plane was alone in the sky over the forest. A full moon lit his way.

19

ALLENDE STOOD with a microphone in front of the twisted wreckage of the still-smoking trucks. Awakened from a dead sleep by an anonymous call, he'd quickly dressed and driven to the area. There he'd met the TSS cameraman working the graveyard shift.

"Light me from the side," Allende ordered the cameraman. "I don't have stage make-up on."

"All right," the cameraman said, adjusting the light, "we have a window in seven seconds."

Allende watched for the hand signals to count down and then began speaking. In the background, firemen were still hosing down the trucks.

"A daring nighttime raid on trucks carrying the Cristos Parchment to a more secure location has resulted in chaos near downtown Caracas. In the background, you can see the trucks that were being used to transport the documents to their new home." He waited, listening to his ear piece.

At the TSS newsroom, his assistant, Marguerite Malagori, had awakened at the same time as Allende, then made her way to the newsroom. She was about to do her first on-camera work. She adjusted her shirt to try to cover her cleavage before speaking.

"That is reporter Gustavo Allende on a live remote near downtown Caracas," she said, showing surprising poise. "Gustavo, can you determine the status of the documents right now?"

The image was split on the screen with Malagori to the left in the newsroom and Allende live at the scene.

"Marguerite, the scene is just now unfolding, but I've asked Lieutenant Jesus Guzman, on-site commander for the Caracas firefighters, to join us."

The camera panned to take in Guzman.

"Lieutenant Guzman," Allende said seriously, "do you know the status of the documents?"

Guzman was fifty years old and stout. With his graying hair, serious air and formal uniform, he fit his job perfectly. A casting agent could not have supplied a better man for the role.

"It appears the trucks were disabled with a high-tech device. Immediately thereafter the boxes were removed and then the soldiers guarding them were hit with gas grenades," Guzman said. "There is no sign of the boxes or their contents."

"How many are dead?" Allende asked.

"No deaths for certain, but all of the soldiers were transported by ambulance to the hospital a few moments ago."

Malagori cut in, much to Allende's dismay.

"Did any of the soldiers have a chance to explain what happened before being taken away?"

"I was just going to ask that," Allende said, turning to Guzman. "Our anchor in the newsroom wants to know if you had a chance to speak to any of the soldiers?"

"One of them," Guzman answered.

"And what did they say happened?" Allende asked.

"He described a lightning raid by a highly trained offensive force. He was in front and could only watch the scene unfold from his rearview mirror. He watched as the boxes were removed and loaded into another vehicle."

"Did he provide any description of the attacker's vehicles?" Allende asked.

"He said they appeared to be a pair of all-black American-made Chevrolet Suburbans."

In the TSS newsroom, Malagori was reading a sheet just handed to her by the night producer.

"Gustavo, may I interrupt?"

"Go ahead, Marguerite," Allende said reaching up and adjusting his ear piece.

"TSS has just intercepted a radio broadcast from the Caracas police. A patrol officer reported he has come across a pair of similar trucks to your description a few blocks from your location. The engines are running but no one was nearby."

"Lieutenant Guzman, I want to thank you for speaking with us tonight," Allende said dispatching the fireman. "Now back to Marguerite in the studio."

The lights went dim as the camera stopped filming.

Allende shouted into his microphone to the manager in the TSS newsroom.

"Give me the address for the trucks."

***

Professionals would leave few clues, Allende thought as he prepared to go live at the scene where the Suburbans had been found. The patrol officer had been smart and had not allowed anyone to climb inside the vehicles. The trucks still sat idling, the clouds of exhaust smoke giving them the appearance of living organisms. Allende stood a few feet behind the open rear cargo doors of the second truck, giving the camera a clear view of the inside. To the right, the chassis of the Orliken fire cannon was visible. So was the back of the driver's seat.

"We are a few blocks from where the army trucks carrying the Cristos Parchment were attacked. In the background a pair of black Suburbans alleged to have been used in the heist sit awaiting inspection by Caracas police," Allende said.

"Any idea yet who is behind this horrible crime?" Malagori asked.

The TSS night producer was just off to the side of the anchor desk, staring at the live feed. He placed his face next to the screen and stared again. Something caught his eye.

"Order the cameraman to come in close on the inside of the truck," he shouted to an assistant.

The man radioed the instructions and a second later Allende was no longer visible. Now the fire cannon and the velour backing of the driver's seat filled the screen. There was something there. The manager scrawled out a note and ordered it taken to Malagori, who received and read the note on camera. Off-camera but unaware of this, Allende was answering her prior question with a negative.

"Gustavo," Malagori interrupted, "the producer has noticed some markings on the rear of the driver's seat. Could you peer inside and see what they might be?"

Allende turned and stared through the rear doors. A minute passed before he turned around again and spoke.

"It looks like someone took his finger and made marks on the velour fabric," he said finally. "I am unable to make out the writing."

Back in the studio the producer had taken a single frame of picture from the tape that had just been recorded. Next he copied the image onto a sheet of paper and studied them. The letters had all the earmarks of Arabic.

"Find me someone who speaks and reads Arabic," he shouted to the newsroom.

Right then, a captain with the Caracas Police pulled up and ordered Allende to back away from the trucks.

20

"GOT IT," a technician at Fort Meade said, pulling the image off the tape.

He handed it to the supervisor, who fed it into a scanner and waited as a computer sorted through a database. He didn't have long to wait.

ALLAH IS GOD, the computer returned.

The supervisor turned to his side, where another analyst was furiously punching commands into a keyboard.

"Clear skies over Caracas," he said. "No need for Smokey."

Smokey was the NSA code name for the single satellite under NSA control that could easily peer through clouds with perfect definition. It was a good thing it was clear, because if they'd needed to reposition Smokey it would take another hour. The control room at Fort Meade was nearly the size of a football field. It featured floor-to-ceiling screens that showed the track of the satellites or images beamed from them in pictures thirty feet tall.

The telephone next to the supervisor beeped and he answered.

"The satellite shot is set up, sir," a technician across the room said.

"Pan the area around the trucks and then come in at the windshield at forty-five degrees and magnify."

"You want the serial numbers on the dash under both windshields, sir?"

"Exactly," the supervisor said.

***

At the same instant the satellite was shooting the first images, the TSS producer was handing the sheet with the image on it to the Muslim night janitor. The janitor's mouth was full of green leaves and his other hand held a chipped cup. He spit in the cup.

"Allah is God," he said.

"Are you sure?" the producer asked.

"There is no God but Allah and Mohammed is the prophet of Allah," he said repeating the Shahabad, or Muslim statement of faith. Of that, I am absolutely certain. As to those letters on this sheet, I am reasonably certain that is what they say."

"Thanks, Tarif."

It was time to decide. The producer spoke to the now-filling newsroom:

"We are going to go with it."

Malagori and Allende had been repeating what scant information was available, while at the same time filling minutes with another reporter who had been dispatched to the hospital where the injured soldiers were taken. They had already repeated the story a dozen times, simply changing the way they worded the information. And now they were praying for something else to break. A sheet of paper was handed to Malagori.

"Allende," she said interrupting. "We have a breaking development."

The camera showed Allende, who stood waiting.

"TSS has analyzed the writing on the seat back of the Suburban truck. We now think we know what it reads in English," Malagori said.

Allende thought to himself that Marguerite was catching on fast. She was slowly leaking the story, building the tension. He had to keep an eye on her—or she could become a threat to his job.

"What does it say?" Allende asked.

"We believe it reads: 'Allah is God,'" she said dramatically. "Since you covered the unrest in Azerbaijan for TSS, there is no reporter better qualified to comment on what this might mean."

Allende had not reached his vaulted position as a reporter without the ability to cross the line from reporting facts to stating opinion. He began to improvise.

"Muslim rebels have long wished the rest of the world would reduce Jesus Christ to the status of prophet. Perhaps this is their way of leveling the playing field for religion," he began. "Recently..."

***

"TSS is now reporting that they believe Muslim radicals might be behind the theft of the Cristos Parchment," the NSA analyst for Venezuela shouted across the room.

The NSA night supervisor was standing near the huge screens watching. The satellite cameras were focusing in on the first serial number. It flashed across the screen ten feet high. A dozen pens wrote it down even though it was being stored on tape. The second number appeared and the people in the room again wrote it down.

"Trace the serial numbers and find out where they came from," the supervisor said. "Then get me General Fairbanks. The National Security Council will want to know about this."

21

TAFT STEPPED to the door of the Citation jet, then onto the steps where he waved his hand to a nonexistent crowd like a rock star on tour. His last mission had ended and Taft was on top of the world. The CIA officer standing behind him laughed.

"My people?" Taft asked. "Where are my people?"

"We're secret agents, remember," the CIA man said. "Now quit screwing around and get off our plane. I'm tired and I want to go home."

In spite of Taft's antics, the CIA man had grown to like the agent from the competing agency. He'd even gone so far as to offer Taft a job with the CIA when his retirement came through. But Taft would have none of that, explaining that he was out of intelligence work forever. The two men walked side by side through the night air to the terminal.

Just then the terminal door opened and Larry Martinez walked out.

"Honey," Taft said, "I'm home."

"Don't ask, don't tell," Martinez said.

"My partner, Larry Martinez," Taft said to the CIA officer. "And we are joking."

"You've got a good hand here," the CIA officer said to Martinez as he opened the door. "He pulled our ass from the fire."

Martinez simply nodded.

Taft shook the CIA agent's hand. "Be sure and write."

The agent shook his head and walked away.

Once he was gone, Martinez reached for Taft's bag.

"How was the blue blood to work with?" Martinez said, referring to the CIA habit of hiring from Ivy League schools.

"He's a good guy—the real deal," Taft noted.

The two men walked through the small private terminal and then out onto the awning-covered driveway in front where Taft's Jaguar sat waiting.

"You asked me to charge the battery," Martinez explained. "I figured the best way would be to drive it here."

Taft opened the driver's door and climbed into the seat while Martinez crammed Taft's bag into the rear. Once Martinez was in the passenger seat, Taft turned the key and waited as the engine rumbled to life. Then he adjusted the radio to the oldies station and slid the Jaguar into gear. Releasing the clutch he pulled away from the terminal. An Otis Redding song seeped from the speakers. They were a block away from the airport when Martinez spoke.

"There has been a development," Martinez said. "The Cristos Parchment was stolen."

"Is this your way of congratulating me?" Taft said. "You can just tell me I did a good job and I put a little something extra in your paycheck."

"The fakes you planted were stolen," Martinez said, "in what is being described as *a daring raid by highly trained operatives*. They hijacked the truck carrying the papers to their new home."

"No way," Taft blurted.

"True story," Martinez said. "Venezuelan television has pinned the crime on radical Islamic terrorists."

"How did they decide that?"

"One of the terrorists was doodling with his finger on the back of the driver's seat of the assault vehicle."

"Fingerprints?"

"Apparently everyone was wearing gloves."

"So you are telling me a crack team ambushes and steals probably the most valuable papers ever recorded by mankind—but then out of boredom one of the men doodles on the back of a seat with his finger and leaves a clue."

"Hard to believe," Martinez agreed.

"Bullshit is more accurate," Taft said.

"I kind of thought that too. But so far our side is treating it as true."

Taft drove along quietly thinking.

"Removing the evidence," he said after a pause, "makes more sense."

Martinez nodded. "There you go thinking outside the box again. No one know you made the switch and everyone still thinks those were the originals."

"Exactly. Let's just say someone planted them originally and knew they would not stand up to detailed scrutiny. So they grabbed them back, thus preserving the integrity of the documents. All you would have then is the opinion of the scholars. Tough to argue they are not genuine then."

"Brilliant," Martinez said, "then blame the theft on Arab terrorists—everyone's current favorite villain."

Taft laughed.

"Take it further. What if they planted a few clues the CIA missed on the duplicates. They might be sitting there right now realizing what they have stolen back are fakes. But they would have no idea who has the genuine article."

"It could be the old double-whammy of misinformation. Beautiful."

Taft pulled off the highway and then turned down Martinez's street. A few seconds later he pulled up in front of his partner's house and braked to a stop.

"I spoke to Marie on the cell a while ago. She made you some sandwiches," Martinez said as he opened the door, "in case you were hungry."

Taft reached back to his bag then unzipped a side pocket and removed a silver spoon.

"Thank her for me, Larry," he said, "but I'm dog-tired. I think I'll pass."

He handed Martinez the spoon from Venezuela. "Give her this with my love."

"Fair enough," Martinez said, climbing from the seat, then bending down.

"When does Benson want to see me?"

"Seven a.m.," Martinez said.

"Good," Taft said. "Let me go home and get some sleep. We'll discuss our theory with him in the morning. Oh, and I have a surprise for you tomorrow."

"Clues?"

"That would take the fun out of it."

"Fair enough," Martinez said. "I'm glad you are back home safe. A fitting end to a fine career."

"I thought so too," Taft said out the window as he pushed on the accelerator and pulled away.

22

"WE HAD TO wake someone up at home but we have the information," an NSA analyst said.

"The Suburbans are built in Ohio by a company named Armored Coaches. They are favored by dictators and despots, along with the usual Arab sheiks. Due to the nature of their product and the addition of the Orliken, each sale must be approved by the Director of the Bureau of Alcohol, Tobacco and Firearms."

"Let me guess," The NSA supervisor said, "South America? No. Persian Gulf? I've got it. It was a Venezuelan drug lord."

"That's three wrong guesses," the analyst noted, "The pair went to Executive Response in South Africa."

"The army-for-hire company?"

"Exactly."

"How the hell did they get to Venezuela?"

"We're working on that, sir," the analyst said rising.

"Find out who hired Executive Response while you're at it."

***

Marty Thompson stared at the desk clerk. He had just been told that a pair of detectives from the Caracas Police had been looking for him.

"Did they say what they wanted?" Thompson asked.

The clerk understood enough English to understand the question but he said nothing. Reaching in his pocket, Thompson removed a fifty from a wad of bills held in place by a thick rubber band. He slid the bill across the desk.

"You sell armored vehicles, right?" the clerk asked, "limousines and Suburbans?"

"Yes," Thompson said.

"I think they want to talk to you about the robbery."

Thompson had spent the day at the home of one Venezuela's corporate moguls. He'd heard nothing about any robbery.

"What robbery?" Thompson asked.

After the clerk explained, Thompson reached back in his pocket and peeled off stack of hundred-dollar bills. Thompson held them in his hand as bait.

"Give me my passport."

He had locked his passport in the hotel safe.

"I can't," the clerk said. "The police took it."

Bypassing the elevator and running up the stairs, Thompson quickly collected his bags and raced toward the American embassy as he had been instructed by his company.

***

In his office at the Venezuelan Capital the current President was huddled with his advisors.

"The Muslim ghetto is on fire and there have been nearly a dozen people lynched already," an advisor said. "The anger against them seems to be growing."

"What time is Cristos speaking?" The President said.

"In an hour," another aide said.

The President turned to the head of the Federal Security Service. "I want you to take charge of this situation. An hour after Cristos speaks, I will declare martial law from sunup to sundown. Use whatever force you need to. I want this situation back under control."

"It's going to look like you're trying to thwart Cristos," one of the aides noted.

The President rose and walked over to the window and stared out. On the horizon, through a crack between the buildings, he could see the glow of fires burning.

"I don't care," he said firmly. "People are dying that don't deserve it and this situation has gotten totally out of control. Alert the U.S. ambassador to our intentions."

Turning from the window, he stared at the head of the Venezuelan military.

"Secure the armories place your troops on alert and await further instructions," The President said. The Venezuelan general rose from his chair.

"We will need fuel for the tanks, sir. Our stockpiles are depleted."

"I'll release the strategic reserves." The President reached for the telephone.

***

The crowd numbered roughly a million Venezuelans. They thronged in and around Parque del Este and spilled onto the side streets for miles in every direction. Most were white Christians, Orthodox, Roman Catholic, or Protestant.

There were few people of color in the crowd and almost none that were Jewish or Muslim. The non-Christians were scared. Along with the fires in the Muslim quarter, the Jewish section of Caracas had been singled out for hatred. Doors had been marked as they were in Nazi Germany, and widespread street harassment and beatings had been reported.

Whoever had stolen the documents and left the Islamic message had unleashed evil. It was as if the seething hatred of failure and poverty that had gripped Venezuela since the economic collapse had finally found a common enemy. Blame shifted from the system of government to outsiders who had poured into Caracas in the past decade. It was not the Venezuelan citizens or politicians who had brought down the once-great country—instead it was those that sought salvation from a different God. That which was good was becoming bad.

Religious persecution, that most ancient and ugly of prejudices, had found a home.

***

The set that was erected in the center of the park was elaborate enough to host any rock band. A large center stage was elevated ten feet in the air with four separate adjacent stages dropping down like plateaus from the heavens. There were four massive towers topped with speakers, two flanking the main stage and two on the lowest level. The wall of speakers was augmented by smaller ones strung throughout the park and side streets, attached to trees and streetlights. And still more equipment was at center stage, including smoke generators, laser lights and pyrotechnics. A humble man would have been disgusted.

Behind a large black curtain, Vincente Cristos stood with his eyes closed. He was dressed in a black banded shirt with white collars and cuffs, giving the appearance of clerical garb. His pants were black, his wool long outer coat the same. His black polished shoes had lifts making him appear even taller and in his hand he held an ancient-looking Bible. The light backstage glinted off the ornate jewel-encrusted cross that rode on a thick gold chain at heart level.

"One minute, sir," an assistant said quietly.

Cristos counted off the seconds then strode through the curtain into a spotlight.

"Good evening, my friends," he said to thunderous applause.

23

AT FORT MEADE, an analyst checked the volume levels and nodded to his supervisor.

"Perfect," he said.

Scattered throughout the crowd were U.S. agents with microphones to monitor crowd response. Backstage, a Venezuelan, bought and paid for by American intelligence, had hooked directly into the live feed to beam to a satellite. The NSA was listening and recording the speech with a two-second delay.

***

"Venezuela enters a new era. A golden era of discovery and progress," Cristos said to the crowd. "It will be an era of leadership with divine possibilities—an era of renewed strength and power. It will mean resurrection for our country—and a rebirth for our homeland."

Applause erupted that rattled nearby windows and swept across the crowd like a gusting wind. Instead of divine forgiveness, he sought retribution.

"Muslim terrorists have taken our proof, but true faith cannot be silenced. True faith is believing in that which cannot be seen. Look to me to lead. Look to me to take you to the Promised Land."

***

Inside the briefing room at the National Security Council, the leader of the free world sat listening to the transmission. Their faces were ashen and sullen.

"This is not good," The President of the United States said.

In Caracas, Cristos had spent the last few minutes talking of a time in the future when Venezuela would triumph. Pandemonium gripped the crowd. So he played his trump card. The laser lights began to scan the heavens, lighting the layer of clouds over Caracas, while at the same time trails of smoke began to pour from the generators. The climax was near.

"I stand before you as the Son of God and man," he said to the crowd.

The stage erupted with twin explosions of light and noise from the pyrotechnics on each side.

"And ask my country to allow me to use my divine powers with the heavens above to take charge of your troubles and ease them, to bring prosperity and faith to a land that has suffered, to bring glory back to a people who so richly deserve it. We will go forth boldly and crush our enemies and seek salvation."

The pyrotechnic cannons were firing at timed intervals during the speech.

"I am the Messiah," said Cristos. "Do not fail me."

The finale began with twelve giant tubes of explosives discharging their ordnance. Each tube held six aerial rockets as large around as a man's head and six feet long. The rockets streaked skyward and exploded over Caracas in a fireworks display of red and orange and yellow. Cristos walked back behind the curtain. Thirty seconds later he was seated in the back of a helicopter, which quickly lifted off and swept over the crowd.

That night there was no order in Caracas, only chaos.

***

"Talk to me," The President of the United States said.

Unlike most of his time in office where he allowed corporate advisors and hangers-on determine his courses of action, he was taking an unusual and hands-on interest in the affairs in Venezuela.

"The President of Venezuela has warned us that he is declaring martial law in one hour," the Secretary of State said.

His second-in-command at the State Department spoke next. "The Knesset is meeting at this hour in a special night session," he said. "The Israelis want him to guarantee safe passage to anyone who wishes to leave the country. If he does not provide for this, Israel is considering using force to arrange a safe harbor inside Venezuela for anyone Jewish who feels threatened."

"And how do they expect to do that?" The President asked the CIA director.

"Our intelligence indicates that the plan is to have a secret location near Caracas spread through their people through word-of-mouth. Once they have assembled they will erect a defensive perimeter and begin to ferry out those that want to leave."

"Sounds like suicide," The President said "The Venezuelans will crush their forces."

"That is a distinct possibility," the CIA director said, "but when have the Israelis not been ready to die for their cause?"

"Their actions will inflame the entire Middle East," The President said.

He turned to the director of the Defense Intelligence Agency.

"General, you've got contacts in the Persian Gulf. What are they saying?"

"The Saudis will provide safe havens for any Muslims that want to flee," the general said. "And they've promised any amount of funds necessary. They will buy the Muslims their freedom if need be. Then they will be picked up by vessels in a sea lift, like when Cuba fell."

"Besides martial law, where's the Venezuelan President on all this?" The President asked.

The assistant CIA director spoke. "He wants a solution..." the man began.

"I'll bet he does," the President said caustically.

"But he's caught in a trick-bag. If he suspends the coming elections, he'll be hunted down and hung. If martial law doesn't work and he moves against his own people with sufficient force to quell the unrest there will be a lot of his people dead."

The door opened and an aide to the Secretary of Defense entered and handed him a note. The President waited while he read.

"What is it?" he said, when the Secretary of Defense looked up.

"The Chinese have fired on one of our guided-missile destroyers near the Spratly Islands. The ship reports nearly one hundred dead and injured. The captain advises the vessel is taking on water and is in danger of sinking."

"Move quickly," The President said. "I want a worldwide show of American strength against the Chinese. Have the diplomats explain that anyone who moves against Venezuela will face U.S. intervention. Serve notice the world is on hold for a time until these messes can be sorted out. Next, get the Navy any help they need and save those sailors. That's all."

The room began to empty. The President motioned to General Benson to remain.

"General," he said quietly, "you had better hope that the theft of the Cristos Parchment was not a copycat response to Taft screwing up the switch. If I find out it was, I'm going to cut your agency and its budget off at the knees."

"Yes, sir," Benson said.

"I need some answers."

"Yes sir," Benson said, saluting.

After the room was clear the President reached for the telephone and dialed a number in Texas.

24

TAFT AWOKE, uneasy, in his home along the Potomac River.

He rose from his bed and took a few steps to where a mini-refrigerator was built into a cabinet. When he had remodeled his house, he'd combined two of the smaller bedrooms into his master suite. Along with the cabinet that stretched across one wall and his king-sized bed, there was a chest for clothes, a large walk-in closet and a pair of chairs around an oval table. Reaching into the refrigerator he removed a bottle of pineapple juice, flicked on the sound system and walked naked into the bathroom.

Taft had gone all-out decorating his bathroom. The floor of the huge room featured large Mexican tiles covered with thick plush cotton mats. Along one entire wall in a semi-private enclave was a pair of sinks set in cherry-wood cabinets along with mirrors, antique medicine chests and a pair of tall houseplants. The toilet was trimmed with gold and had come from an elegant old Washington D.C. hotel that was meeting the wrecking ball.

Standing over the toilet, he relieved himself and walked back and stared in the mirror. He was a little pale—the result of too much time indoors. A full-length tanning bed lay outside along one wall but Taft was short on time. Instead he walked into the bathing area, which held a large tub with jets and a separate shower with twin heads behind a glass wall. He selected the shower and turned the knobs to hot.

He started to wash just as the compact disc player flipped over to Leo Kottke. Guitar music began to flow from the speakers. His sixth sense rarely failed him. If he felt uneasy, there was probably a good reason, something to do with work.

Rinsing the shampoo from his hair, he stared at an old railroad clock on the wall. He had just enough time to dress and make the seven o'clock meeting with the general. The telephone rang as he toweled himself dry. Taft reached for the bathroom extension.

"Wake-up call," Martinez said.

"Just got out of the shower," Taft replied.

"I'm leaving now," Martinez said, "want me to pick you up anything?"

"If you're stopping anyway, grab me a protein bar and a banana."

"Anything to drink?"

"I'll get some coffee at the office."

"Fair enough," Martinez said. "Now get a move on or you'll be late."

"Then get off the phone," Taft said and hung up.

Moments later, dressing rapidly, he looked into a mirror on the closet door, then tied his tie and put on socks and polished black shoes.

"Not bad," he said out loud to his image in the mirror.

25

GENERAL EARL Benson had not slept past five in the morning for thirty years. Today he had risen at four thirty, made some notes in his home office, and then arrived at the NIA headquarters at five forty-one. After checking the overnight news, he was sipping the third cup of coffee this morning. His second-in-command, Richard Albright, sat in the chair across from his desk.

"More problems in the Philippines," Albright noted. "There are roughly twenty dead in the mass demonstrations."

"They should have never pardoned the ex-pres," Benson said.

He was referring to Philippine president's recent decision to give a former president a full pardon and release him from jail, where he was serving time on corruption and graft charges.

"Whatever happens," Albright said, "they need to regain control. We could use a safe harbor with this new problem with China."

"Shouldn't have given back Clark Air Force Base," Benson added.

Benson was flipping through the pile of papers left on his desk by the overnight supervisor. One was a satellite photograph of the *USS Marshall Islands*, the guided missile destroyer that was struck by Chinese fire. He handed the photograph to Albright.

"I checked just before I came in here," Albright said. "The latest report is one hundred and twenty-two dead and forty-six injured."

"And the Chinese ship that fired on them?"

"The official word is that the ship is missing," Albright noted, "but the fact is one of our Los Angeles-class submarines lit it up with a pair of high-explosive torpedoes."

"Good," Benson said.

"That could mean war," Albright said.

"I doubt it," Benson said. "We have been tracking that ship for months. It's not officially a Chinese navy vessel. They claim it is a privately-owned ship."

"Equipped with a wave-top missile delivery system?"

"Their claim is a bit of a stretch," Benson admitted.

"So the Chinese can't officially complain," Albright said, smiling.

"Not only that—Taiwan was testing one of the new submarines we sold them in the same area. So China isn't even sure it really was us that retaliated," Benson said.

"I love this job," Albright said. "Nothing is ever as it seems."

Benson scanned his notes and sipped from his mug.

"Dick," he said, "the game is Venezuela. This thing with Cristos could potentially involve most of the world taking sides."

"A modem Crusades," Albright said, nodding. "The idea is horrifying."

"Exactly," Benson said, "the Middle East heats up. Next India and Pakistan follow. Europe is still unstable from immigration since the fall of the Iron Curtain, and you see what is happening in the Philippines."

"The Philippine population is eighty-five percent Roman Catholic," Albright noted.

"Religion sometimes breeds terrorism," Benson said, "of the worst kind. I want you to monitor this carefully and don't be afraid to look inside our own country."

"We are not allowed to operate on American soil," Albright observed.

"You know how to cover our tracks," Benson said. "Tie any investigation from overseas to home."

Just then Benson's speaker buzzed.

"Yes," he said to Mrs. Mindio, his long-time assistant.

"Agents Taft and Martinez are here," she said sweetly.

"I'll get on it right away," Albright said, rising.

"Keep me posted, Dick," Benson said, "and on your way out tell Boy Wonder and his partner to come on in."

26

"HE CAN count to a hundred," Mrs. Mindio was telling the pair of agents.

"That would be, what?" Martinez asked, "your fourteenth grandchild?"

Martinez, being a father himself, remembered such things. Taft had no clue.

"Fifteen," Mrs. Mindio said.

Just then the door opened and Albright stepped out to usher them in. Martinez handed back the picture of the grandson, then followed his partner inside. General Benson rose from his desk, shook the agents' hands, then motioned to chairs and offered them coffee.

"Okay, John," Benson said, "tell me exactly what happened."

Taft's explanation took a full five minutes. The steward came with the coffee and left before he had finished.

"The President chewed my ass," Benson said when Taft had concluded. "He thinks the second theft was a copycat robbery and it wouldn't have happened unless you had been caught in the act."

"That's bullshit," Martinez blurted. "What did the President want John to do? Shoot the guard in the head? He was just an old man."

"Thanks, for the support, Larry," Taft said, staring over at his partner.

"No problem," Martinez said.

"You two quit screwing around," Benson said sternly. "I agree there was nothing else you could do. However, the problem that was created remains."

The three men sat silently for a moment.

"Well," Taft said finally, "I guess it's time for my surprise then."

"Oh boy," said Martinez.

"What do you mean?" Benson asked.

"I bugged them—the crates of documents that were stolen," Taft said.

"So this is the big surprise," Martinez exclaimed. "I thought you finally got a pet or something."

"I had some with me for the Albornez mission so I thought, why not?" Taft said. "I stuck one into the wood on the bottom of each box after leaving the forgers. Other than us three, no one else in the world knows about this."

"Damn, Taft," Benson said slowly, "you never cease to amaze me."

"Please save your applause," Taft said. "Larry has something to tell you."

***

Imagine searching for three separate pearls inside three oysters somewhere in the world. It could have been that that hard, except for one saving grace—the bugs had a unique frequency. Even with that small advantage the task would be difficult. The listening devices had a limited effective range—one needed to be reasonably close—or have something that could sweep over a large area.

"The NSA reports the satellites just don't have the necessary equipment," Dick Albright said.

General Benson stood next to a large detailed wall map that covered one entire wall of his office. He traced an outline with a wooden pointer, noting Europe, Asia and Africa with a sweeping gesture.

Albright, standing next to Benson, nodded.

"An Air Force Dark Star can fly this entire area in less than twelve hours," Benson noted. "It may return with a lot of stray targets, but it's a start," Benson said.

"I'll file a request," Albright said.

"Good," Benson said, "report back as soon as you know anything."

"Yes, sir," Albright said as he walked from the office.

***

A strange aircraft left the hangar at Edwards Air Force Base in California. Light gray in color like the sky after a rain, she was shaped like a triangle from the top and a small pyramid from the back. Small wheels on stout landing gear allowed her to roll towards the runway. Pulse engines gave her propulsion—the kind that left a contrail like donuts on strings at high altitudes. Her two pilots were dressed in space suits. One was a colonel, the other a major. They were two of twelve men in the world qualified to fly the odd-shaped craft. The flight surfaces of Dark Star were computer-controlled as was the extensive instruments housed in her fuselage.

The pilots came into play only for training—or problems.

"Runway Five West," the Colonel said. The voice-actuated controls instantly responded and the plane moved in place.

"Tower, this is Dark Star One," the Major said. "Request take-off and unlimited ceiling clearance."

"Granted," the tower responded.

"Dark Star initiate take-off," the Colonel said a second later.

The craft rocked down the runway and lifted into the air. A mile past the end of the runway, it rotated and headed straight toward the heavens. In less than an hour the plane would start snooping.

27

"THE IDEA THAT Jesus had children is ludicrous," televangelist Billy Ray Simpson said.

"What I heard was Cristos claimed he was descended from the family of Jesus," said George Schaefer, head of one of the Lutheran denominations, "that doesn't always mean a child."

The meeting had been called by J. Thomas Melton and was held in the executive offices of The Evangelical Church of Believers. While not the meeting was not officially sanctioned by the governing bodies of the Protestant denominations, most of the mainstream churches had seen fit to send emissaries.

Nearly thirty men sat around the massive solid-wood conference table. Atop the table were silver pitchers of ice water, glass pitchers of orange juice and three large fruit baskets. In front of each chair were crystal glasses, china plates for the fruit rinds and, strangely enough, crystal ashtrays. J. Thomas Melton liked to smoke—and as this was his building—he allowed smoking in areas away from the public.

"This is not new," noted Harold Delville, a progressive Methodist minister noted. "Historians have raised the question over the years and some have argued it is true."

Simpson was an old-school fire-and-brimstone preacher—a fundamentalist who would not hear anything save his own interpretation of the Bible. He straightened the wide lapels on his vanilla-white suit and snorted.

"Shoot Harry," he said, "if you Methodists had your way you'd close all the places of worship and just run outreach centers for drug addicts and out-of-wedlock mothers."

Delville was just getting ready to tell Simpson what a backwoods hillbilly ass he was when Melton interrupted.

"Cut the sniping," Melton ordered.

Everyone in the room turned to him at the head of the table.

"We have a real problem here," he said. "If this is true we may be all out of work."

Jim Gentry, a minister at a progressive church in Boulder, Colorado, raised his hand.

"Yes, Jim," Melton said.

Gentleman Jim, as he was known in professional religion, had built a strong following in the West by preaching a message of tolerance and forgiveness. He continued to attract a following from people disenfranchised with what might be considered normal religion. He picked his words carefully.

"This is one of two things," he said quietly, "either the worst thing to happen to organized religion—or the best."

"How do you figure?" Chet Evans asked. Evans was a country preacher from Tulsa with twenty thousand followers.

"Let's just say for a moment Jesus did have children," Gentry said.

"He didn't," Billy Ray Simpson said.

"Shut up and hear him out, Billy," Melton said, "unless you're ready to sell the Gulfstream."

This was a personal attack. Everyone here knew how Simpson loved his Gulfstream jet.

"If he did," Gentry continued, "and we try to brush it off or cover it up, we are going to meet some major resistance. It would be every other religious scandal times ten. People don't buy hiding religious secrets anymore. They want to think everything is aboveboard and they made their own choices what to believe. So, let's say for a minute, just a minute, he did have children. So what?"

"So what?" blurted Temple McPherson, an up-and-coming charismatic preacher from North Carolina blurted. "Christ not being mortal is the basis of all we've been selling for two thousand years."

Melton had cards up his sleeve. But he would never tell anyone else.

"There is more than one way to skin a cat," Melton said. "Let's hear him out."

"What," Gentry said, "if only to help our congregations during this trying time, we acknowledged this might be a possibility."

Delville was more reasonable than most and warmed up to the idea.

"What about the virgin birth?" Delville said. "There are a couple of passages in the Bible that talk about the birth—but so what? We could still acknowledge the virgin birth, but add that for the son of God to experience the entire realm of human existence he needed to be a husband and a father."

"And he still rose to heaven after the crucifixion?" Simpson said, warming up now.

"A miracle," Gentry said. "We all believe in those."

A light was coming on in McPherson's mind.

"Jesus as the son was blessed by God to have a beautiful wife and kids and brothers and sisters," he said. "That would play with my demographics. A son who died so man could be free. A man who preached a message for yesterday and today. I like it and I could sell it."

Billy Ray Simpson hated to be left out of anything—particularly a profitable idea.

"The Scriptures could be interpreted that way," he said slowly. "If we explained that the facts of marriage and family were left out until the time was right for man to be able to appreciate and understand the ramifications."

"A secret for the new coming time," Gentry said, smiling, "A secret that holds the keys to a happy stress-free life. Family values, love for your fellow man. A Jesus who was a little more like the people that support us. The message could be very powerful."

At the head of the table, J. Thomas Melton was puffing and nodding.

"Jesus was more like you than you knew," he said slowly. "That saying is mine, by the way."

"What would Jesus do?" McPherson said easily. "If he had the same problems as you—a spouse, children, and a difficult job. I am beginning to like this."

"We can turn a negative into a positive," Gentry said.

"We'll probably get a whole bunch of new people in the pews because of this," Simpson said.

"They'll come to hear the new message," Chet Evans said. "And they will come in crowds. They will at the least want to see if mainstream religion can accept new ideas about ancient history."

J. Thomas Melton removed another Camel cigarette from a silver case, lit it with an expensive lighter, and inhaled. The smoke curled around his head.

"This could jump-start our churches like nothing since the threat of nuclear war," he said slowly, "and we don't need to scare them to get them to listen. Let's put this down on paper. I need my computer."

If there was an angle, any angle, Melton would work it over.

A black porter who had recently started working for the church stood along the wall with his arms folded. He walked over to the wet bar, removed a laptop computer and carried to Melton.

"Thank you, Franklin," Melton said. "Now could you have the kitchen rustle up some coffee? I have a feeling we are going to be here awhile."

Franklin nodded. He'd hurry back. He didn't want to miss a second of what was happening. The quicker they figured out the plan, they quicker the meeting would end and he could get out of here.

28

INSIDE THE HANGAR at Edwards Air Force Base, Dark Star's computer was being downloaded into a mainframe. An operator from the NSA loaded a program then entered commands. Two seconds later, a map of possible targets appeared on the screen. There were twelve in total, but nine were quickly eliminated as emissions from U.S. military listening posts. The three that remained were concentrated in the United States.

The operator opened a screen on the computer that connected him with the NSA headquarters at Fort Meade in Maryland. He waited until his commanding officer appeared on the screen.

"What have you got?" the officer asked.

"I think we've got a lock," he said. "I'm transmitting now."

He pushed a button and the map raced across the country over fiber-optic lines.

"Got it," the officer said a second later.

***

"What's the latest?" the President asked.

"Sir," The Secretary of State said, "China is still claiming the attack was an accident. As for their own ship, they're blaming Taiwan."

"Have we got Taiwan protected by the Theater Missile Defense System yet?"

The Secretary of State motioned to an Air Force three-star general.

"Mostly, sir," the general said, "and we're staring them down across the straits. At any one time we have as many as thirty bombers on maneuvers between the two countries."

"Diplomacy?" the President asked.

"The Chinese are not ready to face us head-to-head," the Secretary of State said. "In a few years that might be different but for now we're sure they are just shaking their swords."

"Good," the President said. "We can turn to the rest of the world now. What is the situation in the Philippines?"

"The government cracked down," the director of the CIA said. "The country is under control."

Everyone knew it was back down to one main issue in the world.

"What about Cristos in Venezuela?" the President said.

"He has the election in the bag," the director of the Defense Intelligence Agency noted. "With the support of both the military and the people."

"What about the revelation he may be the descendant of Jesus?"

"It seems to be taken with cautious optimism," the director of the CIA noted.

"And what about here at home," the President pointed to the FBI director.

"A few religious zealots are shouting blasphemy," the FBI man said. "Just to be safe, we have a man inside an informal religious conference being held to hash out the a course of action."

The President was surprised. He was not happy but it did not show.

"And what does your man report?"

"The participants are forming a policy if Cristos is in fact the descendant of Jesus."

"So the religious gurus are not fighting this?"

"Right now it seems they're going along with the flow," the FBI director noted.

"Then what is our major problem?" The President asked.

The Secretary of State tapped a pencil on the table and thought before speaking.

"Come on, anyone?" The President asked.

"Sir," the Secretary of State said, "the major problem is one we've all thought about but no one has verbalized. What if other countries with a Christian majority vote to follow Cristos? He could become the de facto king of the world. What would follow might be religious wars not seen since the days of the Crusades."

"One world government," the President said slowly. "That displaces the United States as leader of the world. That could be truly horrifying."

The President paused before continuing.

"In the last day I've given this a lot of thought. I was beginning to think the discovery of the Cristos Parchment could herald a new era in the world—an era of unparalleled peace and understanding. Now I'm not so sure. This is the worst time for a revelation like this."

All those gathered were quiet.

"Mr. President," General Benson said. "I don't know if this helps or hurts but my agency did something that might have some bearing on this situation."

"Go ahead," The President said.

"I would feel better if only you knew about this for now."

The President ordered the room cleared.

Benson explained.

29

MARTY THOMPSON was dressed in ill-fitting pants and a shirt one size too small. The American embassy in Caracas had at first been accommodating but it was not a clothing store. Not only that, in the past few hours the mood in the embassy had decidedly chilled. Thompson wanted to tell them what they wanted but he wanted assurances first.

"Can you get me back to the United States?" he asked the CIA case officer.

"If we want to," the man said slowly.

"You can't tell my employer," Thompson said, "or I'll lose my job."

"I could just call Venezuelan Intelligence," the case officer noted, "and tell the Marine guards to toss you on the street. I'm sure the Venezuelans have a few ways of making you talk."

Thompson was screwed and he knew it. He just wanted to save face if possible.

"If I tell you," he said, "can you get me on a flight home tonight?"

"Can," the CIA man said easily. "Don't know if I will."

"Come on, man," Thompson said, "give me something."

Just then the door to the small room the men were in opened and a medium-height sandy-haired man entered. The embassy official had been hiding behind a two-way mirror in the next room and had monitored the progress.

"Hal," he said to his partner, "take a break."

The CIA man stood up and stretched, then walked out of the room without a word.

"Kids," the older sandy-haired agent noted, "they have seen one too many movies."

Thompson nodded since he wasn't sure what he was supposed to say.

"Get us some coffee," the older agent shouted.

He then turned to Thompson. "I'm Paul Hyde, the senior agent around here."

Thompson shook the proffered hand.

"Here's the deal, amigo," Hyde started to say as the door opened and a steward brought in a tray with a pitcher of coffee and a pair of blue CIA mugs. The server left quickly and closed the door.

Hyde reached into his pocket and withdrew a pack of Marlboro Reds. Sliding one into his mouth, he clicked open a Zippo lighter, lit the cigarette and motioned with the pack to Thompson. Though he had quit years ago, Thompson took one and bent over so Hyde could light the end.

"I don't really give a rat's ass if you were working a side deal your company didn't know about," Hyde continued. "I don't care if you were in Caracas on a sex tour. I don't care if you were smoking a joint using the American flag as the spark. What I do need to know is who the hell paid for the pair of black Suburbans involved in the robbery."

"Will you get me home?" Thompson said, taking a drag and then coughing lightly.

"Shit, yeah," Hyde said.

"Okay. I originally sold the pair of Suburbans to a South African company but they wanted to trade up. My company doesn't take trade-ins so I worked a side deal out to sell the old ones here in Venezuela and order them a new pair. I timed the deal to go down when I was due to be here in Caracas anyway."

"How much extra did you make?" Hyde asked.

"Seventeen thousand plus my regular commission," Thompson admitted.

"We know who originally bought them," Hyde said, stunning Thompson. "Executive Response."

Thompson suddenly realized he had little to bargain with. At the same instant, he wondered what else they needed from him.

"How were you paid?" Hyde said. "Answer that and you have your get-out-of-jail free card."

"As soon as you put me on a plane," Thompson said, "and I'm safely out of Venezuelan airspace."

Hyde snubbed out the Marlboro and drained the cup of coffee.

"Hal," he shouted to the wall.

The door opened and the first agent stood at the door.

"Take Marty to the airport," Hyde said. "And get him on the first plane to the United States."

"Then what, boss?" Hal asked.

"Wait until he leaves."

"Now, like I said, Hal here will take you to the airport and make sure you leave the country safely. But right now I need you to explain how you were paid," Hyde said.

"I said once I'm on the plane," Thompson said. "And out of Venezuela."

"I don't have time for that," Hyde said, "So you can believe me we will do what I said—or I could shoot you in the knee right now."

Thompson glanced at Hyde. It didn't feel like a bluff. Slowly he nodded his head with all the enthusiasm of a dog swatted with a newspaper. Then he told the agent exactly what he wanted to know.

"Have a safe flight," Hyde told Thompson when he finished.

30

ONCE DARK STAR located the general area, satellites could pinpoint the emissions from the bugs. They were now within blocks from the parchments.

"This is all Greek to me," a NSA technician wearing headphones said quietly.

His partner, sitting next to him in a truck designed so the entire roof was a receiving dish, smiled then removed his headphone and checked the recording level on the banks of the recording devices.

"Funny choice of words," he said, "but rumor is these documents are not Greek but an earlier language."

A disc popped from a recorder. He slipped it into a plastic case and knocked on the window to the cockpit, then handed it through a now-open slot. The man in the driver's seat attached an identifying tag, then opened a hatch in the truck's floor. Just inside an open manhole leading into the sewer, another agent clung to a ladder with a small fishing net, waiting to catch the case.

"Morning, Mikey," the agent in the truck said.

"Morning," the agent in the sewer said.

"Want some breakfast?" the agent in the truck said.

"I think I'll pass," Mikey said, motioning with his net. The agent in the truck dropped the disc case into the net, then watched for a moment as the other agent scrambled down the ladder to the main sewer line. He would then travel down the line and pop back out some distance away.

"Thank God for seniority," the agent in the truck muttered to himself as he slid closed the hatch in the floor of the truck.

***

In Caracas, the Venezuelan President was holding a conference with the U.S. Secretary of State. The Secretary of State had learned over the years that the direct approach was always best.

"Mr. President, the United States is concerned about the continued state of martial law," the Secretary of State said slowly. "It seems to be hindering the police ability to respond to the unrest."

"Who is screaming the loudest?"

The Secretary of State smiled a thin smile.

"Everyone. The Israelis, the Arabs, the right, the left," he said. "There's a lot at stake here."

The Venezuelan President considered this.

"I was planning to lift the curfew and end the martial law this evening," he said. "I am just waiting for extra troops to arrive from the countryside. They will be in place soon."

"Thank you," the Secretary of State said.

"May I ask you something?" the President said.

"Certainly."

"How deep is your administration involved with Cristos?"

The Secretary of State considered this carefully.

"Quite honestly, Mr. President," he said, "These revelations were as much of a surprise to us as they must have been to you."

"Could you tell me what information you have assembled about Cristos?"

"Afraid I can't," the Secretary of State said.

The President smiled.

"Have you made any plans for what you do if you lose the election?" the Secretary of State said.

"As far as guests go," the President said, smiling, "you've yet to cheer me up."

"I want to express my apologies, Mr. President," the Secretary of State said, "for any indiscretion."

"Why do you ask about my leaving?" the President said as he rearranged himself in the chair and glanced at his favorite paining on the wall.

"Our President spoke to a few friends at a university. They contacted some rich donors who agreed to fund a chair for you at the school. If you wish to take asylum in the United States, you have a highly-paid position waiting for you."

"What would I have to do to earn my keep?" he asked.

"A few lectures, world traveling, that sort of thing."

"A kind offer," the President said as he rose from his chair and stirred the fire with an iron poker. "But let's hope it doesn't come to that."

31

CIA ARCHAEOLOGIST Harry Duke stared at a scrap of the recovered Cristos documents through a microscope. Every detail had appeared proper for the time and date. So far everything had checked out. If he was ordered to end his investigation right now, he'd have to conclude the documents were genuine.

Why, then, did he doubt them so? From the first second he'd touched the boxes and the papers inside he'd smelled a phony. Maybe his intuition had grown stale or maybe he wasn't as skilled at his job as he had thought.

Adjusting the magnification, he stared at the scrap again.

What was that tiny piece attached to the parchment like a speck of pollen from a budding flower? He rubbed his eyes and stared again. Probably nothing. Or was it? He turned on a desk light and searched in a nearby toolbox for a pair of tiny tweezers.

***

Taft sat in his office with his feet up on his desk. In the last few years, the numerous injuries he had suffered as an NIA agent started to be felt more often. He had installed a spa at his home and had taken several vacations to hot-springs resorts for therapy but the simple fact was the cartilage and deep-tissue damages he had suffered would cause him pains from here until the end of his life. This growing pain was one of the costs he would have to pay for serving his country.

No one tells you that at the start, Taft thought. No one tells you that because no one listens. When they came to him and asked him to consider joining the NIA, he was full of pride and patriotic vigor. He would be part of the people that made his country remain great, and protect it from foreigners determined to destroy the cradle of freedom and democracy.

It was all a good story he and the others told themselves.

The truth was that both here in the United States, and in every other country round the globe, those nationalistic thoughts were a well-polished lie. Most organizations are simply about power and control. The more power they can gain, the more control they can exert over people and their choices. It was no different for communists or capitalists, socialists or fascists. Systems, be they ideological or religious, corporate or government, were all about controlling people and moving them toward a common goal that benefitted those that ran the organization.

Taft had fought and killed communists who believed in their system as much as he himself did in his. Like toy soldiers they had been placed into death struggles, and in the end it had mattered little or nothing at all. It was a shill game. Those at the top wanted more power and wealth and the methods they used were to make the population fearful and confused. Wars against other countries diverted attention away from the fact that someone was always robbing the cash drawer. What a convoluted and disturbing journey. Taft's throbbing knee was a victim of this game—his throbbing mind, another.

"You want some ice?" Martinez asked after walking inside the office.

"Is that some new drug the government has developed?"

"Frozen water," Martinez noted.

"Maybe if you put some booze with it."

"You've never been much of a drinker."

"I figure I'll need a hobby in retirement," Taft said. "Perhaps it will be alcoholism."

"You're still on the payroll until the President signs your exit papers."

"I could just leave," Taft said.

"They could not pay you your pension too."

Taft smiled and considered this. Like most employers, the NIA had added stipulations after he had taken his job and performed his duties for years. A few years after 9/11, when the various agencies started performing duties that had previously been denied them by law, they started to amend their employment contracts. Many of the new clauses dealt with employment separation. At Taft's level, the President was required to sign a form releasing the agent. This was to insure that the country was always adequately staffed with trained agents, like the military stop-loss measures used during the Afghanistan and Iraqi wars.

The second was the ability for the NIA to deny or stop pension payments if an agent disclosed anything his or any other governmental agency had done while he was employed—no matter if the acts were legal or illegal. This effectively rendered any possibility of whistle-blowing null and void. No agent would risk a pension he had spent years earning. This addition to the contract had the unintended consequence of increasing illegal activity by agents. One reason was that there was now little chance of ever being caught for an illegal act. Another was that it became imperative that an agent steal as much of the funds from his mission as possible in the case that somehow his pension was denied or suspended.

As field agents like Taft dealt in large amounts of cash, skimming was simple. Taft had heard a story that an agent from the CIA was believed to have stolen nearly four million in cash that was given to him for bribing a pair of key Iraqi officials. Reporting that he had paid them off, he then used less than one hundred thousand to have them killed by Islamic militants. No one could verify if they had been paid prior to their assassinations so the payments were recorded as paid as ordered.

One of the largest hauls was a portion of the forty billion dollars that the Federal Reserve sent to Iraqi at the start of the U.S. occupation. Most of the funds came from monies seized from Saddam Hussein prior to the start of the war. Pallets of bills, each weighing fifteen hundred pounds and divided into bricks by the value of the currency, were shipped from Andrews Air Force Base outside Washington D.C. to Baghdad. To make the cash easier to use, the bricks of hundred-dollar bills were wrapped with gold seals, while brown seals were used for the fifties and purple for the twenties. Nothing smaller than a twenty was sent as the money was designed to be used for Iraqi rebuilding and not change from a merchant cash drawer. Once the pallets were unloaded from the C-17 transport planes and a receipt was signed by the Iraqi officials on the runway, the money was no longer tracked. Taft had spoken to agents who bragged that upon leaving the airport, more than a few of the trucks were diverted to other locations and the cash divided up.

Taft found stealing disgusting but he was beginning to understand why it was common. In the last thirty years, and more so in the last decade, the moral fiber of the United States had been constantly eroding. It was as if morality was being manipulated as a national policy. First, corporations went on full-scale attack on the average worker. Unions were busted and an unspoken policy promoting low wages was instituted by the Federal Reserve System. Since the Federal Reserve System is a private corporation with perhaps the ultimate power to affect the economy, this policy was at odds with what was morally right and correct for the American working public.

Of course private corporations would want lower wages—that allows them greater profits and thus a greater pool of money to be used for wages and benefits. Unfortunately wages and benefits in a private corporation are determined by a small pool at the top so in almost all cases, the higher wages and benefits were funneled to a few executives at the top. Wages for the average workers declined dramatically while those at the top made obscene wages and benefits packages that would make a major prince or a minor king blush in embarrassment.

The public witnessed this and decided that if the rich were being allowed to steal, they would attempt to become thieves themselves. Attendance at MBA programs soared. What the hopeful future robber barons did not understand was that those ultra-high-paying jobs went not to those with merit, but to a handful of handpicked families within the existing system. Willingness to allow their fellow citizens to be robbed was not enough to guarantee anyone entry into the elite. The problem became that by the time the average person realized the college sham, they were saddled with debt from student loans and any job they could find paid too little for repayment. Their salaries were so low because with their prior support, wages in all sectors had been slashed to the minimum.

By turning their back on their fellow man for a buck, they had gutted a system they themselves had believed they would never need. Complaining about an auto worker making a decent wage had cost them a chance for a decent paying job themselves. The public had been deceived to be sure, but because of their own greed they had walked directly under the guillotine.

By the time the financial collapse and the housing crisis came along, most of those that had supported the system now in place were having doubts, but by then it was too late. As the values of their investments in all things from houses to education devalued, they were stuck. Watching different rules being applied to the banks and financial corporations only rubbed salt into the wound. Some began to understand there was one system for the elite and another for themselves. It seemed thievery and bad behavior was rewarded. Television shows about vacuous celebrities with no skills or redeeming values abounded. Something for nothing became a dream as doing the right thing had been proven to be only for suckers. Taft had watched the decline in morals with great alarm. More than most, he had believed in the dream of his country. Time and time again he had placed his life on the line for what he believed were real values and now he was seeing, and not just since his mind-opening accident, that what he thought was real, was a candy-coated lie.

He looked over at Martinez.

"Good thing I have my own money," Taft said smiling.

It was true. Taft had made money off land in Colorado, the value of his house in Maryland had returned—not all the way but enough—and over the years his investment in stocks had proved lucrative. He understood from the start that the stock market was simply a casino with another name, and he bought and sold frequently, usually selling out before the plunges. If he liquidated all he had now, he would be worth close to a million. Not robber-baron rich but enough to live comfortably for the rest of his life, even if they took away his pension. He had benefitted from the corrupt system—but he never confused cronyism with capitalism.

***

"You did what?" the President asked Benson.

"Agent Taft added a few locators to the box containing the reproduced Cristos Parchments," Benson said. "The Air Force tracked them to a general area with Dark Star and then the NSA computer whizzes gave us an exact locate."

"I never ordered that," the President noted.

Benson stared at the President. He was reacting to the good news in a very unusual way.

"It was well within the scope of my authority."

The President was silent for a moment as he thought.

"Where are the documents?" he asked finally.

"Houston, Texas."

This was the exactly what the President had not wanted to hear. The seconds ticked past.

"Well, it's obvious," the President noted, "that you need to immediately turn this over to the FBI. This administration has had enough problems with the domestic-spying scandal. We don't need intelligence agencies that are not allowed to be operating on America soil to be caught right now."

Benson nodded. This was the first time his agency had ever been thwarted from going anywhere by this President. It was like they had been involved for years in a heated war firing repeatedly on the enemy and now being told that there was a line that bullets could not cross.

"Yes sir. Shall I…" Benson started to say.

"I'll call the FBI," the President said quickly. "Right after I speak to the head of the NSA and order him to call off his men. As for your agency—I want you to stand down. Anything pertaining to Venezuela or Cristos is now off limits."

Benson nodded. Something had smelled wrong so he had prepared.

"I understand, Mr. President. Will there be anything else?"

The President shook his head.

Benson bent over to rise and placed his hands on the underside of the desk as if to lift himself to his feet. He pressed something up into the wood.

As Benson left the room, he could see the President was concerned.

Sam Walker touched the end of his finger, the one missing the tip, to the end of his nose. Leland Hobbs had learned over the years that something funny was coming.

"That damn salesman over at SPS contacted me. They want cash to keep this moving forward," Walker said.

"They have seemed to do their job," Hobbs said laconically, "least so far."

"I guess they have earned out so far. The big payday for them and us is when our man takes over."

"Sounds like bag-of-cash time," Hobbs noted. "I can sneak away from my wife if you can convince yours you need to take a secret overnight trip. We can deliver the cash in person, then party."

"Only a couple hours to Miami on the jet."

"Should I call and have our man there make arrangements?" Hobbs asked.

Walker nodded yes. "Let's snag an extra package of currency when we go in the cash vault, for fun money."

Inside their high-rise office in Houston, the men had a bank-sized vault. It required both men to enter combinations to get it open. Inside were tens of millions of dollars in different currencies along with gold bars and coins and the same in silver plus platinum, diamonds and more than twenty paintings by old masters. Walker and Hobbs wouldn't know a Manet from a Monet, but they had experts and they always knew a good investment.

"Just one extra brick," Hobbs said.

Both men rose and started down the hall toward the vault.

"Sam?" Hobbs asked.

"Yeah, Leland?"

"Is there more Yayo in the vault?"

"I made a trade with some Peruvians just last week," Walker said, "and they threw in a chunk about the size of a softball."

Hobbs nodded. They reached the outer door and punched in their codes.

"That should work," Hobbs said easily, "unless it turns into a longer weekend than we planned."

Walked reached the vault door. It was polished steel and covered the entire wall. Blocking the lock with his back, he spun the dial and entered his part of the combination. Then he moved away and stared at the wall while Hobbs entered his portion. A second later there was a mechanical clunk and the bolts began to retract. A few seconds later the door opened.

"If you call our man down there and make the arrangements for accommodations and whatnot," Walker said, "I'll call down to arrange the talent."

Hobbs entered the vault and grabbed a rolling cart already stocked with some black nylon gym bags. Pushing the cart over to some steel shelves, he began to load the SPS payment and a little extra. Walker stared over at a painting hung on the wall.

"That thing creeps me out," he said.

"If it hadn't had gone up fifty million," Hobbs said, "It would creep me out too."

32

ADOLPHO FIORINI sat to the side of the Pope and his vast council of advisers. The room was lit by dozens of candles, and the smell of ancient wax mixed with the scent from aged rugs and oiled furniture. Pitchers of red wine were placed along the length of the table, as were small demitasse cups of espresso and square glasses for iced water.

"The existence of a wife and family for Jesus has never been decisively proven," Fiorini said easily.

The Pope nodded. His Italian came with an accent and while he chose he words carefully, it was obvious he was more modern than any pope that came before him.

"But then we haven't looked that hard," the Pope noted.

"No reason to prove," Fiorini agreed, "what we do not want to know."

The room was silent save a fat and noisy fly that buzzed near the head of the table.

"It seems coincidental," one of the Pope's other advisers said, "that the parchments turn up at the same time there is an election. And, that they are in Venezuela."

"God works in mystery at times," the Pope said.

"It is not that unusual they would be in Venezuela," Fiorini said. "The Welser family obtained the colonial right to the country from Spain. They formed Klein-Venedig beginning in 1528, only two years before the Augsburg Confession."

"Which gave great weight to the Lutheran Church and started the Catholic Church losing so many to Protestantism," the Pope noted.

"It has been rumored both the Welsers and the Fuggar German banking families were tied into the Knights Templar. And it has been said the Knights Templar could prove Jesus's true identity," Fiorini added.

The room was silent. The fly began buzzing again and soon was flying near the Pope's head.

"So there is a possibility this all might be true," the Pope said.

No one answered him for the longest time. No one truly wanted to know.

***

Not long after the trip to the vault, the Hobker Petroleum jet rose from the runway at a private airport near Houston. Walker and Hobbs were served drinks by their longtime flight attendant. She then disappeared into the pilot's cockpit, where she would remain until called. Hobbs was on the phone negotiating the sale of some oil properties while Walker worked another phone, lining up some people to meet up with in Miami. The sun had set and only a tangerine glow was left on the Gulf of Mexico as the jet headed out across the water. The engines vibrated and droned on and soon the pilot could see lights on the Florida coastline ahead.

"You going for stone crabs tonight?" the pilot asked his co-pilot.

"I planning on doing whatever my boy toy wants to do," she said.

The pilot nodded. The two had worked together for almost three years now.

"Did I ever tell you that you have become a slut?"

"Coming from a boring married man like you," she said, "that is low praise indeed."

"It is Miami," the flight attendant piped up. "Sin City East."

The pilot and co-pilot nodded. Truer words had yet to be spoken this night.

"We are landing at Fort Lauderdale Executive?" the co-pilot asked.

"As usual."

"The bosses planning to drink their way down the beach again?"

"I just fly the plane," the pilot said.

***

Just under a hundred miles away inside the aged bar on North Bay Island, Burke Taylor was drowning his sorrows.

"Hardly fair," Taylor said, "after I came up with that brilliant plan."

Strategic Planning Services, in an effort to cut him out should the deal in Venezuela unravel, had informed Taylor earlier this afternoon that his services would no longer be needed. Along with his accumulated retirement funds and a small severance, he was given the choice of a month's pay or a company-paid month long stint in a rehab facility. Taylor, not truly wanting to stop drinking, had wisely chosen the month's pay.

"Wasn't that *our* plan?" Hemingway laughed.

"What really sucks is that the plan," Taylor said, "appears to be working perfectly."

Hemingway finished the bottle of Coors in front of him, then barked at Dolinda. She immediately began preparing a Salty Dog.

"Think of it from my point of view—this is the second time my plot has been stolen and once again someone else stands to make millions."

Taylor took a large drink but said nothing.

Dolinda slid the drink in front of the writer and he winked at her. As she walked down the bar, Hemingway spoke under his breath. "I have a feeling if we ever did hook up you wouldn't see me for days. Shame it will never happen."

"You being gone for days wouldn't be unusual," Taylor said. "I've noticed you tend to disappear frequently."

Hemingway ignored him. Taylor finished his sixth cranberry and vodka and motioned to Dolinda for another.

"You want something different?" the author asked.

Taylor shook his head impatiently.

"I'm actually getting sick of drinking," Hemingway said.

"I just think this is wrong," Taylor said, ignoring the comment. "A month's pay isn't shit. SPS is billing the oil company millions. Maybe tens of millions."

"The golden rule," Hemingway said. "He who has the gold rules."

"Maybe I'm looking to the wrong source to make this right. Maybe the oil men would pay me to keep quiet. I mean, once I explain I came up with this idea in the first place."

Hemingway took a large sip and squinted from the grapefruit-juice tang. "In the first place, I came up with the idea, and in the second place you don't sound like you know who these guys are."

"I could find that out."

Hemingway waited. A Talking Heads song was playing on the jukebox.

"How drunk are you?" Taylor said at last.

"You know me." Hemingway stared at the large selection of bottles behind the bar, trying to decide. "I sometimes wake up drunker than this. Are you thinking we go to your office and find out the identity of those oil men?"

Taylor wasn't sure if that had been what he was thinking. But now it sounded okay. "We could make a little trip up the island to our office building."

"What about security?"

"Surprisingly not much," Taylor said, "and everyone should have gone home. We just take a quick troll through the computer files and maybe we can solve the mystery of who is paying for the Venezuela operation."

"Didn't they take your keys and cards when they fired you?"

"I wasn't fired," Taylor said. "My contract was not renewed. And to answer your questions, I had duplicate sets of keys and entry cards made so I could come and go without record. The card is under the name of an agent who is assigned to the South Pacific—he hasn't visited the office in years. Maybe never."

Hemingway said, "For tonight that would work, but tomorrow when the security log is scanned they will know the South Seas man did not show up unannounced. Even the worst television detective would suspect you before the commercial break."

"Yeah, but by then we will have the name of the company."

Hemingway motioned to Dolinda, who came down the bar and took the order. She headed off to make the drinks. Neither man spoke.

"Well," Hemingway said, "I guess if you need my help...."

"We probably ought to take a couple drinks to go."

"Your office is two blocks away."

"Yeah," Taylor said. "But it takes a minute for the computer to boot up."

***

The Hobker helicopter was waiting only a few yards from where their jet pulled to a stop.

"I like being rich as much as you," Hobbs said, "But isn't a limo enough even for Miami?"

Walker motioned for them to approach the helicopter. The rotor blades had just started turning, and the tall and lean Hobbs ducked down a little too much. He crabwalked to the rear door, with Walker holding the nylon bag of cash directly behind him. Once they were seated inside with the door closed and the headsets on their heads, Walker answered.

"This was the salesman's idea," he said over the din. "SPS has a helicopter pad on their roof. We're a little early"—he glanced at his gold Rolex—"but I'm sure they are waiting."

"Okay," Hobbs said, "let's have the pilot take us down Miami Beach on the way so we can gawk at celebrity houses."

"Whatever you want, partner."

***

The team of Taylor and Hemingway parked next to the SPS building at a breakfast-and-lunch joint that was now closed. Making their way through an alley, they entered the building through a rear door Taylor thought would be safer. The building was deserted and that was good.

The pair stumbled along, whispering in the loud tone used only by drunks.

"Where's your office?" Hemingway hissed.

"Up top," Taylor said, "But we need to use the stairs. The elevator probably has cameras."

"Probably?"

"I don't know."

The two men made their way up the emergency stairs. As the climbed the stairs, both began sweating from their foreheads and under their arms.

"This is a workout," Hemingway said.

Once they reached the top floor, they exited the stairway and then made their way down to Taylor's office using the light from their cell phones. Once there, Taylor twisted the knob and found it unlocked. They entered.

"Damn," Hemingway said, "Nice view of the water."

To the north was a string of islands and, eventually, Bal Harbor. A few boats floated on the back bay, their red-and-green lights twinkling atop the sheen on the water.

"Seniority," Taylor said, "but that's all gone now."

He quickly booted up his computer and began searching for the name of the company. Almost ten minutes passed before they heard the approaching helicopter.

"Wonder what that is?" Hemingway asked.

***

The helicopter lowered down to the roof pad.

"You want to do this?" Hobbs asked.

"Yeah, it should go quick," Walker said. "I'm sure for a big payoff like this, they will be waiting."

"I would be," Hobbs said.

"I'll go see if the door is open," Walker said. "I bet they are just inside."

Before Hobbs could comment Walker opened the door to the helicopter, bag in hand. At the door leading from the pad inside, he twisted the doorknob and then as it opened turned back to Hobbs and made a thumbs-up sign. Then he walked inside.

"What the…" Taylor started to say as he heard the door at the end of the hall open.

Walker found a light switch as soon as he entered the building and switched it on. The hallway lit up and he walked quickly down the hall with the nylon bag over his shoulder. Drunks move slow but had they been sober they would still have not had enough time to hide. Walker came abreast of their office and stopped.

"How come you are sitting in the dark?"

For boozers, the lies flow as quickly and easily as the booze. Combine alcohol with a writer and you have a recipe for prevarication not easily matched.

"Breaker blew," Hemingway said. "We're working on it."

Walker said, "My partner is out in the helicopter. Here's the payment you wanted." He handed over the nylon bag.

Taylor sat speechless at his computer.

"It smells like booze in here."

"I don't doubt that," Hemingway said. "How about you? Are you planning to down a few yourself?"

Walker laughed. He liked this guy. "You got that right."

"What kind of club you looking for?"

"Something with cold drinks and hot women," Walker said smiling.

"Start at Mirabelle's on South Beach," Hemingway said. "Just watch out to make sure the women are actually women. Check the hands and Adam's apples."

"Would you like to go with us?" Walker asked, "Be our tour guide?"

"I would," Hemingway said. "But we'd better take care of this."

Taylor was silent but amazed at Hemingway's ability to improvise.

"I understand."

"You need a receipt or something?" Hemingway asked.

"Do you need to count it?" Walker asked.

"Hell," Hemingway said easily, "what is business if there is no trust? Besides we know where to find you if we need to."

"And us, you."

That was not entirely true but Hemingway didn't bother to correct him.

"Be good out there," Hemingway said, extending his hand to shake, "and by that I mean bad."

"Will do," Walker shook, then turned to leave.

Hemingway smiled at Walker.

"I know you talk," Walker said pointing to Taylor.

"Good evening," Taylor blurted.

Walker paused as if he was going to say more. He decided against it. "All right then."

With a slight nod, Walker walked out of the office.

Taylor and Hemingway listened to the sound of steps in the hallway then the door open and close.

"So," Hemingway said finally, "are you finished?"

Taylor was clutching a scrap of paper with the information written down.

"We should probably get out of here," Hemingway said.

A second later, with Hemingway hefting the bag, the two men raced down the staircase. The trip down required considerably less time than the journey up.

***

Walker climbed back into the helicopter and slid on the headset.

"Have you ever heard of a place named Mirabelle's?" he asked the pilot.

"Definitely hot," the pilot replied.

"Anywhere nearby to land?"

"About a block away," the pilot said, "but there is no place for me to stay. It's a drop-off landing pad only."

"Don't worry," Hobbs said, "we'll call our limo to meet us there."

"Here we go then men," the pilot said as he rolled on the throttle and pulled back on the collective. The helicopter rose up from the pad. Next the pilot nudged the cyclic forward and the nose dipped down. The helicopter started out over the island and then the back bay between them and South Beach.

"Drop go okay?"

"No problem," Walker said. "Now for the fun part."

***

As the helicopter lifted from the rooftop pad, one of the SPS owners was waiting for the drawbridge to lower so he could drive on the causeway to the island. In the distance, he could just make out the Hobker Petroleum colors and emblem.

"What the hell?" he said out loud.

He reached for his mobile phone.

***

"I say," Hemingway said as soon as they got in his car, "we reconvene at my condo for drinks and decisions."

Without waiting for an answer, he slid the car into gear and pulled down the alley. Driving a couple of blocks, he turned onto a back street then drove into his condo parking garage from the rear entrance. Waving at the doorman and still clutching the nylon bag, he and Taylor rode up the elevator. The piped in music in the elevator was from the eighties. Hemingway tapped his feet as they rode to the top. Hemingway unlocked his door and motioned for Taylor to walk inside.

"Now," he said closing the door. "Speak."

Taylor had already walked to the bar and started gulping scotch from the bottle.

"Man," Hemingway said, "I can't take you anywhere."

Taylor wiped the back of his hand across his mouth to clear the scotch away. "Can you explain to me what that was all about?"

Hemingway walked over the bar and glanced at the bottles. Then he walked into the kitchen and took a large ice-cold can of Australian beer from the refrigerator. He popped the top and walked back into the living room.

"He mentioned something about a payment. Shall we see what it is?"

Taylor sipped again from the bottle.

"I have expensive crystal scotch glasses over there," Hemingway said, "the square ones. There is no need to drink from the bottle."

He walked over to the nylon bag lifted it onto an end table, unzipped the zipper, and peered inside.

"Well?" Taylor said, remaining near the bar.

"I'm no expert," Hemingway said, "but I think it is two million dollars in hundreds. Funny, it didn't seem to weigh that much."

"We just…" Taylor started to say.

Hemingway looked over at him. "Buddy, you don't look so good. Why don't you take a seat over there on the couch?"

"I…."

"I'll get you some ice, You just sit down."

***

The owners of SPS searched their offices and found the computer record of Taylor accessing the files. After a heated discussion they called the main switchboard for Hobker Petroleum and asked to speak to Walker or Hobbs. The switchboard operator notified her supervisor, who relayed the message to Leland Hobbs's cell phone. At Mirabelle's, the oil men had bribed their way to the best table in the house right near the dance floor. Hobbs stepped away to find a quieter place to call back.

"This is Hobbs."

"You are in Miami?"

"Of course. We dropped the cash off with your salesmen," he said, "just like you asked."

At the SPS office the two men stared at the speakerphone. There was no way they could explain the request for a cash payment had not come from them. No way without looking like idiots.

"We're just making sure the transfer went smoothly," one of the owners lied. "Could you explain how it went down?"

"Just a second," Hobbs said. He motioned Walker away from a tall Brazilian his partner was trying to seduce. After Hobbs explained, Walker grabbed the telephone.

"There were two guys waiting in an office. I handed the bag to them."

The owner of SPS asked a few more questions.

"To your salesman," Walker repeated.

The owners of SPS glanced at one another. They had no sales department.

"So you handed it to...."

Walker wanted to get back to the Brazilian. He interrupted.

"You know, the tall blond dude," Walker said. "The other man had red hair and was at the computer."

The SPS men asked a couple more questions.

"Yeah, red hair and a face like a cadaver. Like he avoided sunlight."

The SPS men had no idea why the oil men referred to Taylor as a salesman. Perhaps it was just a manner of speech. Like how some call employees their workers. They still didn't know how much money had been delivered but they could find that out when they confronted their former employee. And then they found also find out about the other man. It was probably just one of Taylor's drunk friends he brought along for support. Bad luck for him. Now they would need to deal with both men.

Walker said, "So the payment is made. We delivered it to your building as agreed. You boys finish this deal up successfully and you get the rest."

The owner of SPS said he thought that sounded fair.

"Then, if you want to join us, we're starting at Mirabelle's. You're welcome to join us."

They thanked him but said they had a few things to take care of tonight.

33

TAFT HAD considered calling one of his girlfriends, but in truth he felt more like being alone. Since his electrocution and the coma, the insights he had gained made him introspective. He was bothered by the fact that he had seen images of the President coming to present him an award and using it as a cover to meet up with his girlfriend for a rendezvous. After all his sacrifices, if this was true—it cut him to the quick. All that plus his coming retirement made him feel slightly uncertain.

These were traits he knew most women abhorred. Taft had always attracted the opposite sex because of his primary traits of self-confidence combined with an ironic sense of humor. These were probably both self-protective mechanisms. If a man deals almost daily with the fact he might be killed at any time, he can either laugh it off or go crazy in short order. His self-confidence was simply a result of not yet dying in spite of the myriad of times he should have.

Tonight might just be better alone. Taft sat in the jetted spa, soaking his tired and sore muscles. Then he meditated for nearly forty minutes to try to clear his mind. Neither truly helped him relax, so he popped a bowl of popcorn and found the stupidest comedy he could locate to watch. Dumb comedies relaxed him. The laughter and absurdity let him forget his woes for a time. Ferrell and Myers together. It had to be a laugh riot. Getting comfortable on the couch, he settled in for the duration.

***

No one with a good deal of moral fiber was elected president nowadays. The game had long ago shifted from serving the people to serving the special interests that paid to place you in power. The amount of money necessary for someone to move through the ranks to even gain enough experience to be in a position to run for congressman, senator or ultimately president made it a certainty that a person was required to sell out early and often. It is said that everyone serves someone and the President of the United States was no exception.

This President had run on a platform of family values, yet he cheated on his wife frequently and gambled with great regularity showing his real platform to be hypocrisy. He decried drug use but had a cabinet filled with prescriptions that he regularly mixed with alcohol. His children, who he frequently trotted out for photo opportunities, did know him well enough to like or trust him. And his wife, who had threatened to divorce him way back when he was a governor, stayed for the money and a promise to be free as soon as he was out of office. Even those that had moved the pieces around to place him in this position of power and trust didn't care for him a great deal.

He sat alone in his office just past ten at night and no one missed his company.

"You," he said, his voice slurring, "It's me."

"Yes," the voice said with a smooth Southern accent.

"You got messed up in some big stuff," the President noted. "I hear some stealing was involved."

Damn. Not much to say about that.

"My spies traced them parchments right back to you."

"How'd they…"

"Some little electronic device," the President said, sipping a whiskey and ginger ale to go with the anti-depressants and swig of cough syrup he had taken for a possible cold. "Anyway, the entire affair with the stealing and the Muslim stuff has caused me a great deal of distress. You need to distance yourself from this affair. If anyone traces this back to you and then finds our connection, I will be screwed."

"I needed to know…" the other man said, "for me."

"Don't get all that way with me," the President said. "You are as much a salesman as me. What does it matter what we are selling? Real or imaginary, it pays the same."

The telephone line was silent for a moment.

"How do I get rid of them if they are bugged?"

"I understand the box is bugged, not the papers. Keep the papers if you want but destroy the boxes."

"How soon will that be safe?"

"I called off the hounds," the President said, "so do it now."

"You have my word."

There was a pause.

"If your word is as good as mine," the President said with a chuckle, "I'd like something else."

The telephone line went dead.

***

The lights from Miami Beach twinkled. Hemingway and Burke Taylor sat in chaise lounge chairs on his balcony, pondering their choices. Hemingway was not sure how much to discuss. His friend was very drunk. Maybe it would be better to talk about it all later.

"We can be assured that whoever it was with the bag of cash has already identified you."

"You too," Taylor noted.

"I look like thousands of other guys," Hemingway said, "People come up to me all over and claim they know me—I just look familiar. You on the other hand are probably one of the few red-haired employees of SPS and certainly the only one fired today."

"My contract was…"

"Enough of that. You were fired. Then for good measure you decided to rob your ex-employers. I doubt they will give you a good reference."

"The robbery wasn't planned," Taylor said, "and that was more you than me. It was a crime of convenience."

"Aren't all crimes?"

They were quiet staring out at the lights and sipping their drinks.

"What should we do?" Taylor asked.

They were quiet for a moment.

Hemingway said. "I have an idea. You wait here."

Hemingway walked back into his office and sat at his desk. It was time to call a man that had been his friend and mentor for decades. Hemingway had become a writer because of him, had his first breaks because of him and still leaned on him when he needed to. They were not as close as they once had been, but Hemingway knew if push came to shove he'd probably help him. He even had an idea of what he might do. Taking a few deep breaths, he dialed the number.

"Hey boss," Hemingway said, "it's me."

"Long time no see," Malcolm Driggs said. "You ever going to visit?"

"Soon."

"I'll believe that when I see it," Driggs said. "How you coming on the drinking?"

Since moving to Miami he had made a few drunken calls late at night. The two had known each other too long to lie to one another. It wouldn't work.

"About the same. You weren't asleep?"

"No it's only nine here," Driggs said. "I'm not that old yet."

"Good."

"You lonely or do you have something you need to talk to me about?"

So Hemingway explained what he needed him to know.

After a pause Driggs said. "Sounds like you've been busy. I told you that you needed to blow off that plot theft. It was unfortunate but it happened. Don't keep going back to it."

"You didn't have your million-dollar idea ripped off."

"No I made a million off mine."

The line was quiet. Driggs knew he had cut a little deep. "Well, old buddy," he said. "You have a hell of a mess."

"Can you help?"

Hemingway was pretty sure what Driggs might do.

Driggs thought for a moment. "I've got someone I can call," he said, "owes me a favor. I'll give him your number and then you've got to take it from there."

"I'll…" Hemingway said. "Guess I'll wait to hear from him?"

"Hang tight," Driggs said, "help is on the way."

"Hey, boss," Hemingway said quietly. "Thanks."

"You're like the child I never had," Driggs said. "If I'd had one that was always a pain in the ass."

The line went dead and Hemingway sat back in the chair. He walked back onto the balcony. "You want a fresh drink?"

Taylor nodded. "What's the plan?"

"I used my phone-a-friend. Now we wait."

The call came twenty minutes later.

The party listened to the story, then wrote down Hemingway's address and telephone numbers. Admonishing him not to leave his current location, he said he'd be there the following morning.

"Stay put," he advised, "but if something starts feeling wrong move quickly to another location. If you need to reach me, call this number." He rattled some digits. "It connects to me wherever I am. Otherwise bury your head in the sand and wait for me to arrive."

The telephone disconnected and Hemingway explained the conversation to Taylor.

"I'll run home," Taylor said, "long enough to grab my toiletries and a fresh change of clothes."

"I think that is a really bad idea," Hemingway said.

Sometimes it is impossible to argue with a man who has been drinking.

"An hour and I'll be back."

Hemingway paused. There were several things he needed to explain to his friend. But he decided they could wait until he returned.

"Be sure and grab your passport," Hemingway said.

"Why?"

"You might need it."

Taylor nodded. The old spy looked sick, nervous and shaky as he walked to the door.

"Hurry back here, man."

34

VINCENTE CRISTOS stared into the mirror. His jaw was hurting from a low-level infection that had permeated the bone. He touched the tip of his finger to the thin scar, then dabbed on some makeup to cover the mark. His hair was showing a touch of brown so he added some lightener. No one wanted to elect a man showing age or not in his prime.

There was six days before the election and his handlers had made it clear that, other than a few more carefully choreographed speeches, he was to remain out of sight until the results were clear. Several of his close aides, those that had supported him from the start, complained about his isolation but since he had flooded his campaign with the new blood they were ignored. The old guard had been appalled when Cristos hired the consulting firm from the United States to manage his campaign shortly after the revelations as to his lineage appeared. Cristos explained to them as a group that he felt the campaign might now become ugly, and there was no one better trained in ugly politics than a United States campaign-consulting group.

When his three closest aides sought a personal meeting to argue their case against the move, Cristos had refused to meet with them. Since that day he had refused any other face-to-face meeting with old staff or old friends. He was like a rock star that had achieved blinding fame and then tossed over his old friends for a new set of sycophantic hangers-on. Those close to him muttered their disdain but they had no choice but to go along. They had tied their futures to Cristos, and if they left now their rewards would be nothing.

Cristos walked out into the living room of the suite they had rented in the high-rise hotel in Caracas and looked down at the American glancing down at his cell phone. The man looked up.

"I'm going to need some companionship," Cristos said.

The man nodded. Then he pointed the tip of his finger to his eye. Cristos got the message and walked back into the bathroom.

***

John Taft had taken the earliest flight from Washington D.C. to Miami, then rented a car and drove down to North Bay Village. Buying a pair of coffees at a drive-up kiosk, he parked on the street outside Hemingway's condo building. After surveying the area, he slipped into the freight elevator to avoid detection then exited on the author's floor. Dialing his telephone number, he told the author he was outside.

***

Miami Beach Detective Robert England was standing on the pool deck of the beachfront condo building. His partner, Christie Tamarino, walked over with a paper sack containing coffees.

"Six more feet and he would have made the water," England noted.

"These old buildings have deeper pools," Tamarino said, opening the sack and handing him his coffee. "Damn insurance companies now make everyone have those shallow ones. They heat up in the sun easier."

England nodded and popped the plastic top of his cup. Looking around, he found a trash can and walked over and tossed it inside. A large splash of red now turning brown was textured with flesh on the tile. The remains of a chaise-lounge chair sat nearby. The body had been bagged up and removed, but four men wearing full hazardous-waste suits were cleaning up the rest of the mess on the deck and in the now-drained pool.

"The first people on the scene report there was a strong odor of alcohol from the body."

"Suicide?" Tamarino asked, sipping her café con leche.

"Or accident."

"Anyone check the front-desk cameras?"

"Who would do it except us," England said. "There isn't enough homicide detectives in this town to keep up with the demand."

England glanced down and noticed a small blob of bloody flesh atop his finely polished shoe.

"You have any napkins in that sack?"

Tamarino nodded and handed him one. England spilled a few drops of coffee onto the paper and wiped the blob off his shoe. He walked back to the trash and tossed the wad inside.

"This guy's everywhere."

"Do we know who he is?"

"Downtown is working on that."

Tamarino nodded. "I'll go check the cameras and see if there is anything interesting."

"I'll go up to the apartment and see what it looks like up there," England said.

Tamarino stared up at the sky. "Kinda muggy today."

"Storm is coming in," England agreed.

An hour later, the viewing of the desk cameras showed the deceased arriving in the early morning, then a pair of men showing up a few minutes later. The cameras had not filmed either group leaving. A search of the apartment showed signs of a struggle that moved from the living room onto the balcony. Maybe the guy returned home drunk and tore up his own possessions–England had seen that before. Then in a fit of anguish or poor balance, jumped or fell from the balcony. Maybe the two unknown men were tied in—love or money being the usual motives. England was glancing down at the pool deck from the balcony when his telephone rang.

"You want to know who this guy is?"

"Okay."

So the dispatcher told him.

***

"For real," Taft said. "Plot stealing? I always read in those 'you can be published books' that was not a problem."

"That's what they want you to believe," Hemingway said. "Books, movie scripts, whatever. There is only a trio of publishing houses anymore and I think those three are all tied together. They own the writers and they can make or break them like old Hollywood."

"Bizarre," Taft said.

The two were sitting in the living room. Hemingway had laid out the story. Every snag, bump and twist. Driggs had told him the guy could be trusted and that was enough for him. The nylon bag of money was on the floor between them. A news helicopter started hovering across the bay near a beachfront high-rise. Taft motioned for them to walk out on the balcony.

"That's my friend's building," Hemingway said.

"Since he was due back hours ago, I doubt that is a good sign."

Hemingway walked back inside and flicked on the television. There was a story about a possible unidentified suicide. A jumper from one of the higher floors. There was no description of the party but Hemingway knew it was Taylor.

"His place was on a high floor."

"Listen," Taft said, "I can't tell you what I'm planning to do. What I will tell you, as a favor to Driggs for helping me in the past, is that I'll help you. That sound fair?"

"Okay," Hemingway said.

Taft looked the author over. "You sure sobered up fast."

Hemingway nodded. His mind and his body felt clear.

"First, the stolen money minus one hundred thousand goes with me. By now they know it was your buddy that robbed them but they don't know about you. If SPS doesn't have a video of you it will take them time to put together you two are friends. First we create a cover story that after you left the bar that evening, you two split up and you went somewhere else. As soon as the police confirm who is dead and if it proves to be your friend, who we are pretty sure it is, then we need a place for you to hide out. The story will be that you were distraught and decided to go to rehab. The medical privacy act will make that difficult for them to check all the facilities. We get you to a safe location and you wait it out. By that time whatever is going to happen will be over."

"Taylor mentioned that his company acted on my idea. Do you know anything about that?"

Taft was silent.

"Are you going to steal the rest of the money?" Hemingway asked.

"I'm no thief," Taft said.

"Where should I hide?"

"Somewhere with very few observation cameras," Taft said. "I don't know how tied in this company is yet. You say they are ex-intelligence. That is never a good sign. There are numerous observation cameras in most major cities. I think you should buy a car for cash and take to the road. When you stop to fill it with fuel, wear a hat and glasses. Don't stay at any of the major hotel of motel chains—use only small local inns or bed-and-breakfasts. Also lay off the booze, starting now. If you get stopped for drunk driving there will be a computer record and I can't guarantee I could spring you from jail before they reach you first."

"You don't need to worry about the drinking."

"You should," Taft said. "Right now I need you to pack your computer and any other electronic device that leaves a trail. Then we need to exit this building by the fire escape."

Hemingway nodded.

As the two were climbing into Taft's rental car, a pair of men entered the bar, which had just opened for the morning drunks. The bartender on duty had been off for a few days but it didn't matter. He was trained to answer no if ever asked if someone had been at the bar. And it didn't matter if the person being sought was sitting right in front of him.

After securing Hemingway a serviceable automobile and several disposable mobile telephones, Taft sent him on his way. And although he had the authority to order the security guards at the airport not to examine his baggage, Taft decided that traveling by plane with a large bag of cash might draw attention, so he bought a trio of smaller canvas bags and split up the money.

Next he telephoned the rental car company and asked for a car that could be dropped in Washington D.C. The company directed him to an office on Biscayne Boulevard, where he switched the car he had originally rented for one the company didn't mind going north.

After stashing the bags of cash in the new rental car, Taft stopped for a breakfast burrito, then entered the Florida Turnpike for the drive to the railroad terminal near Orlando, where he would drive his car on board the Car Train for the overnight trip to the northern terminal in Virginia near Washington D.C. Since today was Saturday and he was not due back to work until Monday, he doubted if anyone even knew he had taken the trip to Florida at all.

***

England met Tamarino on the pool deck.

"Guess what?"

"He's not dead?" Tamarino joked.

"Good one," England said. "But almost as good."

A pair of men dressed like undertakers sporting hidden submachine guns walked toward the pair of detectives.

"He was a spook," England said before they reached them. "And my guess is we have nothing more to do here."

The first agent flashed a polished gold badge that featured an eagle and a holographic identification plate with a picture and name. The name probably wasn't real but the picture was close enough.

"I'm Special Agent Hall," he said seriously, "and this is Special Agent Wilbanks."

Wilbanks was staring at Tamarino's paper cup of coffee.

"We have been ordered to take over this investigation."

Tamarino said, "I've always wondered. Who exactly orders you to do that?"

"Washington," Hall said.

"The dead President?" England said.

"Let me ask you something," Wilbanks said quietly.

"Go ahead."

"Where'd you get that coffee?"

"Place about a block away," Tamarino said, "On the right-hand side. Strong but good."

"Café Cubano?"

"The best."

"So are you relinquishing control?" Hall asked.

England was silent for a moment.

"I'm not sure we ever had control," he said. "But whatever it is, it is all yours now."

England and Tamarino turned to walk away.

"One more question," Wilbanks said.

The pair of detectives stopped.

"Do they take cards?"

"No," Tamarino said, "but there is an ATM on the way."

"Appreciate it."

The detectives walked through the exit and onto the street where their car was parked.

"The dead president?" Tamarino said as they climbed inside. "Good one."

"Spies," England said, "they are always so self-important."

Tamarino started up the cruiser and placed the air-conditioning dial on full-on. Mist poured from the vents, making them feel they were inside a rain forest.

"Muggy, muggy," England said.

Tamarino placed the cruiser in drive and pulled out. "So what do you think killed him? Revenge or regret?"

"Probably," England said, "a little of both."

35

JOHN TAFT watched as his car was loaded onto the car train. The two million in plastic-wrapped cash bricks had been stashed under the seats and spare tire and bungee corded into place. The hiding places were crude but it was no concern. Taft was not smuggling heroin. If, for whatever reason, a police official wanted to search his car Taft could simply order him to stop—or, better yet, just show him the money and explain that the shipment fell under the Official Secrets Act and that the officer would be wise to forget they ever met. Taft wondered if he would miss such power once he retired.

Once the car was safely aboard the train, Taft was directed to the sleeper car he had reserved. After stashing what little luggage he had, he summoned the porter to fold down one of the beds so he could lie and stretch his back. The quick flight from Washington to Florida last night, followed by the morning meeting with the author and the fast drive up to Orlando to make the mid-morning train, had tired him. Since the electrocution and coma, his muscles had never fully recovered. As the train pulled from the station, he figured he would rest and then eat a nice lunch in the dining car.

***

At the same time Taft was relaxing his back, Sam Walker was snorting a line of cocaine out of the belly button of a supermodel from Suriname. The woman was milk-chocolate brown with bright white sclera surrounding her green iris. Walker had spent some time between snorting and licking the woman and noticed that she tasted of the sea. They were on the wooden deck surrounding the spa located on a balcony of the largest penthouse suite at the most expensive hotel on South Beach.

Leland Hobbs had been involved in a heated debate about capitalism with a woman from Amsterdam he had brought home from the club. After much argument, they seemed to reach an agreement both could live with and in the last few minutes she had slid herself into place onto Hobbs. They were gently rocking back and forth as she uttered strange praises in Dutch.

"Lee," Walker shouted across the deck. "When you get done over there, can you call room service and have them send up breakfast?"

Hobbs was busy at the moment and said nothing.

***

At the bar on North Bay Island, Dolinda had arrived for an early morning shift. She answered the phone and listened.

"Okay," she said at the end.

The owner was doing inventory and looked over.

"What is it?"

"The writer just called," she said. "He said he spent the night with a girlfriend but he heard about Taylor earlier this morning. After what happened he decided he'd better take a trip to the farm for awhile. Said he has no idea when he'll be back—if ever."

The owner nodded. Over the years, customers came and went. Some drank themselves to death, some just drifted away. And while he always missed a good customer, he knew there were thousands of others that would fill his place.

"You ever bang him?"

"Never did," Dolinda said.

"A little upscale for you."

Dolinda said nothing but the comment hurt.

***

"We haven't got shit," one of the owners of SPS noted.

"If you hadn't had rushed Taylor," the other one said, "and sent him over the edge, we could have questioned him and perhaps located the funds."

"Whoever party number two is, he has our money."

"With only a vague description and nothing much to go on," the man said, "we have about as much chance in finding this guy as we have of a snow storm this evening."

"Hell of a night for the surveillance cameras to crap out."

"I told you they were doing that for months," he said. "You didn't want to pay to have them fixed."

"Hell, they only cover the doors anyway."

"It would have been something."

The men were silent.

"I guess we shouldn't have fired him."

"Ya think?"

***

Larry Martinez was sitting in his home office reading another research paper about the possibility that Jesus was a mortal man who had sired offspring. The arguments were compelling. If one removed the unusual attributes attributed to Jesus, it could be argued that most all the other major religions were similar. There was one God, some type of afterlife, and the necessity to do good deeds while here on earth.

The problem was that religion was not about reason but beliefs. And Martinez's strong belief had clouded him from accepting the fact that Cristos might in fact be descended from Jesus. This made any true investigation into the unrest in Venezuela almost impossible for him. He placed the book aside and started a recording. He carefully began to watch the early campaign appearances of Cristos.

No one had notified him the NIA had been ordered off the case.

***

Later that afternoon the President sat in an office at Camp David with his National Security Adviser. His wife and children were away on vacation, and he had managed to smuggle one of his girlfriends onto the compound and stash her away in a cabin. He needed to do at least some work to justify him coming here, so he was receiving an update on the Venezuelan affair.

"The persecution of Muslims and Jews continues," The National Security Advisor Lester Marks noted, "but the overall fallout from the revelation has decreased."

"How so?" the President asked.

"The religious leaders have toned down the rhetoric," Marks said. "Like they are awaiting the outcome of the election."

The President saw his opening.

"I ordered the NIA and NSA to cease their investigations," the President said casually "And I think we should see if the CIA is sniffing around."

"Easier said than done," Marks noted, "Ever since their agent was outed, they have taken a decidedly defiant attitude to be ordered around."

"Cut their funding."

"We can't," Marks said, "but I'll have a talk with their director."

The President noted and glanced down at the files on his desk.

"Sir?" Marks said. "Don't you think it is important to ascertain if Cristos is the real deal? We are always preaching free-and-fair elections and here we have a clear chance to help another country have just that."

The President was silent for a moment and just looked at Marks as if he were an idiot.

"Venezuela has always been a thorn in capitalism's side," the President said carefully, "Particularly the last couple of presidents. If we can get anyone else in power that seems like it would be good for the country."

"This is a democratic republic, not a capitalist nation," Marks said. "Capitalism is one economic choice available to us—it is not a constitutional mandate."

"I had a feeling when I appointed you that you being from California would pose a problem," the President said. "The business of America *is* business."

Marks violently disagreed but said nothing.

"What else do we have?" the President asked.

"You need to sign the retirement approvals." Marks slid over the file.

There were three and the President read each one carefully. Two were men that had been assigned top-secret satellite technology jobs and the President had neither ever heard nor met either. The last was for Taft.

"John Taft," the President said, reaching for a pen. "Seems like he was always involved in something."

"He was Benson's go-to guy," Marks agreed.

"I heard stories of him before I was even elected."

"He has served his time with distinction."

The President quickly signed the form.

"How long after retirement do we monitor these men? With their knowledge and special skills they are an entirely different breed of men."

"With some like Taft," Marks said, "limited monitoring occurs until death."

"Dangerous even as old cusses," the President said, smiling and handing Marks back the file.

"That brings me to another point," Marks said, "We had an ex-CIA agent die sometime last night in Miami. He retired eight years ago but was on a ten-year watch list."

"Ten years?" the President said. "Did some things but nothing that would change the balance of power if revealed?"

"Something like that," Marks agreed.

"What is the procedure?"

"He's ex-CIA," Marks said. "I think we should let them handle it."

"You can discuss the matter of their dead former agent," the President said, "when you find out if they are still investigating the Cristos affair."

Marks nodded. He wondered why the President seemed so insistent about Venezuela.

***

Taft watched through the window as the land rolled past. What had once been orange groves and fruit orchards was now mixed up with housing developments and strip malls. The movers at his house were probably finished packing by now. After having listed his house for nearly three months, the real-estate agent had recently closed a deal with a couple from Michigan whose company was transferring the wife to a new job in suburban D.C.

When Taft had been called away to Florida at the last minute, he had asked the agent if she would supervise to final loading of his furniture. As the sale had been a surprise and Taft had not yet received his clearance for retirement, everything he owned was going into storage. He was a man without a home and soon would be a man without a job as well.

That was fine with him. His world was crumbling anyway. He was planning to take a trip around the United States to plan his next moves. Taft was one of the lucky ones. He had the financial wherewithal to live anywhere he desired. His plan was to search for a place that felt right.

Taft often wondered if he had missed one of a human's great pleasures by never remaining in a relationship. He wondered what, short of a life of leisure, his new path would follow. Long ago Taft had learned not to dwell on anything personal too long or his mind would beat the thoughts to a gruesome death. So, with the Florida groves giving way to the Georgia swamps, he started to concentrate on the Venezuelan problem again.

***

The CIA archaeologist Duke stared at the finding from the laboratory analysis again. They had checked and double-checked, so he finished writing the report and sealed it inside an inter-office envelope to be delivered to his superior's desk by Monday morning.

Scientifically trained people like Duke usually refrain from dealing in absolutes. Even so, this one had seemed to be a slam dunk. The fleck on the Cristos Parchments he had located was unusual. It had appeared like pollen at first because of the coating. Nasal mucus or, more colloquially, snot, had surrounded a small almost perfectly round orb of methamphetamine. The snot contained a small amount of blood, presumably from the naval cavity, and that had been further analyzed for blood type and DNA markers.

Duke was pretty certain that no ancient scribe was snorting meth. First, it had not been invented. Methamphetamine was created during the Second World War. Second, the snot was recent, and the genetic markers indicated it came from an Asian male.

***

The kidnapped man now believed the worst part is the uncertainty if you will live or die.

A pair of criminals sat at a table in the kitchen of a run-down apartment in Caracas. In the bedroom was their captive. Over the last few weeks the man being held prisoner had gone through a change in appearance. Without a razor he had grown a beard, and without a haircut his hair was more scraggly. It was his eyes that had changed the most, however. They now had a mournful air that replaced the twinkle of optimism that had been present since birth. Confinement combined with the realization that freedom is but an illusion that makes everyone go through soul-deep changes. Changes that might never be reversed.

By replacing the original handlers several times in the past weeks with progressively stupider ones, the people in charge had managed to start the process of scrubbing the operation. The two men now playing cards did not even know who they were tasked with watching. They had been told he was a foreign terrorist and that they were not allowed to speak to him directly. They had been told he was a menace to their country. They had been told a pack of lies.

"I don't know why they just don't kill him," the younger and stupider of the two men said.

"Perhaps he holds some secret information."

"But no one has come to question him."

"I would guess," the younger man said with a serious air, "they need to let him stew for awhile. That's what I have seen on television shows."

The other man nodded slowly, then reached into the pile of cards on the table.

***

John Taft had managed to stretch the knot out of his back. He was sitting in the dining car, picking at a soup-and-salad lunch. Had he known the President had signed his retirement papers, he might have celebrated.

Instead he was wrestling with his future. The Venezuelan affair should have been truly none of his concern at this point. He should just let whatever might occur just happen, but the situation was nagging at his mind. If what the author had told him was true—and he had no reason to doubt that—a corporation abetted by a rogue spy-for-hire firm was subverting the will of an entire nation of people and fixing an election.

Whatever anyone might feel about the country of Venezuela and their politics that was wrong.

The author had explained that the man who had delivered the money to them had flown to the rooftop by helicopter. It should be easy enough to trace that down. The writer also stated the oil man had asked for a night club and was recommended Mirabelle's. That was another way to determine his identity. Maybe Taft should dig around and find out who was behind the plan.

Pushing aside the half-eaten salad, Taft smeared butter on half a roll and bit into it. He was washing down the bite with a slug of iced tea when his telephone rang.

"I've got something for you."

"Give me a couple minutes," Taft said. "I'll call you back from a more private location."

Taft slipped a bill on the table for the waiter and walked through the rail cars back to his cabin. Once inside he listened to hear if anyone was in the cabin to the front but it appeared quiet. Then he dialed Martinez.

"Cristos does not appear the same man," Martinez said without preamble.

"How so?"

"Both his facial structure and physical appearance seem magnified. As if he is larger and his facial features more prominent."

Taft had yet to tell Martinez of his trip to Florida.

"Maybe he is simply growing into the role as the descendant of God," Taft said. "Like a politician that appears more magnetic when he is speaking to a crowd."

"Or somebody replaced the real Cristos with a doppelganger."

They were both quiet as they considered this.

"I had to take an emergency trip last night," Taft said. "I'll explain later. I'm on my way home right now. Can I ask you to do two things for me?"

"You know you can."

"First, drive over to my house and make sure the movers got everything packed and the real estate agent has the place locked up."

"The second?"

"Find out who leased a helicopter that landed Friday night on a high-rise on Seventy-Ninth Street in Miami. More specifically the town of North Bay Village. It's an island between Miami and Miami Beach."

"That should be easy enough."

Taft was silent for a moment. "Do that on the hush, Larry."

"I assume you mean finding who leased the helicopter."

"Yeah," Taft said. "You're welcome to tell whomever you like you about my house. On Monday it won't be mine anymore."

"What else, old buddy?"

"A voice print from the new and old Cristos would be nice."

"And I thought I might have a weekend off."

The telephone went dead and Taft sat for a moment watching the scenery roll past.

36

THE DIRECTOR OF THE CIA had about as much use for the current President as a cat has for a pet dog. First, in an effort to further his own goals, the President had exposed one of the CIA's longtime agents. In the second place, the President had taken to using his agency as handmaidens to private industry—particularly for his friends and large donors. Third, in the pursuit of other investigations, the agency had come across proof of bribes paid, infidelities with numerous women, and a wanton and repeated disregard for presidential decorum. The director was not a prude—if the President cheated on his wife, that was a moral issue, not an agency matter. The problem was the President was so indiscriminate that he opened himself up to infiltration by female enemy agents.

"So what have we got?" he asked his three closest advisors.

"Special Agent Duke, one of our agency archaeologists, discovered a"—the man consulted his notes—"mucus-covered granule of methamphetamine on the original documents the NIA agent retrieved from the museum in Caracas."

"So," the director said quickly, "the Cristos Parchments are most likely fakes."

The advisor nodded. "He has retrieved a DNA sample and he is running it through a database."

"Probably won't get a hit," the director noted, "as the rest of the world is too smart to allow a national DNA database to be set up. What else?"

"A former agent died in Miami Beach. Allegedly fell from his high-rise condo balcony. He was a known heavy drinker and had retired eight years ago."

"Retired, or went into private practice?"

"Went into the private sector for a company called SPS."

"They are a lesion on the face of society," the director said. "Both of the owners were kicked out of the agency for multiple incidences of low moral turpitude. What was the name of the agent?"

The advisor consulted his notes. "Burke Taylor."

The director nodded. "Red was a friend of mine back in the day. He was one hell of a good second-tier agent until the drinking got the best of him. What has our investigation uncovered?"

"The agents on the ground have examined the video surveillance tapes from the front lobby and are reasonably sure that the two owners of SPS visited Taylor shortly before the incident."

"Get me a match with DNA or fingerprints to be sure it was them," the director said carefully. "Then report back to me ASAP."

The advisor nodded, gathered up his notes and left the office.

"What else?" he said to the third man.

"As soon as the armored-car salesman gave up the bank we sent an agent to investigate. As it was the weekend, they needed to break inside but they retrieved the name of the owners."

"Well?"

"It was exactly as we thought."

The director shook his head back and forth. "What has my country come to? We have private citizens trying to overthrow governments, people who should stand for good doing bad, and a political system so financed by big-money interests that a fair and decent man or woman has about as much chance of being elected as they would winning the lottery a dozen times in a row."

The room was silent.

"The National Security Advisor asked me if the CIA was involved in any of this," the director said.

"How did you answer?" his senior advisor asked.

"That I had no idea," the director said, "what he was talking about."

***

That night for the first time since the coma, Taft slept soundly. Maybe it was the motion of the train as it raced through the countryside. Maybe it was the knowledge that he would soon be retired and away from the stresses of his job. Perhaps it was that his house had sold and the closing fast approaching. Possessions have a way of restricting one's freedom without them ever knowing. More likely it was because he was coming to a series of decisions about his future life, and sometimes when a path is clear, so is the mind.

The following morning Taft awoke early, and shaved and showered in his compartment. Then he made his way to the dining car. No tables were available. He was looking for a place to wait when he noticed an older woman motioning to him. He walked over and smiled down.

"You're welcome to sit with me," she said easily. "The waiter has yet to take my order."

"Thank you." Taft slid into the booth.

The woman appeared to be north of fifty but her obvious wealth and good breeding made an actual age impossible to determine. Her eyes were clear, her smile broad, and her body toned and trimmed. She looked into Taft's eyes, then farther down the dining car.

"Here he comes," she said, smiling.

"Miss Maggie," the waiter said, wiping a fluffy white towel over the already spotless table, "I am so sorry. You know how we get rushed at this time."

"This is my friend…" Maggie started to say before realizing they had not been introduced.

"John Taft," he said. "This lovely lady was polite enough to allow me to join her at the table."

The waiter nodded. "I know you want coffee, Miss Maggie. How about you, Mr. Taft?"

"I'd love some."

"I already know what the lady wants," the waiter said. "Do you need a moment to decide, sir?"

"Cheese omelet, crispy potatoes, sliced tomatoes, no toast."

"A man who knows what he wants." Maggie noted as the waiter walked off to fetch the coffee.

"I take it you come here often."

"My husband and I used to ride the train down every few months," Maggie said easily. "We had a vacation home in Cedar Key."

"You said 'had,'" Taft said. "Did you sell it?"

Maggie was silent for a moment. A wave of sadness swept over her face. "Once my husband passed away," she said, "it just wasn't the same. This is my first trip on the train without him."

"I'm so sorry," Taft said. "How long has it been?"

"Not quite a year," Maggie noted.

The waiter returned with the coffee a silver pitcher of cream and a ceramic bowl with sugar cubes.

"I can tell you were very close," Taft said after the waiter had left.

"And I can tell," Maggie said wisely, "that you have never had such love."

Taft was quiet. "Work has…."

"No need to explain," Maggie said.

There was a moment of quiet as they sipped the coffee.

"What did you and your husband do for employment?"

"We were, and I still am, part of a dying breed," Maggie said easily. "Labor lawyers."

"You will pardon my ignorance," Taft said, "as to any changes in that. I've worked for the same employer almost my entire life."

"What do you do?"

Taft could have lied—it was a reflex for him when asked what he did—but for some reason he answered her question directly.

"Spy," he said quietly, "The actual term is intelligence officer or Special Agent."

"Truly?"

The waiter returned with a tray of food. Maggie had the steel-cut oatmeal with fresh fruit and yogurt. After arranging the food, he refilled their coffee and water and retreated.

"No kidding," Taft said after taking a bite of the crispy hash browns, "I don't know why I told you, however. I usually make up something."

"People naturally trust me."

"Plus I'm retiring soon."

"Congratulations."

"You said labor law is a dying breed," Taft said. "Tell me more."

"How much time do you have?"

"I've got nothing until the train pulls into the station."

"Here goes," Maggie said. "You may need to take notes."

Taft smiled.

"My husband and I came to understand—we are not certain when exactly—the government, or more accurately the democratic system, was taken over by a wealthy elite that probably works together."

Ever since the coma, unusual circumstances kept cropping up. Taft felt there must be a reason.

"That is pretty far out there," he said, "but just for argument's sake, when do you think this occurred?"

"I'd say as early as nineteen hundred, as late as the Great Depression. From there the octopus just continues to strengthen and grow. This concentration of power comes at a great cost to ninety-nine percent of the other Americans. People are starting to see it. But it may be too late."

"Most people have larger homes and more toys than ever," Taft noted, "so how bad can it be?"

"They have debt," Maggie said. "They own nothing. This was planned to offset and divert attention from the fact that for the last thirty years, the real wage people receive and more importantly what it will purchase, continues to decline. As the elite were moving toward control they worked with the banks to allow free and easy credit. For a decade or more, the average working man received increases in their credit-card limits to hide the fact they could not pay the balances on what they owed. Nor could they live on what they made. People were taking on debt on credit cards for the basics like food and medicine."

"What about the stock market?"

"Part of the plan for business to screw the worker was to steal their pensions and replace them with self-invested individual retirement plans. This policy of businesses seizing their employees' pensions and using them for their own purposes was outright theft, yet the government stood by and allowed it to happen. By making the average worker take a position in the stock market they could steal trillions, as the game is theirs. It is exactly the same as owning a casino—you hook people on gambling, then sit back and reap the profits. Then every time you create a crisis you can steal more. People who could once look forward to a comfortable old age are now reduced to near-poverty at retirement. Without a defined-benefit pension, the average worker is simply a sheep to be shorn and no one is more adept at stealing than the thieves that run the stock exchanges."

Taft smiled. "Okay, what about housing values? Some did okay?"

"Only if you timed it perfect, never borrowed against your home, and had an excellent-rate short-term mortgage or paid cash. Then when you sold you would need to move to a smaller place or an area that was substantially cheaper. Like the scam that brought about the last crash. The stock market had a great deal of corporate investors such as banks and insurance companies. When the crisis of September eleventh occurred and the markets were closed for nearly a week, the losses were so severe that the economy would have been plunged into a depression with more than a few banks and insurance companies declared insolvent. As the entire scam of fiat money and the U.S. selling trillions of dollars in bond is based on faith, the failure of these major institutions would have brought down the sham system. So the government inflamed the housing market to divert attention."

"You are saying the economy was broken years before the Lehman collapse and the housing bubble bursting?"

"It has collapsed many times and it has been reinflated like a leaky balloon. The Arab oil embargo and Nixon going off the gold standard come to mind. But let me get back to housing for a minute. After September eleventh you might remember the President coming on television and begging people to spend money. People were scared and holding on to what they had. With the U.S. economy based seventy percent on consumption, only a few more months of that and the country would have been in a depression. That would have led to even less spending, and so on."

Taft sipped from his cup.

"Over thousands of years it has become apparent that the quickest and easiest way to make people act is greed. The talking heads began shouting real-estate appreciation. This would also lead to construction, which put people to work. It was a simple idea. If you are in dire straits and need to falsely inflate the value of something, go for the largest asset. If that is rising, workers and consumers think things are great and they won't notice the further erosion in their employment conditions and they can return to spending. Go for the touchdown pass and worry about the consequences later—it was that bad. The banks dropped all pretense that anyone needed to be qualified to buy a home—a pulse and enough money to pay their fees was enough. Mortgage lending increased substantially while standards dropped to their lowest level ever. It was a free-for-all that increased demand, as so many people entered the market that could have never before, that prices skyrocketed."

"What's wrong with that?" Taft asked.

"Let's look at the basics of home ownership first. Along with mortgage rates, which at the time of the housing bubble were running around six percent, there is the cost of taxes of one to two percent per year. Add in maintenance, remodeling and updating costs. New kitchens and baths and ordinary repairs add another one to two percent. Just do the math—a three-hundred-thousand-dollar house today needs a thirty-thousand-dollar redo within fifteen years. There are carpets, roofs, driveways and whatever, and that doesn't include the ordinary replacing of the appliances. It all adds up but almost no one figures that into the equations."

"You always hear I bought my house for one hundred thousand and sold it twenty years later for two," Taft said, smiling. He was enjoying Maggie's banter. The older woman was sexy and smart.

"Except with a twenty-year mortgage at six percent, the total of payments was two and a quarter and you paid probably thirty thousand in taxes, not including updating and repairs."

"Does the average consumer understand this?"

"Hell no," Maggie said. "It's on the documents, but the banks and lenders have trained everyone to look at the payments and repeat the stories of houses going up. At best, unless you can pay cash, a house is a forced savings account with a negative return. That and you personalize it more than a rental house. The other thing people don't consider is even if they timed it perfectly and sold their home when the market was screaming, if they want to buy another one in that same area it also has increased in value. Then there was the second-mortgage outrage."

"That never made any sense to me."

"Mortgage money was so free and easy that people would borrow on the falsely inflated value of their house to buy themselves expensive cars, boats or take vacations. If they took on another first mortgage they were effectively financing their trip to Mexico for twenty or thirty years. It was insane as an economic principle—but people went for it. They took on greater and greater debt. And then the prices began to fall."

"A bunch of people lost their houses," Taft noted.

The waiter came over and refilled their coffee cups.

"A bunch of average Americans lost everything," Maggie said. "After they lost their jobs, most poured their retirement savings into making the mortgage payments, as they had been told 'real estate never goes down' and they expected it to rise up again. They were honest and wanted to pay their debts but the problem was that the system was designed from the start to fleece them. Then, to add insult to injury, while the banks got bailed out for their part in the destruction and the elite retained and actually increased their funds, the average American was left to fight it out in a job market that offered even less pay and benefits than before. It was a no-holds-barred assault on the middle class and it decimated them as effectively as a plague."

"So what about labor law?" Taft said. "Your specialty."

"From the time people employed one another," Maggie said. "And that has not been very long. The employer has always attempted to keep wage costs low while at the same time retaining all control. Back in the Old West, the mining companies or railroads, which were large employers, retaliated against unions organizing by bringing in immigrants. We think the flooding of the labor market by Mexican nationals is new but it is an old tactic. The railroads brought in Chinese, who would works cheaper until laws outlawing their immigration were passed. The mine owners brought in southern Europeans to replace the northern Europeans, British and Welsh miners who began to demand safe working conditions and an adequate wage. Until the immigration problem is dealt with, the average worker does not have a chance. The only way a worker can demand and receive a fair and adequate wage is through collective bargaining. If an employer keeps changing workers and not allowing any form of representation, people will continue to receive less and less."

"What about control?"

"Employers continue to dumb down jobs," Maggie said, "and not train people. The unions trained workers so they had a sense of self worth as well as valuable skills they could take elsewhere if the conditions deteriorated—the elite hated that. They also had the ability and right to strike—and that was simply too much for those that control capital. They believe themselves to be better than the lowly worker and thus they must always be in control. Do you know right now who is the largest employer in the U.S.?"

"The government?"

"I wish," Maggie said, smiling. "The big discount store. They neither pay people much nor do they promote stable and secure full-time employment. Do you know what the largest company was forty years ago?"

"I'll stay with my guess. The government?"

"AT&T. The phone company was a regulated monopoly so they could offer great wages and benefits. Second was General Motors and third was the government. If it was like that today, the average worker would be in a lot better shape. The entire deregulation movement was a fiasco. The elite convinced a gullible public that if they would allow them to remove all regulation, things would be better. That was a bright shiny lie—prices rose, service levels declined to the level of absurdity, and workers got screwed on wages. Did you know being an airline pilot or flight attendant used to be a great job, or that if you worked as a telephone installer for AT&T you could actually send your children to college? The only people that deregulation was good for were the guys at the top. CEO salaries have skyrocketed while the assets held by the extremely rich have reached levels that signal a coming revolution. The entire public in the United States has been fed a bill of goods and they lapped it up like a kitten at a bowl of milk."

"Who exactly is behind it all?" Taft asked carefully.

"That's what I would like to know. Do you have any answers, secret agent man?"

"No," Taft admitted. "I've only been open to the possibility since I was recently electrocuted."

"Sometimes someone has to be laid off, sometimes they have to lose their house," Maggie said, chuckling. "First I've heard about electrical shock, however."

Taft looked into her eyes.

"Me and some other people," Maggie said, "are trying to look behind the curtain. If we figure it out, I'll let you know."

Taft nodded. It was odd but it felt as if they had been destined to meet. They were both quiet.

"I waited a year out of respect for my husband," Maggie said quietly. "Now could you please take me back to your cabin?"

Taft slowly grinned and they rose. He reached down and helped Maggie from her seat, then led the way back to his cabin. She needed the attention of a man. So Taft did all he could for her.

"You going to be okay now?" he asked over an hour later.

Maggie leaned over and kissed him. "Great."

37

TAFT WATCHED AS the rental car was driven off the train car. Once the car was parked, he walked over to it with his single bag. Opening the trunk, he tossed his bag inside before he slid into the driver's seat and twisted the key. Automatically he drove in the direction of his home before remembering that the movers had already come and gone and it was empty.

Like a judo chop to the neck, it hit him hard. He was homeless and unemployed. Homeless and unemployed by choice, but still, the effect to his ego were similar to what others in similar situations might feel. There was a sense of not being attached to anything. Of familiar rituals now gone. Of uncertainty as to what each day might bring. Taft, trained to analyze and understand emotions, recognized his symptoms and began to deal with the problem analytically.

"I do have enough funds," he said aloud. "And more when my house closes tomorrow."

As soon as he said those words, he felt better and began planning his future moves. He'd figure out where to stash Hemingway's cash. Figure out a place to stay overnight. Then he'd do some long-term planning. For a moment, he analyzed how the wave of despair had swept across his mind and he felt for the millions of others who had faced much harder choices and did not have the resources he had to use. He thought to himself of people in turmoil. How did they cope?

***

At that exact instant half a continent away in Houston, J. Thomas Melton was preparing to address that very question. The chorus had warmed the crowd and the computer whizzes had manipulated the lights and heat and sound to bring the crowd to the point he wanted. Now all he had to do was deliver his magic. He sneaked onto the side of the stage and stood exactly on his marks, which were taped to the floor. The chorus ended, then there was complete silence. Then a thin tendril of light from the heavens descended and lit his face. The beam grew until Melton's entire body was bathed in a stream of unearthly light. His arm was thrust in the air as if pointing to God. He leg was cocked as if he was some new form of rock 'n' roll singer and preacher. The crash of a gong filled the hall. Melton broke his pose and began to move, with the light following close behind. Slowly the entire hall filled with the glow.

The meeting with the other religious leaders was all a sham. His plan was simple but diabolical. After first convincing the other churches to profess moderation, he would go on the attack.

"Jesus is the son of God, not some son-of-a-gun," Melton said.

A chorus of amens rose up.

"Not some son-of-a-gun ordinary man who had a wife and children. We wish he could have experienced such pleasures—but that was not his fate. He was sent here to pay for the sins of man. He was sent here as your salvation."

The crowd was warming now. More were shouting their agreement.

"There are bad people," Melton said, "other religions behind these falsehoods coming out of South America. Trays will be sent down the aisles for your donations. The Evangelical Church of Believers is planning to send a congregation to Venezuela to stand against these lies and we need your financial support to make it happen…"

***

As soon as he heard these words, a black man at the rear of the stage dialed a telephone number and spoke quickly.

"He's gone off the deep end," he said quietly. "I'd recommend action."

"Along with everything else," the voice said, "we didn't need this right now."

"How about me," the black man said. "I've been assigned to this idiot for some time now."

The voice on the telephone was silent. Finally he said, "Time to raid the vault?"

"Now is the perfect time."

"Two agents will meet you downstairs and help with your extraction."

"So I'm finally done here?"

"Yes."

"Good because if this cracker treated me like a house slave one more time, I was going to slap him until his capped teeth fell out."

"Grab the package and get out," the voice said. "I'm going to put you up for an intelligence medal."

"Thank you, master."

"Quit screwing around, Franklin," the voice said, "and make your exit."

**

Melton was barely concealing the enemy now. "Those religions who deny his divine existence—those religions that see him as a prophet, not the savior. Those religions and the people that practice them must awaken. Awaken by whatever means we find necessary."

***

Franklin, the CIA agent posing as the porter, made his way upstairs to the vault. Sometime in the first week of his employment, he used an electronic keypad device to open the vault door and record the combination. What he had found inside was disturbing.

Trays of collector coins, stamps worth millions, and cash in different denominations shared space with plastic-sealed magazines about J. Thomas Melton. There were articles about his work with the poor—a slap in the face considering how much illegal loot he had inside the vault—and articles about his close friendship with the President. Melton was listed as the President's spiritual adviser. There were gold strips and bars, precious stones and jewelry and titles to real estate, cars and boats.

It seemed that one side of the vault was a shrine to his ego. Framed photographs of his first churches, robes and other clothing he must have worn. Photos and newspaper articles chronicling his rise. There were records of Melton's arrest for possession of marijuana when he was younger, which had been removed from police files and hidden. There was the certificate from his first marriage, which ended in divorce. No one knew he had ever been married before but Melton's people sent her a check every month to keep quiet.

Most disturbing was a collection of pornography and photographs, most featuring Melton with a variety of women. This was hidden off to one side. The greed and disturbing detritus from the life of a man who pledged himself to good deeds and helping others less fortunate.

Franklin quickly opened the vault door, took the legs off the box, and prepared the box to be moved. Using a small camera built into the lapel of his suit, he recorded the contents of the room quickly, then reached for his phone.

"Still a go?"

"The other agents are downstairs."

"Have them deploy on the north side."

"Done."

Grasping the box and placing the poles under his arms, Franklin walked out of the vault, closed the door and spun the dial, then made his way down the hall to the back stairway and started down.

***

Melton had been extolling his followers when his telephone in his suit pocket vibrated warning him the vault had been opened. He had several different tones programmed so he was not absolutely positive it was the vault. Even so, he was deep in his sermon of lies and could not have stopped even if he wanted.

Melton's forehead was becoming slick with sweat. Over the years, members of his congregation had come to believe that this was a sign that God was inside Melton. They believed this because Melton's people had spread the rumor. The fact was the sweat was most likely from alcohol as Melton consumed at least a fifth of whiskey a day.

'There are enemies all around," he shouted, "enemies who believe different...."

***

Franklin was at the lower floor and made his way toward an emergency-exit door. As he turned backwards, he bumped his buttocks on the bar that opened the door and leaned outward. The door opened into blinding sunlight. Franklin saw a nondescript car parked on a side street across a great expanse of grass. As he trotted toward the car, the doors opened and a pair of men climbed out. One stood by the driver's door, ready to jump inside and drive while the second raced around to open the trunk. Then he started to run toward Franklin, who was balancing the poles under his arms with great effort. The man took the poles and the two raced over to the car. As he placed the box on the rear seat, Franklin saw a pair of church security sedans headed their way.

"You men have any way to disable those cars?" Franklin asked as he climbed into the rear seat.

The man in the passenger seat nodded as the driver slid the sedan into drive and pushed down on the pedal. They headed through the parking lot, with the security cars catching up. The passenger tossed a package out the window.

Franklin turned and looked out the rear glass as the package hit the ground. The package exploded, sending thousands of razor-sharp triangular obstacles onto the ground directly in front of the pursuing cars. Seconds later, with their tires shredded, one slid into the other and stopped. Steam poured from under the hood as the security guards tried to climb out.

The nondescript sedan careened onto the road outside the massive church. A few minutes later it pulled to a stop where a semi-trailer with the door open sat waiting. After removing the box and poles, Franklin and the passenger climbed out. The driver drove up the ramp into the semi and shut off the car. Leaving the keys inside, he climbed out and walked down the ramp. The passenger of the sedan was now behind the wheel of an SUV. With the box and poles safely stashed in the rear and the switch of vehicles completed, they pulled away.

A few moments later the truck driver had the ramp stowed and he too pulled away.

***

Melton quickly made his way to the vault after finishing his sermon. The cameras clearly showed Franklin entering the vault and leaving. It was obvious he knew the combination. It was also obvious he knew exactly what he had come for. Melton made his way to a nearby office and dialed a telephone number.

"I need you to find out who just robbed my vault," Melton said.

"You idiot, I told you to get rid of the boxes," the voice said.

Melton's ego had expanded over the years and he was not used to being talked down to.

"There is also information about me and you in there," Melton said.

"Why the hell wasn't that destroyed," the voice said. "Lord knows both of us required quite a scrubbing before we got into all this."

"For old times' sakes," Melton said.

"More like you might need to use it against me."

Melton was silent.

"You made a huge mistake," the voice said coldly.

The telephone went dead. Melton had no idea what might happen next.

***

Taft was standing next to a monument in a cemetery in Maryland. He stared down at the words on the marker. Tears no longer spilled from his eyes at the sight. It had been years since that had happened. Instead he had taken to smiling and remembering the good times. The cemetery was old and rarely used anymore. The two of them had found it on a bicycle ride in the countryside one day long ago and she noted how it was such a peaceful place that when she was gone, Taft had decided this would be her place for eternity. He came here several times a year to clean the monument and pluck the weeds. He looked around to be sure he was alone, then nudged the marble side of the

monument. It gave way to an open space inside. Taft stuffed the bags of money inside.

***

At the same time, hundreds of workers were using pressure washers to clean the rows of seats inside the largest soccer stadium in Venezuela. More than one hundred thousand people could fit inside. For tonight's speech the streets nearby would be jammed, and outside another group of workers were hosing down the pavement. Millions of gallons of water would be used for cleaning the area, thousands of ushers, tickets takers and security forces would be working, and hundreds of radio and television stations across the globe would carry the message.

One man required all this preparation and at this instant he was carefully dyeing his hair.

In an age of immediate media and worldwide exposure, Vincente Cristos was at this instant the most famous person on the planet. Reporters had swarmed throughout Venezuela, interviewing anyone who could shed light on the man.

Even before the revelation he might be related to the son of God, when he had first announced his candidacy for the presidency, his past history had been sparse at best. He never spoke of his childhood claiming the future was the real story. He had served one term as a congressman from a rural area where it was difficult to find anyone who knew him well before running for president, and as a congressman he did little of note. He was unmarried, seemingly without friends, and had nary a neither black mark nor gold star on his record.

In short, he appeared to be the perfect candidate even prior to the revelation.

Plucking one of his eyebrows with tweezers, Cristos glanced at his hair one last time and walked from the bathroom of the hotel suite into the living room. Tonight's speech had been laid out carefully on the coffee table in front of the couch, and he sat in his robe and picked it up. First he read through the text slowly, then, once he had the words down, he rose and paraded about the room, reading the text and practicing intonation and hand gestures. This practice would last for hours. Until he believed he could extract the emotions he needed from tonight's crowd.

***

General Earl Benson, the director of the CIA, and the National Security Advisor sat in the Oval Office. As it was late Sunday and there was a football game on the television he wanted to watch, the President was both distracted and irritated.

"He's a private citizen," the President said. "I cannot tell him what to say."

"We understand he is your friend, Mr. President," Benson said. "As my agency's mandate is to combat terrorism, we need to inform you that J. Thomas Melton's sermon is divisive and has the potential to cause actions to be taken against the United States. Although we were formed expressly without a state religion, most of the rest of the world views us as a Christian nation and may attempt to retaliate against our country for the words of a private religious leader."

"We were formed as a Christian country…" the President started to say.

"Sir," the CIA Director noted, "we were expressly not. The Constitution and a variety of other documents state that freedom of religion is one of the founding tenets of the United States."

Both Benson and the CIA director were astounded that when alone, the ignorance of the President was so easily visible. The man was like a puppet. When he had rehearsed and there was an audience, he was fine. He could repeat the lines he was given and as long as no one asked a probing question or for further information, the President was fine. When forced to discuss new topics or make analytical decisions, the man was clueless.

"Sir," Benson continued, "Melton was one of your largest donors as well as bringing you the massive block of votes from the religious right that put you in this office. We know you speak to him frequently. We are asking you, if you could ask him, to tone down the religious rhetoric."

"If this Cristos fellow turns out to be a phony," the CIA director said, "Melton can jump all over it, right now however he needs to keep quiet."

The President nodded but agreed to nothing. He knew more than he was saying, but so did the director.

"Is that all?" the President asked.

It was not, but everyone knew they would accomplish nothing today.

As the two men walked to their cars under the portico, the CIA director turned to Benson.

"Do you have time to come by my office now?"

Benson simply nodded. "I'll have my driver follow you over."

Moments later, both men were in an elevator for the private ride up to the CIA director's office. The CIA director turned to Benson.

"So Earl," he said. "How about I send out for some coffee and sandwiches."

"I could use a whiskey."

The elevator stopped.

"I don't need to send out for that," the director noted.

Once they were settled in the office and food and libations served the director turned to Benson.

"J. Thomas Melton had someone steal the Cristos Parchments your agent planted."

"So I heard."

"We had an agent inside," the director said. "I ordered him to steal them back. They should be downstairs by now. Do you want me to have them sent up?"

"No reason." Benson said. "My question is, are they real?"

"That's what I wanted to speak to you about."

Benson waited.

"We think a company named SPS created them for a client."

Neither man was yet ready to completely disclose what he knew.

"The intelligence-for-hire firm from Miami?"

"That's the one."

"My agency has had issues with them before."

"Mine too," the CIA director said.

"Do you know who the client is?"

"We think it's Hobker Petroleum."

"So because their oil-drilling rigs are nationalized by Venezuela, they decide to take over the country?"

"We are still putting the pieces together," the Director admitted.

"Aren't the two owners of Hobker tied into the President?"

"As close as fingers on a hand."

Benson took a slug of whiskey while the director took a bite of a chicken-salad sandwich.

"Aren't our two agencies supposed to have an inter-governmental rivalry?" Benson said. "And not to work together?"

"That's the beauty of this operation," the CIA director noted.

"What's that?"

"After we are done there will be no credit to fight over. I won't want anyone to know what we did—and neither will you."

Benson reached for a sandwich. It was obvious he was going to be here awhile.

38

THE ENTIRE stadium was rocking from the huge crowd stamping their feet. Spotlight on the street swept back and forth illuminating the clouds. There was a palpable sense of urgency and furor as the people awaited their savior. Slowly a repetitious drumbeat came over hundreds of speakers. The rhythmic sound grew in volume and cadence. A single pinpoint of light lit up on the stage and then expanded into an orb three feet into diameter. As the crowd was transfixed by the light, Cristos slid in from the right. Then all at once, he appeared in the light. Cupping his hands together, he shrunk the light down to a pinpoint. Then he flicked his hand to the side, tossing the light away.

As if the sun had ignited the stage, it was flooded with light from every direction. The drums grew louder and faster. Cristos spread his hands in a circle then brought his hands slowly down to his sides. The light diminished until just his upper body was illuminated. The drums ceased.

"I am the son of the seventh son," he said powerfully.

Chaos that ran through in the crowd as people lost control of their emotions. Tears streamed down faces and cries of joy rang out.

"The other countries," Cristos said, "those that claim to lead the world, are not Christian but bastard nations. Hodgepodges of mixed religions and mixed values. If elected I will lead a Christian Venezuela. A nation that others in the world will idolize for our single-mindedness of purpose. A nation under one God. A nation ready to receive God's bountiful blessing."

The crowd was erupting in a frenzy.

"I am here to lead you," Cristos said, "Here to move Venezuela into first place in the world. Here to…"

***

The CIA Director and Benson had finished their meeting only a half hour before the speech. That left Benson little time to make it back to the NIA. A technician sent a live picture from the stadium directly to the director's office and an interpreter was sent in to translate.

"This is not good," the director noted at Cristos's mention of the first pure Christian nation.

"I guess this decides it then," Benson said quietly.

***

Martinez telephoned Taft just as he was leaving the cemetery.

"Do you have time to stop by my house?"

"I'm not doing much else," Taft admitted.

"Have you had dinner?"

"Nope."

"I'll have Marie save a plate."

"Thanks."

"You in the Jaguar?"

"Rental car."

"I won't ask."

"Be there in under an hour."

"I'll be here," Martinez said.

Two hours later, Martinez stopped the disc. The pair had watched the footage a dozen times. A plate with the remnants of a meatloaf and mashed-potato dinner sat off to the side of the desk. Taft was sipping from a large bottle of Italian mineral water.

"Excellent observation," Taft said, "The differences between the two are so subtle that at first they are barely obvious."

"Whoever did this knew that someone would have to carefully study the clips and even then it is doubtful anyone but a professional would make the connection in the limited amount of time before the election."

"The guys that arranged this are pros," Taft admitted.

"At first it was the mannerisms that caught my eye. The little subtleties everyone has that makes them different. The new Cristos was slightly different. It was almost imperceptible but it seemed as if his attitude had changed. He went from sincere to what I began to perceive as acting."

"I see what you mean."

"His physical appearance is very close," Martinez added, "but it is slightly off."

"Unless they could have cloned him, it's as close as one could get."

"Are you convinced like I am?"

"He's a fake," Taft said. "I agree with you one hundred percent."

"Then we have a problem."

"How's that?"

"From what I heard, the President ordered intelligence to stand down on this."

Taft was quiet.

"Forget that for a minute," Martinez said. "What's the deal with the rental car?"

"I brought it back from my trip to Miami."

"You fly down and drive back?"

"I met a nice lady on the train."

"What train?"

"Allow me to explain."

***

After the speech concluded, Benson smiled at the CIA director.

"I'm headed to my office. I'll be there all night if you need me."

"I doubt I'll be going home anytime soon," the director said. "Feel free to call on me if the need arises."

Benson made his way down the elevator to his waiting car. Once inside used his secure telephone to call Dick Albright.

"Meet me at the office ASAP."

"I'm already here," Albright said "And I've watched the speech several times already."

"Good," Benson said "Because you're not going to believe what the CIA just told me."

"Sunday at the CIA," Albright said, "how quaint."

***

Martinez sat back in his chair once Taft finished. Taft took a last slug from the mineral water.

"Small world. The author that helped you with the Tesla affair calls and asks a favor and it turns out someone he knows might have be the inspiration that created this entire mess."

"Some crazy drunken idea," Taft noted, "and someone actually does it."

"It's not done yet."

"When I called you and asked you to trace…."

"Helicopter was leased by Hobker Petroleum," Martinez said. "I have a file there on the desk with the information."

"You are just so efficient."

Taft scanned through the documents. "Hobker is closely tied to the President."

"The Hobbs in Hobker calls the President, Johnny Boy."

"I hope not in front of other people," Taft said. "It's one thing to sell out. It's another to be obvious."

"Everyone loves whores," Martinez agreed, "just no one wants anyone to know they use them."

"That's not entirely true," Taft said. "There is that one Hollywood actor."

Martinez laughed. "There is an exception to every rule."

"So friends of the President hire a company to overthrow the government of a sovereign country by staging a fake election to put their man in charge. All because their oil rigs were nationalized. Now we believe our President has knowledge of this and orders the intelligence into the matter shut down. Now this entire mess is threatening to start a religious war that might rival the Holocaust."

Martinez said. "That sounds about right."

"I'm glad I'm retiring," Taft said. "This country has gone to hell in a handbasket."

***

Albright was listening intensely to Benson, who was relaying the same information.

"The CIA thinks a company named SPS out of Miami somehow perpetrated the scam taking place in Venezuela. They would probably let it go but they think the owners of SPS were behind the murder of a retired agent."

"We always protect our own," Albright noted.

"They believe a company named Hobker Petroleum hired SPS to perform a coup d'état as payback for the country nationalizing their oil rigs."

"I've run across Hobker before," Albright said. "They seem to think they have immunity from any international laws since the President was elected. They tried to have the leader of a small African nation killed last year and a puppet government put in his place."

"Yes," Benson said. "I remember now. We learned of the plot and warned the leader. He and his country are some of our only allies against terrorism in that region. He's almost tougher on the Islamic terrorist than we are."

"Exactly," Albright said. "We could never prove it, but all clues pointed to Hobker being behind the plot. We wanted to go farther in the investigation but we were called off by a call from the National Security Adviser."

"He's a puppet of the President," Benson said. "No experience in government whatsoever and he was appointed by the President. What was he before he came to Washington?"

"His family are big citrus farmers in Florida."

"Well that definitely qualifies him," Benson said sarcastically.

The two men were quiet.

"There is another development," Benson said. "The Cristos Parchments that were taken in the military-style raid?"

"Do tell"

Benson said. "They ended up with J. Thomas Melton."

"The right-wing religious nut case."

"You mean the respected religious leader who counsels the President, don't you."

"How in the world did he manage to pull off the heist?"

"It was done by a company based in South Africa."

"But of course," Albright said.

"The CIA swiped the documents back."

"That was fast."

"They had a man inside Melton's operation for some time."

"Why?"

"Apparently even before Cristos, he has been trying to stir up trouble with both the Muslims and the Jews. Something that will give the President a reason to take action against them."

"What on earth for?"

"Because," Benson said quietly, "as you noted so accurately earlier, he is a right-wing religious nut."

"And both Hobker Petroleum and J. Thomas Melton are presidential friends and advisors."

Benson motioned to the bottle of bourbon on the desk. Albright shook his head.

"You know all these problems caused by influence are just going to become worse," Benson said after pouring himself two fingers. "In the nineteen-eighty election, the total raised for the presidential election, all the parties included, was something like one hundred and sixty two million. What was it in oh-eight?"

"Something like one billion, seven hundred million, if I remember right," Albright said.

"Since the population in 'eighty was two hundred and twenty million, and had only increased to three hundred and five million in oh-eight it pretty obvious that the average citizen is not putting people into office any longer. It's the corporations, the PACs and the money packagers. Each has their own people—hell, they have probably been grooming them for years—and each group expects those they elect to do what they want, when they want."

"In oh-ten the average winner of a Senate seat spent hundreds of millions to win."

"You know as well as I do, Dick," Benson said, downing the bourbon, "that it is different than when we started into this game. The new politician is, for the most part, an unqualified, sometimes borderline stupid, bought-and-paid-for minion of whatever groups gave him money."

"I miss the old Washington," Albright said. "Some of those guys actually cared about doing what was right for the country."

They were both silent for a moment.

"Waxing nostalgic will get us nowhere," Benson said. "We need to figure out what if anything we do about this Venezuelan conundrum."

"We do anything and we are going directly up against the President."

"He can cut us and our agency off at the knees."

Benson rose from the desk.

"Not if we cut him first."

***

Because of the excitement of what they had discovered, Taft left the Martinez home before he remembered his house was empty. Without a firm idea of his night's accommodations he drove around for a half hour, thinking and planning, before he found a chain hotel near the airport and checked in.

After carrying his single bag up to the room he opened the door and threw his bag on the folding stand in the closet. Then he flopped down on the bed and flicked through the television channels. Taft felt unsettled but somehow the anonymity of the hotel—so similar to the thousands of others he had stayed in during his career gave him comfort. In less than an hour, he was sound asleep.

***

The President was drunk.

After earlier hanging up on Melton, he'd started drinking and stewing until he dialed him again.

"So you thought it might be a good idea to steal the most important religious documents of all time?" the President said.

"If they are real they could ruin us both," Melton said. "Without the religious right, you are just an old cokehead that washed out of everything you ever did."

"You always were a nasty son of a bitch. And a phony too, I might add. You believe in God Almighty for one thing—how much money you can make off your hypocritical ramblings."

"And you are so high and mighty?" Melton said. "You preach free markets and bail out your friends and contributors you preach goodwill and Christian values, then allow companies to pay slave wages and ship their workers jobs' overseas if they can save a bunch and make their earnings numbers so the executives stock options are worth more and they can sell out."

"What did you plan to do with the Parchments?"

"Prove they were fake," Melton said, "before that idiot in Venezuela has me and all my colleagues looking for a new gig. I happen to like my jet—and everything else this life affords me."

"Well, J. Thomas," the President said menacingly, "that is something I could not have let you done."

"Why not?"

"Because other friends of mine are involved," the President admitted, "and they have more to offer me than you."

There was a twinkling of ice in a crystal glass.

"Don't really matter," Melton said. "I had them all photographed and enough negatives to raise questions with any reporter. And it so happens I have one in mind."

"Don't do it."

"Remember when I said there was some, shall we say, unsavory items about you in the vault?"

The President was silent.

"It turned out the thief didn't touch those at all, old buddy," Melton said quietly. "So I'd quit threatening me, if you don't mind."

There was a pause.

"You know, I do still mind."

The line went dead again. Melton bent down and sniffed powder from a mirror. The President dialed another number on his telephone and had a brief conversation.

39

TAFT AWOKE COMPLETELY rested. He showered and checked out, then packed his bag and made his way down to the rental car. Once inside the car in the parking garage, he opened his secure telephone and dialed a number.

"This is John Taft," he said when the voice answered. "I wonder if I might pay a little visit in an hour or so."

The voice asked a couple of questions, then disconnected.

Taft drove to a nearby restaurant and ate a light breakfast with several cups of coffee. Steering out of the city, he drove into suburban Virginia down country roads littered with hidden cameras. Approaching the gate in front of a tree-lined driveway, he bent forward and peered out the windshield to make absolutely sure the camera had a clear picture of him. The gates slid open electronically and he drove up the drive and stopped the rental car in front of the house. The door opened and a man with a MAC-10 machine pistol on a strap peered out. Seeing Taft alone and nothing amiss, the man motioned him inside.

"I don't even want to know why you are here," the man said.

"Probably better you don't."

"He is in the sun room," the man said, "just finishing breakfast."

"Appreciate the favor," Taft said.

Taft wove his way through the old plantation house to the rear where the sun room sat off the kitchen. He walked through the door and stared at the man seated at a table.

"Remember me?"

"How could I forget," Albornez said, smiling. "By the way, I still smell like fish."

"Good cover, you must admit."

"I would have done the same."

Albornez motioned to a seat and Taft sat down. When the Venezuelan motioned to the pot of coffee, Taft nodded and was poured a cup.

"Just checking on your most recent extraction?"

"I have a couple of questions I need to ask you."

"Why not," Albornez said, "That is all I have been doing since my extrication."

Taft nodded.

"Is this about the recent events in my country?"

Taft nodded again.

"How can I help?"

"Point blank, I think someone kidnapped the real Cristos and substituted a fake. I believe someone is trying to steal the election in your country and if whoever this is continues with their current course of actions inciting religious hatred and furor, the world community will turn against Venezuela. I was wondering if you might be able to help me stop it."

"As you might have guessed, I am no great fan of the current administration in my country."

"True," Taft said. "But I think you'd agree that your countrymen deserve at least a fair election."

"That, my friend would be a first."

Taft was quiet. "At least, then, one not fixed by an American corporation."

"I guess I can agree with that," Albornez said.

"Then who could have kidnapped Cristos and made the switch?"

Albornez thought for a moment. He needed to get this right.

"As far as the switch I don't know," Albornez admitted. "That must have been planned and executed by this corporation you speak of. As far as the kidnapping, if it was not Venezuelan intelligence—and I would have been privy to it if it was—it was most likely a man named Dieter Marcos. He is the leader of the Caracas underworld. He's half-German and half Venezuelan, and a criminal genius."

"Do you know where I might find him?"

"I know every home, stash house, apartment, office or other building he used in Caracas. I was planning to put together an operation to take him down before I was stopped."

"Why were you stopped?"

Albornez was silent.

"A bribe, a favor, who knows," he said. "That is the problem with my country and one of the reasons I had had enough and sought to leave. Money is power and power is everything."

"Would you be interested in accompanying someone back to Caracas to show them these places?"

"There is not a chance in hell," Albornez said easily, "but I will write them down for you. Names, addresses, even nearby landmarks. If Cristos was kidnapped and a switch was made, chances are Marcos was behind it—and if he was, Cristos will be held at one of the locations I will list."

Taft nodded. "Let me go locate a pad of paper."

"I could use some more coffee as well."

***

Sheila Armstrong was an Australian national working for an American newspaper owned by an Australian media magnate known for far-right politics and loose editorial standards. His newspapers and television stations were equal parts sensationalism and lowbrow jingoistic dreck. Since it seemed the mentality of the average person had declined of late, it was easy to see why his empire had proved so successful.

Armstrong was a large woman—not fat, just large. Raised on a far outback sheep station, she stood almost six feet in height and weighed some one hundred and seventy-five pounds. She was not unattractive but was lacking in curves. Her more-than-ample chest was lost in her broad shoulders and the transition from waist to hips was a straight line. Raised on a diet of Australian attack journalism, her work lacked any form of subtlety. Armstrong sought scandal, not story, and scintillation, not substance. That was probably why she found herself at a Houston coffee shop at six in the morning across from Melton, who had obviously spent the night wired and awake.

"It doesn't work that way," Armstrong told Melton.

She had finished a plate of bacon, eggs home, fries and a fruit cup and was considering a slice of pie. Melton had ordered the same but had barely touched his plate. He kept pushing the food around but never taking a bite while keeping up an endless stream of banter.

"I'll give you the story of your life," Melton stressed again, "but you cannot use it unless I give you the okay later."

"Reporters are not insurance policies," Armstrong said.

"That's not…" Melton began to say but then he realized she and he knew both knew that was true.

Armstrong finished the food and chugged some coffee. They both waited as the waitress came over to refill her cup. Once she was out of earshot, Melton spoke again.

"What if…"

Armstrong was beginning to realize one of the United States' more recognized religious leaders was either scatterbrained or high. Or both.

"Someone gave me copies of the stolen documents that tie that candidate in Venezuela to Jesus."

He had just blurted it out. That was not the purpose of this meeting but he needed something to make the reporter start doing his bidding. He had photocopied the papers and hid them in the vault away from the boxed edition.

Armstrong took notice. This was starting to be interesting.

"Where are they?"

"That's not as important as the fact they are fake," Melton countered. "Jesus had no children."

"Can you prove that?"

Melton seemed high but what seemed to be trying to say was he would give Armstrong the Cristos story—all she had to do was not run another story unless he needed her to. Odd, she thought, but intriguing.

"Go over the deal again," she said.

"You hold off on a different story," Melton said. "My insurance story, so to speak. I let you examine the proof but you don't run anything unless I give you the go-ahead. If you do that, I'll give you the dirt on Cristos."

Armstrong thought for a moment. What story could possibly be bigger than Cristos?

"That's a deal," she said quickly.

"I'll need it in writing."

"You'll have it."

Armstrong could not for the life of her figure out what Melton could think was remotely as important as the Cristos story. One man's punch is another man's poison.

"Okay then," Melton said, pushing away his plates. "My driver will take us to my office and we will draw up the contract."

"Right after, you will show me the copies of the Cristos Parchments?"

"Right after," Melton agreed.

***

It would be naïve to think that corporations did not use assassins. As the large corporations have become de facto governments that operate across borders and regions and sometimes dealt with people of questionable morals and values, it became a necessity for them to have people they could call if trouble arose. Lately these assassins were even being used to avert future problems.

Trigby Tubbs had worked for more than one recognizable company. A poor boy from a working-class family in northern

England, he had learned at a young age his world was neither fair nor just. If you came from his station in life, you would need to take what you wanted from life by force or guile. To avoid a jail sentence for petty theft, he had enlisted in the British Army at age nineteen. Along with vivid lessons in brutality doled out by his training officers, Tubbs had learned how to take human life at close or long range. Sent numerous times into Ireland when the country was in strife, he had a half-dozen confirmed kills before he was twenty-one.

As soon as his enlistment period ended, Tubbs went freelance. For almost a decade the Arab world kept him busy. Mostly he was hired to eliminate radicals that might oppose their monarchies but occasionally he was hired by one prince or another who sought to have a competing relative killed, or a prostitute silenced after she threatened to talk. But then corporate power erupted and the gentleman's idea of business went the way of the typewriter in less than a decade. Once the first company sought to remove an impediment by force, it seemed they all jumped onto the bandwagon. Isn't the first rule of business that a company must grow to compete, and if your competitor has an advantage, you must either steal it or do a close copy? Steal a patent or kill a person—both had become rather common now.

Today, like most times, Tubbs was not even completely sure who had retained his services. He had been asked to trail a person and report exactly what they were doing. When Melton and Armstrong walked out of the restaurant, he snapped a photograph and sent it over his cell phone to another number. Then he followed Melton's chauffeured car at a safe distance.

***

About the same time Melton and Armstrong were leaving the restaurant, Albright received the copy of Taft's retirement papers that the White House had sent by messenger. He dialed Benson, who was in his office, and shared the news.

"Why don't we call the Golden Boy and his partner in," Benson said, "and let them know."

"We need to find Martinez a new partner," Albright said.

"Find a new agent. An up-and-comer."

"Then Martinez will be out in the field," Albright said. "Taft always kept him away from that."

"We can worry about that later," Benson said. "I was approved to offer Taft a consulting job for the next few years if he wants it."

"I got a feeling he'll turn you down cold, boss."

"Schedule a meeting and see."

"I'll do it."

Taft was halfway through his house closing when Albright's assistant sent word. The meeting was in two hours. If the title clerks didn't drag this out he would have a cashier's check for his house in hand before he was due at the NIA headquarters. He texted over his acknowledgement.

Martinez was driving into work when he received word. He sent back his confirmation as soon as he pulled into the NIA parking garage.

Albright resumed scanning the world events. Cristos's speech had caused rioting and uprisings in several spots on the globe. Venezuela had declared martial law as soon as the speech ended, so once the crowd was back in their homes there was less fallout than expected. Several dozen Muslim and Jewish homes were burned but there were no reported deaths.

In spite of the presidential order, the NIA was supporting the various Arab countries, which, along with Israel, were evacuating their people from inside the country. So far Venezuela was not impeding repatriation efforts. The NIA had a couple of agents in Venezuela watching and reporting, and the NSA and NRO had numerous satellites over the country watching. The Venezuelan presidential election was set for the day after tomorrow.

***

Tubbs read the message twice. Whoever his target was meeting, it was not a healthy meeting for either. Within minutes of him transmitting the photograph of the pair, someone had obviously identified the woman. Tubbs was ordered to keep both of them in sight.

Tubbs waited for further instructions as he followed Melton's vehicle. When the next message he received specified that all communication devices and handwritten notes needed to be seized, Tubbs quickly figured out she was a reporter. Tubbs had come across this scenario before. It had not turned out well for those involved. They turned into the parking lot of The Evangelical Church of Believers headquarters. Tubbs could see it would be impossible to follow them inside without being detected. It was still early and most of the lights in the building were off.

Tubbs drove to a nearby street with a view of the building and prayed for the best. He could see parts of two sides of the building, and those sides were the ones that looked away from the highway toward a park and nearby woods. Tubbs hoped that whatever office the two were going to was on the good side of the building. He waited patiently. Luck was on his side. A light, perhaps from a hallway, was turned on. Tubbs carefully pointed a parabolic microphone at the lit window and dialed the adjustment knob.

"Here?" he heard a female voice say.

"You cannot come in the vault, it is private. Wait here and I'll bring out the documents."

Tubbs heard a chair being moved and shuffling. A few minutes later he heard footsteps returning, then the sound of a packet of paper being slapped down on a desk.

"Here are the Cristos copies."

"So how do you know they are fake?"

"I don't know what you think of me," Melton said. "But at one time I was one of the foremost experts on the history of Jesus."

"And?"

"Only about me and three or four other scholars know this," Melton continued. "But the Romans changed the calendar within Jesus's lifetime. If you did not know this, these genealogical records would be perfect. Almost too perfect. However if you compare the ages they list, and the years they list as births and deaths, you will find them a couple of years off. You'll need to start at the present time and go backwards like I did. Then you'll realize the dates simply do not add up."

"And the archaeologist in Venezuela had no way of knowing this."

"As I said there are only five men in the world privy to this information and one of those men is over ninety years old and in poor health, so really it is four."

"And none of them are in Venezuela?"

"One is an Islamic scholar in Riyadh, Saudi Arabia, a specialist in ancient languages who helped unravel the words. One is a Dutch millionaire whose hobby is biblical archaeology and who financed my efforts years ago when I was a young student. Besides me, the last was at that time a graduate student and now a professor in England. I can assure you we all agreed to keep this quiet unless absolutely necessary."

"And you find Cristos an absolute necessity?"

"I think without speaking to the others this definitely qualifies."

Armstrong was impressed. It all added up.

"I will have what you say checked out. If it all jibes, we will run the story ASAP."

"Now here is the second part."

Tubbs heard a ruffling of papers.

"That's not?"

"It is," Melton said. "And they are many other indiscretions from arrests to drug involvement pictures inside. Now as we agreed you must sit on this unless I expressly ask you to run with it—or if I turn up dead."

The room was so silent Tubbs could feel it through the microphone.

"So you…"

For whatever reason the microphone began to act up. The sun was now firmly reflecting off the glass windows and more people were arriving at work and that might have been the reason. Sunspots, skips off the Ionosphere or other electronic signals in the area, might be others. Whatever the case, only snippets of the conversation could be gleaned.

"Only if…"

"….or something…"

From there on the speech was so garbled that no words could be discerned. Less than a minute passed and the room fell silent. Tubbs waited and watched. In a few moments the woman exited the building alone and climbed into the chauffeured vehicle. Tubbs made a split-second decision to follow her. The route led back to the restaurant.

The woman climbed out and headed for a small sports car. Tubbs kept back a safe distance but had her always in sight. He saw her place a cell phone to her ear.

"Meet me at the office in an hour," Armstrong told her assistant. "I've got something big."

"What is it?"

"I'll tell you when I get there," Armstrong said, "but I was called out to a meeting before I had a chance to shower. This will be a long day so I'm going to stop by my place and tidy up."

"What should I do before you get here?"

"Get me all the research on Vincente Cristos that is available."

"I'm on it."

Tubbs watched as she drove down a residential street. In front of a tidy duplex, she parked and went inside one of the units. Tubbs drove a couple of blocks away and parked. He then made his way through several backyards until he was at the rear of her house. Testing several windows until he found one slightly open, he wedged a plastic card inside and sprung the latch. The bushes in the backyard shielded him enough, and at this time of day most people would either be at work or on their way. Tubbs climbed inside.

Tiptoeing from what was obviously an office to the hall, Tubbs could hear the sound of water in the shower. Turning left, he made his way into the living room and entry. The packet of documents sat on a chair near the front door. Tubbs made his way back to the bathroom. Then, slowly, he opened the door and reached inside.

***

Taft had just enough time. He had already checked the car in and settled the bill, and now he stood outside with his single bag at his feet. Down the street he saw the cab approaching and he hoisted the bag.

"Where to?" the cabbie asked after Taft climbed in with his bag.

"Capco Mining." Taft rattled off the address.

"Good enough."

Taft quickly sent a text to the security office of the NIA that he would be approaching the front of the building in an ordinary cab. Then he sat back and enjoyed the ride. For some reason he felt free. Perhaps it was being relieved of the burden of homeownership. Perhaps it was that he was almost certain Benson and Albright were calling him in to inform him that his papers had come through. Whatever the case, he was in an upbeat mood in spite of Albornez's disclosure.

Pulling up in front of the NIA Headquarters, the cabbie said, "Capco Mining."

Taft got out. Moments later, near the front door, he looked at the hidden camera so he could be positively identified. The door opened. Taft walked in and made his way to the elevator and rode up.

At Mrs. Mindio's desk, he stopped and smiled down.

"Hello, John," she said sweetly, "You are a few minutes early and Larry is not here yet. Can I get you a coffee or something?"

Taft thought for a minute. Since becoming an agent, he must have drank a million cups of coffee.

"Do you have any tea?"

"What type?"

"I'll let you pick."

Mrs. Mindio headed off to the kitchen and returned a few minutes later with a cup with a bag dangling off the side.

"Darjeeling."

"I trust I'll like the tea better than I like the place."

"I remember that," she said, sliding back behind her desk. "We were all very worried for you."

Taft nodded. Words were not needed. They might make the memory more real.

"Whoa," Martinez said as he burst into the outer office. "You beat me to a meeting for the first time."

"First and last," Taft said, "if it works out right."

Martinez started to ask about the closing. Just then a voice on the intercom requested they go inside. Albright was already seated at a chair, and he motioned for them to sit.

"Congratulations, John," Benson said. "The President signed off this weekend then sent the papers over by messenger bright and early. He included a personal note."

Benson handed Taft the note. He quickly scanned it and slipped it in his pocket.

"It was a short thank-you," Taft said, glancing at Martinez.

"I thought it might be a gift card or something."

"At this point your pension can start if you want," Benson said. "Lord knows you have earned it. You can also wait for a higher payout. Human Resources will go over all that with you."

Taft smiled.

"Do you have any immediate plans?" Benson said. "Moving, travel, settling down anything."

"Nothing firm, sir."

"I'd like to discuss an idea."

Benson handed across the desk a form with the terms of the offer to be a consultant. Taft quickly looked it over and handed it back.

"Thanks to both of you," he said. "It's a generous offer. I think it might be better for me to just make a clean break. I know that upon retirement some of the agents feel they might miss something and want to keep their nose in it, but I think I'll be fine. I'd like to reserve the right to change my mind, however. Who knows how I'll feel in a couple months. For right now though, I just need some time away from all this."

Benson and Albright nodded. Then Albright reached out his hand and shook Taft's.

"You were the finest agent I worked with."

Benson rose and extended his hand and they shook.

"Ditto."

"Come on," Taft said, smiling, "You're going to hurt Larry's feelings."

"Trampled on is more like it," Martinez said.

"Before I go," Taft said, "there is something Larry and I discovered I'd like to share with you."

40

"ARE YOU BOYS even authorized to be here?" Sam Walker asked the agents.

Leland Hobbs was silent, but over time their wealth had made both men feel they were above mere laws.

"How about we ask the questions," the older agent said. He had been subjected to every form of intimidation from torture to threats of firing. Two obviously hung-over Texans did not bother him much.

"We could telephone the President," Hobbs said, now out of patience. "He's an old friend of ours."

The older agent forced a grim smile. "You could have an engine failure in one of your jets, too," he said quietly. "I'm just saying."

Only moments before Walker and Hobbs had felt they were masters of the world. Now even their friendship with the President didn't seem to deter these men.

"I'll ask you once more," the younger agent said. "Did you hire a firm named SPS out of Miami?"

Walker looked at Hobbs. "We need to speak to our lawyer."

"Now you're just pissing us off," the older agent said.

***

Taft's master-forger friend from the CIA was sitting in the director's office.

"How did you find out?" he said, his façade crumbling as fast as his future.

"There was a speck of meth you had snorted with blood on it," the assistant director noted. "Since every CIA employee has their DNA on file, it wasn't exactly difficult."

"I have money troubles," Lee said.

"Who doesn't?" the director said.

The assistant director was trying to figure out how much time Lee might receive. He brought his mind back to the present.

"So a company contacted you and asked for the fake parchments," he said. "Paid you in cash, then we sent you over to fake your own fakes?"

"That's about it."

"What was the company?"

"No name was given."

"How much cash of the payment do you have left?"

"A little over ten thousand in my safety deposit box."

The director reached for a telephone and dialed a number. Two minutes later two beefy security agents walked into the office.

"Take Lee here to his bank and retrieve the money from his safety deposit box and bring it back here," the director said, "If he tries anything like not cooperating or trying to escape, shoot him in the back."

The two agents nodded.

"Does your wife know?" the assistant director asked Lee.

"Nothing," Lee said. "Not about the drugs or the money or any of the other shit I've done."

"We'll cover the rest later," the director said. "Now go retrieve that money."

Two hours later the CIA had traced the serial numbers on the hundreds as going to a bank on North Bay Island, Florida. Now they knew for certain who had hired Lee.

"So," the director said, "we are sure that Hobker Petroleum hired SPS and SPS hired Lee."

"I guess we can be certain the parchments are fake now."

"I was certain Jesus had children," the assistant director joked.

"I didn't know if the revelation was real or not," the CIA director admitted.

"We also know that the two owners of SPS killed Burke Taylor," the assistant director noted.

"Plus the copies of the Cristos Parchments were stolen by a team hired by J. Thomas Melton, then stolen back by us. And the documents are fake as per Lee."

The two men were silent.

"It just so happens the President, who ordered us to discontinue our investigations, is friends with Walker and Hobbs as well as Melton."

"He sure picks shady friends," the assistant director noted.

The intercom buzzed and the director's assistant spoke. "General Benson from the NIA for you."

"Put him through."

Benson came on the line and the two men exchanged greetings.

"So what can I do for you?" the director asked.

"As you know, the President explicitly ordered my agency off the Venezuelan affair," Benson said.

The director was silent.

"But not yours, if I assume correctly," Benson continued.

"We have yet to be involved," the director said, "as far as the President knows."

"One of my agents is retiring…"

"John Taft," the director said. "We keep apprised on the presidential signings."

"Yes," Benson said. "He was involved in this business. This morning, before he received notice of his approval of retirement, he spoke to a former Venezuelan intelligence officer he was tasked with bringing to the U.S. recently."

"We weren't aware of that."

"Nice to know some things are still secret," Benson said. "It seems he and his partner studied footage of Cristos from a few months and weeks ago and then more recently and are convinced there has been a substitution."

"We will look into that," the director said.

"The Venezuelan intelligence officer suggested who might have the capability to pull off such a substitution."

"Who might that be?"

"Taft wants to meet you in person," Benson said, "and talk about that."

The director was silent for a moment. He stared over at the assistant director, who nodded.

"So agent Taft has his retirement papers so he no longer technically works for the NIA," the director noted, "and that would not be a violation of the President's orders."

There was a pause. "Can't see how it possibly could be," Benson said slowly.

"I'll welcome his call."

"Thanks for the courtesy," Benson said before disconnecting.

***

"You didn't stop by here?"

"You said you would be here in the office in less than an hour," the assistant noted. "Why would I bother to drive over there? By the time I went to your place and returned you would be here."

Armstrong had a towel wrapped around her ample body. Water was dripping down on the hardwood floors on her living room. When she first exited the shower she noticed her cell phone was gone. Certain she had taken it in the bathroom with her, she nonetheless searched the other rooms. As soon as she entered the living room she noticed the packet of information had disappeared as well.

"Somebody followed me and took the evidence."

The line was quiet for a moment. "Most likely whoever you spoke to had second thoughts," the assistant said logically. "Who else would have known you even had anything?"

The logic was brilliant. And it made Armstrong furious.

"I'm going to talk to this joker again," she said, "and I want you to meet me."

"Where?"

"Meet me at the headquarters for The Evangelical Church of Believers."

"I don't think we have time for a sermon."

"I'll be giving the sermon," Armstrong said.

***

"You need to put your foot down," Walker said. "We are only days away from pulling this off."

"There is only so much I can do right now."

"The largest oil reserves in the world, Johnny Boy," Walker said, "that's what we are looking at. Plus we basically own our own country. I guarantee we'll have a better job for you than the one you have now. No Congress, reporters or the religious right to kiss up to."

"I am the President. But there is only so much I can do."

The President was juggling Melton's threats against his deal with Hobker Petroleum. He wished he could just crawl in a hole and hide, but bad things haunt people at the least opportune times.

"You're the president," Walker said. "We got you that job because there is nothing you can't do."

"I was assured by their director that the CIA was not involved in this Venezuelan mess."

"Well," Walker said, "they sure as hell want to know about Miami and SPS."

"Maybe your hired hands screwed something up."

"We flew back to Houston but we are stopping there again on our way to Caracas. I'll find out."

"I need to get off the line," the President said. "I have some other issues."

"Make plans to come visit us in a couple of days. Show the world you support the new regime in Venezuela."

"I'll see what I can do," the President said, and disconnected.

Walker sat looking at the telephone. It was him and not the help who ended conversations first.

***

J. Thomas Melton was hungover and wanted to go home. He sneaked out the back door as his staff began to arrive and had his driver take him to his luxury condominium. Melton and his wife had a marriage of convenience and had not shared the same bed for years. His children, who neither hated nor liked him, but more accurately barely knew him, were either in college or graduated and the illusion he was happily married was easier to keep up now.

Before the children moved on, Melton had needed to be seen occasionally at the family home, a two-story suburban with an actual white picket fence and a rose garden. His wife was a perfectly trimmed-out Texas lady who would never leave the house without hair fixed and makeup carefully applied. She so thoroughly hated her husband that since the children were gone she had banned him from the house. When not at his condo, Melton spent most of his time in Cancun— where his debauchery could be kept quiet—and Vail, which big money had started and still ruled.

His driver dropped him off and he was making his way on his private elevator to the top floor where his unit was located. He wondered if it was worth calling a prostitute for a house call. Melton was hungover but sometimes that made for a fun time.

Tubbs had left Armstrong's duplex and returned to Melton's headquarters. He had sent several messages back and forth to his handlers as he sat watching the chauffeur, who was waiting with the engine running. When Melton emerged from the back door, Tubbs had followed the car at a discreet distance. Now he sat in the parking lot of the luxury condo awaiting instructions.

***

"He met with a reporter?" the President asked. "And he gave her information about me?"

"Don't worry. The people we hired managed to retrieve the documents."

"What was it?"

"There was a packet of papers detailing how the Gregorian calendar was wrong and biblical times needed to be corrected. Parts seemed to argue against a family tree of someone. Then there was information and pictures with you in them."

"Bad?"

"Not if you feel oral sex and snorting drugs can help your political career. There was some other stuff we should probably leave unsaid."

"I was young."

"We all were once."

The President was quiet.

"I'm sure these were not the only copies."

"I would tend to agree. They usually aren't in cases like this."

"Can you…."

"We will take care of it," the voice said.

The President sat in the Oval Office. A beam of sunlight came through a window and illuminated the now-silent telephone in his hand. This day was not turning out to be the best.

***

Taft's legs were vibrating. Benson had telephoned the Air Force and arranged a ride for him to Houston in a C-17 cargo plane. The plane had been configured as a troop transport and Taft had stretched out across a row of seats on his back for most of the ride. The vibration and drone of the engines had been like an electric massage chair. Once the C-17 had dropped him at Hobby Airport, Taft found his rental car sitting on the tarmac with the keys inside on the center console. He started the engine, turned on the air conditioner, and watched as white mist that looked like smoke poured from the vents.

As the rental car cooled, Taft looked over his maps and building plans. First stop was the headquarters for the Church of Evangelical Believers. Taft steered the rental car from the airport and down the interstate. A block from the headquarters, he climbed out and walked around to the trunk. Inside were several duffel bags with zippers. He opened the first and removed a uniform shirt from the local natural gas company that serviced the headquarters and a disposable white jumpsuit, and put them on. Next he removed a small weed sprayer, a respirator and an electric detection wand. Another zippered, tightly folded bag went inside the jumpsuit. The rest he walked toward the headquarters. He made it appear he was inspecting the lawn as he got close to the building.

Once at a side door, he waited until no one was nearby, then attached a device that read the card scanner and opened the door. The device automatically erased any sign the door was breached. Tossing the weed sprayer in the first trash receptacle he walked past, Taft placed the respirator over his mouth and climbed the emergency stairs. Once at the level with the vault, he took out the wand and flicked it on. In truth it measured nothing, but all the controls from light bar to beeps and warning siren were adjustable. Taft started to sweep it back and forth as he approached the receptionist. She looked up for her desk with alarm.

"Why are you still here?" Taft said, his voice muffled by the respirator. He unzipped the coverall and pointed to the patch on his shirt. "Gas leak. Just go down to your car for now—when you see me exit, it will be all clear. Don't take the elevator down—sparks and all."

The sight of a uniformed man breathing through a respirator was enough to get the receptionist to her feet. Taft followed her to the staircase and watched her descend, then returned to the room where the vault was located and used the device to open the outer door. Then he walked toward the massive steel vault door.

Taft attached a device to the door, then placed its earpiece in his ear. The sound was similar to being in a hollow room. He could hear the tumblers as he spun the dial. There was a definitive thump as he hit each correct number. He pushed up the lever and the door unlatched.

Inside, Taft found copies of Cristos Parchments and a file on the President. He removed these and placed them in the bag. Next he attached flash-explosive tape to the other file boxes. Using a small bag of explosive dust from his pocket, Taft spread the contents about the vault, then took the fake detection wand and set the timer for a half hour. He placed the timer on a trail of explosive powder, walked back out of the vault, and shut the door. The explosion and almost instant fire would flash-burn the remaining documents before the sprinklers in the vault began spraying. By the time the flood of water started, anything in the vault would be ashes—and whatever was left would be turned to mush.

Taft ripped off the disposable white coveralls and hid them in a trash chute on a lower floor. A moment later he crossed the parking lot. The receptionist climbed from her car, but Taft motioned her to stop.

"I'd go to a restaurant for the next hour and let that floor air out," he said. "I'm going to my vehicle to call in the readings."

The receptionist started to ask a question but Taft was already across the parking lot. Once back at the rental car, he called Martinez.

"Headquarters is done," he said. "I'm headed for station two— monitor fire and rescue there should be calls of a fire and the sprinkler deploying shortly."

"Got it," Martinez said.

Taft drove toward Melton's condo. He knew this part of the operation would be trickier. Parking to the side of the building, he removed the uniform shirt, knotted a tie on his dress shirt, and took a sport jacket from the bag. He packed and carried another bag toward the elevator and the doorman's desk.

The research department at the NIA had discovered one of the residents, a rich older lady whose family had made its fortune in copper mines, had frequent unattached male visitors that were understood loosely by the staff to be personal trainers. Taft approached the doorman's desk, smiled his best male-escort smile, and slid a fifty-dollar bill into the doorman's hand.

"Don't call up," he whispered. "The deal is I'm supposed to break in."

The doorman had heard kinkier so used his key to let Taft into the elevator.

"Have fun," he said as Taft walked into the elevator. Taft gave the man a half smile that signaled it was just work.

The fact that the copper heiress had secured the top floor had always galled Melton. As his following had grown so had his ego. Several times he had offered to buy the woman out. Each time he had been rebuffed. Taft rode up to the top floor. As the elevator stopped, he popped open the control box. After placing a small antenna on the controls, he dialed Martinez, who read the make and model of the elevator and the control box. Martinez sent a signal to the box that reprogrammed it to allow Taft to control it at will.

Taft pushed the button for Melton's floor below. The elevator opened directly next to Melton's condo. Taft slid the respirator over his mouth, then placed another unlocking device on the door and waited until the lock was sprung. Melton was back in the bedroom, sleeping through the sweaty dreams of the hungover. Taft placed an aural amplifier in his left ear so he could monitor Melton's sleep as he broke into Melton's safe. In a few minutes, Taft was riffling through the contents.

Taft secured the documents and left the apartment. He didn't know that the elevator had been called to a higher floor, however, and no lights had given him an indication. When the door slid open a woman of unknown age, dripping in jewels and holding a small poodle in her arms, stood there. She had been rebuilt by doctors numerous times over the years and there was nary a wrinkle to be seen. Her hair was Texas-big and piled in waves and layers atop her head, and her makeup looked like it had been applied by someone in Hollywood. She smiled a smile of pure lust.

"Hi, honey," she said like the serpent speaking to Adam.

"Ma'am," Taft said, walking inside.

"I haven't seen you around here before," the woman said as the doors closed.

"No, ma'am," Taft said.

He moved closer to her to show that he was far from intimidated.

"What do you have in the bag?"

Taft didn't answer. "We'd need to have a drink before I could tell you that."

They were almost to the ground floor before Taft noticed the control-panel door open and his antenna inside. He reached over, ripped off the antenna, stuffed it in his pocket and closed the control-panel door.

"So much shoddy workmanship nowadays," he said easily.

The doors slid open and Taft reached for the woman's arm.

"May I help you out?"

She smiled. "So gallant."

Taft started walking across the lobby floor. He turned to the doorman and shrugged as if to say that the plans had been changed. The doorman had learned to ignore such things. He nodded and returned to the game he was watching on a portable television.

Taft walked with the woman out the doors and to a nearby grass area, where she let the poodle down. Another man approached. He barely glanced at the two as he made his way under the awning and opened the doors to the lobby.

"Sugar," the woman said, "about that drink."

Taft smiled. In another time and another place it might have been different.

"I think I'll regret saying this, but that drink will need to wait for now."

Clutching the bag of documents, Taft made his way out of sight. In a few minutes he was in his rental car and headed back to the airport.

***

Trigby Tubbs tried a more direct approach than Taft. At the doorman's desk, he flashed a fake Houston detective's badge and ordered the doorman not to call upstairs. Using his own master elevator key, he rode up to Melton's condo and knocked on the door. When the still sleepy, hungover and now angry Melton opened the door, Tubbs roughly pushed him inside and stuffed the barrel of a gun in his mouth.

"How's that taste?" he said.

A tear began to form in the corner of Melton's eye. A few days ago he had seemed on top of the world. Now he was being bullied. Melton had a pretty good idea who had sent the man.

"What do you…." Melton tried saying with the barrel in his mouth.

"Open your safe."

Melton was confused. Maybe this was a garden-variety robbery.

"It's back there." Melton pointed down the hall.

Tubbs removed the pistol from his mouth and followed him down the hall. As Melton approached the safe, he could see the door was ajar.

"Did you…."

"Shut up."

Tubbs waved the gun. "I need everything you have pertaining to Venezuela or the President. Hold anything back, and I will return."

Now Melton knew for sure who had sent the intruder. He glanced inside the safe but everything pertaining to those two topics was already gone.

"Someone has…" Melton stuttered. "There is nothing here."

"Is everything at your office?" Tubbs asked.

Melton thought for just a second. He had a strong feeling the man was planning to kill him before this was all over. If he could drag out the time and string the man along, he might have a chance.

"Yes," Melton said.

Tubbs nodded. Then he reached in his pocket, withdrew a hypodermic needle, popped off the protective cap and jammed it into Melton's neck before he could react.

"Then I don't need you anymore, do I," Tubbs said quietly as he reached for Melton.

As soon as the massive dose entered his bloodstream, Melton went limp. Supporting him by the shoulders, Tubbs dragged him back to the bedroom. He placed drug paraphernalia around the bedroom before feeling for Melton's pulse. It was slow and weak—no wonder, considering the amount of heroin Tubbs had injected.

Melton's eyes tried to focus on Tubbs but to no avail. His mind was reliving all the bad things he had done. Then his breathing slowed and his heart stopped. Tubbs left the room and rode down the elevator.

"He wouldn't answer the door," he told the doorman.

The doorman had watched the light that tracked the floors the elevator stopped on. Melton was not one of the doorman's favorites. The evangelical leader who preached kindness to others had always treated him like dirt.

"Do you want to leave a card?"

"I'll try back later," Tubbs said as he walked out.

41

TWO DAYS BEFORE the election, the media was predicting a sure win for Vincente Cristos. In anticipation of the historic event, reporters from more than one hundred and fifty countries had descended on Caracas. Backstage at the soccer stadium, where Cristos was due to give his acceptance speech, a dozen special-effects masters were choreographing the entire affair with an emphasis on drama and pageantry.

The removal of the Muslim and Jewish Venezuelans from the major cities had led to a decrease in religion-motivated hate crimes. The country seemed to have calmed and it seemed that most Venezuelans were in a festive mood. Never before had the country been at the forefront of a movement with the eyes of the entire world upon it. There was a descendant of Jesus in the flesh and he was a native Venezuelan. It was almost too much for the average citizen to withstand. Sales of Venezuelan flags, t-shirts with a map of the country, or seemingly any other trinket that showed national identity went up a thousand fold. The national anthem *Gloria al Bravo Pueblo* or *Glory to the Brave People* was being aired on radio stations at least every hour. Scarves, bandanas and hats with the national colors were almost impossible to find.

Predictions indicated that more than seventy-five percent of Venezuelans would be watching the results and listening to Cristos' acceptance speech. It was estimated that worldwide observers might number a billion people. No event yet in ancient or modern times could rival the sheer size and impact of this event.

Mostly overlooked in all the hoopla was the effect on the average Christian. Early prognosticators had imagined the effect from the revelation to be everything from wide-scale hysteria to the end of modern civilization. Instead, it seemed that people had accepted the idea that Jesus may have been more man than previously thought. For decades, psychologists would debate this phenomenon, but for many it was a simple truth: the mechanics of the who and why of Jesus were never as important as the how. The lessons he had imparted, the message of peace, love and respect for fellow man, overshadowed all else. As these ideas, and not the startling idea of a less-than-miracle birth, started to be discussed more openly and frequently. The initial divisiveness between religions started down a path to moderation.

If only this newfound acceptance of other ideas would prosper.

***

Walker and Hobbs cared nothing about actions starting a possible age of religious enlightenment. They cared nothing of the millions of soul-searching people, or the thousands affected by the violence that had been wrought on people of non-Christian religions. They were bored and barely recognized the esoteric results of their scam—they were, and had always been, motivated solely by money and power.

It was in this state of mind that the two returned to Florida. Their plan was for them to party until the evening prior to the election, fly their private jet to Caracas, and take up temporary residency. From there, they would direct the future of the country they felt they had rightly bought and paid for.

"Place those over there," the party planner said, pointing.

This party and the one that would follow, a rolling wave of debauchery and excess, were unusual for Walker and Hobbs. In all their years of business, through thousands of successful deals, never once had the two men celebrated success prior to the actual outcome. The usurping of an entire country was their largest and ultimately greatest accomplishment, so for this they broke their rule.

"I think we can put the horse before the cart," Walker had said.

He explained to Hobbs he had hired a hip South beach party planner to coordinate their Miami stay. The planner had seen excess before. Newly rich eastern Europeans with more funding that style. Drug lords, potentates of African nations and Arab sheikhs away from their many wives. The Texas oilmen seemed determined to outdo them all.

The planner had rented a water front house on a small island off South Beach. Party guests would be ferried back and forth to the island by replica Venetian gondolas. At the shore landing were a line of limousines to carry home intoxicated guests.

A baker's dozen of B-list celebrities had been paid, either through lavish gifts or promises of future support, to attend. The attendees would include few fading rock stars, a pop sensation who owed more to the fact her act was more a pedophiliac dream than a display of musicianship, and several television actors with canceled series and doubts about how they would make their mortgage payments. Local celebrities also abounded. There was the host of a local cooking show, two straight-from-the-swamp reality stars from a show filmed in the nearby Everglades, and a local golf pro with an instruction segment on the local news. Most everyone, from the guests to the planners to the waiters, knew the hosts were friends of the President, and that also brought out a few politicians seeking fun and favors.

"What do you figure this will cost?" Hobbs, the more logical and reined in part of the duo, asked after climbing into a limousine next to the jet.

"A couple of million," Walker said, popping open a beer from a refrigerator between the seats.

Hobbs nodded. That was not too bad.

"We can repay ourselves early next week when we have access to the Venezuelan treasury."

"I'm curious, how big is the army and navy?" Hobbs said. "I've always had an affinity for the armed forces, as you know."

Like most right-wing capitalists who were hawks, neither Walker nor Hobbs nor anyone in their family from the time their ancestors had first immigrated to this country had actually served in the military. They could rattle sabers when the time came, but that was easy when no one you actually knew might die. They were chicken hawks who thought war was fought on a movie screen.

"Maybe we can make you a general," Walker said.

"Or an admiral."

"An admiral." Walker finished the rest of the beer in one long pull, tossed the bottle into a waste can, and reached for another.

"Did you order a large goodie bag?" Hobbs asked.

"Should be inside the trunk. Yayo, some really fine weed, mushrooms, Ecstasy…"

"I don't think I ever tried that," Hobbs said.

"We used to call it MDMA."

"Put that way, I have had some."

"I don't know what all else," Walker said. "I told our trusted dealer to send down a box filled to the brim. As far as liquid refreshments, the order to the liquor store was five figures. I even had some absinthe flow in from New Orleans. The planner has a rum distillery being installed. An attendant will make rum at the party and send the guests home with mini-casks for further aging."

Hobbs smiled. "We sure have moved up since the days of warming cans of spaghetti and meatballs on the engine of the first rig."

"That we have."

Walker rarely looked back but if he had, he would have realized much of their success was based on the fact they had made friends with the right people. They had been working men for only a short time. Both men had quickly realized how the game worked: favors and payoffs.

The elite talked deregulation but were involved in the most closely ruled industries in the world. They spoke of low taxes and less governmental interference but the public subsidized their industry with numerous wars, protection of shipping lanes, and the not-infrequent overthrow of foreign dictators. That Hobker Petroleum was planning to swing the election in Venezuela was nothing new. It had already been done in Iraq after World War II, and Iran not long after. Any leader of an oil-rich country that did not go along with the rules was removed either with force or fraud. The same held true with other industries as well. Competition was an often-bantered-about concept of capitalism but in truth it was rarely practiced.

The limousine arrived at the boat landing, and Walker and Hobbs were ferried across the water. They watched a half-dozen workmen stringing lights over dozens of tables on the outside deck overlooking the water. In the kitchen, a chef was supervising a crew of eight preparing food and snacks for the next two days.

By nine that evening the party was underway. At first it was much like any other rich person's event. Fine food and drink; much talk of recent trips and faraway locales. By midnight, most of the politicians and happily married folks had left, and the denizens of the night began to emerge. At three in the morning, the first guest vomited into a shrub on the grounds and shortly thereafter dwarves with mirrors strapped to their head and bowls of cocaine began to circulate. With the wave of a hand, the little person would walk over and the guest would have a portable mirror for snorting at just the right height. It was so very convenient.

By four, people—men and women, men and men, women and women—began to pair off and create other combinations. The master bedroom upstairs began to take on the look of a movie set for an adult film. Clothes were strewn about, and moans and grunts were growing louder.

Walker was looking off the deck at the water and debating how low taxes spurred economic development with a professor from a West Coast liberal arts college.

"Trickle-down is shit," the professor said, "more like piss-down."

"We had boom times back then," Walker said.

He reached down and adjusted his belt.

"The energy policies of the prior President had resulted in historically low energy costs," the professor noted. "Whenever that happens, the economy does well."

Walker started to argue but his eyes rolled back in his head and he grunted.

"Thanks," he said as a tall Amazon rose from her knees.

"Glad to do it," a surprisingly low voice said.

"Yeah," the professor screamed.

A few seconds later he zipped up his pants and resumed the conversation.

Hobbs was being more of a gentleman. In a bedroom, he was allowing a slim black woman with gigantic breast implants sit atop him. She was muttering things about Hobbs being a slave master and forcing himself on her, but she had led him by the hand into the bedroom.

At just that minute downstairs, a hip-hop singer with an entourage of a dozen arrived at the boat landing. There were a series of gunshots like the rapid popping of popcorn. Walker adjusted himself and wandered down to see what was happening.

"I swear," one of the entourage said. "It was an alligator."

Walker walked over.

"I'm Sam Walker. This is my party."

"Tiny Jimmy," the seven-foot-tall singer said.

"What's going on?" Walker asked.

"One of my people thought they saw an alligator and took a shot."

"Where?" Walker said to the man still holding the handgun.

The man pointed and Walker thought he could catch a glimpse of the reflection off the creature's eyes. He looked at the man holding the gun.

"Give me that."

The men hesitated, but when Tiny nodded, he handed the gun over.

Walker waited for the reflection again, then emptied the gun at the spot on the water. There was thrashing as the alligator was struck, then a slow rolling over on its belly, which glinted white in the dim light.

"All right," Walker said, "let's go party."

***

Taft was glancing down at the country out the co-pilot's window of a CIA light jet.

"Good thing we were passing through," said the pilot, a woman of thirty. "This sure beats the hell out of commercial."

Taft nodded. The woman was obviously still enthralled with her job and the world of intelligence. "How long have you been with the CIA?"

"I got my political science degree three years ago and joined then the company sent me to flight school for a year."

Taft smiled and looked back out the window.

"You ever fly?" she asked.

"Army, helicopters."

"Who do you work for?"

"NIA."

"The Secret Spooks," she said, trying to show her knowledge of the game. "Who is that super agent they have over there?"

Taft had climbed into the plane as it touched down on a cross-continent flight. Once he boarded, the pilot had rolled back onto the runway before they'd had a chance to make introductions. He'd sat in the rear for a time before asking if he could join her in the cockpit.

"What you heard was probably just rumors," Taft said quietly.

The woman glanced across the cockpit. Almost every career has groupies. Spies were not any different. The NIA was at the top of the food chain.

"No kidding, NIA," she blurted out. "I can't wait to tell my co-workers I flew you around."

Taft looked back out the window. He was thinking about taking a road trip around the country. Maybe he would rent a car. Or drive one of his motorcycles.

"Rumor is one of your agents killed a Chinese spy with a blow dart," she said, "then drove a stolen car to the border with Viet Nam and made his way to safety."

Taft smiled. His life had become a pulp action-adventure novel. The problem was it wasn't true.

"Sounds like someone just made that one up."

The pilot had a square face but was not unattractive. She looked like a woman who had grown up in the Midwest with a lot of brothers. She paused, unwilling to let the conversation die.

"I wonder," she said. "Since you look like you've been around awhile, could you give me the number-one thing I should be aware of as I go through my career?"

Taft thought for a few moments.

"Things are never what they seem," he said, "except when they are."

Knowing that she was probably going to continue talking, Taft stretched his arms and smiled.

"It was good talking to you. I'm going to head in back again." He squeezed his way out of the seat. "And try and grab a few minutes of shut-eye."

"I know how that is," the pilot said.

The problem was that she didn't.

***

The director of the CIA sat in front of General Benson's desk. Taft had transmitted copies of the files taken from Melton back to the NIA. Inside his briefcase, he carried the originals sealed in plastic so that the NIA forensic team could see who had handled them.

"Not good," Benson noted as both men finished reading.

"I've got no desire to besmirch a well-respected religious leader," the CIA director said. "But Melton is drawing way outside the boxes here. He's having teams of mercenaries steal religious documents and he is trying to blackmail the President?"

"The President didn't wear white to his wedding, did he?"

"Melton has him tied into Hobker," the Director said. "That for sure links him to SPS and the Venezuelan thing if not directly, only once removed."

Both men were silent. They had no desire to interject their agencies into politics. But that seemed to be happening more and more as the years passed.

"You said your agents are convinced that the Cristos running for office is a fake," the Director said quietly.

"And you think our next move should be to try and see if he the genuine Cristos is still alive."

"Exactly."

"Who do you want to send?" Benson asked.

"Your retired agent seems to be able to do the impossible."

***

Special Agent John Taft was trying to relax when the alarm on his briefcase sent a buzz to his watch. He flipped open the case and raised an antenna, then tuned the screen with a dial.

An image of General Benson in his office along with another man appeared on the screen.

"John," Benson said, "this is the Director of the CIA."

"Good afternoon," Taft said.

"We'd like to speak to you about something," Benson said.

"I'm retired," Taft said. "I told you that when you asked me to come down to Houston."

"The papers you uncovered are explosive," Benson said.

"It's obvious that a private company is trying to overthrow Venezuela," the Director noted.

"I'm sure that has happened before."

"John," Benson said quietly. "You haven't read what we have. We have a bad player in the Oval Office. This entire affair had created religious strife that the world at large can ill afford right now."

"Maybe it's true," Taft said. "Jesus was more man than was thought. So what? If we intervene we may be covering up a long hidden truth. Then what?"

Both men on the other end were silent.

"We want you to go to Venezuela and find out of the real Cristos is still alive," Benson said ending the debate.

Taft could say no. He was no longer an active agent. The time was now. But after years of following orders, he had a hard time saying no. "How soon?"

"There is twenty-four hours to find him if he is alive, release him, and get him in front of the media so he can tell his story," Benson said. "Then the voters of Venezuela can decide who they wish to believe."

Taft said, "Wasn't the NIA and the CIA ordered off this case by the President?"

Taft stared at the screen. The two men's faces were blank.

"That's why it has to be you, John," Benson said finally.

Taft shook his head back and forth as he decided.

"Divert the plane to Miami," he said, "and arrange for another pilot to join us for backup. Then get on the horn and find a bank that will open."

"What for?"

"I'm going to need twelve million in cash," Taft said. "A half million an hour ought to get me the information I need. If it can be done, I'll find a live Cristos or a dead body we can display."

"Big bribes?" the CIA Director said.

"In an economy fueled by oil," Taft said, "grease always works."

***

After Taft finished the arrangements, Benson looked over at the CIA director.

"You got men that can handle SPS and the oil men?"

"It would be an honor."

"My agency will take care of Melton," Benson said.

The buzzer on his telephone sounded.

"General, Mr. Albright needs to see you right away."

"Send him in."

The CIA director rose to leave but Benson motioned him to sit back down.

"Is this pertaining to the Venezuelan affair?" Benson said after Albright walked in and was seated.

"Yes."

"Go ahead," Benson said.

"We just received a news reports that J. Thomas Melton was found dead a few minutes ago by one of his assistants that had been sent to his apartment to awake him for his evening telecast. I know you just sent Taft down to visit him."

Benson buzzed Taft again.

"What else, sir?" Taft said when the screen came on.

"Melton was just reported dead," Benson said without preamble.

"He was sleeping when I was there."

"You sure?"

"I didn't climb in and snuggle with him, boss," Taft said. "But the breathing over the mini-microphone coming from the bedroom was reasonably regular."

"Was anyone else there?"

"Not that I'm aware of."

"Thanks," Benson said. "I'll send down a team of agent to see what we can find out."

"Twelve million," Taft said as he turned off the screen.

42

THERE COMES A TIME when the cheating spouse, the gambling addict, the drug addict or alcoholic knows that they might finally be held accountable. It is a time when they feel remorse for their numerous wrong decisions. Some have the flop sweats, liquid rolling from their forehead or chest, as if the sweat can wash away the lies. Some develop tics and twitches, shaking hands or quaking muscles. Some become angry and some become sad. And some feel nothing.

"Your operative retrieved everything the reporter was given?"

"Yes."

"And copies," the President said, "There were…"

"Mr. President," his receptionist said over the intercom.

"I left instructions not to be disturbed."

"Sir, J. Thomas Melton is dead," the receptionist blurted. "It just came over the wire services."

"Thank you," the President said quickly.

This was hardly the reaction the receptionist was expecting. She put the reaction down to grief. Melton and the President were known to be close friends.

"Melton is reported dead," the President said to the other party. "Now as I was asking. What about other copies in his home or office safe."

"The operative reports there were none."

The President knew Melton and this was almost impossible. The man put on rubber gloves to wash fruit. Chancing having only one copy of anything was out of Melton's character. Still, because of the nature of the documents and his involvement, there was a slim possibility this was true.

"Your man is sure?"

"Double-checked."

"And his computers?"

"Wiped and washed so clean the NSA couldn't find anything."

There was silence for a moment.

"I'm worried about the reporter," the President said finally.

"We checked. She did not have time to transmit anything," the voice said. "She met Melton, received the documents, went home to shower before going to the office, and that is when our man snatched them—while she was in the shower."

"She still has an inkling of the contents," the President said. "At least on a tertiary level."

The line was silent again.

"We will take care of it, sir," the voice said.

Far down in the basement of the NIA, an older retired agent listened to the conversation and texted Benson. Then he settled back in to continue to listen to the microscopic bug that Benson had pressed into the wood under the desk.

***

Sheila Armstrong had a story without proof. A tale without substance. An unsubstantiated, uncorroborated un-article. She was sitting there trying to figure some angle when the news came on the television in the office that Melton had been found dead. In that instant, she felt a fear that cut through her spine like a knife through fish guts. She rose and raced for the bathroom. She vomited, then ripped her pants down as her bowels let loose.

Her assistant cracked the door to the ladies' room and shouted inside.

"You need anything?"

"Air freshener and breath mints," Armstrong said tiredly. "Close the door. I'll be out shortly."

The assistant waited in the hallway until Armstrong emerged. An odor of fear still enveloped her. "Where is your family again?" she asked. She was banging him on the side but couldn't remember much of his history.

"Cedar Rapids, Iowa."

"Like the movie." Armstrong walked toward her desk.

They sat.

"I don't think Melton dying is a coincidence," Armstrong whispered. "I recommend you take a prolonged trip to visit your family."

"Wouldn't that be obvious?" the assistant said. "I mean that would be like taking an ad out—my boss told me everything."

Armstrong had watched too many movies. And movies are not reality.

"Maybe you're right," she said quietly. "But I'm going on the run."

"Are you going to tell the editor?"

"No," Armstrong noted, "I'll take emergency leave—dead family in Australia or some such nonsense. There is no reason to reveal any of what happened to anyone else."

"When are you leaving?"

"Right now."

Armstrong rose from the desk. She was not one to coddle a decision.

"Keep me posted," the assistant said.

Quickly driving back to her duplex, Armstrong did not watch to see if she was being followed. That was a mistake. The person who was trailing her figured he had plenty of time to make his move. He sat down the street studying the duplex through binoculars and listened to her enter with a parabolic microphone.

Armstrong flung a suitcase on her bed and hastily packed. When it was stuffed, she sat on the suitcase until she could fasten the zipper.

Farther down the block, another car pulled to a stop. The man inside removed a set of binoculars and began scanning. This man did not concentrate on Armstrong's duplex. Armstrong walked out of the duplex, opened the hatch on her sports car, and jammed the suitcase inside. It barely fit inside. The suitcase reduced her rear-window visibility. Scrolling through the songs on her potable music device, Armstrong selected a rock-and-blues band and turned up the volume. Then she backed out of her spot and drove forward, still unsure of where she was going.

As soon as Armstrong was at the end of the street, the first car pulled out and followed her at a discreet distance. The driver had not had a chance to make a plan, so killing Armstrong would be a matter of opportunity. Those thoughts weighed on his mind enough that he never bothered to check if he was being followed himself.

The driver of the second car was trained to avoid detection.

Driving through dense Houston traffic, Armstrong navigated the looped freeways, then headed north. She drove for a few hours, then stopped at a gas station off the highway, filled the fuel tank, and bought a cup of coffee. He mind was occupied by fear and she noticed no one following her. The road finally left the city and entered a rural area. Armstrong continued driving.

After another hour, the coffee sat heavy on Armstrong. She noticed a sign for a rest area and pulled off the highway. The killer, who had been concentrating on the reporter and awaiting his opportunity, accelerated and also exited. So did the third car, which until now had remained well back, out of sight. The driver saw the killer leave his car and walk quickly toward the women's side of the restroom.

Stealth is good when needed, but being bold and direct is often better. As the killer slipped under the awning leading to the door, the man in the third car simply accelerated, jumped the curb and drove over the grass toward the restroom door. He slammed the car into park while it was still moving, then ran toward the door and drew a handgun from a shoulder holster.

The killer had made two mistakes. The first was that he liked to kill and relished the chase. Because of that personal flaw, he had only concentrated on the intended victim and never considered that he might not be alone. The second was he felt the killing was a game and instead of just marching in and pulling the trigger, he wanted to slowly stalk Armstrong. He liked to see the fear in his victim's face. The killer was just outside the wall of the stall when the second man burst into the restroom.

A professional never hesitates. There was no reason to shout warnings or draw out the battle. He had heard the recording with the President and knew Armstrong was targeted to die. The man in front of him was not there to have a conversation. As soon as he entered the restroom and saw the killer turn toward him, he fired three quick shots from his silenced weapon. Head, neck and heart. At such close distance, the trio of shots could have been the basis for a training film.

The brain shot made the killer incapable of further of further movement and he dropped onto his knees and fell forward in slow motion. Armstrong, who had heard the commotion, sat on the toilet frozen in fear. A second later the tip from a polished shoe was seen under the door.

"I'm Franklin," a deep voice said. "I'm with the CIA. If you want to live come with me."

Armstrong finished and pulled up her skirt. She slowly opened the door and peered outside. A black man stood off to the side, weapon still in his hand. A spreading pool of blood was flowing from the head and body of a man face down on the concrete floor. The black man motioned for her to come closer as he pushed a number on his phone.

"The current location of my vehicle is a rest area." Franklin knew they had a satellite link to his location already. "The threat was neutralized. Notify the locals to secure the area and have a wet team remove the body. I doubt there will be any identification—he looked like a pro. I'm securing the protected party now and I'm going to have her follow me away from this scene. Once her vehicle is secure I'll remove her to a safe spot."

He ended the call and turned to Armstrong.

"Follow me in your car," he said. "The local police will check tapes and note your car as being here in their report. Shortly after that the people that want you dead will access the report, see that your body was not found at this scene, and know you may have survived. By stashing your car, it will buy us a little more time before they are sure you are still alive."

He motioned with his weapon toward the door.

Armstrong, tears running down her cheeks, led the way out.

***

John Taft supervised the loading of the CIA jet. He had called Martinez with a list of food and supplies he'd need. With Martinez's usual efficiency, everything was boxed and ready to go. The cash, in plastic-wrapped bundles, was between seats in the jet's center row. He then unrolled a sleeping pad out of the supply pile and threw a blanket and pillow over the top. Taft planned to catch up on his sleep atop the pile of money. Taft and the female pilot were waiting for a co-pilot to arrive when a pizza delivery van drove onto the tarmac near the plane.

Taft climbed out, walked over to the van, and took the boxes. Handing the driver a hundred-dollar bill and waving off the change, he carried them back to the plane and climbed inside. The pilot had already supervised the fueling, done another pre-flight, and was inside the cockpit with the door open.

"Pizza?" Taft asked.

"Sure."

"Come back here," Taft said. "The forward table is still open."

Taft piled the pizzas on the table. As the pilot sat, he walked back through the plane climbing over the stacks of cash to the very rear. Grabbing glasses and some ice from the galley along with cans of soda and napkins, he climbed back over the cash and slid behind the table.

"You don't look like a diet kind of gal," he said.

"Stuff tastes like chemicals. Sugar is much better."

"Let's dig in," Taft said.

After chewing a few bites, she said, "This is good."

"Found this place years ago," Taft said. "It seems like I have go to restaurants all over the world now. It always bums me out when a favorite closes."

"Do you ever become sick of life on the road?"

"It seems I've always been moving," Taft said. "I went from my parents' house to a college dorm to the Army and into this. It's been years since I had any kind of stable home to come back to."

"That's tough. What did you miss the most?"

Taft thought for a moment.

"I would have liked to have a dog," he said with a touch of regret in his voice. "I always had one as a kid but with my lifestyle I knew it would not have been fair to have one as an adult."

"That's sad."

"I'm still pretty young," Taft said with a chuckle.

They were quiet as they ate.

"Do you know how to get us into Venezuela?" Taft asked, "The CIA is not exactly welcome there."

"There is a remote airfield a hundred or so miles from Caracas nearer the coast. I'm going to need to come in low over the water, then perform a quick landing. They told me they arranged to have a truck meet you there. As soon as you deplane, I'm going to turn around, take off, hightail it to Central America. There I'll wait for further instructions."

"Like coming back for my body?" Taft said. "If this plan fails."

It was par for the course. Taft would need to figure out how to do the impossible.

"I hope the help they arranged down there is good," Taft said finishing the meal and closing the box.

"I wouldn't know," the pilot said. "I just fly the plane."

"How long until your co-pilot arrives?"

"They said one to two hours," the pilot said. "That will put us at the airfield in Venezuela just before daylight."

The jet was plugged into shore power and the climate control systems were keeping the plane cool and comfortable.

"I should probably try to nap then," Taft said. "That's lesson two—always grab sleep when you can."

The pilot walked over to the exit door and peered out. The refueling and provisioning was completed and they would not be disturbed until the backup pilot arrived. She reached up, pulled down the clamshell doors and secured them closed.

"Relax," she said. "I'll do guard duty."

***

The President was drinking. The story of his God-given abstinence had been a lie to get him elected. He was a bought-and-paid-for shill from the time of his first election to the governorship. He worked for those that pulled the strings, but he was never truly sure who that was. He was the mouthpiece for their drivel, the spokesman for their aims.

In return, he lived a life of luxury and opulence and was looking forward to even greater wealth when he left the Presidency and no longer had to report his income. The President had never really had any morals to speak of—witness to that was that even a man of limited intelligence would have figured out over the years he was throwing the average American into the chains of poverty with the policies he promoted. But he never gave that much of a thought. He had his and wanted more. If others in the country suffered for his gains, so be it.

Still, by directly ordering the killings of the reporter, even he knew he had crossed a line. He had ordered troops into needless conflicts to enrich his corporate friends but that never bothered him—they had been poor enough and stupid enough to sign up for such duty. Melton's death barely bothered him. That was quid pro quo. The man had tried to blackmail him and that had backfired. So goes the world. But the reporter was an innocent. And that needed some alcohol to forget.

***

Tears were streaming down Sheila Armstrong's face as she drove from the rest area. Like most Australians, she was skeptical of government and doubting of institutions of most types. This may have stemmed from the settlement of her county by criminals, outlaws, rogues and adventurers. This national doubt was woven into the fabric of the country and had allowed her country to avoid the outright takeover of politics by corporations such as had happened in the United States.

Armstrong, like many in the world, had viewed the United States through rose-colored glasses. America had always seemed somehow better than everywhere else—a place where anyone could rise to the top, a country where right and wrong and fairness reigned. She knew now that was all a polished lie. But the realization that the United States was rotting away was not why she was crying. Armstrong was crying because as soon as she accepted that fact, she had accepted the fact that she was probably dead.

If the country was completely corrupt, then the black man who appeared to have saved her was most likely not looking out for her best interests. He wanted something. Either information or silence. Once that was achieved he would take his leave. Armstrong knew her only chance was to make it back to Australia, to Oz. As soon as she got home, she could figure out her next move.

In the movies, electronics always work, files can be downloaded in seconds and no one is ever out of reach. The reality for a field agent is usually different. Franklin attempted to report back to the CIA after calling for the cleanup crew, but his phone was malfunctioning. He had a backup phone in his bag in the trunk, however. He flashed his lights at Armstrong so she would pull over.

Armstrong looked in the rearview mirror to see the lights flashing, but she was not sure of the meaning. The two vehicles were in an area of wooded hills and numerous small towns. A sign indicated an exit two miles ahead, but the exit was not visible as the road wound through the trees and brush. In the rearview mirror, she saw the CIA agent waving his hand as if she should pull off on the shoulder. Armstrong slowed and pulled over.

Franklin pulled in behind her and shut off the engine. He thought about explaining his problem to Armstrong but decided he would grab the phone first and then tell the reporter the plan. He raised one finger to indicate he'd be right back, then walked back to the trunk and inserted the key.

Armstrong, running on pure adrenaline by this point, watched in the rearview mirror. Something felt wrong. He was stalling her. She was sure he was going for a weapon. Armstrong decided he was planning to end it right here on the road away from the rest area. So she placed her car in gear and rapidly accelerated. The sound of her driving away was buried in the noise from the passing semi-trucks and other traffic.

Franklin located the bag with the backup telephone and dug deeper for batteries. He turned on the phone. No bars.

Meanwhile, Sheila Armstrong raced toward the nearest exit then got off and drove under the overpass before stopping. She got out of the car, ran up the steep-sloped concrete footings for the bridge, and found a spot to hide and watch oncoming traffic.

Franklin decided to tell the reporter to stop at a convenience store. There, he'd flash his badge and borrow a land line. He reached up and closed the trunk—and noticed the reporter's car was gone.

If he had been a man prone to profanity he would have cussed. Instead, Franklin jumped in his sedan and raced up the interstate. His eyes were directly ahead searching for the sports car and he raced past the exit without a thought. Armstrong watched as he passed. Then she descended the steep slope and pulled her car back onto the interstate in the opposite direction. A few miles back, she had noticed a secondary highway leading back toward Houston. She exited the interstate onto the highway and raced south toward the airport.

Meanwhile, Franklin drove at a high rate of speed north. There was no sign of the reporter. Ten minutes later, a highway patrolman flashed his lights at the speeding agent. Franklin pulled to the side and climbed out, figuring he could use the patrolman's telephone. The problem was this: for the Texas highway patrolman, a large black man approaching his cruiser was not a good sign. Texas is part of the South and old prejudices sometimes die hard. The highway patrolman shouted over the intercom for Franklin to get back in his car. The black man reached inside his coat, removed something and waved it around. The highway patrolman called for backup, and another patrolman a few miles away raced south, then turned on the cross-over and pulled in behind Franklin.

Franklin yelled that he was CIA and flashed his badge. But the two patrolmen had heard a million stories before. They followed their procedures and carefully subdued the suspect. By the time they had the angry agent in handcuffs and called in his badge for verification, almost twenty minutes had passed.

"You men need to escort me to the nearest telephone," Franklin said.

"We have radios."

"This is past the point where I feel comfortable broadcasting this over open airwaves."

The patrolmen led them to a store a few minutes away. Franklin called to report what had happened. With all that was happening, the reporter was not the highest priority. By the time it was reported to a supervisor that could make a decision, it was too late. Shelia Armstrong had stashed her car at the airport and bought a ticket on the first international flight available. The ticket was not direct to Australia but it was out of the United States. As an Australian citizen, the CIA could not flag her passport. Armstrong traveled across the globe over the next day and a half with no one following. By the time she reached Sydney and safety, she was a changed woman.

43

THE CARRIBBEAN IS beautiful. It is even more so near Venezuela. Taft had awakened atop his bed of money as the plane neared Aruba. In the galley, he brewed a pot of coffee and drank a cup. Then he went the cockpit and asked the pilots for their orders.

"Two, both black," the pilot said.

"How long until touchdown?" Taft asked.

The co-pilot, who was acting as navigator, replied, "A half hour, forty minutes."

The jet had dropped down and was only a hundred feet above the crystal-clear water. Taft peered out the window as he walked back to retrieve the coffee and saw a pod of porpoise breaching. The arching motions as they raised their blowholes to exhale was a smooth symphony of grace and beauty. Taft decided as soon as he was finished with this job, he'd take a beach vacation for a few weeks. Just relax and suntan for a change.

The truck waiting at the airstrip was registered to the Venezuelan army and bore markings but it had never been assigned to a motor pool. The CIA had simply paid off the appropriate clerks to reassign it to a nonexistent unit and then make it disappear. Every two years they rotated this and a few dozen other vehicles throughout the country in and out of inventory so they always had clean trucks should the need arise. Agents did this same maneuver with vehicles, boats and aircraft in nearly one hundred other countries across the globe.

This particular truck was a newer four-door medium-duty with a canvas covering over the rear cargo area. The man in charge of the operation on the ground was a mid-forties Venezuelan named Gustavo

Valencia, who had been CIA-trained and on the payroll for nearly two decades. His brother had been an officer in the army and had been killed when he refused to go along with the coup that had raised the former President to power. Because of that, Valencia hated anything to do with the current or former regime.

Valencia had carefully selected eight of his specially groomed men. All of them hated the government, and each was highly trained and would die if needed. By using its power and contacts, the CIA had spent decades amassing money and power in almost every country on the globe. The men knew that if they were killed in service to American intelligence, their families would never want for money. They also knew that if Venezuela found out they were working for the CIA, they would be tortured and never seen again.

Gold or lead—it was the way intelligence had always done business.

The thirty minutes passed with Taft staring out the window. There were a couple of things bothering him about this case, but he could find no resolution or answers. In the last few minutes, he cleared his mind and stared at the blue of the water as it became increasingly shallow. A moment later, Taft caught sight of the shoreline.

"We are close," the co-pilot yelled back to the cabin.

Thicker trees and foliage interspersed with swampy ground gave way to low hills rising up as they traveled inland. An occasional road was hacked through the jungle, but mostly the area seemed deserted and remote.

"We are going to make a pass over the field," the co-pilot shouted back.

On the ground, the men milling outside the truck looked up as the plane roared low overhead.

"No one has landed or filed a report on this airfield in two years," the pilot said to the co-pilot, "but she looks sound."

"Hell," the co-pilot said, "I'm sure we pay someone to keep it up."

The pilot headed out over the jungle, then turned and once again. As soon as she was on her downwind leg, she slowed and dropped the flaps. Quickly reversing the thruster, she slowed right at the end of the runway and carefully turned the plane around. As the jet slid to a stop, the Venezuelan truck was already driving down the edge of the runway.

The co-pilot unbuckled his seatbelt and climbed out of his seat.

"Safe and sound, Agent Taft," he said as he walked over and unlatched the clamshell door.

Taft walked toward the door as it was lowered, and climbed down. The ground leader approached. In case the mission had been compromised, Taft had his knife and handgun with him. The man approached and extended his hand. Taft did not take it but instead uttered a single word.

"Fidelity."

Taft had randomly selected the verification.

"Allegiance," the Venezuelan replied.

This particular exchange had been taught for only a single year— the year the Venezuelan agent had attended school. Even if he had been tortured, it was doubtful he could have exposed all the hundred oaths and counter-oaths the agents had been required to memorize. Taft had been required to memorize four thousand of them. The oaths and counter-oaths had never been written down and although rarely used, this crude and non-computerized method of recognition had never been compromised.

Taft extended his hand. "Glad to know you never forgot."

"Some things," the Venezuelan said, "one never forgets."

"John Taft."

"Gustavo Valencia."

The pilot poked her head out of the door. "Agent Taft," she said, "the longer we are on the ground, the more nervous I become."

"Mr. Valencia," Taft said, "I have brought a large sum of cash along. Do you have something like a tarp we might cover it with?"

"Agent Taft, please call me Gus. At least until such time I assume the office of general," Valencia said, "which will be about the time we climb into our truck."

Taft smiled and chuckled.

"And as to your issue with the funding, I was alerted and brought along an appropriate container."

Valencia stepped back from the jet and motioned to four men holding a polished mahogany casket. They walked forward and placed it carefully on the ground at the jet's doorway, then retreated.

"I think it best the men are not aware what is inside," Valencia said. "Even the best of men can become distracted if they dwell on money."

"How about me and the pilots form a line and hand the packets out to you."

Valencia reached down and opened the top of the casket. "Ready when you are," he said, smiling.

Twelve million dollars in cash took six minutes to secure in a coffin. Once Valencia had armed the device, which was designed to secure and track, he motioned the four men to take the coffin and secure it in the back of the truck. Then he handed Taft a Venezuelan military uniform. Taft quickly dressed and tossed his other clothes back in the CIA jet. The pilot was already back in her seat. Taft thumped his hand against the fuselage. The pilot gave him a thumbs-up, and the co-pilot stepped over and began to raise the door.

"Good luck, Agent Taft," the co-pilot said just as the door closed.

Taft walked away toward the truck as he heard the engines on the jet start up. He had just climbed into the rear compartment of the truck with Valencia when the jet taxied down the runway. In seconds, it was in the air and lost in the jungle, with the receding sound from her engines reverberating and disappearing into the dense growth. In the front of the truck, the driver turned back to Valencia for instructions. Next to him was another soldier with an automatic weapon. Valencia handed a package of black armbands to the soldier in the passenger seat.

"Have the men place these on their arms," Valencia said, "and tell them they may now display rank."

The soldier took the package, then climbed out and walked around to the back of the truck.

"Everyone is ready," he said in Spanish once he had climbed back in the truck.

Taft's uniform already had his rank and badges attached. Valencia pinned his on his epaulets and spoke to the driver. "Okay, we can leave now."

Soon they were bumping down a jungle road. "We meet up with a paved road soon," Valencia said. "It will take us to Maracay, then on to Caracas."

Taft nodded.

"I'm sure you can speak Spanish or they would not have sent you. Can you do a convincing drunken officer lost in grief?"

"Do you plan on us being stopped?" Taft asked.

"Doubtful with us flying the general's flag from the front fender, but you never know."

"If someone cries enough, no one wastes much time in further inquiry."

"True enough," Valencia agreed.

***

Agent Franklin was about to board a flight to Washington D.C. when his telephone rang.

"She is out of the country," the voice said, "and no longer our problem."

Franklin stepped away from the crowd of people to a more private area.

"How was the cleanup?"

"That went smoothly," the voice said. "The team got in and out with nary a problem."

"Nary?"

"Very lyrical, I thought."

"Any idea who he was?"

"We have a few ideas," the voice said. "We are just awaiting the fingerprint identification."

"So this is it for me in Texas for a while?"

"Seems so."

"Good," Franklin said as he listened to the first boarding call, "because this place sucks."

"It's a whole 'nother world," the voice said repeating a state tourist slogan.

"They can keep it,' Franklin said before disconnecting.

***

Just under four hours after landing, Taft and his team had reached the home they would use as their headquarters in Caracas. After backing the truck up to the garage and finding it too tall for the door, Valencia ordered the soldiers to remove the casket and secure it inside. A pair of guards was assigned to watch over it. Since none of the soldiers had been involved when the coffin was filled, they had no idea what was inside. They only knew that if there was a person inside he was a large man. The twelve million weighed two hundred and sixty-four pounds.

"What now?" Valencia asked after Taft had cleared the garage, removed four million of the cash, stuffed it into a duffel bag, then reassigned the soldiers to guard the stash.

"Do you have a portable air conditioner in the house?"

"I think there were a couple in the back bedrooms."

"Have one of your men bring one out to the garage and get it running."

"The soldiers…" Valencia began to say.

"If they think there is a body inside," Taft said, "they will be uncomfortable thinking it might heat up. Plus the guards might as well sit in cool air. Once that is done, I want the guards rotated every four hours. Is the top securely fastened?"

"Locked—with you and I having the only keys," Valencia said.

"Good," Taft said.

Valencia walked into the house and ordered the air conditioner moved from the back bedroom to the garage. He joined Taft, who had walked through the house onto the screened-in front porch.

"Is that Audi one of ours?" Taft pointed to a high-performance sedan on the street.

"Yes," Valencia said. "Armored and ready, as are the two SUVs behind it."

Taft nodded.

"You and me in the Audi," he said. "Have the rest of the men follow behind in the SUVs."

"Where are we going?"

"To bribe some people." Taft smiled and raising the duffel in the air.

***

"Hell of a conundrum," General Benson noted.

He and the CIA director were inside Benson's office. Along with all the shielding that had been built into the walls to avoid any type of detection, Benson had turned on a small jamming device that would scramble anything spoken. At this instant they were one of very few people on the planet who could not be heard or seen.

"If we expose the President and his association with the oil men and that blows the election for Cristos, we chance having the same socialist or some other anti-American leader being elected in Venezuela," the CIA director noted.

Both men thought for a moment.

"It is almost simple, if you think of it," Benson said, sipping from a glass of water. "Either we cut out the cancer in our own country or we try to save a patient we aren't related to a thousand miles away."

"It is hard to believe the President is so stupid to think that his own intelligence services don't monitor all his communications."

"I heard a recording. One of his aides actually told him as long as he used disposable cell phones there was no way he could be identified. Forget that I stuck a bug in the wood under his desk."

"Burner cell phones," the CIA director said with contempt. "We figured out that game a decade ago. It just goes to show you what happens when a President assigns all of his top jobs to close friends and donors. The people he has working for him for the most part are clinically brain-dead. By the way, the bug was a nice touch."

"Wasn't that aide running an equipment rental outfit before the President elevated him to government service because his father was a large donor?"

"The press release said equipment rental," the CIA director noted. "It was truly portable toilets, upscale portable toilets."

"I didn't know there was such a thing."

"For outdoor weddings and the like."

"So we have proof the President is tied into the oil men who are attempting to overthrow Venezuela," Benson said, "and he ordered Melton and the reporter silenced. That seems enough to me."

The CIA agent was quiet for a moment. "Plus he revealed my agent."

"So this is truly a vengeance thing," Benson said with a thin smile.

"You'd do the same."

"True," Benson said, "but it's nice we have all this other dirt to justify digging the grave."

"Here's what I'm thinking," the CIA director said quietly.

***

"I think it is time you take care of our man," the voice from the United States said.

The man on the other end chuckled.

"Your voice sounds different this time," he said. "Not tinged with booze."

"You cannot believe how old that got."

"Does that mean when you come down here you won't be enjoying cocktails with me?"

"If I never taste or even smell alcohol again it will be too soon."

"Is everything going according to plan?"

"Yeah, such as it is," the voice said. "My guess is they have dispatched an agent to Venezuela by now."

"Is it who you think?"

"Hard to say. I called his partner, told him I had an emergency, and asked that he contact me," the voice said. "That was a few hours ago. If he calls back, we'll do a trace then I'll know for sure where he is located."

"But whoever the agent is, you are certain they will be coming for me?"

"That would fit the plot," the voice said.

'So I'd better go take care of our boy as soon as possible."

"I think it's time. To uncover the package."

***

Taft was driving away from the house in Caracas in the Audi, followed by the SUVs.

"So what do you know about Dieter Marcos?" he asked Valencia.

"He is loved by the people," Valencia noted. "A Robin Hood-type character who funds programs for the poor."

"I heard he is ruthless."

"From what I could gather he only uses brutality against other criminals," Valencia noted, "and only when they refuse to join up with him and follow his code of honor."

"Code of honor?"

"Marcos and his gang have rigid rules as to their conduct."

"Kind of like the Mafia?"

"Sort of," Valencia agreed.

"Maybe that explains why…" Taft drifted off as he rounded a corner and had to quickly squeeze between a large truck and a stone wall siding the road.

"Like I told you, I'd be glad to drive. The traffic in this city is insane. The rich actually commute by helicopter."

"We'll switch in a bit," Taft said.

"You were saying?"

"We had intelligence that your government was investigating Marcos and then the agent in charge was ordered to stand down."

"In Venezuela that might have been for a thousand reasons," Valencia said, "not the least of which might be incompetence or laziness."

***

Dieter Marcos opened the door to the apartment and peered inside. One of the guards had a handgun trained on him but lowered as soon as he recognized who it was. Marcos placed his finger to his lips, indicating silence, then motioned for the guard to bring his partner into the living room. When both men were inside he motioned them toward the door quietly. Once outside the apartment, he whispered that they should go down to the street and meet with one of his assistants, who would take them to a safe location. With several of his guards stationed in the hallway and on the stairs, Marcos opened the door with a bag in his hand and walked into the apartment.

In the bedroom, a man sat on the edge of the bed. At the sound of the door opening, he looked up at Marcos. His face was gaunt and his eyes seemed dead and resigned. His normally tanned skin was pale and his smile more grim than happy.

"Is it time?" he asked simply.

"Yes," Marcos said.

The man rose from the bed.

"Your Excellency. I have a bag with toiletries and such along with a set of clothes you can change into," Marcos instructed. "I hope this experience was not too harrowing."

"I know it was needed for my absolute safety. Now I know what our political prisoners and kidnap victims feel like."

"It was necessary," Marcos agreed.

The man walked closer to the door. He extended his hand and Marcos took it, shook it, then drew the man closer in an embrace.

"A carefully woven web of deceit snares many a man," he said grandly.

***

Valencia had radioed to the SUVs to take the lead as they drew closer to the first hideout. As soon as they pulled to a stop, the soldiers jumped out and secured the interior and exterior. By the time Taft and Valencia walked inside there were a half dozen men clustered around a table in the kitchen. Their hands were palms down on the table with arms extended. Surprised, it seemed not one of the men had time to retrieve their weapon. Valencia's men were standing around the kitchen table with handguns pointed down.

Taft burst into the room and said in Spanish, "We mean you no harm. We are only seeking Dieter Marcos."

He watched as the men at the table kept their arms and hands outstretched as ordered but glanced at one another in some unspoken language. It seemed they were all weighing their options.

"Who is in charge here?" Taft asked.

One of the men, older and with one eye going cloudy, spoke up. "I am."

"We can go through an entire scene here," Taft said, "where we threaten you and perhaps shoot a few of your men to make sure you understand the seriousness of this situation, but I would rather not do that. I need to speak to Marcos—see him in person. And I'm willing to pay you men one million in United States currency if you will tell me where he is currently located."

"Hundred-dollar bills?" the leader inquired. Hundred-dollar bills were the preferred currency of all worldwide criminal enterprises.

"Yes," Taft said.

The scene around the table was almost comical. It appeared as all the criminals were reaching for the pot of chips at some strange card-less poker game.

"Can you take me to another room to speak?" the leader asked Taft.

Taft nodded at Valencia, who motioned for one of his men to help the leader up and guide him by the arm into a back bedroom. Once there, the man spoke.

"Can you make it one million, four hundred thousand? I need four hundred for me and two hundred for each of my men."

Bumping up the price of treason. Taft liked this man.

"Are you sure you know his location?"

"Absolutely."

"You know if you deceive us we will return."

The man nodded. Taft wondered why the man seemed less than nervous. He figured it might be some Latin American cultural difference. In South America, bribery was more common.

"Half now," Taft said wisely, "and half when we find him."

"Can we trust you?"

"What choice do you have?"

"I'll need to speak to my men."

Taft motioned for the guard to lead the man back to the kitchen. Once he was seated with his hands flat on the table he spoke. "Men, I know many of you were angered when our leader fined us for the unsanctioned robbery at the airport. Taking all of the proceeds as a fine was wrong. We now have a chance to even the score. If you agree, then raise your pinky finger from the table."

All the pinkies rose save one. Then slowly that last one arched upwards.

"Sorry," the man said in Spanish. "I broke that finger as a child and it has never healed properly."

"Then it is agreed," Taft said.

"Yes," the leader noted.

"We are going to need to take your weapons at this time," Taft said. "While a couple of my men take them out to the trucks, I will retrieve the funds."

In a few minutes Taft reentered the kitchen. "Where do we find him?"

The leader gave him an address. Valencia wrote it down and nodded at Taft. It was a real address.

"Once I hand over the cash," Taft said, "I want you all to remain at this table for five minutes to give us time to exit your neighborhood. Do we have an agreement?"

"We have an agreement," the leader said.

Taft dropped the bundles of cash into the center of the table. He walked out, followed by Valencia and the rest of the guards. A moment later they were in their vehicles and on their way to the address, which was located across town.

Back in the house, the leader listened to the noise of the Audi and the SUVs recede. Then he reached into the cash pile and tossed bundles to each of the men.

"The deal is we get to keep half."

***

For humans there is no greater threat to survival than arrogance. That afternoon as Hobbs and Walker awoke sticky, sweaty and hung over, they wanted nothing else than to climb under a rock. Instead, Hobbs's telephone rang.

"Now look, I'm having second thoughts about this entire affair. There must be some other way to get you those rigs back."

Hobbs was standing in the kitchen of the rented mansion in Miami. He walked over to the refrigerator and opened the door. There was a pair of tennis shoes on a shelf as well as a partially filled cardboard case containing green glass bottles of beer. He grabbed one and twisted off the top.

"Johnny Boy," he said, "this operation is way too far along to stop now."

He took a large slurp from the bottle, then let out a slow burp.

Benson and the CIA director were watching gauges on a computer as an NIA voice actor trained in impersonations did a nearly flawless job of mimicking the President. Benson gave the man a thumbs-up and a smile.

"Look here, there is already a media push for me to comment on the death of J. Thomas Melton," the actor said, reading from a script, "and you know how I hate speaking to the public at any time. You add this trouble in Venezuela you men are stirring up and soon reporters will be camped out in front of the White House."

"Melton's dead?" Hobbs said. "I hadn't heard."

"Where the hell are you?"

"Miami," Hobbs said, "and watch your tone. If it hadn't been for me and Sam getting you that last-minute influx of cash donations, you would have never been elected."

The CIA director nodded. Venezuela and illegal campaign cash admitted. A few more disclosures and the President and the oil men might as well wear a noose around their necks to dinner.

"Let me talk to Sam."

Walker was bent over, snorting cocaine off the counter in the kitchen. He finished and slurped from a glass holding a mimosa.

"I guess Melton is dead and Johnny Boy wants to speak to you," Hobbs said, handing him the telephone.

Walker took the phone. "Where are you calling from?"

"Don't worry," the actor said, "I'm on a disposable. You've got bigger problems. That guy you had me call didn't do his job with a reporter."

"Look here, Johnny," Walker said. "Me and Lee had a rough night. That and we have to fly down south tonight to take over a country. We're going to be busy for a few weeks there…."

"I told your partner I thought you'd better figure some other way to get those rigs back."

"It's way past the rigs, Johnny Boy…." Walker started to say.

Benson and the CIA director were motioning with their hands for the actor to get back to the killings.

"Whatever," the actor said. "This man you referred me to did not do his job and now I'm at risk."

"Look," Walker said, taking another sip of the mimosa, "you wanted a killer and that's what we gave you. If Tubbs did not perform all of the jobs you needed done, then most likely he's dead himself. You need to find another contractor to deal with his reporter, whoever it is. Now we've got to hang up. We've talked way too long this morning about things one should not speak of over a telephone."

With that Walker disconnected.

***

"Big balls, hanging up on the President," the CIA director said.

"Good," Benson agreed, "he'll need them in prison."

The voice actor removed his headphones. "How was it?"

"It could not have been more perfect," Benson said.

"Thanks," the actor responded, rising. "Will there be anything else?"

"Can you do a Texas accent?"

The actor smiled. "Dallas?" he asked with a little Western-and-Southern mixed twang. "Or Houston?" he asked in a different western speech pattern.

"You'll be speaking to a reporter," the CIA director noted.

"Considering the quality of reporters nowadays," the actor said seriously, "it probably doesn't matter much."

***

Taft read the secure message from Martinez. The Miami author had asked—insisted, Martinez said—that Taft contact him. Since they had a long drive across town and Valencia had decided that he should take over piloting the Audi, Taft scrolled through his telephone memory and dialed the number. The phone at the other end rang a half-dozen times, then mysteriously went dead with no answering message.

44

"WE NEED TO move immediately," Benson said. "Tomorrow is election day in Venezuela."

"I agree. The men I have covering the oil men heard them call their pilot and ask him to file a flight plan for this evening from Miami to Caracas," the CIA director said.

"That seals it."

"Let's do it," the director said, reaching for the phone.

He uttered a single word then turned the phone off.

Outside the headquarters of the FBI in Washington, D.C., a CIA agent entered the lobby, flashed his badge, and asked to be taken up to an agent. A guard quickly led him to an elevator and within minutes he was delivering the recording and the written proof tying the President to Hobker Petroleum and Venezuela as well as the murder of Melton.

At that same instant other agents fanned out to the television, radio and newspapers to deliver similar packets of information. Within a half hour, the telephone line to the White House spokesman was flooded with calls. Minutes later, the President was informed that there was a crisis.

"Did you collaborate with an oil company?" the spokesman asked, glancing at his notes. "A Hobker Petroleum? In an attempt to throw the coming elections in Venezuela?"

The President glanced at his spokesman. His handlers had selected the man—as much for his skills in evasion as his knowledge of a fair and open media. But the President had never cared for him—they shared almost the same amount of pomposity.

"Excuse me for a minute." The President walked to a small bathroom off to the side of the office.

Once inside, he removed a vial from his pocket with a tiny silver spoon attached to the top by a thin chain. A moment later, the President placed the spoon, now heaped with white powder, next to his left nostril. The powder raced off the spoon like a vacuum had been flipped on into the President's nose. He repeated the process with the other nostril, and then reached for a tissue and wiped off the area under his nose. He stared into the mirror. His eyes were a touch watery and his cheeks a little flushed, but in general he felt he looked good.

He returned to the Oval Office and sat. "That would be an issue of national security."

The spokesman stared at the President. He was acting a little strange.

"Were you or anyone from your office involved in the death of J. Thomas Melton?"

The President ground his jaw a little. Something was dripping onto the back of his throat and he swallowed. "Melton was an old and dear friend of mine."

"That is not an answer, Mr. President," the spokesman said. "And I will be ripped apart by the media if I answer that way."

"I thought we control the media now?" the President said. "Since I signed all those orders relating to national security and terrorism? Just tell them to mind their own business. I only have a few more months left in my term, then whoever wins the election can deal with those monsters."

The spokesman was a handpicked shill but he also knew a free and fair press was important.

"These monsters, as you call them," the spokesman said, "have been unleashed by something. In all the time in my position I have never seen them as riled up over anything as they are with these allegations. Telling them to go away is not going to work."

Just then the intercom buzzed.

"I asked not to be disturbed," the President said into the speaker.

"You'd better turn on the television," the Vice-President said quickly. "Russian station."

The spokesman found the station on the Oval Office TV. The station was secretly funded by the Russian government but designed for Western audiences. Recently the station had become a thorn in the side of the United States government and big business.

"That is amazing," one of the anchors was saying.

"If you are just joining us," the other anchor said, "once again here is a recording we just obtained. Our experts have run analysis on the voice and believe it is the President of the United States. By voice-printing the other voices on a computer, we matched them to an interview on one of the business channels. The two other men who spoke to the President are believed to be"—he stared down at his notes—"Leland Hobbs and Samuel Walker. The two men are the principals in Hobker Petroleum, one of the largest multinational oil companies in the world. Let us play the tape again and then…"

He paused and pointed to the other side of the studio where several men and women were quickly filing in and taking seats around a conversation pit.

"We will discuss this with the panel of experts we have called in to the studio."

The camera switched back to the anchor desk and the two men turned toward the screen. There was a graphic that showed up and down bars that moved as the voices rose and fell.

"Johnny Boy," the voice began, "this is too far along to stop now."

Then the entire conversation that Benson and the CIA director had recorded was played over.

The spokesman listened carefully then turned to the President, who had walked closer to the television and was staring as if it was a tiger about to leap across and rip out his throat.

"Please accept my resignation," the spokesman said. He walked out.

***

As soon as their office in Houston called Walker and Hobbs to report the news, they flipped on the television and watched. Before the recording had even finished, Hobbs was on his cell phone to their pilot, ordering him to amend the flight plan so they could leave immediately. They chugged their drinks and made more for the road, then raced for their limousine.

The local field office of the FBI was closer to Miami International Airport. As the limousine pulled through the gate and started down the tarmac toward their jet, Walker and Hobbs could see a pair of black SUVs sliding to a stop in front of their plane. The doors opened and agents with weapons drawn approached.

"Turn around," Walker screamed.

The driver twisted the wheel and the long white limousine wallowed through a turn to the right. Walker tried to balance the cocktail in his hand to overcome the lean of the limo but some spilled on his hand. He slurped it off his skin and then turned to Hobbs.

"Ideas?"

"Bahamas?" Hobbs said quietly.

***

"Stop at the stash house so we can grab some more cash," Taft said to Valencia.

The day was mostly clear with the humid haze that so often enveloped Caracas. A storm was forming out over the ocean but it would be some time before it made land. The sky overhead was crisscrossed by jet contrails and commuter helicopters.

"All those helicopters look like angry birds."

"Most of the larger high-rises have heliports these days," Valencia said as he turned on a side street closer to the hideout.

Once at the hideout, Valencia ordered the guards out of the garage as Taft unlocked the coffin, disarmed the alarm, removed two million more in cash and placed it in a duffel. Once he had re-secured the coffin, he turned to Valencia.

"Let's head to the next stop."

Outside, the noise from a turbine helicopter grew louder, then faded away.

Taft and Valencia walked back out to the Audi and, followed by the trucks, drove to where they were sure Dieter Marcos was hiding.

***

"Look!" the man said to his team in English. "I don't want anyone harmed. We make our way through the backyards undetected. Once there, don your masks, throw the canister through the window, then wait three minutes."

The men had climbed from the helicopter, which had touched down in a park near Taft's hideout.

"You copy that, men?"

The leader was folding duffels and placing them into a pack with other supplies. He slipped it onto his back. "Let's go."

The team made their way carefully through the neighborhood undetected. Once they were in place alongside the house, the leader motioned for them to don their masks. He made another motion for a pair of men to pull the pins, then lob gas canisters into windows in the house and garage. Watching the timer on his cell phone, he waited for the three minutes, then ordered his team to enter the house.

Kicking down the doors, they found two men inside unconscious from the gas. Then the leader walked through the house and garage.

"That must be it," he said, pointing to the coffin.

One of his team approached the coffin and swept an electronic scanner back and forth. It beeped and a red light was illuminated.

"Can you disarm it?" the American asked.

The man studied it for a few minutes. "It is embarrassingly simple. They must not have expected experts—this would only protect it from someone without knowledge in devices of this type."

From his pack, the expert removed a black metal box the size of a pack of cigarettes. He folded out a small leg from the rear so the box was angled like a small speaker might be. He faced it toward the casket, then motioned for the other man to turn around with his back to the casket.

Flipping a switch to start a thirty-second timer, the man turned his back to the casket. There was an increasingly louder whine, then a bright flash of light, as if a high-intensity strobe had been lit.

"It's disabled."

"How did that…"

"Scrambles the circuits. Takes in the other device's signals and sends them back at varying speeds. I can go into more detail if you want to write a book about it." He laughed.

The leader grinned. "Kind of busy right now."

He stepped over to the casket and examined the lock, then looked back at the other man.

"Do I have to do everything?" he joked.

This time he used brute force, jamming a black composite survival knife into the crack in the door and wrenching it up until the wood shattered and the lock gave way.

"That's one way," the leader said as he removed his pack and removed the duffels. He and the other men started to quickly fill them with cash. They were just finishing when one of the team burst into the garage. "Time to go!"

The leader gave a sharp whistle and another man entered the garage.

"Grab a bag," he said.

The four men carrying the cash-filled duffels made their way out the rear door and started running through the backyards to the helicopter.

"You know," the leader said once everyone was seated, "for a bunch of civilians you're not too bad."

"We all did our time," the man with the electronics expertise noted. "Now we do it for us."

"Sir?" the pilot asked over the intercom.

"Better head to the wait zone," the leader said. "If we head to our next destination now we are going to be early."

"Yes, sir," the pilot said.

Then the leader reached for his cell phone and plugged it into the headset so he could hear over the noise of the helicopter. He dialed a number and spoke.

"I haven't had a chance to call you since I got confirmation," the American said. "But it is definitely going to be him."

"We'll go easy," the voice said.

"Don't go easy, D," the American said. "I don't want a hair on this head harmed."

"I understand," the other man said easily.

***

Dieter Marcos was watching news coverage of the Presidential recordings. He turned to the other man in the room.

"I wonder who was behind this?"

The other man pondered this. He had shaved, cleaned up and dressed in a collared shirt and a pressed pair of slacks. On his feet were highly polished shoes, and on several of this fingers were rings containing large precious stones.

"Excuse me," Marcos added. "Your Excellency."

The man thought for a moment. "Most of man's actions are either for money, revenge or love."

"Can this harm our plan, your Excellency?"

"Can the actions of man alter fate?" he asked quietly. "That is a question that has been argued for centuries."

***

Taft was speaking to Martinez, who was revealing the allegations against the President.

"That's about par for the course," Taft noted. "Now my ass is hung out to dry. I'm in a foreign land launching a covert op when worldwide media has just disclosed that our government, our President at least, is attempting to manipulate their elections and place his own man in charge."

"I'd pull out," Martinez advised.

Taft considered this.

"Let me hit this next stop, then I'll decide," he said. "If I can capture Marcos, I might be able to determine if the real Cristos is alive."

"I don't know why you would even care right now."

For an instant Taft considered turning around his caravan, returning to the stash house, taking the remaining cash, and disappearing. It wasn't so much duty to his agency that made him hesitate—since the electrocution, he doubted most of what the intelligence agencies and his own government now stood for. It was more curiosity. What if Cristos was alive, and what if he was a descendant of Jesus? Taft had to know—even if his life would be endangered in the attempt to find out.

"I've got to know," he said to Martinez at last.

Martinez paused. "That's not like you, John. You've always been content to be a cog in the wheel. Often the cog that drove the wheel, but you always left the ultimate picture to others."

"I told you after I was sprung from the hospital, I'm a different man."

Martinez had been partners with Taft for a long time. He had learned that when he gave him a direct order, it almost never worked. Still, for the sake of all they had gone through, he tried.

"John," he said forcefully. "I want you to get the hell out of there."

"That's the first time in a long time I've heard you cuss," Taft noted.

"I mean it, man. Pull out. We can figure this out back here in the states."

"One more stop, Larry," Taft said, "and if it comes up short, I'll have you arrange transportation for me out of here."

Martinez had a bad feeling but he did not want to jinx it.

"One more stop, then call."

"Will do," Taft said.

***

The actor who had been hired to play Cristos watched the news broadcasts with growing concern. The United States intelligence services had been involved in numerous coups and attempted coups over the years, and few people harbored any illusion they would not try again. As he watched the broadcasts he dialed the number for the man that had hired him. No answer. He went down the list, dialing everyone involved with the plot. Not one person was available.

His suite had been manned since he started by numerous security officers and handlers. In fact, the entire top floor of the hotel where they stayed was populated by advisers, media experts and future cabinet members.

He walked into the living room of the suite and found it empty. A half-eaten club sandwich on the table and a glass of iced tea was still sweating as the ice melted. He walked through the rest of the suite and found it empty.

Opening the door, he peered out and down the hall. The guards usually stationed there were absent. He tapped on the first door down the hall but no one answered. Across was a door propped open by a suitcase. He opened it up and found the television on a news station and the recording of the President of the United States playing. Clothes were littered about the suite as if the person inside started to pack but then decided just to leave. The fake Cristos didn't bother to check any of the other rooms. He simply raced back to his suite, secured his passport, what cash and credit cards he had available, and raced out into the hallway again. He had made his way to the elevator. The light indicating the floors was starting upward toward him.

He had a premonition, so he raced to the stairway and started down at a dead run.

***

Taft and his team stopped in front of the house where, he had been told, Marcos was being harbored. The house was on a quiet residential street that seemed deserted. Four of the team clustered around the front door as one of the men popped the lock. Like a pack of dogs, the group entered. Though it could not be heard outside over the sounds of the boots on the floor, there was a series of puffs, then the muffled sound of the men crumpling to the floor.

Taft, Valencia and the remaining team members ran for the door, not knowing the men inside had fallen. From behind them on the lawn, a man popped up from under a hatch that was buried in the ground under the drip line of a tree. There were several quick puffs of air escaping and then the others fell as if they suddenly needed sleep. Taft glanced around. Then he heard a voice from inside.

"You'll need to raise that weapon in the air, Mr. Taft," the voice said.

Taft looked around. Resistance was futile. He raised his weapon and stood on the front porch. A man walked out the open door from inside the house. He reached up and took Taft's handgun.

"I'm Dieter Marcos," the man said. "Please come inside."

45

THOUGHTS RAN THROUGH Taft's mind at the speed of light but the jumbled fragments always came back to one thing. He had been caught on his last mission after retiring from a lifetime of successes. Why had he gone back to the well one last time? Beads of sweat popped out on his chest and forehead, the oily sweat of failure and regret. He was a hardened realist since his electrocution. His lifetime of positive attitude had given way to the harsh light of what was. Not what might be.

His immediate future would contain torture and death. The torture he had faced before. The death would be a first. Marcos motioned with his gun toward the rear of the house as a pair of men filed past to retrieve the bodies. From the rear, Taft could hear a voice.

"Good," the voice said. "I believe it was in the plan."

There was quiet.

"Yes," the voice agreed, "and thank you."

Taft slowly entered a kitchen. Marcos motioned for him to sit down at the table. Taft complied and then stared as the man who had been talking on a telephone turned toward him.

"Please excuse my rudeness, Mr. Taft," Vincente Cristos said. "That call was about my usurper. Apparently when the news of your President having involvement in this affair was aired, the man tried to escape and go underground. Some of our people are bringing him here now."

Taft sat stunned, looking at Cristos.

"Also, another team recovered the stash of bribe money you had hidden in the casket," Cristos said.

Taft was beyond shock but tried not to show any emotion.

"Want some tea?" Cristos asked.

Taft paused, not knowing how to answer. "Sure."

One of the men in the room started to walk over to handle the duties, but Cristos waved him away. "My ancestor washed the feet of the poor," he said. "I can surely make tea."

Cristos filled a pot. Then he turned around.

"Your people are fine," he said. "They were struck with darts containing a fast-acting nerve agent that put them to sleep. Their only injuries will be from their falls. We have a doctor here and he's checking them over and taking their vital signs. I assure you they will be treated fairly."

"Thank you," Taft said, rather surprised.

"I understand you were badly injured recently," Cristos noted. "Electrocution, if my memory serves me correctly?"

Taft—his injury, recovery and almost everything else about him—was as highly classified as any U.S. governmental secrets. For Cristos to know anything was astonishing.

"I was," Taft said easily.

"I offer my condolences," Cristos said. "Man seems to be constantly beset by challenge."

Taft remained silent.

"Would you like me to call you by your real name?"

Taft, who had long ago forgotten he was someone else, said nothing for a time.

"No," he said finally.

A man walked into the kitchen. He was dressed in a suit and carrying a clipboard.

"Sorry, your Excellency," he said. "I just wished to inform you that the press conference is arranged for six p.m. That will give the population time to digest the information and have time to reflect prior to the polls opening tomorrow."

The tea kettle whistled and Cristos arose.

"Thank you," he said kindly.

Cristos poured hot water over the tea and let it steep in the pot. He carried the pot and a pair of cups over to the table. Then he smiled warmly at Taft.

"I'll pour this in a minute. Would you like to hear the story?"

Taft nodded.

"I am the leader of an ancient order that traces its lineage back thousands of years. Tales passed down over that time tell stories of our leadership of mankind. It seems…"

Cristos stared at Taft. The American had said nothing but Cristos had acute senses.

"You wish to ask me a question?"

"So you claim to be the descendant of Jesus—the son of the Son of God?"

"I make no claims," Cristos said. "Others have done that already."

"But…"

"If this helps you cope, it is thought I descend directly from James the Just, who was Jesus's brother. My uncle paid for the sins of man. There is but one; may you find Him now."

As soon as Cristos uttered that last phrase, a tingle raced down Taft's spine. He felt content.

"Since time immemorial, man has sought the answer to a question that does not need an answer. He has spent trillions of hours, suffered billions of deaths and supplied millions of false solutions to this riddle. The question is this: Is there something more than this of which I am aware? And the answer should never have been considered for more than a millisecond, of course.

"Only man, of all the creatures that inhabit this planet or orb or spot in space, could have the ego to consider that they were alone. Alone and possibly the highest life form. By even considering this question, man for centuries shows his ignorance. Everyone at some point for sure when a child has felt the divine breeze from something both greater than—and better than—themselves," he continued.

"But we choose not to embrace this feeling that we know to be true, and instead allow our cluttered minds to weave and reweave this gift of knowing until we have killed the very thing that is within each and every person. Our egos make us try to supply an answer—yet as I have said, there is no question. The power is; and it is good."

Cristos continued: "Once and for most it happens at an early age, we start down the path to seeking the answer to the question, we gradually lose the ability to feel and recognize what is all around us. Shortly thereafter people take an evil turn. Some much more than others, but all somewhat try to become masters of their own universe. They, with increasing regularity, they begin to believe that they can manipulate the real and thus through their actions make it unreal."

"That which is inside us, outside us and around us, is a gift that requires no explanation. To do so takes the essence of the gift and reduces it to but another problem to be solved, another job to be performed, another riddle needing explanation. And as soon as people attempt to explain a feeling and make it into words, the process is corrupted and abuses occur. The abuse can be simple—you believing another knows better who to follow. Or severe—you raising a sword to slay those that believe differently. From good feeling, true feelings, come many bad things," he said.

Without missing a beat, Cristos poured two cups of tea. Taft was in the present. He did not feel fear or anxiety. And for the first time, his mind was neither formulating measures or counter-measures.

"My ancestors were blessed with one unusual trait," Cristos continued. "They never lost the overwhelming sense, the unwavering knowledge, that there was something out there that transcends man. My people never needed to scream they know there is a higher power, because it so inhabits our flesh that the question need not be even considered. He is here now with me, and with all others who open themselves up to the feeling. Do you feel that of which I speak?" Cristos asked, turning to Taft.

Taft did not feel the presence of a higher power—not right then. What he felt was the unwavering feelings that Cristos radiated.

"I feel that you feel it is true," Taft said.

"So, over the centuries, do others," Cristos noted. "So my … I guess today it would be referred to as a gene pool—my gene pool of ancestors, while not prophesying, were often asked the meaning to different questions as they traveled the lands of nations long past. Other men, as is their way, wrote these conversations down—often if not always adding their spin to the statements. Some of these chance meetings and random statements grew into fantastical tales, which later were used to control man. You see experts, whatever their ilk, are created so man is made to feel that they are incompetent to supply the answer. Nowadays, modern man has taken it to the extreme. The more involved the story, the more experts can interject themselves and further sever man from their feelings. Religion is ripe with this problem. People are told what to believe and how to believe it. The higher power simply is—there are no complicated instructions needed. And that brings me to religion versus faith."

Cristos continued: "Faith is simply the unerring belief in a higher power. Religion was created by man and grows ever more complex. Religion is someone else's man-created answer as to how a person might find that which is already there. Religion claims to offer help so one may find faith; however, the very nature of a series of rituals and doctrine in fact usually drives a wedge into the process of true faith itself."

Another man walked into the kitchen and leaned over and whispered into Cristos' ear.

"Your men are all fine, Mr. Taft," he said. "They are being given food and water."

"Thank you."

Cristos nodded slightly.

"So let me move us closer to the present time, if I may. For tonight I must do the one thing my people have avoided for all these thousands of years. I must come forward and reveal at least a little of who I am." He looked over at Taft. "You are puzzled as to why we have never done this sooner?"

That was exactly what Taft had been thinking.

"One of the greatest gifts of man is the gift of self-will. This, although a gift, is also the source of all of man's ills. Self-will requires that we find a higher power on our own and that for most is almost an impossibility. Self-will allows man to simply turn to the higher power, to give up that gift so he could be unburdened enough to feel. But the gift becomes tinged by man with thoughts and manipulations so that for most it can never serve its true purpose. Instead of surrendering the gift so they might receive the feeling, they wrap the attempt up with a thousand doubts and rituals and requirements that they are not surrendering but negotiating. Why would man attempt to negotiate with what is absolute truth? It defies logic."

"Self-will," he continued, "is both the savior of man and the element of his destruction. And once my family took a position, revealed who we were—be it at the time of the Crusades, the Reformation, or when Hitler seized power—we would have, by the very nature of self will, run the risk of manipulating man. Manipulation must by her nature, include control. We have known forever that as soon as we reveal ourselves, many will bind themselves to us as surely as if they wrapped chains around their wrists and offered themselves to us as slaves—whether figuratively or literally. We over the centuries have used teaching and not rote obedience as our rule. Believe what you will as long as the belief is your own, has been our guideline. We have had to watch as thousands of others abused the will of man and imposed their own philosophies in an attempt to gain control while we remained quiet. And they have succeeded."

Cristos took a sip of the tea, now growing cold, and then looked into Taft's eyes.

"You wonder what is different now. Why this time and this place?"

That was Taft's thought.

"Man has always beaten back the evil before we felt like we needed to intercede," Cristos said. "And by felt I mean to imply the higher power had given us guidance to stay hidden. Now at long last has come a time we felt sure might never arrive. The higher power feels that the evil is beginning to gain an upper hand and if not directly confronted might corrupt man forever."

"In the last few decades, greed has increased in proportions never before seen. A few have too much while others grow ever poorer. The systems of control honed through debt have grown so great that many people in both the civilized and uncivilized worlds are but one step away from catastrophe, should those that hold the ropes choose to form a noose and start to push. Instead of admiring those in the arts and sciences, studies that advance and further the growth of man, the powers of evil have created celebrities whose main virtues seem to be self-centered behaviors and extreme avarice. There are few people of morals gravitating to leadership roles and those that do are corrupted through psychological methods that target the base desires all people possess. In the past these desires could be denied by a good person if they arrived in a normal form," he preached.

"Now through targeted manipulation and recordation of the acts, those that seek the ultimate control of man can select the people that rule the countries that they have made increasingly reliant upon one another. Self-will and self-governing have given way to simply: You are either with us or against us. There was a fine candidate for President of your country thus removed from the running a few years ago. The takeover is almost complete but it is not yet too late. It may still be reversed and an age of enlightenment never before seen can arise on this planet. If we do nothing, we as humans will be led down a path from which we may never recover. It is that serious." Cristos paused and took a sip of tea.

"This is so serious," he continued, "that the very tenet of all that my family has stood for over these past thousands of years must be tested. The question is this: does revealing who we are alter the balance of self-will—the greatest gift given by our higher power? Not long ago I was posing this very question to a mortal man and the message I received from our higher power nearly jolted me from my chair. I was in a most unusual place for introspection with a most unlikely person to have triggered such a revelation but still it occurred, was real, and did not lessen or alter over time. Call it a revelation or a message from the heavens or even a false prophecy, but whatever the case, we started immediately to act and the events set into effect have led us directly here, to this time and this place."

A robed man walked into the kitchen and whispered into Cristos' ear.

"That is good news, indeed," Cristos said, smiling. "He can help fill in Mr. Taft further when he arrives."

Taft sat quietly.

"I need to go now to prepare for my speech," Cristos said. "Soon someone will arrive that can complete the story and answer any questions you might have."

With that, Cristos arose and left the kitchen.

Taft had no idea why he was being treated as an integral part of a puzzle and not a prisoner of war.

46

WALKER AND HOBBS did not make it far from the airport before being captured by a pair of agents from the CIA and NIA under the direction of the CIA director and Benson. After a few hours of interrogation and threats, their statements were recorded and they were turned over to the FBI. Their betrayal of the President was detailed and complete, and led all the way back to the President's first run of office. He had been a bought-and-paid-for shill from the beginning. Media manipulations and bribes, along with blackmail against those that ran against, him had raised him quickly up the political ladder. His fall would be faster and even steeper.

***

The President walked the grounds of Camp David. He had asked to be brought here just after four p.m. when he received word that Walker and Hobbs had been taken into custody. Neither his children or his wife had wanted to come along. Both barely knew the President. Now with the scandal breaking in full force, they simply wanted to distance themselves from both the President and his name. There had been perks to being the wife or child of the President, but the cost had always been greater than the reward.

The President was not a smart man, but he was wily. He understood almost instinctively that there was no way to be saved from the problems he had created. He had done the dirty deeds and there was proof. For the first time in a lifetime of bad behavior and evil acts, he would be required to pay a price. His wealth and privilege had not prepared him with any form of personal character. His was a soul devoid of the skills needed to weather adversity.

Throughout the afternoon, when his transgressions became more widely known, the outcry for his ouster had grown. Even the other right-wing billionaires, who helped his election through the use of sham organizations and relentless media advertising, were powerless to stem the tide. Within hours of the news breaking, the opposing political party was calling for serious charges that could lead to life imprisonment. In the last hour, a quorum of the leaders of his own party were calling for his resignation. It was clear that even if he stepped down right now and had his Vice-President take over, a pardon was unlikely to come. He was going to jail or worse.

He dropped the glass of bourbon he was sipping and it shattered. The Secret Service man hurried toward him but the President walked away toward the cabins.

***

Benson was inside his soundproof office when the telephone buzzed and the receptionist notified him that the CIA director was calling.

"Benson," he answered.

"I pulled both our agencies out of the mix and brushed off the tracks."

"Hell, better wash the tracks to be certain," Benson said.

"Let me rephrase that," the director said quietly. "Everything was scrubbed clean. There is no way anyone can tie anything back to either of our agencies."

"You don't think we will need to go back in and fan the flames again?"

"During my reign I've never seen anything like this in Washington," the director sighed. "This is a wildfire that neither needs or would respond to further tending."

"Good working with you," Benson said.

"Likewise," the director of the CIA said before disconnecting.

***

At two separate homes along the intra-coastal waterway near Miami, police cruisers sat with engines running. In the first cruiser, a pissed-off Christie Tamarino, still dressed in her swimsuit under shorts and a top, was questioning the patrolman.

"Hey," the patrolman said to Tamarino's aggressive questions, "I just showed up to a report of a heart attack. When I called in the name, they cross-referenced it to a case you may have worked. That's all I know."

"Did you notice anything unusual?"

"I called the coroner right away," the patrolman said, "and I backed out quick so as not to disturb the scene. As soon as the coroner arrived he pulled out a camera. He probably has pictures of the entire scene by now."

"So that's it?"

"I can tell you the guy had been dead a few days."

"How?"

"Unless he reads newspapers from days ago, the one in his hands was from Friday."

"Good eyes."

"It's not just the detectives that detect."

***

At the other house Robert England was faced with a similar scene. What was the chance that both of the principal owners of a company that was also involved in a suspicious suicide they had investigated had somehow died in the same manner at roughly the same time? He could have called a bookie friend to run the odds but he knew they were astronomical. He also knew deep in his heart that there was foul play involved and that it would never be solved. He reached for his cell phone.

"I have the assistant coroner over here," he said. "What do you say we don't screw up any more of our day off?"

"Makes sense to me," Tamarino said.

She hung up the phone, twisted the air conditioning in her personal car up a notch, and spun around to return to the beach. She just hoped she could find a spot to park.

***

Hours before the rally was to begin, the seats in the stadium were already filled. As more people funneled into the area the surrounding streets filled to capacity. Farther and farther back the lines of people stretched until more than a million waited. And still the lines grew. Cristos and his team scrambled to keep ahead of the ever-growing crowds. They persuaded business and apartment buildings to help supply fresh water. Every portable toilet in Caracas—even ones already in use at construction sites—were confiscated and brought rapidly into the crowds. Leased trucks slowly drove forward through the masses of people, delivering supplies and trained first-aid responders while electricians worked feverishly to erect loudspeakers on power poles.

The revelations that the President of the United States had conspired with an oil company to foist Cristos onto the Venezuelans had been met with equal parts horror and disbelief. In a country where the United States had attempted to overthrow their government numerous times, people were divided between believing that Cristos was who he said he was and believing that he was an oil-company plant sent to sway the election.

Whatever the case, everyone in Venezuela wanted the truth prior to the next day's voting.

Backstage, there were considerably fewer handlers than when the fake Cristos spoke. There were only a half dozen of the Knightly order that protected and supported Cristos, along with three close advisers. Cristos was alone in his dressing room. He had no illusions about the importance of tonight's speech. His life quite literally might depend on the outcome.

Of the advisers, two had been born in Europe—one in Switzerland, the world's oldest democracy; the other in France, the first country to shake off the bonds of royal rule. The third was born in the United States, a country with a shaky democracy. He was perhaps the most important of the trio, as he alone had finally set the events of the possible ascension of Cristos into motion. It was he who quietly entered the dressing room. Cristos was at an altar, praying. He waited until Cristos finished.

"Your Excellency," he said as Cristos arose and walked over.

"Did you complete your mission?"

"It is not complete until you are elected President," he said, "but what you asked me to check into was done."

"And?"

"The crowd has been tended to and made as comfortable as we could," he said. "As for the general mood of the country, there is both anger and doubt but I believe that will dissipate once the full story comes out."

"It is always about the story with you," Cristos said with a wry smile.

"You knew that," the American said, "from the time we first met."

Cristos was quiet for a moment. He looked into the other man's eyes.

"So it all comes down to this," he said at last. "Will the truth win out?"

"I would say I'm afraid so," the other man said lightly, "but I am not afraid. I am confident. The people will listen to you and respond favorably."

Cristos nodded.

"Before I go," the adviser asked, "do you require anything?"

Cristos shook his head.

"Then I shall take my leave as we discussed."

"Do you think you will be able to convince him?" Cristos asked.

"No idea," the American said quietly, "and his approval or disapproval is not needed anyway. I just feel since he offered to help me and has acted honorably he deserves a full and complete explanation from me. Either way he will be well taken care of as we discussed."

"I liked him," Cristos noted.

"I would imagine most do."

Cristos extended his hand and the adviser lightly kissed it.

"Be well, my King," the aide said before turning and leaving.

***

Taft was confused. Nothing right now was making sense. He and the others had been fed a sumptuous meal before being taken to separate rooms of the house. Televisions had been brought to each room and there seemed to be no restriction on what they might watch. The available stations were making much of the disclosure in the United States of the President's indiscretions, and there was also great debate about Cristos and his coming speech.

Taft scanned the room as he had been trained to do and found there was no chance of escape. Whatever they had planned for him, there was little he could do to affect change. His mind raced back and forth over scenarios and events, decisions he and others had made in this case, and possible outcomes. No clear picture emerged from the fog.

After his meeting with Cristos, he wanted to believe the man was who he said he was. Taft, an expert at deception, had seen or felt nothing to indicate that the man was lying. But if he wasn't lying and the coverage about the United States President was true, then Cristos was merely a puppet of the big oil interests. The riddle continued to play over and over in Taft's mind as he lay fully clothed atop the bed.

***

Martinez was sitting in Benson's office. Dick Albright was in a chair next to him. Benson's face showed his concern. Albright was running over the possible courses of action.

"How many hours again?"

"Three now," Martinez said. "We had an hourly check-in protocol in place."

"And Taft, you said, arrived safely and had control of the funds needed to propel the mission? You are certain he was on his way to intercept the primary target when we last heard from him?"

Martinez started to answer but Benson's intercom interrupted.

"Sorry," his receptionist said, "but you will want to hear this."

The call was put through to his speaker phone. "This is Gary Weedlin, sir. I was assigned to today's debriefing with Albornez. When I arrived, both his handlers had been disabled and he was gone."

Weedlin was speaking rapidly. He was a longtime agent and rarely riled.

"Are the other agents…"

"They are fine, sir. Albornez jumped them and tied them up and placed them in the basement. There was no reason to suspect he might run, so we had a lax security protocol."

"How long ago did this happen?"

"Last night. Since he arrived, Albornez has always slept until afternoon," Weedlin noted. "He said right from the start that he had awakened up early every day of his career and now he was retired he wanted to stay up late and sleep in. We adjusted our schedule to serve his needs so the debriefings never began much before six p.m. I always arrived at least a half-hour early to see if he had any special needs before we began. Usually it was only a Cuban coffee and I would send one of the guards out. I arrived at the house about five twenty p.m. and found it empty. I quickly called in backup and searched the home. That's when I found the guards in the basement. They claim they were jumped sometime just after nine last night."

"And we didn't have systems in place to check on anyone at the house until you arrived?"

Albright interrupted. "I'm to blame for that, sir," he said. "We had the guards on three-day twenty-four-hours-per-day shifts. In the past we found that works best. Both the guards and the subjects like the continuity. As Agent Weedlin noted, there was no reason to think he might bolt. Who takes the risk of turning double agent, then slips away from his only chance at security? It doesn't make sense. The guards are primarily there to protect the person from retaliation from his own country. As far as I know, Venezuela never attempted to locate or silence Albornez."

"So he has a twenty-four-hour head start?" Benson said.

"I'm afraid so, sir."

"I'm sending Mr. Albright to the scene to assume command," Benson said. "You stay there and assist in any way possible."

"Will do, sir."

The speaker went dead. Benson watched as Albright left the office.

"This adds another layer now, doesn't it, Agent Martinez?"

Martinez was worried about Taft and it showed.

***

Inside the stadium, the giant screens used to show goals and game highlights suddenly lit up. Bathed in blue glow, the seated people turned. Suddenly a recording started. It appeared to be a security camera from outside a home in the hills at the edge of town. Black SUVs roared up and stopped and armed men jumped out. A few minutes later a man was dragged from the house. The video clearly showed it was Cristos. Next the screen went blank and a Spanish translation of the U.S. President speaking to Walker and Hobbs was played. This video and the audio alternated back and forth. On the streets nearby the video was not visible so an announcer narrated what was being seen. Whispers spread through the crowd.

Exactly at six p.m. Cristos walked onto the right side of the stage while the fake Cristos, who had been captured attempting to leave the hotel, was led by guards on to the left. The real Cristos was dressed in a long white flowing robe, while the fake Cristos was dressed in a suit as befit a pawn of big business. Cristos watched as the crowd reacted.

"To have hope given and then wrested away is the cruelest of cruelty," the real Cristos began. "Now if you will allow me, I will explain what truly happened."

***

Taft was watching the beginning of the speech when the door to Taft's room opened and a man walked inside. Taft stared in surprise at the visitor. Of all the possible angles or likely scenarios, this was one he had not seen coming.

"Hey there," Hemingway said. "We have this being recorded. So we can talk now if you want."

Taft sat mute.

"I want you to know that you can leave or stay," he said. "I have a large sum of money awaiting you and a jet that will take you and your men back to the United States."

He had left the door to the bedroom open.

"But if you'd like," he said, smiling, "we can retire to the living room where I'll explain all this."

Taft was so stunned he forgot to answer.

"I've got snacks," Hemingway added.

Taft was still in shock but he rose and followed the author out to the living room.

Once they were seated, a houseman arranged various appetizers on the coffee table. The television was showing Cristos's speech with the sound turned off. The houseman asked for their drink orders.

"Have a drink if you want, Mr. Taft," he said. "As for me I've sworn off alcohol. I had to drink so much in Miami to fit my cover that I was near to suffering liver damage."

Taft asked for a beer.

"You just thought I was a drunk? Don't worry, that was a mistake made by more than a few."

The houseman brought the drinks and set them on coasters before retreating.

"So if you'll allow me," Hemingway said, "I'll explain this entire affair. Then I have a proposal for you."

Taft just nodded. The surprise was still washing over him.

"I didn't come to writing spy books without experience. My story is different than yours but similar in some ways. I was raised in a military family, a brat as they say, and was in college when I was approached. I now understand this is common. They look for certain types of service brats, ones whose parents have secret clearances. They think they are conditioned to keeping quiet plus most of the background work has already been completed since military personnel and their families are already vetted for security clearances. Why go through the process twice? This little cost-saving idea was part of the much heralded government-efficiency push that took place in the late nineteen eighties when I was recruited. Anyway let me back up a few years. The House Select committee on Assassinations, which was led by Senator Church from Idaho, changed the world of intelligence rather radically as I'm sure you know. It's a shame a lot of the young people haven't studied enough history because this was an important event."

Hemingway took a bacon-wrapped water chestnut and chicken-liver appetizer and ate it.

"Man, I love rumaki. Who was it that said, 'those that ignore history are doomed to repeat it?'"

"George Santayana," Taft said, "but that wasn't the exact quote."

"Thanks. Anyway, you remember the Church commission decided that both Kennedy and the Martin Luther King assassinations were most likely conspiracies? And more importantly, they exposed numerous CIA involvements in nefarious schemes including assassinations, drugs, mind control and a host of other seedy activities. Some people actually got in trouble; a few of the old guard were retired and the intelligence agencies had to agree to stronger Congressional oversight."

Hemingway took a sip of fruit juice and continued.

"So what did the intelligence agencies do? Well, they could have followed the guidelines Congress ordered, this being a democracy and all, but of course they decided to skirt the law wholeheartedly instead. That's where the guys like me come in. If the CIA was being watched and the country was rapidly moving to control by the large corporations and the rich, why not simply form numerous private companies and corporations to do the dirty work? So that's what they did. Ultimately this was reflected most completely in the most recent Middle East war, which was as much run under the guidance of corporations as the U.S. military. I guess that is kind of fitting, considering the most recent actions were mainly a war for the control of oil. Anyway, by the time I was approached, the private war or intelligence corporations had begun but the movement was not yet in full swing. I was somewhat of pioneer. Shrimp?"

Taft reached over, grabbed a few, and placed them on an appetizer plate.

"Now understand the deal I was offered is similar to yours, but different. For example, I never was listed as an employee of the government, or received the benefits you had, but I was highly paid and, interestingly enough, trained at some of the same schools as you were. I can fly a plane or a helicopter, drive a boat, truck or motorcycle and shoot, do advanced demolitions and kill men with my bare hands, maybe as well as you and your kind can. I just never had the blanket that, if caught, my government would bail me out."

"That's changed a little," Taft said.

"The guy in Pakistan who was working for the private company," Hemingway agreed. "I followed that with interest. Anyway, I ran weapons to various factions, participated in the overthrow of a couple of nations, and then began to realize it was all a giant shell game and slowly pulled away. I had stolen enough money to live a life of leisure if I chose to do so—not investment-banker rich, but enough to ski and play golf and drive new cars. I did that for a year before I grew as bored as a rich widow. You'll see what I mean now that you are retired.

"I was sitting around on a beach one day reading a truly bad paperback thriller when it hit me. I could write this shit. It really didn't matter what I called my career as my childhood friends—the people I went to school with, even my own family for the most part, thought I was a salesman. That was the cover I used to explain my long absences and wads of cash. Salesmen need to travel, and the good ones are highly compensated. You know how it is. If you lie for a living, soon it becomes very easy to convince anyone of anything. So anyway, I wrote a novel. A friend's father was involved in business with an author who had just had a hit, so he introduced me. I showed him the novel and while he mentioned it was not the worst he had seen, it wasn't good. He also told me that was the time when most people give up. That pissed me off enough so I wrote another, then another, each time showing them to him. Gradually they improved until I was as good or better than most of the people out there."

"Driggs," Taft said.

"Exactly. The stories I could tell you about that. I love the man but every crazy claiming to be in intelligence found him. He, like a lot of the dudes that write thrillers, wanted to think they are somehow involved in the game. I could never reveal to him what I had done;

most of the stuff was still hot and he had a difficult time keeping his mouth shut when he drank. I could just imagine it—I tell him about one of my missions and he accidentally spills the beans. I finally start to relax my guard and some crazy Columbian shows up and slits my throat because my author buddy slipped up. No thanks. As far as he was concerned, then and now, I used to be a salesman. By the way, I'd like to keep it that way."

"Understood."

"Anyway, I'm writing my own stuff, then seeing a change in the market, we agreed I'd co-write books for him. You see, since the advent of the mega-bookstore, an author became a name brand. It's like the grocery store—there are a lot of varieties of soda under the two big brands, but try to find a smaller root beer from a family-owned business and the grocery stores don't carry it. Books became just like that. He and I jumped into the co-writing game early.

"Anyway, I'm making a few bucks and learning how to write the perfect thriller, when I come upon the plot of a lifetime—Jesus had children! There were several non-fiction books out but I put them in the same category as the legends of the lost city of Atlantis or Bigfoot. Even so, I immediately realized it would make a great fiction thriller so I began to research it from all sides. I'll return to that in a moment."

Hemingway placed some cheese on a cracker and stared at the television for a moment. Cristos was in full swing, and when the cameras panned to the crowd it was obvious he had them under his control. He smiled and turned back to Taft.

"The timing seemed perfect. I had just finished a co-writing book for Driggs and I'm biting the bit to start on one of my own novels. But then just as I finished my novel something reared its head that changed everything for me."

"My guess is he spilled the beans on your plot," Taft said.

"I never figured it out for sure. Anyway, like I said, Driggs loves to talk. I don't think it was on purpose but somehow he lets slip my plot to the editor at the publishing house we were using. It was probably just him making small talk. Whatever the case, that's what happened."

"I'm surprised given your background you didn't seek vengeance."

"I wanted to believe it wasn't malice. We had been friends—I thought—and I didn't want to believe a friend would do that. Hell, even now I still consider him a friend. Anyway, other than the money I lost—and that was substantial—it really doesn't matter. My research into the novel took me somewhere else that needed more attention than writing potboilers."

"Cristos?"

"Exactly. That and the fact that the country I loved and served— and I think what I did for the U.S. is equally as important as some of the missions you performed—has been taken over by a non-democratic cabal comprised of the rich and powerful."

"I've felt some of that myself in the last decade."

"According to what I have been uncovering, it goes back farther."

A man walked into the room and bent to whisper in Hemingway's ear. The author nodded.

"But back to the story. As soon as I found Cristos, and was convinced of his lineage, I came down here and approached him. He denied everything but over time I put together a mountain of evidence. It was a damn good thing he was here in Venezuela, one of the few places that has not been totally taken over by the Corporatists—that's what I call the shady groups that are taking over the world. Once I finally was able to convince Cristos to come forth, it was simply a matter of setting this all up."

"What..." Taft stuttered. "You set this..."

"Bingo," Hemingway said. The author reached for the remote and turned the sound on.

Cristos was speaking:

"We realized that the United States would intervene as soon as I came forth. We knew not how they would move, but we knew they would stop at nothing to keep me from being elected. Working with a very smart friend of mine, we created a campaign of disinformation and deceit that would rival their own. The evidence is irrefutable. I am descended from Jesus's family. I ask tomorrow that you vote for me and allow me the honor of leading our country forward in the future…"

"This will tell us where we are," Hemingway said quietly.

"Now is the time…" Cristos shouted.

"*We are the people*," the millions inside and outside screamed in reply.

"Sometimes truth can overcome," Hemingway said, smiling. He turned down the sound again.

The houseman walked into the room. "The chef is preparing the sandwiches you love."

"Oh, excellent! Mr. Taft, do you eat pork?"

Taft nodded.

"Bring him one as well, Luis."

The houseman made a small bow and backed from the room.

"You said you set this up?" Taft asked.

"What do you think—you're the only spy in the world?" Hemingway laughed.

47

AT CAMP DAVID, the President of the United States had been drinking increasing amounts of liquor. He had watched Cristos' speech, which had been translated into nearly one hundred languages and broadcast worldwide. Even before the speech had concluded the President was convinced he would not only be found guilty but severely punished.

He had not tried to manipulate another country or some tinhorn dictator—he had, by his assistance to Hobker, tried to place a torch to a larger field. A field that was larger and stronger than borders on a map, a field of divine righteousness that had served as a compass of good for over two thousand years. A man of God—no, *the* man of God.

The President had no illusions as to his fate.

As often happens to the rich, greedy and powerful, he found himself alone when his time of utmost crisis was upon him. Over the years anyone who had come close to him had been trampled or repelled by his personality and abrasiveness. His family, so distant from his life as to almost appear as actors, felt no remorse about his downfall. Any friends he might have had in the past had long ago been chased away. Business and political acquaintances wanted nothing to do with him—they had only tolerated him for what he might do for them. Even his dog, a prop to appeal to the voters, was in Washington D.C. The dog resided at the home of one of his staffers, where he was loved and walked daily. The President only saw the creature when he was unveiled at a photo op designed to stress the President's Everyman image.

At ten that evening, the president ordered a limousine and was driven into a bad part of the capital, where he ordered his Secret

Service agent to enter a house and secure him cocaine. By midnight he was back at Camp David and becoming more intoxicated. By the time he asked the switchboard to start placing calls for him to various world leaders, the Air Force officer in charge of "the football," the briefcase containing the launch codes for nuclear and biological strikes that was never more than a few yards from the President, called his superiors and asked for the Nixon Protocol to be implemented.

The Nixon Protocol was named for the former President, who as he was being hounded to leave office in the wake of the Watergate affair, showed enough instability that he was secretly removed from being able to use nuclear options. The military temporarily assumed control until such time as an acceptable government official could be arranged. Tonight they were forced to do the same.

At six a.m. the following morning, the President was wired on cocaine and drunk with alcohol, and ordered the Secret Service to prepare the skeet range so he might open the day with shooting clay pigeons. The man in charge of the detail had not been ordered to ignore any of the President's requests so he warned the others to stay clear and drove the President to the range in a golf cart.

The President had shot and reloaded a dozen times, striking only one of the flying targets, when he demanded the Secret Service agent drive him back to his cabin so he could use the rest room. The President told the range master controlling the skeet range they would be right back, then climbed into the seat cradling the twelve-gauge shotgun in his lap.

"Sir," the Secret Service agent said casually, "could you break that open so I can verify it is not loaded? I wouldn't want it going off on the ride over or back."

The President flicked the lever to the side and the double barrel side-by-side hinged open. He showed the Secret Service agent the chambers. Pulling out the two spent shells, he tossed them to the ground. The Secret Service agent nodded and drove to the cabin and parked in front. He was waiting there when a few minutes later, he heard the sound of the shotgun firing.

Leaping from the golf cart, the agent raced to the door and twisted it open. In time the agent would be forced to take early retirement because of the image that would haunt his mind for the rest of his life: the President seated on the toilet, with the top of his skull neatly blown off. The shotgun had fallen from his mouth after firing the fatal shot and the President had a large grin like that worn by a circus clown. One hand was still facing up with the thumbs-up sign the President had made famous when campaigning. Chunks of skull, mists of red blood, and gray, wispy brain matter dusted the wall behind the toilet and the divider alongside that led to the bath and shower.

The Secret Service agent swallowed the bile that rose in his throat and reached for his radio.

***

Hours before the polls in Venezuela opened, everyone knew it would be a record turnout. It would be midnight before the last people, at the busiest polling stations in Caracas, had a chance to vote. By noon, exit polls from the rest of the country and those that had already voted in the capitol showed Cristos to be the clear winner. It was not even close. Nearly ninety-five percent of all votes cast had gone to him and the concession speeches from the other candidates began long before the polls were due to close.

As the concession speeches started to air, the television station began to report the news that the President of the United States had been wounded in a hunting accident. Less than an hour later they reported that he had perished from his wounds. It had been decided, by whom it was never clear, that the fact that the President had committed suicide would be buried inside a false story: he had been bird hunting at Camp David when he had dropped his shotgun and it had discharged with deadly consequences. World leaders began to make arrangements to attend the lavish ceremonies that would follow, and that diverted some attention from the change of government that would be taking place in Venezuela.

The former President of Venezuela made his call to Cristos, congratulating him and promising an orderly transition of power, then started planning for leaving the country to accept the offered job at the think tank in the United States.

The country he was leaving behind was in shambles. Inflation was officially running over twenty percent but in truth was closer to fifty. The infrastructure was failing and crime rate, particularly violent crime, was one of the highest in the world. There were a litany of other problems but nothing had progressed so far that they could not be reversed.

Venezuela would move into the future with a major advantage few other countries had ever had—an incorruptible and charismatic leader who believed in the dignity of man and the honor of service to mankind. Venezuela also had the largest oil reserves in the world, and with the prices as high as they were and demand as China and India modernized skyrocketing, Cristos could in short order make the economy the envy of the world.

Cristos agreed to pay the men that had assisted Taft before his capture—though they were technically traitors to their country. He then paid to lease a private jet to fly them directly to Virginia, where the CIA would pick them up. Cristos asked Taft if he would stay another night, as he wanted Hemingway to speak to him further. Taft agreed and retired to the larger mansion where Cristos and his team had taken residence to await the official results. When Albornez showed up at the house, Taft was past surprise. He simply walked out to the spacious pool deck and lay on a chaise lounge chair alongside Hemingway, who was visiting with a trio of beauties who someone had invited.

Hemingway asked the ladies for a few moments of privacy, then turned to Taft.

"My country—our country—has been taken over by a group which we have yet been able to positively identify. They subvert any free and fair democratic process to achieve their own agenda, which is power first and money next."

"When did this happen?"

"We are still working on that but the group behind this may have existed since the start of time. In the United States they were beaten back and did not reemerge with power until the Depression, when they began their push to corrupt the government again. FDR was old and becoming tired and he tried to fight them off, but once he passed away, they grew even stronger. Eisenhower warned of them; Kennedy died from them, and since that time they shielded behind corporations and a fake banking system, they have grown ever stronger. The people of the United States are suffering and if no one acts quickly the takeover will be complete."

Hemingway paused and stared directly into Taft's eyes.

"Cristos has many friends throughout the world that will help us, for he too knows of the danger of one overwhelming force on this planet. Groups have been hunting his family for longer that your or my ancestors have existed."

"You are asking me to oppose my government?"

"Your government, my government, no longer assists," Hemingway said forcefully. "It has been subverted and taken over like some Third World coup on an island no one knows exists. Worse thing is, it was done directly in front of her own citizens."

"How did you meet Cristos?"

"I was researching the novel," Hemingway said. "I began to come upon documents in Germany, Spain and later here in Venezuela that shed light on the truth."

"Why you?" Taft said. "If these documents have existed for so long, why was it you that uncovered them?"

"I never said I uncovered them," Hemingway said, taking a sip from a bottle of cola. "Thousands of people have probably seen them over the years, maybe tens of thousands. I merely put it all together. Look at it this way—everything in life is geared toward specialization, especially now. Generalists have no place. Anyone that read these papers in the past would have looked at them only from their point of interest or expertise. The movement of a family to a scholar studying immigration would become an immigration statistic to further their thesis. They might only care why not who or who not why. Since scholars are for the most part—the only people other than writers who examine old documents—the chance of proof of a theory evolving is much larger than the truth coming forth. It has been that way for a long time."

"You are saying this was never uncovered because no one ever looked for it?"

"Basically," Hemingway admitted, "my being average was the key. Had I been a genius I would have read into the documents my own truth. Me, being me, was simply trying to find a story."

"It makes sense."

"Cristos is who he says he is," Hemingway said. "But would it matter if he wasn't?"

"A descendant of James the Just?"

"Brother of Jesus Christ."

Taft pointed to a silver ice bucket that had colas chilling. Hemingway nodded and handed him an opener. Taft pulled one from the icy water and squeezed off the lingering droplets with his hand, then popped off the top and took a sip.

"So what does that mean?" Taft said.

"As near as I have been able to determine, his family has the ability to more directly have contact with whatever forms the higher power. God, is what I call it—or others use other names."

"So Cristos has a direct link to God?"

"More direct than anyone else on this planet, as far as I can determine," Hemingway said quietly. "I'm sure there is much, much more to it than that, but I don't have proof. Hang around him long enough and you will see coincidences galore. As if the unseen hand of God is showing himself."

Taft was quiet. He had already seen more than one coincidence as of late. He sipped from the cola and glanced across the pool to where the trio of ladies lay in the sun upon chaise lounges. They were stunning, truly beautiful.

"I have a lot less of a problem buying Cristos and his family power," Taft said, "than the story that our government has been subverted by some worldwide octopus organization."

Hemingway nodded. What Taft said was expected.

"Once I discovered Cristos, it took some time before he acknowledged his true identity. Eventually he showed me some files his family had amassed over the years. They were compiled from throughout the world, but the ones he agreed that I could show you now pertain to the United States."

"And if these files convince me?"

"Then I'd like you to work with me to attempt to stop these people."

Taft was quiet. "It can't hurt to look."

Hemingway smiled.

"John Taft—always pushing ahead. Cristos has the files at a different location and it will be tomorrow before he can send someone to retrieve them. If you haven't noticed, today is election day, which I think in time will be one of the most historically significant days in the history of man. What do you say you and me simply relax and enjoy it? I'll get you the files tomorrow. You read through them and if what I offered is not of interest, the jet will be back from dropping off your team and we will fly you home to the U.S.—no harm, no foul. Does that sound fair?"

"Relax and enjoy," Taft said easily staring across the pool. "I guess I could."

***

As the sun set set over Venezuela and the election results continued to be announced, the crew went about its duties at one of the drilling rigs stolen from Hobker Petroleum. The rig operated twenty-four hours a day, seven days a week. As the lights scattered throughout the rig flicked on to beat back the growing darkness, a cheer arose in the dog house—or control center—as the final results were announced.

48

TAFT HAD AWAKENED after a night of civilized celebrations. Joining Hemingway on the pool deck, they both sipped coffee.

"I ordered us omelets with hash browns and orange juice," Hemingway said. "Once the chef has it prepared, one of the housemen will bring it over to us."

Taft nodded. "I like my hash browns crispy."

Hemingway motioned to one of the housemen nearby and relayed Taft's request.

One of Cristos's aides approached. "Sir," he said to Hemingway, "we have dispatched one of our men to retrieve the information that you seek. He will return here shortly with what you requested."

"Thank you."

The aide turned and walked away.

"He's rather formal," Taft observed.

"He speaks eighteen languages," Hemingway said. "I'm sure he had difficulty with switching tones and nuances from one culture to the next. I know I would."

Taft stretched. "I don't think I've danced that much in years."

"I've found most of the South Americans much more joyous than us dour Americans," Hemingway said. "Most parties in the U.S. I've been to lately consist of people discussing real estate values, stocks or the cruises they've been on. No one is having any fun, it seems."

Taft and Hemingway were finishing breakfast and and lingering over coffee when a man walked over and set a cloth-wrapped package the size of a file folder in front of Hemingway. He bowed slightly and backed away.

"Here you go." Hemingway slid the package over to Taft. "Just raise your hand if you need anything and the houseman will come over immediately."

Hemingway rose and walked away as Taft untied the strings holding the cloth in place. Pulling the cloth apart he opened the first file folder. It was titled METHODS OF CONTROL.

He began to read.

The oldest documents were on the top of the pile. Each section had a page or two from a historian/archivist explaining the history of the document and where and how it was acquired. The first section contained copies of parchments several thousand years old. These were written in a language Taft had never seen but were accompanied by a complete translation. Said to have been recovered after a battle in Mesopotamia prior to the beginnings of Christianity, they had been "secreted in beautifully tanned soft goatskin then placed inside a turban the warrior wore wrapped around his head."

Taft read the translation:

> For us to be the one we must allow all the other savages on this life to always feel there is no one in charge. The only one they can feel rules all is an illusionary God. (Undecipherable due to blood stain) for our family may find other families. These families will be rewarded but their power will be ours.
>
> There must be many people of many types as this world as shown by the shadow on the sun and moon is round. But this makes this world finite and with limits. That should make it easy

to be controlled. But having a known limit means that if we control what all need we control all.

The family is all; the others are naught. All things are given and taken by us. Anything else is an illusion. We make and break and keep all confused.

We send out (translation difficult, closest to-) *ambassadors to different parts of this earth to make pacts with all others. Anyone who opposes this we slay.*

Taft read through the rest of what could be most accurately described as guidelines. They seemed an early form of a recipe for world domination through bringing in others in different parts of the world, so these others might enslave their own people and cede ultimate power to this unknown group. The first four on the parchment were most disturbing to Taft.

The first made mention of the need for an imaginary God that many could believe was all-powerful so they could deflect attention from themselves. Had they actually helped create religion as a shield for themselves? Taft wondered.

The second showed that they knew of the finite earth and plan to exploit that; shades of Thomas Malthus thousands of years later.

The third seemed to indicate they would have a policy of taking and giving to confuse man and keep them on edge. Did they mean food, water, the tools to make life easier? Taft wasn't sure.

The fourth passage seemed to indicate that they would form a pact with other families that would answer to them. Was this the beginning of royalty?

The next few hours Taft read forward through time. Occasionally the houseman came out with iced tea or pots of coffee. When Taft would go inside to use the restroom, two men would appear from just out of sight and stand guard over the documents until he returned.

There were numerous documents about the founding of the United States. At first they seemed to give little chance that the colonies could shake off the far richer and militarily superior British. Once the tide began to change they issued a number of manifestos explaining how they would infiltrate the new democracy and wrest away control.

> *These people are beggars and revolutionaries. They fight for scraps while exposing the freedom of their fellow man. We must keep them holding the forced servants. (*Translation: slaves*) so this tears their country to shreds in time. Then we swoop in with our treasury and make them our servants by becoming debtors.*

Taft read more. For the United States, they showed particular disdain, claiming the American people were little more than drunken savages. They stressed the need for continuous wars to let the people always feel the savagery that comprised their souls.

Taft read further. The revolution in Europe of 1848 had a number of documents that had been secured. It seemed that this time may have been their closest to exposure, with attacks on many fronts.

> *We must send the worst of these rabble rousers overseas. Let us profit from this by outfitting ships to take them to the states and farther.*

> *All things we learn from this we can benefit from in less than one hundred revolutions of earth.*

Taft read that last part twice. It seemed they had learned methods of control they were saving for another time. And they felt this time would be in less than one hundred years. That meant they had moved from putting methods in place in the world to allow them to reign, to actively distorting the future in a way that would make them even more powerful.

By the time Taft reached the documents pertaining to the 1890s in the United States, it appeared that they had attempted a takeover of the government, only to be repelled near the end when Teddy Roosevelt took office after McKinley was assassinated. The vast growth of industrialization in the United States had brought many citizens off their farms, where they were isolated and less able to be controlled because of their natural self-sufficiency, to the cities.

> *If we cluster the savages together we can control their purse strings and thus their thoughts and minds; ebb and flow, taketh and giveth away.*

> *We are growing ever closer.*

Taft read the historian's notation.

These were stolen, copied and replaced by one of our loyal followers from Jekyll Island, State of Georgia, United States of America from French Capitalist.

Taft read through another folder until he reached a thick section from the 1920s. These foretold of the Great Depression and the need to beat people down throughout the world to regain control over them. There was a long section about creating a dictator somewhere in the world. They wished to test if people would willingly give up their freedoms for promises of national pride. The plan advocated nothing less than the abolishment of religion, a wholesale subverting of education and a system of secret police forces that would promote citizens spying on other citizens. They also wanted to see if it was possible to rid a country of a certain ethnic group.

Hitler, Taft quickly concluded.

Taft swiftly read through the rest of the documents. It seemed as if they were moving ever faster toward eventual world domination over humans. It was so far-fetched as to be almost believable.

Hemingway had asked the guards to inform him when Taft appeared to have finished.

***

"Cuban?" Hemingway asked Taft as he walked over.

"Sounds good to me."

Hemingway motioned to the houseman.

"How long did it take you to write all that?" Taft asked casually.

"I think you know I didn't," Hemingway said. "But just for fun I'll say this: Scout's honor, I did not write a word of any of that file, and I can tell you it was written by all different men at all different times. No professional writers, however."

The houseman walked over with a cedar box and opened the lid. Taft selected a cigar, as did Hemingway.

Taft said, "So you were a Boy Scout?"

"I made it to Star Scout before I discovered girls and quit going to meetings."

"The stuff about Hitler is spot-on," Taft observed.

"When he invaded the Rhineland in early March of 1936, he sent three battalions across the border. The French could have rounded up enough Parisian chefs to outnumber the German troops and send them running back to Germany in defeat. Instead the French did nothing but explain that the League of Nations would take care of the problem. If Hitler would have been stopped, then it would have been the end of him and the end of German aggression. Someone was telling the politicians how to act and it led to a huge war," Hemingway said.

"Maybe even Gettysburg during the Civil War," Taft added. "Or if the French, British or any other country had recognized the Confederacy, the war would have ended in a stalemate."

"But if that happened the bankers could not have loaned the United States the huge sums of money that we are still repaying."

Taft nodded slowly.

"The *Lusitania*, Pearl Harbor, Tonkin Gulf," Hemingway said. "It's not hard to make the argument that it seems someone is pulling the strings."

Taft was silent. "I don't want to believe it is real."

"I didn't either," Hemingway agreed.

The men puffed on their cigars. Taft took a drink from his half-filled glass of iced tea.

"I contacted your partner, Martinez," Hemingway said. "You were captured during your mission and as a show of Cristos's wanting better relations with the United States, we will be releasing you soon."

"You didn't request a ransom?"

"Venezuela has the largest oil reserves in the world," Hemingway said. "In addition I have your intelligence bribe money. By the way, where is the money I grabbed from SPS?"

"I hid it in a special place," Taft said.

"I never wanted anything to happen to Taylor," Hemingway said. "His death was not part of the plan. I had to use him—in fact my entire time in Miami was setting this all up—but I was going to offer him sanctuary here in Venezuela."

"Right after we first met," Taft said. "The lady on the train?"

"One of my group," Hemingway said. "We needed to gauge your feelings about our message."

"Regrets?"

"Nowhere in the plan did we ever imagine people would so quickly start persecuting people from other religions. I don't know who for sure was writing the speeches for the fake Cristos but he'll pay. That was not foreseen."

"Me?"

"We have people inside your agency monitoring and I was delighted when the NIA picked you for the report and later to extract Albornez."

"He was with you?"

"We requested the Congressional report knowing some agent would be sent here, and Albornez has been on board for some time."

"The support group for Cristos is larger than you let on."

Hemingway turned and stared at Taft.

"Look, we are going after the bad guys, whoever and wherever they might be," Hemingway proclaimed. "They have screwed my country to the wall. I would like you to join us, but if not, we are going to do it anyway. We have nearly unlimited funds and as soon as Cristos is sworn in, the entire Venezuelan government at our disposal. We have a base to come back to where we will be safe, embassies to hide in should we need them, and a mission the world needs done. How much better might it be?"

Taft was quiet. Hemingway knew better than to speak. Taft puffed on the cigar and drained the last of the tea, but still he sat quietly. His mind was racing; going over scenarios and outcomes, the positives and the negatives.

"I will never go against my country," Taft said at last.

"And neither will I," Hemingway promised.

"Then count me in," Taft said.

THE END

Printed in Great Britain
by Amazon